Death in Saint-Chartier

By Ivo Fornesa

Death in Saint-Chartier

a&b

Death in Saint-Chartier

IVO FORNESA

Translated by Allen Young

Allison & Busby Limited
11 Wardour Mews
London W1F 8AN
allisonandbusby.com

First published in Great Britain by Allison & Busby in 2019.
This paperback edition published by Allison & Busby in 2020.

Copyright © 2013 by Ivo Fornesa Rebés
English language translation copyright © 2019 by Allen Young

A CIP catalogue record for this book is available from
the British Library.

First Edition

ISBN 978-0-7490-2444-4

Typeset in 10.5/15.5 pt Sabon LT Pro by
Allison & Busby Ltd.

The paper used for this Allison & Busby publication
has been produced from trees that have been legally sourced
from well-managed and credibly certified forests.

Printed and bound by
CPI Group (UK) Ltd, Croydon, CR0 4YY

AUTHOR'S NOTE

Buried deep within the twists and turns of many a crime novel lies a fact seldom considered by the reader: the plot is inspired by events that, though they may not have actually taken place, have ardently been desired. Such is the case with the novel before us, a story that could well have been real, and which hews closer to the truth than one might wish.

The human mind is complex and gripped by untold troubles, and often mere chance or fear of punishment keeps our darkest desires from becoming reality. These deterrents – and nothing else – are the sole reason many crimes go uncommitted.

Let him who is free from the sin of intent cast the first stone.

FIRST CHORD

THE VICARAGE

The rainy season was at its peak, and inside the vicarage logs blazed cosily in an oversized hearth, wrapping the sitting room in their warmth.

A bottle of chartreuse – the abbot's grand reserve – stood on the desk as a bulwark against any rash or foolish urge to leave the house. Its green hue glowed brighter in the flickering light of the fireplace, as if to prove the wisdom of the motto of the Carthusian monks who make it: *nunquam reformata, quia nunquam deformata* – never reformed, because never deformed. Indeed, some things are so well made and reach such pinnacles of perfection that any attempt to alter them is doomed to failure.

I can't go out, I won't go out, I've got to get started on these memoirs. For Laurent de Rodergues, this line had become a mantra, one he'd repeated each day for the past eight months, ever since he moved to Saint-Chartier. Yet he still couldn't get beyond the first sentence. His writer's block surprised him, because he had a good memory and no lack of material. No, that wasn't the problem. The reminiscences he wanted to set down on paper flowed in mighty torrents in his head, but he couldn't manage to channel them into a story. For several days now he'd noticed an undeniable whiff of failure in the air.

Two things were now abundantly clear: that his life had indeed been exhilarating and unconventional, with an unusually intense combination of adventure and romance; and that the only constant in his life was his inconstancy, which meant that the task he'd set for himself – to write it all down – simply exceeded his capabilities.

True, there were plenty of extenuating circumstances: a lack of inspiration, a location – the Berry region of France – that offered an endless number of attractions and scenic spots to explore, a sumptuous local cuisine that demanded considerable time to prepare and even longer to digest, and neighbours who often popped over for a visit . . . and add to that the card games he couldn't miss at the nearby tavern, the get-togethers and dinners his new friends held in their cosy homes, the pints he could never turn down, the occasional wooing and cooing (and everything that went with it), and perhaps his inability to write was understandable – justifiable, even.

Still, Laurent constantly agonised over his lack of willpower, and he was again reproaching himself when he saw through his window the headlights of a car stopping in front of his door. Cars rarely parked in the small church square in winter, especially so late in the afternoon on a day that would quickly give way to a bone-chilling night. No sooner had he noticed this unusual occurrence than he heard steps on the gravel, followed by a sudden vigorous tapping on his window. The smiling face pressed up against the glass was unexpected, to say the least: it belonged to Monsieur Jablard, and he'd brought along his assistant.

Laurent had only a passing acquaintance with Jablard, a lawyer in Châteauroux whose portfolio of clients consisted mainly of foreigners with interests in France. He was a foul-tempered man whom Laurent, in a flight of mean-spirited literary fancy, had privately nicknamed 'Cocardasse', after the swordsman who takes Lagardère under his wing in the swashbuckling adventure *On Guard*. Ever since he was a child, Laurent had made a habit of finding fictional twins in books or films for people he knew in real life, and in this case, Jablard bore no small resemblance to the actor who played Cocardasse in the film version of the story. Not only did the lawyer seem aware of the likeness, he practically went out of his way to accentuate it.

A large man of around sixty, he had a face that had once been attractive but was now loose in the flesh, with a noticeable wattle hanging from his chin. He wore a spectacular mane of hair, probably his most remarkable trait, pulled back and tied with a tacky black velvet ribbon. On more than one occasion Laurent was tempted to ask about his peculiar appearance, which seemed even more flamboyant in such a conservative region, but he never quite dared, because he feared the answer would be interminable. Jablard had a theatrical demeanour to go along with his striking appearance, though for all that he wasn't a bad person: he had a certain sense of humour and a notable bonhomie, traits that in times like these are nothing to sniff at.

Puzzled, Laurent went to open the door and invite his visitors in.

'Well, this is a pleasant surprise,' he said. 'Please come in.'

As he and his assistant stepped inside, Jablard gave the bottle a look that Laurent couldn't miss.

They made some superficial, practically British chit-chat about the lingering rains in the region, the most recent gossip and the local rugby results. Then Jablard smoothed his hair, looked Laurent squarely in the eye and finally got to the point.

'I suppose you haven't the slightest idea what brings us by today. No doubt from the moment we knocked on your window, you've been dying to know what we're doing here. No, don't pretend,' he said with a sardonic smile, seeing Laurent's reaction. 'We hardly know each other, and here I show up out of the blue in the middle of this cold spell, and with my assistant to boot. It's only natural that you should wonder why.'

'As a matter of fact, I am curious,' Laurent said, and then hurried to add, 'but in any event I'm happy to have visitors on such a dreary afternoon. So tell me, Monsieur Jablard, to what do I owe the honour?'

'A very curious matter, but one that's good news for you, because unless I'm mistaken, you're quite the equestrian.'

Jablard didn't take his eyes off Laurent's face, studying his reaction. As Laurent made no reply, he went on. 'I suppose you haven't forgotten about the tragic incident at the château that took place during that splendid party Shennan threw.'

'Now you've got me intrigued. Why don't you cut to the chase? And yes,' he added, gesturing to the bottle, 'be my guest.'

Jablard, always obedient when given such an order, proceeded to pour himself a drink with the touching generosity of a man who knows someone else is picking up the tab. Then, glass filled almost to the brim, he sat back down on the black leather armchair and gave a roguish smile, knowing his next words would unsettle his host.

'As I was saying, I'm sure you haven't forgotten that doleful day.' He stopped again, perhaps hoping to catch a nervous twitch in Laurent. To no avail: Laurent had spent his childhood in Valparaíso under the care of an old Englishwoman who taught him the secrets of bridge, and his poker face could have got him a job on a Mississippi steamboat. 'Nor have you forgotten who was there that day. In fact, I think you were rather good friends with Madame Shennan.'

Watch what you say, you smug, potbellied arse, or you'll get a slap across the face, Laurent wanted to say. But he concealed his thoughts with an eloquent sarcasm.

'How could I forget? It's still the talk of the town. Saint-Chartier doesn't exactly have the social life of Gstaad or Saint-Tropez, and Shennan's untimely demise is probably the only thing of any note that's happened here.'

He took a slow, deliberate sip from his glass, holding the lawyer's gaze, and added calmly, 'And yes, I was good friends with the couple. With *both* of them.'

Jablard might be many things, but he was no fool, and

13

he quickly saw his best move would be to gallop back to the pastures of discretion and verbal decorum. As a young man, he'd been involved in enough scuffles to guess that Laurent would be quick to raise his hand if he felt offended. So he backpedalled:

'Of course, Monsieur de Rodergues. I didn't mean to imply anything else. Magnificent liqueur, by the way.'

Laurent smiled. He had that rare talent of not attaching importance to what doesn't deserve any, and he quickly put the incident behind him.

'One of my cousins is a Carthusian monk in Slovenia, in the Charterhouse of Pleterje, and every year when I visit him, he gets me two bottles.'

The portly lawyer, a hedonist whose first reaction to the soggy notion of voluntary sacrifice was to reach for his raincoat, looked puzzled for a moment, and could only muster the words, 'Ah – well, I suppose it takes all kinds.'

'Yes,' Laurent shot back, 'even lawyers.'

Sensing that the conversation wasn't going as well as planned, Jablard dispensed with the small talk and asked his assistant, who sat in the corner enjoying seeing his employer humiliated, for the documents that had brought them there.

'Now give me the papers, if you will, Monsieur Devaux . . . but my God, man, why didn't you get them ready earlier, instead of just sitting there like an angora cat?' Clearly, thought Laurent, he wouldn't be an easy man to work for.

Laurent waited with expectation. His alarm bells were ringing loud and clear, for deep down he always knew that one way or another Shennan's death would come back to haunt him. And this visit was the first sign.

The assistant dug both hands into an oversized leather briefcase and with no small effort extracted a bulky dossier that he handed to his boss. Jablard, without so much as a thank you, proceeded to open it and flip through the contents, licking his thumb every few pages.

'Now, as I was saying, I have here the reason we've come by.' He waved some very official-looking papers plastered with signatures and seals in Laurent's face. Then he adjusted his reading glasses and read out in a formal voice: 'I, Madame Mayumi Sayotaki Oden, widow of Carlos Shennan, sound of mind and body . . . blah blah blah, as the sole heiress of the deceased, and in accordance with my late husband's wishes, do hereby give his entire collection of stirrups, spurs and riding gear to Monsieur Laurent de Rodergues, blah blah blah.'

He now understood why the lawyer had been giving him such sardonic looks. Laurent stopped listening and wondered why on earth he'd been given this inheritance. After all, his relationship to Shennan was cordial but entirely superficial, grounded more in neighbourly courtesy than actual friendship. Indeed, Carlos Shennan, though affable and pleasant in the extreme, was the kind of person who always kept the conversation limited to what he wanted to share and never revealed what his listener actually wanted to know.

Suddenly it occurred to Laurent that Shennan's life and mind were like the château he aspired to make his home: full of doorways, hidden passages, underground chambers and tiny dungeons loaded with secrets. He had little time to reflect on all this, though, because his always practical mind had seized on something else the lawyer said: 'his entire collection'. Laurent felt short of breath. He'd seen said collection in full, and it contained hundreds of pieces, perhaps more than a thousand: gleaming engraved silver spurs from Mexico, spurs from Chile with needles arranged in the shape of an enormous sun, gold-ring gaucho spurs from Argentina, thick-shanked spurs from Ecuador and Bolivia. The stirrups, too, came in all shapes and sizes: sets from Japan made of fine lacquerware; from China in coarse rattan or heavy bronze with dragons rampant on the straps; from Mongolia, Tibet and the Mughal Empire; leather stirrups in the Castilian style; and not a few of those impressive Peruvian extravagances that attest to that country's past colonial riches. Without a doubt, it was a spectacular collection, but one he honestly couldn't accept because it simply wouldn't fit in his house. Nor did he want to waste a large portion of his life polishing it, no matter how much the childish side of his brain – the most creative half – yearned to make it his.

'I'm speechless,' said the newly named heir, giving a frown that many women would consider sexy and local men would mock as affected. 'I never thought being written into a will would be an inconvenience, but honestly I don't think I can accept it, even though its contents are entirely to my taste.'

'If you'll pardon me, Monsieur, that's an unwise choice.' The lawyer let his melodramatic side show. 'It's a magnificent collection, and I know you're passionate about riding. Besides, Madame Shennan hasn't the least interest in these things. Think it over, take your time. I'll leave you the inventory with photos of each item, so you can mull it over in peace.' And setting down before him a document that looked like *The Merck Manual*, he proceeded to stand up and shove poor Devaux toward the door. Laurent got up to see them out, and as the lawyer shook his hand, he whispered some parting words of advice.

'Take the collection, don't be a fool. I know an antiques dealer in Issoudun who can offer you a fantastic price should you decide not to keep it.'

As they drove off, Laurent stood there, hands on his hips, now understanding why the lawyer was so keen on him accepting the collection. He looked at the château walls, then went to sit on the church steps, which offered a better angle from which to view the towers and the walled grounds. A line from Tagore came to mind: 'the Taj Mahal is a teardrop on the cheek of time'. The same could be said, he thought, of the Château de Saint-Chartier, standing proudly in the very heart of France after centuries of upheaval.

The image of Shennan's lifeless body flashed through his mind. Laurent himself had found him in the search hastily arranged when some of the guests at the party noticed their host had gone missing. He remembered the scene as if it were a dream – or rather a nightmare. The circular stone tower with its enormous spiral staircases, the absolute silence, a cellar-like chill, and Shennan splayed out on his stomach with his head to one side, a permanent smile etched onto his face. Had it not been for the growing pool of blood, it would all have looked like another childish prank, like one of those jokes that used to make him burst into contagious laughter.

There were no signs of violence, and even his suit remained unwrinkled and unsmudged, its starchy shape unaltered. Thanks to some strange mechanism in Laurent's mind, his first thought was of his own tailor, who was always insistently recommending styles and fabrics that Laurent, just as insistently, would reject, explaining that such lavish expenditures lay neither within his budget nor within his means. No doubt that man would have cried for joy to see how well the deceased wore that cut, even in such gruesome circumstances. Shaking himself out of these frivolous thoughts, he detected something in the atmosphere around the body that defied explanation, a vague whiff of intent. Maybe Shennan, with that savage energy of his, managed in his last seconds to imbue the scene of his death with an air of suspicion, if only to play with everyone's minds, something he found endlessly entertaining.

In any event, in the days that followed, not a single piece of evidence turned up to lead the police to continue their investigation. The detectives and forensic experts unanimously agreed that Shennan had died in a tragic accident most likely caused by his habit of darting up and down stairs. In fact, Laurent recalled that on one occasion, after declining an invitation to play tennis, Shennan confided that he disliked sports but enjoyed going up and down stairs, especially after reading that it was the only physical exercise Cary Grant ever did to keep his figure. After the body was found, Laurent had run into some unpleasantness, but that was a whole different kettle of fish.

As he sat there enveloped in the smoke of the noxious cigars he liked to smoke – a blend of pungent Tuscan and reeking *caliqueño* tobaccos – Laurent de Rodergues let himself be carried away by his thoughts back to his first days in town, in the not yet distant past.

FOOD AND SHELTER

The train he'd boarded two hours earlier in Austerlitz left him at the station in Châteauroux. When he stepped outside, he could see practically nothing on that gloomy February morning except the gate of a girls' boarding school, which inevitably brought to mind the novels of Enid Blyton he used to pilfer from his little sisters. From *The Twins at St Clare's* to the more exciting *Malory Towers* saga, he spent his youth secretly in love with the alluring if contrived characters of Darrell, Pat, and Isabel.

A voice shook him out of his reverie. It belonged to a tall, energetic woman who held out her hand.

'Monsieur de Rodergues? My name is Claudine, and I've got the taxi you requested through the town hall in Saint-Chartier.' She cast a sideways glance at Laurent's small, cheap travel bag. 'Don't you have any more luggage? Or are you just here on a short trip?' Taxi drivers have a variety of interrogation methods, and no doubt the security services of several countries have adopted their techniques for making even the most tight-lipped passengers talk.

'No, on the contrary, I hope to stay here permanently, but the rest of my things will be delivered by the movers.'

The driver's eyes indicated her mind was already calculating how to extract as much information as possible from this outsider – information she'd of course pass on to her divorced cousin in Verneuil, such as the fact that the new arrival wore no ring and looked as tasty as a chocolate *petit chou*. Here in rural France, when it came to husband-hunting, women had to look out for each other: nearly all the local men were farmers who worked endless, draining days, and they weren't always appealing, no matter how romantic the sight of cows lowing on emerald fields looked from afar.

Once inside the vehicle, the driver, who handled her car very well, didn't let up until she'd learnt how he liked his vinaigrette on a duck gizzard salad. The battering ram she used to break through his defences was her praise of his perfect French – though she noted he had an enchanting accent she couldn't quite place.

'Is Monsieur from one of the overseas territories, from French Guiana, perhaps?'

Laurent welcomed the question with a laugh. He guessed at her intentions and decided to have a sense of humour about it. Certainly in the previous places he'd settled down, the rumour mill had been no less active, least of all in Chile, where he'd spent most of his life. Indeed, as Chileans themselves are the first to admit, they're quite the busybodies.

So it was that Claudine gathered all the relevant data: he was forty-five, unmarried, his parents had lived in Indochina exporting tropical woods until they were expelled in 1954 and had to move to Chile, specifically to Valparaíso, where his aunt and uncle owned several flower nurseries . . . As he answered her questions, Laurent took in the flat, pleasant, peaceful landscape of carefully tilled fields surrounded by several wooded areas. These he supposed contained wild boars, deer and roebuck, for he'd read that this was a region with a serious hunting tradition.

The towns they passed by may not have been especially remarkable, but their buildings had a consistent style and an undeniable tidiness. Also evident was that French tradition of preserving the past even when its symbols had nothing to do with the present: there were boundary crosses in every village, monuments to those who had given their lives for the *patrie*, church towers and a general air of undisturbed comfort. When they reached a lookout point, he asked the driver to stop. The little hillock offered views onto an area known as the Vallée Noire, a vast and charming patchwork of dark thickets, green pastures and little villages spread out underneath a haughty sky of the most magnificent azure.

Back in the car, Laurent decided that the best way to avoid repeating his story over and over again was to tell it all now, since Claudine would no doubt relay it in minute detail to every living soul in the area. He didn't omit a thing: his education in a Jesuit boarding school in Santiago, his stifling career as a sales engineer, the outdoor activities that Chile's extraordinary geography offers, the many years he spent working as a guide and ski instructor at high-end hotels in national parks: Torres del Paine, the Atacama Desert, Chiloé, Easter Island, Osorno . . . Obviously, there was no skirting around the question of why he'd come to

Berry, and when the driver learnt that Laurent's grandfather was a Berrichon, she couldn't contain her excitement: an attractive man with local blood to boot! That was too good to be true. In Berry, having a local pedigree, even just a single grandparent from the area, was very important.

Laurent knew that the dreaded question about his future plans couldn't be avoided, though he clung to the hope that he might reach his destination without having to comment. When the time came, all he could do was answer, 'I haven't the slightest idea. For some time now I've wanted a change, to live in a quiet, unfamiliar place where I can think, try to write a bit, ride, eat well and wait for destiny to give me a hint about what I should do next.'

'Well, you've come to the perfect place, Monsieur. Saint-Chartier ticks all those boxes, plus a few more besides. Not only that, you're in the land of Romanticism. Did you know that less than two miles down the road is the manor house that once belonged to George Sand? They hold the Chopin festival there, along with other cultural events where you can meet all sorts of interesting people. And once you get settled, I'd recommend getting a cup of coffee at La Cocadrille, where you can get to know some of the locals and find out the latest gossip. I'm pretty busy shuttling people to and from La Châtre for doctor's appointments, but if you need anything, my cousin Annabelle in Verneuil will be happy to help you out.' She looked at him in the rear-view mirror. 'She's cute as a button, I can tell you that.' Here too, it seemed, the Amazons roamed free.

Laurent saw then that as peaceful as the town was, in

Saint-Chartier, as anywhere else, the demands of the heart were anxious to be met. He sighed. That was one of the reasons he sought refuge here: at his former job he worked in idyllic settings that had left his emotional storehouse overflowing with enough fond memories and bedroom adventures to get him through several winters.

After paying and thanking the driver, Laurent spent a while figuring out which of the keys on the enormous ring would open the gate to the town's vicarage or clergy house. No, his grandfather wasn't a priest – that would have looked rather bad in France – but the *sabotier*, or clog-maker, and his home and workshop sat just behind the vicarage. Over many long years of hard work, he'd managed to save enough to buy the priest's house and annex it to his own, hoping it might one day belong to his only grandson, whom he'd seen only in photos and once during a hurried meal in the Gare de Lyon. The thought of his grandfather filled him with regret. Laurent's father had died when he was still a child, and his mother's financial circumstances didn't allow them to take holiday trips to the Old Continent, so he knew his grandfather only through the stories she told and a few letters and postcards he received. Now he was about to move into a house that the old man had bought for him with the savings of a life spent carving wood to make clogs, and he promised he wouldn't let him down.

When he turned to pick up his single piece of luggage, he suddenly caught sight of a large structure that until then, unaccountably, he simply hadn't seen: the château. He was astonished. Laurent thought himself very observant, and his failure to notice the large wall with turrets standing right in front of him could only be explained by how engrossed he'd been in the chit-chat with the taxi driver. He then recalled reading something about a château in the travel guides he'd looked through, but in France the word 'château' could be used rather pompously to describe anything a larger than a manor house. He hardly expected to find a medieval fortress looming in front of him, so close to what was now to be his home. Awestruck, he stood for a moment in admiration. A man motored by atop a huge tractor, raising two fingers to his brow in a sort of salute. Then an old woman appeared out of nowhere with a quart of milk in an old-fashioned brass container, eyes gleaming as she practically shouted at him, 'Bonjour, Monsieur. You must be the grandson of Monsieur Fanchier. I'm your neighbour, and I knew your grandfather very well. I've brought you some croissants and some milk for your coffee.' Before Laurent could thank her, the lady was already shaking his hand, telling him she'd be happy to help with anything he needed.

A slight breeze, so bracingly cold he shivered, seemed to seize him from the inside, and in his head he heard the quiet voice of experience whispering that he was going to feel quite comfortable in this town.

LA COCADRILLE TAVERN

Some days went by, enough for Laurent to clean the house from top to bottom: it had sat empty for nearly ten years. He bought appliances and everything else he needed that wouldn't arrive in his shipping container, and he made several trips to the town hall to find out how to set up his utilities and fill his tank with heating fuel, since he sensed winter would come rough and rude. Most complicated of all was the purchase of a car, because he was naturally clumsy, and mechanics weren't his strong suit. In a fit of patriotism for his new home, he opted for a Citroën Jumpy van – cheap and efficient and as French as the Andouille sausage from Angoulême.

After a week, once his home had taken on a certain comfortable air, Laurent decided to take a break and get to know his new surroundings a little better. But first he needed to reward himself with a real coffee, if possible with a few fingers of one of those liqueurs that soothe an adverse fate and placate the deities of the home. He remembered the advice he'd gotten from Claudine, the taxi driver, and he headed straight for La Cocadrille, the tavern on the main road through town that he saw each time he drove to La Châtre or Châteauroux.

The tavern stood right next to the police station, up the street from the main entrance to the château. He stopped in front of the château gate, intrigued by the bustle he'd noticed from outside. Covering the building was an elaborate network of scaffolding of all shapes and sizes, while hoists, cranes and a bevy of small backhoes were scattered across the grounds, operated and surrounded by an army of construction workers. Clearly the château was undergoing a thorough renovation, as he saw from the notice that by law has to be posted outside every worksite. He couldn't make out the names of the owner, the architect or the construction company, since the recent endless rains had partly washed out the lettering. But that didn't matter, he thought, for the tavern was sure to be an extension of the taxi: a sort of living local newsletter. From the outside, though, it didn't look terribly promising. With its slate roof and smoking chimney, it was identical to every other building in town. The only thing that stood out was the large sign hanging on the wall, a veritable tribute to traditional French ironworking, emblazoned with a strange mythological creature apparently made up of various animals that reminded Laurent of a velociraptor with feathers.

Nevertheless, what looked from the outside like an unremarkable house turned out to contain a delightful traditional *bistrot*, with little white marble tables with brass footrests and large rusty mirrors in antique gilt frames. Best of all, in spite of the signs forbidding smoking, an undeniable scent of tobacco hung in the air, and suspiciously empty coffee cups sat next to all the drinks the patrons were sipping.

The bartender, a hulk of a man with a head like a Roman bust and receding waves of black hair, didn't look at all out of place in that setting. He wore his white shirtsleeves crisply rolled up to reveal hairy forearms that rested on the bar, and Laurent noticed him looking at him as though he'd been waiting for some time.

'Good morning, Monsieur de Rodergues. I thought you'd never deign to stop by our establishment,' he said, giving his hand an effusive shake. He had the hands of a pelota player. 'I'm Gaston Le Juanch, the owner of this dive, and I can tell you I had a great fondness and respect for your grandfather.'

Then, noticing that the rest of his customers had turned to look, he took the opportunity to introduce Laurent. If anonymity had been one of Laurent's hopes in moving here, he could strike that off his list. Still, he gladly agreed to be treated to a first round in memory of his grandfather, about whom everyone had something nice to say, and he had a nice chat with two old-timers who introduced themselves as friends who used to play belote with him.

Before long he was feeling tipsy but happy. Everyone insisted on buying him a drink to welcome him to town, on the grounds that it was time for the midday aperitif. He downed several glasses on an empty stomach: a sweet concoction of grapefruit juice and rosé, another of crème de cassis and white wine, as well as a pastis or two. Fortunately, the French take mealtime punctuality very seriously, and at twelve-thirty everyone left to go home for lunch. Laurent was used to eating on a Latin American schedule, and after unexpectedly ingesting all that alcohol, his stomach was in no mood for jokes.

When the others had gone, he sat alone chatting with Le Juanch, who turned out to be a crafty old fox and made his coffee a double-double. He downed it, and Le Juanch asked if he'd like something to eat. Even amid the distractions of the drinks and introductions, Laurent couldn't help noticing an enticing and impressively wide variety of tapas and hors d'oeuvre arranged Spanish-style on one side of the bar, behind a pane of glass, and he could hardly say no. He was surprised to come across this bit of Spain here, knowing how rarely the French admit modifications to their culinary habits. Gaston explained that as a young man he worked in Andalusia for a French water-treatment company, and working as a salesman throughout Spain, he'd gotten used to having tapas at bars.

'So whenever we don't want to be understood, we can just speak in Spanish,' he said, half in jest. Laurent raised his cup to that.

Then Gaston explained that the tavern, located as it was in a small town with few customers, offered a simple lunch menu consisting of an appetiser, a *salade du jour* and a traditional, hearty main course. They served no cheese course but did have homemade desserts. Laurent's mind was made up – he didn't even ask what the main course was. He felt at home in this place, and the smells wafting in from the kitchen indicated he was in for something rich and substantial.

He ordered the house wine Le Juanch suggested and sat down next to a large window looking out on to the château.

From there, as the food was served, he watched the progress of the construction. The place had piqued his curiosity, and he'd tried to learn as much about it as he could, but the information he'd been able to find was limited. The Château de Saint-Chartier had, it seemed, quite a storied past, dating all the way back to the seventh century, when a Syrian monk named Carterius – or Chartier, in French – built a monastery fortress under the patronage of the Abbey of Déols. Later it passed on to the Lord and Lady of Déols, who married their daughter Denise to André de Chavigny, a crusader who followed his cousin Richard the Lionheart to the Holy Land and died in combat. A couple of centuries later Joan of Arc even stayed there, according to one historian, since at the time it belonged to the father of one of her lieutenants, a certain Lord Boutillier, and that was why the lone tower was still called the Tour des Anglais. The château survived the Hundred Years' War, and several centuries and lords later it wound up with the Comte de Moreton de Chabrillan, Napoleon's chief aide-de-camp. The emperor's brief stay in the château after his defeat at Waterloo gave rise to the legend of its hidden treasure. In the nineteenth century, George Sand used it as the setting for her novel *The Master Pipers*, and since 1976 the château had been home to the famous Festival International des Luthiers. He had an easier time finding information about this event, an annual gathering of musicians and instrument makers that for over thirty years had been held on the château grounds. The previous year had been its last, because Carlos Shennan, the new *châtelain* – a term for feudal lords that the French still use for château owners – had decided he would no longer host the festival.

He gave many reasons, the main one being the restoration work, for he intended to renovate the building as his home.

From what Laurent could gather, this decision provoked the ire of a lot of the locals, as well as many musicians, artisans, scholars and instrument makers who regularly attended the festival. They'd become his fiercest critics, though it wasn't lost on Laurent that part of their criticism was directed at the new owner's foreign background. In local newspapers, and in articles and columns about the festival, he came across some very pointed remarks about the sale of the château and its buyer, who fuelled all sorts of speculations. He even found a physiognomic study of Shennan's facial features published alongside his photo, signed by a woman using the name 'Thracian Zither'. She went so far in her searing conclusions that Laurent decided that either she was a loon or she was dying to get her hands on the new *châtelain*'s flesh.

Still, after he studied the photo for a moment he could easily draw his own conclusions, since in his life he'd run into more than a few individuals like him. Carlos Shennan was one of those men born with all of the charms Mother Nature has to bestow, and which she so often distributes unfairly. He possessed an angular face and classic Irish grey eyes with a mischievous or cocky gleam. Laurent could tell he was thin but sinewy, with a good figure and skin made leathery by a sun that doesn't shine in the more genteel latitudes. He also noticed a scar over his eyebrow, and another on the bridge of his nose, no doubt due to a type of boxing not sanctioned by the Olympics. But what stood out most to Laurent was his smile: it seemed to defy the whole world. He could tell that the face, while handsome, could swiftly and surely go from kindness to cruelty.

Yes, that was a portrait of a conqueror and a lone wolf. He exuded intelligence, skill and relentlessness, along with a healthy dose of worldliness, of course, and the air of someone who knows how to use his charms. The physiognomist wasn't far off, he thought. What would she say about him? Bah! he snorted. Best not to think about it.

Lost in his thoughts, Laurent didn't hear Gaston approach and quietly set down before him a plate filled with all sorts of *petites bouchées*. He looked down in delight at the little bites and wondered which one to start with when Gaston pointed out the window toward the château park, where two people were engaged in what appeared to be a very heated debate. The one gesturing wildly was none other than Monsieur Shennan. His face was illuminated with a demonic light as he stood shaking a roll of blueprints and shouting at a large man in a hard hat, who did his best to weather the storm.

'It's not an uncommon sight with the head of the Portuguese crew. Who knows what he botched this time?' explained Gaston. 'His employees are excellent, but he's a fool, and I bet Monsieur Shennan's patience has reached its limit. I'm afraid we won't be seeing much of them any more. I feel bad for his four employees, who are wonderful, not to mention good customers.'

'Well, I imagine a restoration project like that isn't easy to oversee. Doesn't he have a construction manager or someone helping him out?' He had trouble getting the last words out, because he'd stuffed a small roasted pepper filled with hot goat cheese into his mouth, failing, in his gluttony, to properly calibrate the time between the end of his sentence and insertion of the *bouchée*.

'Yes, another idiot, a guy from Barcelona by the name of Andrés . . . he had us all fooled at first, but he turned out to be a cheap con artist with a fake engineering degree. Since Monsieur Shennan didn't live here, and his business kept him away, he couldn't keep an eye on him, but as soon as he found out he gave the guy the boot, just as he did with the carpenter, Carlo Melisso, another swindler. Believe me, a lot of people talk bad about Monsieur Shennan, but I've lived in front of the château since I was a kid, and it takes a pair to do what he's doing. If it weren't for him, in a few years the château would have been a pile of rubble.'

Laurent speared a mini sausage with a stick of celery inserted in the middle and wrapped in a piece of fried pancetta.

'I'm not one to judge, because I just got here, but from what I gather he seems to have more detractors than friends.'

Gaston looked at him squarely in the face. 'You can say that again. But you can also bet that none of them are from Saint-Chartier. I'd even wager that none of the people badmouthing him have ever done a thing for the town except attend the festival. Personally, I like him. He's a straight shooter and good drinker, and he's fixing up our monument – because incidentally, here we feel the château belongs to all of us. Your grandfather felt that way too. So Shennan's a foreigner. Who cares? Madame Curie was Polish, Chagall was Russian, Louis de Funès was from Seville, and Yves Montand from Italy. And you're from

Chile, so you probably know that Matta, the painter, was from your country. Same with Jodorowsky. And they were all adopted by France, weren't they? Right now the main thing is to support him so his project is a success, because it'll be a boon for everyone, you can be sure of that. Besides, despite all the grumbling about the festival, I know La Châtre wanted to move it to the Château d'Ars, which is owned by the town government.'

All Laurent could do with his mouth full was nod while his host held forth, especially since he saw nothing to quibble with. But mostly he wanted to give the matter a rest, because the wise diner, if the dish is good, savours his food in silence. Luckily Gaston was a professional and quickly grasped the situation. He apologised for the rant, saying he'd let him enjoy his food in peace while he went to the kitchen to check on the salad and the main course. On the menu today were Berry lentils with rice pilaf, blood pudding and fried onion. Not exactly light fare.

Laurent spent the rest of the time relishing that simple yet superb meal, which concluded with some unreasonably delicious poached pears and a plum liqueur made in house – in a private still, as Gaston whispered in a tone meant for serious matters that require discretion. To tell the truth, he said, with all the regulations and red tape nowadays, you didn't know which hand to wipe your arse with.

A GREAT DANE AND
A CHINESE CRESTED

Saint-Chartier was a small but picturesque town, and Laurent decided to explore the area on foot in a series of outings. After he got his dog, a black Belgian Shepherd he christened Chimay (after the beer of the same name), he set about carrying out his plan with gusto, since his companion turned out to be a tireless walker.

He spent these walks thinking about what his future might hold. He'd arrived in France with luggage and gear but without a clear, definitive plan – just the certainty that he needed a long break from his job and social life. Specifically, he needed to get away from a certain gorgeous but problematic woman . . . and above all from the powerful politician she was married to. It wasn't his fault if he kept meeting unsatisfied women in search of a stud to alleviate their marital troubles – troubles of a largely sexual nature. What else could he do? 'It's a question of patriotism,' said his uncle in Valparaíso, the one who had the flower nursery, stroking his white moustache. 'A Frenchman must never let anyone question our reputation for romantic prowess.'

A new life: that's what Laurent had decided to build, and he believed it wasn't too late. He hadn't yet reached fifty, he was in perfect shape, and he'd never let himself be carried away by any dangerous pursuits save sports. He had no time for drugs, gambling, alcoholism or other vices. Nor did he smoke or eat to excess. In fact, women were his only weakness.

His saving grace was that his interest was not merely sexual. He loved everything about women: he adored talking to them, listening to them, watching them, even going shopping with them. In fact, some of the ones he'd lived with openly mocked him for his obsession with organising their wardrobe.

That was the problem: Laurent fell in love with each and every one. What's worse, he fell in love with them all at the same time. If only he could become – to quote a Nobel prize-winning writer whose name he couldn't recall – a serial monogamist! No, he was a sentimental philanderer and couldn't bear to go without even a single one of his women. But therein lay the rub: keeping them all happy took a physical, psychic and monetary toll on him, and robbed time from everything else, since Laurent, to top it off, was a considerate man who never forgot to call, write, send a postcard or, when his grim finances allowed, buy a gift that was 'simple but heartfelt', as he'd say as he presented them.

No doubt, he needed a long sabbatical, far from the temptations that Latin America offered him.

* * *

First of all, as a form of therapy, he resolved to do all household chores himself and to maintain a Prussian tidiness. Neither cleaning, nor washing, nor cooking, nor ironing posed any challenge, but the house had a tiny yard and came with a small plot in a community garden next to the old wash house, out on the footpath to the town of La Preugne, so he'd set about learning the basics of growing and gardening to keep the landscaping in his small terrain under control. He also found he had to become a handyman, since the rates technicians charged in France were so high that when he received his first bills he nearly died of shock. Little by little he started exploring the daunting array of publications on such disciplines available in bookstores and kiosks, and gradually his intimidation gave way to enthusiasm, as he noticed a certain level of success in his work.

He began to enjoy everything he did, even running into neighbours from the village and exchanging a courteous 'Bonjour, Madame' or 'Bonjour, Monsieur' as everyone in rural France still does when they see each other on the street. And with his two daily walks with the dog, he now had, for the first time in his life, something that could be called a methodical, orderly existence, a prospect that years back would have made him retch.

In the afternoons, right after lunch, he took a route that led down a path by the church and on to the cemetery, and then continued on up to the farm where Monsieur Roger raised his Appaloosa horses. From there Laurent would head down toward the police station, past the tavern and the post office, around the town hall and onto a path carpeted in dense mown grass curiously called the 'Ladies' Path', which led past the Bodard chapel and along the river to the main road.

One peaceful afternoon, not long after starting out on his walk, he heard a huge commotion of dogs barking, little girls squealing and shouting in English, and an adult woman yelling something after them in some incomprehensible tongue. Chimay went tense and pricked up his ears. Suddenly a tiny freak of a dog rounded the corner of a moss-covered wall and shot toward them. A bounding Great Dane came hard on its heels, followed in turn by three girls, each in a multicoloured parka – and not cheap ones, as Laurent, veteran skier that he was, could tell from afar. Running and stumbling after them came an inconceivably overbundled something or other, shouting in a high voice and clearly not in the local dialect. Laurent stood, mouth agape, though in his defence it should be said that he reacted with presence of mind: he'd spent too much of his life doing outdoor sports not to see that the dogs had gotten off their leashes and were heading straight for the road. As he knew, Great Danes are as dumb as they are playful, so the scene could end in a dramatic accident if that gang of dogs and girls made it to the road.

To keep this from happening, Laurent saw that he first had to stop the freakish little dog, which, to judge by its barking, was having a ball. Its breed was anyone's guess: it was a little thing, about as tall as a beagle but much skinnier and mostly hairless, with just a few moles on its body and tufts of fur on its ears and its lower legs, and a crest on the top of its head. It was wrapped in what looked like a doll's dress, in a cheery fuchsia, with – and here Laurent thought he was seeing things – a purse of the same colour slung over its leg, bouncing back and forth as it ran.

Good Lord, he thought, *it takes some nerve to dress up a dog like that out here in rural Berry*. But a tug by Chimay yanked him out of his thoughts and forced him to react. He had to do three things: first, make his dog obey and not bolt off; second, grab the little dog as best he could; and third, and most difficult, not let the Great Dane tear the other dogs – or him, or his clothes – to pieces.

This is what happened: Chimay was restless but stayed put. The little pink creature leapt into Laurent's arms (he had, after all, a certain animal magnetism), and the Great Dane . . . well, there was no way to stop it from tackling him and covering him in mud and strands of slobber as thick as the curtains in the Château de Chambord. At this point Chimay, instead of defending his master, began to lick the muzzle of the mutt or whatever it was in the pink dress. The damned thing must have been in heat, because it seemed to enjoy it and got so agitated and hot that it peed all over Laurent. The Great Dane, meanwhile, managed to slip its rope of a tongue inside the collar of his raincoat. To top it off, suddenly three pairs of children's feet began to kick him in the buttocks and lower back, shouting, 'Dog thief! We'll tell our daddy and you'll be sorry!' 'Let Barbie go, you bad man!' 'Olaf, kill him, he's trying to kidnap your girlfriend!' It should be said that this last instruction, despite shedding light on the Great Dane's name, was none too reassuring.

As if to prove things can always get worse, a delicate little child-sized foot hit him squarely in the jewels, and at that point Laurent realised all he could do was bear it with as much dignity as he could. Clearly the proverb about a good death bringing honour to your life wouldn't apply here. Fortunately for him, someone appeared at his side and began pulling the animals and girls off him.

From the person's tone, speaking now in English, he guessed that it was the bundle wrapped up to the eyebrows he'd seen running behind the girls. Her voice was calmer now, sweet and angelic – although, truth be told, any voice of rescue, even the rum-soaked growl of a pirate, would have sounded to Laurent's ears like the song of a castrati choir.

Freeing him was no easy task, and the girls clearly didn't care one whit that the woman with the heavenly voice was telling them to get off. Even in such a plight, what Laurent most desired was not to get the peeing dogs off him but to see the face that went with that siren's voice. Perhaps the woman in question read his mind, for she unwound the scarf and threw back her hood, revealing one of the most beautiful faces Laurent had ever seen: she was small, with large eyes, golden skin, long earlobes stretched by a pair of heavy gold earrings, a mouth with coral lips and gleaming white teeth. Her smile made abundantly clear how sorry she was about the situation and what sympathy she felt for the man on the ground.

Laurent looked up at her, silently imploring her to sort out the mess, though he knew full well she couldn't. Even struck with Cupid's arrow, he still had enough sense to see that this young woman, a sort of governess or nanny he supposed, was pleading in an unknown language to no avail.

Luckily, just then, through the frigid wind of early March came another voice, clear and decisive, issuing an order that would brook no disobedience. The rabble quieted down, the slobber practically crystallised from fright, the girls leapt off Laurent as if he had the plague, and even the dogs moved a prudent distance away. Only Chimay continued rolling on the ground, eyes fixed on the little dog.

As Laurent, now a mess, got up and tried to pull himself together, another Asian woman walked over, apparently their mother. Tall and thin, she possessed that rare, elegant beauty that has something of the supernatural about it. She had devilishly dark eyes and a face full of angles, each more unsettling, intriguing, fascinating than the last, while her marble-white skin set off the straight, jet-black hair that waved gently as she walked. Everything about her exuded elegance: no doubt her ancestors had enjoyed power and regular meals for many generations, two things that ultimately give their descendants character and great confidence.

When the woman reached the group, she looked at the girls and the dogs, whose eyes were all glued to the ground, and then turned to Laurent with a surprisingly friendly smile. He saw a distinct sense of humour from the edges of her lips and the fine lines around her eyes, which remained firm, even if not immune to time. She extended her hand and introduced herself in proper French.

'Good afternoon. My name is Mayumi Shennan, and I apologise for this mishap. Rest assured it will not happen again. The girls and I are going to have a serious talk.' Saying this, she turned to look at them again, and all three girls were overcome by an identical shudder of terror.

Laurent could tell that the Japanese woman who radiated authority was, in all likelihood, a good mother, meting out intelligent punishments, which also tend to be the harshest. He couldn't help but laugh when he saw the panic written across the faces of each of the girls, and even those of the Great Dane and the little dog.

'It's nothing,' he reassured her. 'Forgive them, please – they've practically done me a favour, since I certainly needed a little exercise,' he said with a smile, apologising for the girls.

Madame Mayumi looked at him fondly, and feigning seriousness, responded, 'You're very kind, and I appreciate your goodwill, but we can't let them get off scot-free after the mess they've made of your clothes. By the way, you've got some saliva and a bit of moss hanging from your ear.' She handed him a tissue. 'And apparently our nanny lost control of the situation.'

When the nanny heard this, a stricken look came across her face. Then, to Laurent's surprise, Madame Mayumi put her arm around her affectionately, and she immediately recovered her calm. It was a strange gesture, as if the girl were like another daughter to her, or a little sister. Finally, Madame Mayumi issued her judgment.

'Still, I think we can overlook it this time, don't you? On one condition: that you come back with us for tea, so we can get those clothes cleaned up. I'm sure we can find something of my husband's for you to wear in the meantime. I think you two are the same size.'

'I'd be delighted, mostly because I suspect you won't take no for an answer,' Laurent replied.

Madame Mayumi gave a hearty laugh. 'You've got a shrewd eye, Monsieur . . .'

'Laurent, Laurent de Rodergues.'

'So you're Monsieur de Rodergues. We've heard of you; you're the new neighbour who just moved into the vicarage. My husband is very eager to meet you. Sadly he's in Châteauroux today, arguing with the architects from the Heritage Office. I'm sure the two of you will have a lot to talk about, such as your experiences in Patagonia and Araucanía – along with the customs and habits of the native women, no doubt.'

When they reached the town hall, a local who was just coming out of the building stopped to stare at them with an unmistakable look of disgust. Putting his beret on his head, he muttered audibly, 'Lovely! Now everyone's become all buddy-buddy.' Then he spat on the ground and walked deliberately away. Laurent had half a mind to run over to him and slap him across the face, and he made a move to do so, but Madame Mayumi grabbed him by the arm with unexpected strength.

'It's nothing, let it go. Only fools think they can be liked by everyone.'

The farmer's attitude and Mayumi's words left Laurent more than a little confused. A gust of frigid air blew over him. He knew her words weren't meant for him. And yet, taken together with the local's scornful remark, it showed that the sleepy town of Saint-Chartier wasn't the haven of peace and tranquillity he thought he'd moved to.

That's the second drop of vitriol she's dispensed in the last few minutes, he thought. Then he began to wonder whether perhaps the life of Carlos Shennan wasn't as carefree or happy as it seemed, at least not domestically – because if one thing was clear beyond a shadow of a doubt, it was that his wife didn't bow down before anyone.

Lost in these thoughts, he walked through the château's magnificent gates, with one girl's hand in each of his own and the third hanging onto his jacket. Suddenly he felt himself being watched. He turned and saw the farmer, still staring at them with a scowl of deepest loathing.

Fortunately, he was distracted by the Great Dane, who gave a woof and set off bounding happily across the château grounds, unaware that the crafty Chimay was trying to snatch his morsel – a vivid illustration that many a romantic betrayal is due less to the villainy of the usurper than to the cluelessness of the usurpee.

As he walked on, Laurent saw that the château was in a frenzy of construction, especially the exteriors and the garden, where several workers struggled to move heavy blocks of stone.

Mayumi and the strikingly beautiful nanny led the way, walking close together and talking softly, until a third Asian woman came running to Mayumi with a worried look on her face and interrupted the conversation. Shennan's wife, always mindful of her guest, motioned for him to follow the girls up the stairs to the large northern entrance. The girls, meanwhile, wouldn't let go of him, tugging on his arm to lead him to their room so they could show him the fossils they'd unearthed during construction. So he had no choice but to let himself be led, while the nanny followed along behind.

The terrace was impressive: it was a huge space of over five hundred square yards, with two doors at the end, one on either side of a central tower. A smaller door, presumably the oldest and perhaps original entrance, led to the tower, no doubt with a cramped spiral staircase.

Laurent suddenly felt a powerful curiosity about what the château looked like from the inside – along with a desire to explore it hand-in-hand with the nanny. Yet Laurent was not naive: by then he knew all too well that the peace of his recent days would soon be little more than a memory. A sixth sense warned him that trouble loomed on the horizon.

IN THE GUEST ROOM

Laurent didn't know how the château would be decorated. He half-expected to find a faithfully restored façade with an enormous exhibition of modern art on the inside, complete with some impossibly uncomfortable designer furniture. These stray thoughts were interrupted when a swarm of servants, all impeccably liveried for their duties, came to open the door for them. At first he felt flattered by what he assumed was an inordinate amount of attention lavished on him, as a guest, but he quickly realised that the maids and footmen were all looking expectantly at Madame Mayumi, who had just crossed the terrace and entered the hall, trailed by the other Asian woman who had gone out to find her. Once inside, the servants crowded around, all requiring something of her and jostling to speak with her before the others.

She calmed them down in a professional tone of voice, or so it seemed to Laurent, though since she spoke a different language with each one, he understood very little. Once she'd reassured the surprisingly large retinue, she issued orders to the nanny to take her daughters upstairs. Before they left, they first made Laurent promise he would indeed visit their room. Then Madame Mayumi excused herself in turn, as she apparently had to go straight to the kitchen to see to some culinary crisis or other.

Laurent, suddenly alone, stood for a few seconds watching her leave, when he felt someone else tugging at his sleeve. He was surprised to see a fourth Asian woman, one who introduced herself as Miss Xiao Li, Mr Shennan's personal secretary. In fluent English she asked him to follow her to a room where he could change clothes so that she could have his washed. Afterwards, she assured him, she would take him to the hunting room for tea with her employer's wife.

As he followed her, he studied her: she was rail-thin, almost brittle, but her eyes contained a world of suspicion. She gave off a scent of clothing that had grown old as she'd worn it. To break the silence, which had inexplicably turned hostile and thick, Laurent tried to make small talk, but the only thing that occurred to him was to praise Madame Mayumi. This was met with an ill-disguised scepticism and a cold, clipped reply. He could easily see, from the way she referred to her, that she felt no affection for her employer's wife. Once he overcame his initial surprise, however, he quickly came up with one possible explanation: as her name indicated, clearly the secretary was Chinese, and ever since the Rape of Nanking in 1937, successive governments had sought to instil in their people a hatred of all things Japanese (even as they welcomed their neighbours' investments with open arms). On further reflection, Laurent decided that Xiao Li's antipathy toward Madame Mayumi probably had other causes, and he recalled a psychological condition aptly called 'secretary's syndrome', which would explain the murky mix of subservience, admiration and idolatry he suspected she felt for her boss.

After all his attempts to strike up a conversation ended in failure, Laurent decided to follow Shennan's secretary in silence. They crossed several rooms and eventually climbed a steep spiral staircase that the French call a *colimaçon*, or snail. On the stairs Laurent noticed two things: first, that Xiao Li, despite her thinness, had fantastic legs; and second, that he was entirely mistaken in his intuitions about the château's interior design. Everything he saw, in the way it was arranged, indicated that whoever decorated the place not only had good taste but was a consummate connoisseur. Nothing clashed, everything was soothing and harmonious, with the unmistakable aroma that comes from a mixture of the ancient, the beautiful and the good, combined with the obviously expensive. As he proceeded through the house he admired pillowy eighteenth-century French and Spanish rugs; Flemish and Gobelin tapestries depicting mythological and sylvan scenes; sideboards inlaid with ivory and mother-of-pearl that held marvellous religious sculptures with exceptional patinas; and a panoply of arms, including one set that particularly caught his attention – a collection of intricate swords and daggers of Hindustani origin, as he read on their bronze plaque. Sadly, though, he had no time for such artistic contemplation, for the secretary had already climbed the stairs with the nimbleness of a lemur, and he had to make an effort to follow her and not lose his breath.

When they reached the third floor, Xiao Li opened the door to a bedroom – one of the guest rooms, she explained, where he could change once suitable clothing had been brought. Just as Madame Mayumi had predicted, he was exactly the same size as Monsieur Shennan.

Once alone, Laurent took a leisurely look at his surroundings. The bedroom was unusually large and seemed to revolve around a fireplace big enough to comfortably roast a Bactrian camel. If Shennan's aim was make his guests feel transported to the very essence of castle life, then he deserved a medal, maybe one of those brutal Soviet badges that Russian generals use to hide their vodka stains.

Curiously, the complete set of furniture added an unexpected note of warmth, though the first-time visitor's eyes could see only the English bed with its enormous canopy and columns so exquisitely carved they left no groove for the turner's gouge. Laurent approached to better appreciate the detailed work in the wood, when he noticed a tray of spirits thoughtfully placed next to the wing chair over a Tabriz rug. It was a welcome amenity, and Laurent, of course, did not hesitate to help himself.

After pouring himself a beautiful glass of Calvados Grande Réserve, he turned to the bathroom, a perfect visual continuation of the bedroom, since the toilets and taps were of brands that specialised in reproducing classic models.

With one hand he raised the glass to his lips, while with the other he ran his hands over the fittings, pausing to consider that the showerhead alone probably cost as much as all the appliances and bathroom fittings in his vicarage. *Well, what's the point of having money if you don't spend it?* he thought. *At least this individual – or whoever's advising him – has a flawless sense of aesthetics.*

Shortly thereafter, wrapped tightly in a cosy robe, Laurent turned toward the door, intending to place the hamper with all his dirty clothes and shoes in the corridor. As he did so, he thought he heard a faint childlike giggling. But that was impossible, because it came from inside the room. Yet after a moment he heard it again, so after setting the basket outside he walked back in, ready to inspect the room from top to bottom. Meanwhile, the giggling grew louder and louder, but Laurent still couldn't find the source.

He was drawing back a curtain when he heard someone clearly call him by his name – and that someone was behind him. He leapt up like a startled cat, as much as his weighty, tassel-bedecked robe would let him, and found himself face-to-face with Shennan's daughters, who stood right there, in his room, doubled over with laughter.

'Scared you, didn't we?' asked one.

'He was scared to death, you could tell,' added the other.

'You look funny in that robe,' declared the youngest without compunction.

Laurent couldn't help but laugh along with them. These girls were quite the little rascals.

'But where did you come from? Were you hiding under the bed?' he asked, to no avail, since their laughter prevented them from responding.

Suddenly the oldest girl silenced them with a motion of her hand. She looked at her sisters, seeming to ask them a question, and finally turned back to Laurent.

'If we tell you a secret, do you promise not to tell anyone?'

'What kind of secret, and why would you tell me if you've only just met me?'

'Because you're nice. And you're like a kid inside, even if on the outside you're a grown-up,' explained the second one.

'Plus you're handsome,' started the youngest, but she didn't dare go on, after the fierce looks of warning from her sisters.

Laurent nodded, not knowing whether to feel flattered or offended by the girls' words. After all, they had just called him childish and easily scared. In the end he raised his right hand and solemnly declared, 'You have my word, lovely ladies, and I assure you your trust does me honour.' And then he performed a palace bow, which they seemed to enjoy very much.

Then the oldest of the sisters took him by the hand in silence and proudly led him to a wooden panel in the wall that she slid aside with ease.

'Look! I bet you'd never notice, right?' she said with an air of satisfaction.

'No one else knows about it, not even Mum or Dad,' added the middle sister. 'You and our nanny are the only ones.'

Laurent noticed right away why no one would have noticed it during the restoration work. In front of the panel stood an ancient silver processional lamp that rested at an angle on the floor, attached by a thick chain to the upper edge of the wainscoting above the panel.

Both this panel and those on either side were quite thick, and as they were in good condition, the restorers had had to do nothing more than clean and wax them, so no one had discovered the secret door.

Laurent leant down for a closer look: behind the panel was a steep, narrow tunnel carved out of the stone, through which only a very slight person could fit, like the girls or their nanny, the one who drove Laurent mad.

'The passage goes straight up to the toy room, next to our bedroom. Tum found it, and she opened it up and has been secretly cleaning it. Every day she sneaks out small pebbles and things in her bag, just like in the movies,' explained the oldest girl, while the others smiled and nodded, each prouder than the last.

Laurent said their discovery was very impressive. It was hard not to feel affection for that trio of adorable little ladies, but the day was getting on, and while he would have liked to stay, he had to get going. With the excuse that he had to finish getting dressed, he suggested they retrace their steps and head back to their rooms – though this happened only after he solemnly swore, crossing his heart, that the secret would die with him. Alone again, he put on Shennan's clothes, which, no doubt thanks to his wife's good eye, fit him like a glove.

Once outside the room, as he shut the door, he felt someone behind him, half-hidden behind one of the enormous columns holding up the ceiling of the landing in front of the spiral staircase.

For the second time in under a half hour, he spun around, this time bumping into an attractive blonde woman of around forty whose clothing, demeanour and scent encapsulated all the poise and confidence of a born-and-bred Parisian.

'Did I startle you?' she asked with a half-smile, holding out her right hand to shake Laurent's. 'My name is Pia de La Tressondière – Carlos's architect. I'm looking over the wiring. Carlos is set on placing a colonial baroque altar from Bolivia on this landing, but there's not enough light,' she explained, brandishing enormous rolls of blueprints.

Laurent found all this information excessive. Even stranger was the architect's liberal use of the name 'Carlos', especially in a country like France, where nearly everyone addressed each other as *monsieur* or *madame*, and formal speech was a way of life.

As she gave him her hand, Laurent performed one of his quick but efficient visual scans. Without a doubt, the architect was a remarkable woman: she had elegance coming out her ears, with an undeniable air of a good girl from a good family, even as her expertly arranged décolletage, never seeming to go beyond the confines of decency, left two hefty mounds of tanned flesh easily discernible, sprinkled here and there with a few graceful freckles. A quick glance at her blue eyes, beautiful and hard, confirmed that this Parisian left nothing to chance, not even those two strands of hair that, while the rest sat atop her head in a bun, hung down gracefully, framing her face like the sidelocks worn by orthodox Jews.

Lastly, he noticed that on one of her meticulously manicured hands she wore a small ring with the seal of a noble family – all very French upper class, and very professional to boot. Already starting to get a sense of what Shennan was like, he had no trouble imagining his work meetings with the architect, both of them leaning over blueprints laid out on a table, while she pointed to this or that space on the paper, and he savoured the scrumptious view of her neckline opening up before his eyes like a water lily.

Laurent deduced that Madame de La Tressondière was not there by chance. He couldn't guess the reason, but nothing in that encounter seemed like pure coincidence. *What interest could she have in me?* he wondered. *Maybe just curiosity.*

Just then, as if she'd read his mind, she asked, despite seeming to know the answer: 'You must be the other New Worlder, I suppose.'

Laurent smiled. 'I see that here in Berry any attempt to keep a secret or remain anonymous is futile. But yes,' he finally answered, 'unless there's a third, I'm the other one. And you? You've got a scandalous scent of Paris about you.'

The architect couldn't conceal a gratified look from what she understood to be a compliment. 'How did you guess?'

Laurent, who was a professional flatterer, took his time. 'No one but a *vraie* Parisienne could be so magnificently reckless as to wear heels like those in a construction site like this, with a mud pit in the yard.'

'Merci, Monsieur,' she said graciously. Laurent smiled to himself. 'Actually I have boots for when I have to go outside, but inside the castle I prefer my shoes. I feel it's a show of respect to my clients,' explained Pia, with a look that let Laurent know without a doubt that she was a true huntress, fiercer than Artemis, with arrows by Hermès or Vuitton.

But Laurent could clearly see that he wasn't her objective, as much as she loved the attention. No doubt she'd lassoed and brought down a larger, more interesting beast. And yet, he thought, he at least didn't come with the cumbersome baggage of three daughters and a wife whose icy gaze could freeze the family jewels off Polyphemus. Still, he felt obliged to continue flirting. 'Then I imagine your assortment of boots must be outstanding.'

Just as she gave a very chic laugh, an angry voice interrupted the flirtation.

'Mademoiselle Pia, what on earth are you doing here? Need I remind you that this is a private area, and that you need to ask me personally for permission to enter? Madame Mayumi has been extremely clear on this point.'

The diminutive secretary stood in the doorway, arms akimbo, with an eely expression frightening enough to send cracks through the twin moons of Planet Krypton. Her lips looked so tense that Laurent was afraid she might sprain her zygomatic muscles.

Pia, embarrassed, tried to mumble an appropriate response, but she couldn't quite get one out. Finally, turning back to Laurent, she forced a smile.

'I don't understand how a man like Carlos can have this scarecrow ordering people around like some sort of political commissar.' And then she walked off, muttering something like *putain de connasse chinoise*.

Laurent was shocked. He never thought he'd see a Parisienne crumple so easily, least of all when faced with this sort of emaciated elf. Xiao Li walked over to him.

'Monsieur de Rodergues, you ought not waste your time with such insignificant people,' she said, urging him toward the stairs. 'Now we must go. Madame is waiting for you in the hunting room.'

As they left, Laurent could hear her muttering under her breath, and even though she did so in Chinese, he would have bet her words were something to the effect that even in the dens of sin of Sodom and Gomorrah that architect would be judged a lewd woman with an indecent profession. As they continued toward the hunting room, Xiao Li explained that when he finished his tea he could leave without waiting for his clothing, since she'd have it sent to his home. Laurent didn't doubt for a second that she would do as she said. Everything about her radiated efficiency, self-control and distance.

Left once again to his own thoughts, Laurent concluded that if he ran into another headstrong woman in the château, he'd be ready to kneel down before Shennan and beg him to take him on as an apprentice in the difficult art of handling the female temperament.

IN THE HUNTING ROOM

What they called the hunting room was an enormous hall of around a thousand square feet that housed an extensive collection of hunting trophies. Stretching from wall to wall in an imposing array were the heads of every horned creature in existence, from the oryx to the gnu to the rare Spanish ibex, mounted on wooden plaques indicating the date and location of the kill. The chesterfield chairs were draped with hides, and before them stood what Laurent reckoned to be the largest open-jaw crocodile he'd ever seen, serving as a footrest. In the hearth a dozen logs crackled behind bronze andirons as big as elephant tusks. African masks decorated the few empty spots on the walls, and the glass cases atop the cabinets contained jewels from North Africa, the Sudan and who knows where else. Assegais, spears, arrowheads, knives and axes were on display everywhere, and not even the ceiling was bare: tribal shields hung from above, their polychrome designs on hippopotamus or cow hide suggesting they came from the Maasais or the Zulus.

Madame Mayumi was seated at a table whose legs, Laurent realised to his horror and amazement, once belonged to a zebra. At the end of the room, arrayed on a shelf alongside some anthropomorphic hairpins, he noticed some very strange figurines that seemed to be looking at him.

'Those are headrests, mainly from Ethiopia and the Congo,' explained Madame Mayumi, seeing his puzzlement. 'But please, sit down.'

He did so, and she poured two cups of tea from a heavy Japanese cast-iron teapot, just as Xiao Li approached to whisper something in her ear.

Once the secretary left, Laurent tried to break the silence.

'Impressive collection,' he said.

'Yes,' his hostess agreed flatly. 'Though I think "cumbersome clutter" would be a better description. Forgive me for bringing you here, but it's the only room where everything is finished, so I thought it would be the best place for us to speak alone.'

'So you're not a hunter.'

'I likely have better aim than my husband, but I don't need to surround myself with trophies. That's more a trait of male insecurity,' she replied, eyes fixed on the lovely, fragile teacup, and the column of steam rising into the air. 'And speaking of trophy hunting, I understand you've just met Madame Pia.'

Laurent looked at her in wonder. Madame Mayumi possessed an impressive self-control, and no doubt an exceptional intelligence.

'I ran into her outside the bedroom. She was checking on something about the wiring on that landing.'

'Quite a peculiar woman, wouldn't you say?' She gave a slight smile, holding the cup in both hands with her delicate fingers. 'Oh, she's a professional, but she likes to pry and seems not to understand the meaning of private property. But let's talk about something more interesting. Such as what brought you to this bucolic little village.'

Laurent made one last attempt to avoid the topic.

'Did your husband shoot everything here? It's an amazing assortment.'

'Yes, he's not only childlike, he's also charmingly obsessive. Though as I was saying, I'd rather we'd put the music room here. All these masks, all these bones and hides – they can't bring us good luck. But do drink your tea, it's very nourishing. It's made with toasted rice.'

Laurent sipped the brew and found that it really did have a flavour unknown to him, a light fragrance that seemed to permeate him with a pleasant warmth.

'I understand why you might find the hall overwhelming, Madame Shennan, but all hunters are like this,' he offered, in an attempt to comfort her. 'And while I don't hunt myself, in my humble opinion I think this room fits in perfectly in a château that looks a bit like a military fortress. One can easily imagine medieval lords riding in from the chase, wild boars slumped over their horses' haunches, and holding gargantuan feasts in front of these fireplaces.'

Madame Mayumi was in no mood for historical reveries.

'You're a good man, Monsieur de Rodergues, and I don't want to take up any more of your time. I just wanted to thank you for how wonderfully you reacted to today's little mishap. My daughters were totally smitten, and we hope to see you often. Rest assured that my husband will want to meet you, too.'

Laurent cleared his throat and replied, 'That's very kind of you. I'd just like to say how impressed I am by the restoration work you're doing on the château. Everyone in town is delighted, since they consider this a sort of local treasure. I'm sure you and your husband are spending like a country at war, but the results will be spectacular.'

Mayumi frowned and shook her head.

'Alas, Monsieur Laurent, nothing is what it seems! Yes, my husband is spending far more than is advisable or necessary, since he'll never recover the money he's pouring into this project. As I said, he has an obsessive personality, and sometimes I'm even afraid that by investing so much he's putting my daughters' futures at risk, which I'm not about to let happen. As for whether people are happy or like us,' she continued, opening a drawer in the table and producing a bundle of letters, 'take a look. These are the messages we've received this week alone.'

Laurent picked up one of the letters at random and read:

Capitalist pig! Don't think you can buy us all out. One day your castle will burn to the ground. Thief!

Madame Mayumi put it back with the others.

'Surprised, Monsieur Laurent? Wait, here's a better one.' She took out a postcard with a few sentences scrawled in a jerky, angry hand:

Chink bitch! You know he's cheating on you, don't you? Of course you do.

Laurent blushed upon reading it, and Madame Mayumi returned the stack to the drawer, adding with a sense of humour, 'I suppose the "chink bitch" is me. People around here aren't exactly experts in ethnography. As you can see, not everyone is so delighted.'

Laurent wanted to come to her aid.

'Please, Madame, those lowlifes are not . . . are not representative. You're a woman of the world, you know there are always some people with sour grapes. Besides, the part about the cheating can't possibly be true; you're a beautiful woman . . .'

'Fear not, Monsieur. I'm strong, and I come from a family that's stronger still. I only worry about these things on account of my daughters – I don't want anyone to harass them. In any case, thank you for saying I'm beautiful. One always likes to hear that at my age. And now please be off. It's a gorgeous afternoon; it'd be a pity if you missed it.'

Mayumi gave him her hand, and this time Laurent thought it proper to kiss it.

'*Au revoir*, Madame Shennan. I hope to run into you again soon in town or in La Châtre.'

Outside, he crossed the broad terrace with its worn red granite flagstones and decided to walk home around the right flank, in order to see the part of the garden blocked from view from the street. The construction outside was quite noisy, and it occurred to him the new windows must be thoroughly soundproof. Nothing could be heard inside the château, and no doubt the reverse was likewise true.

Walking by the large wooden doorway at the base of the terrace, he caught sight of Pia, who now had boots on, and he couldn't fail to notice that even these were dazzling. She was speaking to a gentleman of a certain age, probably a supplier, and pointing to a wall with some damp patches on the newly applied cladding treatment. Pitying him, Laurent quickened his pace and returned her rather indifferent wave goodbye.

The château park or garden was probably eight acres at most, but it looked as though it would soon become a very interesting spot, as he could see from a project diagram posted on a bulletin board. On the ground nearby some planters and plants were waiting to be given a home. Laurent looked around, and in the areas bordering the cemetery he could see half a dozen people digging and preparing the ground for them. Nearby stood a thin, young, beautiful woman inspecting some bulbs, oblivious to his presence. Her enormous eyes were as dreamy as they were sad.

Laurent turned down the pathway to the right, which threaded through various families of giant ferns, making him feel he'd entered some sort of Jurassic garden. Just then a sudden shiver came over him. The spot was beautiful and would no doubt become more so, but there was something in that garden he couldn't put his finger on, a *je ne sais quoi* that caused him to shudder. He didn't put much stock in omens, but he had the unmistakable feeling that something dreadful had occurred, or was occurring – or worse yet, would occur very soon.

He again looked around him, unable to find the source of this foreboding. The sun shone gently through the plants in a pretty dappled light. He chalked it up to his imagination, clicked his tongue in self-reproach and continued on his way.

THE RIDING SCHOOL
IN LA BERTHENOUX

Men have their codes of friendship, action and conduct; in Laurent's case, he felt an affinity with Roger, the farmer whose property lay on the border of Saint-Chartier and Nohant-Vic, and they quickly forged a good relationship.

Roger and his wife Isabelle not only worked from sunrise to sunset, tending their fields, orchard, chickens, rabbits, cows and goats, and making an excellent chèvre cheese, they also kept various breeds of horses. He was surprised to learn they had Appaloosas, an American breed descended, like mustangs, from the horses the Spaniards lost or the indigenous people took in the early days of the conquest. Appaloosas are good horses, docile and strong, and Laurent liked how their spots set off one of his saddles, an ornate Mexican piece that a client had once given him.

It turned out Roger had been a professional jockey, educated at the school in the Château de Chantilly, though as much as he loved horses, he never had time to ride. Laurent eventually decided to buy a horse on instalments, a three-year-old grey mare with black spots ringed in white that he decided would answer to the name Malinche. Of course, Roger offered to stable and train her, but Laurent was well aware that his neighbour's good intentions were no match for his endless daily responsibilities, so he found a more practical solution. The owner of the Château de la Vallée Bleue, a local hotel, told him that just five miles away, in La Berthenoux, there was a riding school run by a lovely woman who had once won the Miss Berry pageant. Given these qualifications, Laurent decided a visit to the riding centre was now de rigueur.

The drive from Saint-Chartier to La Berthenoux was one of Laurent's favourites, regardless of whether he went through Verneuil or spent twice as long going through Saint-Août. The landscape along the way was a veritable cross-section of rural France: tilled fields, sweeping pastures full of cattle – mostly Charolais – farmhouses with slate or clay-tile roofs, hawthorn or rose hedges dividing the lands, highway shoulders neat and well maintained. Best of all was the wildlife that in other countries is almost impossible to see: hawks perched proud and sphinx-like atop lamp posts, white cranes calmly pecking in ponds, enormous beavers scurrying away in channels and irrigation ditches, red squirrels, tottering hedgehogs, bristly boars and, above all, deer of all kinds: fallow, chamois, roebucks. Groups of them would often cross the roads, stopping what little traffic there was, but their grace and beauty made the driver forget his initial irritation at the interruption – and in any case, Berry isn't a place for urgency or haste.

Whenever he drove, Laurent had a longstanding habit of putting on *cuecas*, rural Chilean folk songs. Many Chileans would find this practice incomprehensible, but he was an aficionado, both because of the essentially good memories of his adoptive country, and because he liked the lyrics and tunes, which he always sang along to in his dubious voice. With a soundtrack that went from 'El viejo lobero' to 'Gallo de la Pasión', he arrived at the riding centre. There he had negotiated with Caroline de Flalois a fair and equitable arrangement: she'd take care of Malinche for free, and in return he'd let her use the horse with her students. From what he'd seen, most of them were girls, and that reassured him, since girls tend to be more empathetic and careful with horses than boys.

Caroline was, just as he'd heard, a beautiful woman, and very tall. Yet her appeal really came from her spontaneous, natural kindness: it was impossible not to notice that she was a good person. She'd recently married, much to the sorrow of the men in the region. And in the opinion of some women, her husband, Pierre, possessed similar qualities. Their estate covered sixty hectares on a hill that offered good views of the surrounding area, and while the farm wasn't exactly an ode to orderliness, it had its charm, with a jumble of carts, sheds with various animals, two Mongolian yurts for extended stays, setters barking at everything, horses of different breeds and sizes and of course children – plenty of children. Kids who love horses are never in short supply, and Caroline, her kindness notwithstanding, had the rare, enviable gift of authority, and she knew how to use it.

One day Laurent took a long ride with Caroline, Pierre and another couple they were friends with, Lilly and Hervé. By the time they returned it was already getting dark, so they decided to set up a barbecue right there in the little yard at the riding centre, opposite the house. It quickly became apparent that Pierre was the expert in such matters, so the others, after pitching in with the preparations, sat back in their chairs overlooking the valley, well provisioned with cups full of warm punch.

'Make yourself comfortable, Laurent. There's someone coming I want you to meet, a good friend of mine who also lives in Saint-Chartier. She's gorgeous, and I just know you'll adore her,' said Caroline with a wink. Laurent wasn't fussy – he didn't even know the meaning of the word – and being single in the French countryside was revealing itself to be something wonderful: everyone insisted on introducing him to women.

As the scent of blood pudding and white sausages filled the air with an invitation to gluttony, the conversation turned to the Château de Saint-Chartier and its new owners. All the questions ultimately were addressed to Laurent, who after all lived there and had a front-row seat.

'It never ceases to amaze me how endlessly curious people are about the château,' he said. 'After all, France is teeming with châteaux – they're everywhere you look. Near Saint-Chartier, off the top of my head, I can think of Montgivray, Sarzay, d'Ars and many more besides.'

'True, there are a lot,' Caroline conceded, 'but they're almost all owned by the same old families, or by the municipality or regional governments. Some of them do draw attention, like the Château de Magnet, which people said was bought by some sort of group or cult that wanted to recreate the Middle Ages. In the end it all turned out be just rumours, and the owner is apparently a gentleman who came into it by chance.'

Pierre brought over a tray of roasted kidneys seasoned with parsley, garlic and a dash of sherry.

'The unusual thing about the one in Saint-Chartier,' he chimed in, 'isn't just that there's so much history behind it, it's that it's getting such a radical facelift, and is now home to a sort of United Nations of people from all sorts of places. On top of that, there's a constant stream of lorries going in packed with mysterious crates from all four corners of the earth. There's even something strange about the people working on the restoration. And the cherry on top is Monsieur Shennan.'

At the mention of that name, Caroline and her friend Lilly couldn't hold back a giggle. Then they stopped short, hearing someone approach, their footfalls audible in the leaves and brush.

'Shennan? He's a bastard,' said a voice from the darkness. Everyone turned at once, and Laurent was literally blinded by the singular beauty before him, immediately aware that he had perhaps just reached a watershed moment in his bachelor's life.

Caroline got up to embrace her and, taking her by the hand, introduced her to everyone else.

'This is Yael, a very good friend of mine. She's a potter, and she doesn't live far from you, Laurent.'

Everyone else had clearly already met her, though the

men's eyes showed that excitement that's always stirred in the presence of beauty. Not only was this woman a potter, she was living proof of the biblical theory that in shaping human clay God sometimes liked to show off.

Her green eyes had that rare ability to pierce whomever she spoke to, shoving them to a perilous sea of insecurity. So it was that as she said hello to everyone one by one, the normally self-assured sweet-talker Laurent could only manage to mumble a pathetic, 'My pleasure.'

The new guest accepted the glass of red that Pierre offered her and inserted herself into the conversation with a smile.

'As I was walking up here I heard you talking about something very interesting. Please go on; I want to know everything there is to know about the château.' Turning toward Laurent she added, 'And since you're a frequent visitor, I hope you can tell us quite a bit.'

Then she sat back in her chair, holding her glass with both hands, and looked at him squarely, awaiting a reply.

'I don't know why you think that,' Laurent said in his defence. 'I've only been there once, and very briefly. What I do find strange, though, is that I've never seen you in town. If we'd crossed paths with each other I'm sure I would have remembered.'

Hervé, Lilly's partner, could hardly repress a grin.

'We're all quite certain you'd remember if you'd seen her.' Lilly shot him such a withering look that he had no choice but to keep quiet.

By this point Laurent had started to recover his courage. He gave a laugh and shot Yael a rather cheeky glance. She held his gaze for a moment before replying.

'I don't often leave my workshop, which is right on the square, next to the house of that Scottish couple who spend the summers there. But I've seen you strolling about this way and that. Apparently you have plenty of free time, or not many responsibilities, which is something to envy or to pity, depending on how you look at it. In any case I have a small, lovely garden in the back, and I spend a lot of time there.'

Laurent noticed that the rest of the party followed this exchange with rapt attention, and he wanted to put a stop to it. The only way he could think to do so was to quickly recount his experience with the inhabitants of the château, since they appeared to be so interested. He told an entertaining tale, and their silence was interrupted only by their laughter at some of the details. As Laurent spoke, he couldn't help stealing glances at Yael: he really wanted this woman to like him. True, he was a bit taken with the Shennans' nanny, but only because she possessed a perfect beauty and inspired a gentle desire to protect her. But he now realised he hadn't thought of her even once since he'd left the château. Yael, on the other hand, was like a climbing ivy vine that digs its roots in and takes out your heart before you even realise it.

Laurent could tell she noticed him looking at her. She didn't look his way but smiled and seemed to adopt a pose that would aid his contemplation. Her hair was a tangle of violently black curls, her eyes were dark green lined with long lashes, her skin had a true olive tone that nevertheless contained a hue different from anything he'd ever seen before. Her features were flawless but bore a certain hardness. He studied the earrings hanging from her ears – antique, made of gold filigree, they looked beautiful on her. Laurent was lost in thought as the others commented on one of the details in his story. Suddenly it dawned on him.

'This may sound odd, but by any chance are you Jewish?'

Everyone went silent, and for a long time only the crackling of the embers and the grease dripping onto the fire could be heard. Yet Yael didn't seem bothered in the slightest. On the contrary, she gave a broad grin. 'How did you know?'

The rest of the group looked much more relieved at her reaction, and even Caroline pointed at her with a bite of sausage and said, in a joking accusation, 'You never mentioned that to me. I thought you were Lebanese, or a pied noir. How could you tell, Laurent?'

'She reminded me of one of those biblical engravings by Doré. I could even imagine her in the same dress,' explained Laurent, perhaps betraying his attraction.

'I'm impressed,' said Yael. 'You're right, even more than you know, because I'm a Yemeni Jew. Well, my parents are, and we must be the purest line that exists, ethnically speaking, because we've been in Yemen from time immemorial without intermixing, unlike the Sephardic and Ashkenazi Jews. If you saw pictures of my grandparents, you really would be looking at characters from one of those engravings Laurent had in mind.' Now Yael looked at him with an expression of greater respect. 'I'm really very impressed. But I interrupted you – please go on and tell us about your visit to the château.'

'There's really not much more to tell. Just that, aside from the spectacular decor, the biggest surprise was the threatening letters Madame Shennan showed me.'

'The what?!' everyone all asked in unison – everyone except Yael, who leant forward with a look of unabashed interest.

Laurent proceeded to give a detailed account of the content and tone of the letters Madame Mayumi had shown him. He asked them what they made of it.

'Well,' began Pierre, 'it's true that the festival had a large following. After all it was the most famous, or perhaps more accurately the only international festival of its kind. People came from around the world, and among traditional music aficionados, there was no one who didn't know about it. Some thirty thousand people gathered there every year for thirty years – for specialists, it was quite an event. And the Château de Saint-Chartier was the ideal place for it, since it's where that George Sand novel is set, *The Master Pipers*. In the book musicians hold their initiation rites in the castle's underground chambers.'

'How's the new site working out, in Château d'Ars?' asked Lilly.

'It seems to be doing well,' replied Pierre, without hesitation. 'D'Ars has the advantage of having a huge forest park, which provides plenty of shade for the exhibitors. They always used to complain about how bad the lack of shade in Saint-Chartier was for their instruments. Besides, the municipality of La Châtre, which owns the château, is thrilled. Some of the organisers may not be, like Monsieur Gimbault. He felt the event belonged to him, and now that the municipality's gotten behind it, he can no longer just do as he pleases. And he might not turn as much of a profit any more, which would explain the nasty grudge he holds against Shennan.' He paused to take a sip and then went on. 'The nice thing about holding the festival in Saint-Chartier was that the town's right there, and it's one of the prettiest in the area. And of course the castle walls are impressive. But all is not lost: apparently Shennan is an avid collector of rare instruments, and he's stated on more than one occasion that Saint-Chartier could host some of the festival's events, at least the smaller ones, and that he'd even fund some others. In fact, last year, after they finished redoing the slate roofs, he hired several bagpipers to play from atop the tower, and I got the chance to attend. It was magical.'

'Indeed,' Lilly agreed. 'Even if there's always someone who wants to stir up trouble, because they're jealous or not right in the head, I bet whoever sent those awful letters to the Shennans isn't from Saint-Chartier. I think except for a few people, everyone realises the château urgently needed renovation, and that moving into a half-deserted castle isn't the same as moving into someplace inhabited. Everyone I know in town is delighted about the project, and delighted with the Shennans.'

'There's a newsletter put out by a couple of musicians called *La Cordophonie*,' added Hervé, in one of the rare moments when his mouth was empty. 'They used to be very involved in the old festival and have apparently been sidelined in the new one. I'm sure that's got their bile up. What were their names, Lilly?'

'The Monattis – Jeannette and Claude Monatti,' said Lilly, clearly making an effort to recall their names. 'But they're not bad people, just a bit fanatical about their hobbies. Maybe the festival was the only interesting thing they had in their lives. The first few newsletters they put out were pure vitriol, but I think by now they've calmed down.'

'What you have to understand, Laurent,' Caroline began to explain, 'is that this is a very sleepy part of the world. Even the sheep are bored. And all the activity at the château now is like a movie. Besides, since the festival changed location, probably the most exciting thing going on around here is the Pumpkin Fair in Tranzault. So when someone like Shennan comes along, who's dashing, debonair, entertaining, an eccentric millionaire whose fortune is shrouded in mystery, and who turns out to be a world-class skirt-chaser to boot . . . well, it's only natural for him to become the subject of all the gossip.'

Yael followed everyone's words carefully, and Laurent could have sworn she was clenching her jaw. *Maybe she's one of those man-haters who fly into a murderous rage at the very idea of a Don Juan*, he thought.

'They say he's not particular,' added Lilly. 'He doesn't care about caste, race or class. Or age, size or marital status. The motto on the flag he flies is "Anything with a skirt".'

They all laughed, and Pierre, always circumspect, added further details as he set a plate piled with beef tips on the table.

'I'm not surprised people don't like him, what with all those stories,' he said. 'Remember what happened with that woman in Lignières.'

'What happened?' Yael pounced, with an eagerness that surprised everyone present.

74

'Apparently Shennan had a full-blown affair with a woman who runs a bakery in Lignières,' said Pierre. 'They say she's gorgeous, and it was just one more of her many dalliances, even if this one raised the biggest scandal. Anyway, as much as he preferred discretion, she apparently found it titillating to make a show of things. Some people say she did that to get back at her husband for a previous affair. Whatever the reason, from what I've been told, every time she took a lover she made them go to her bakery to buy bread – specifically to buy a baguette *chabanette*, the loaf with two little horns at each end, horns being a symbol for a cuckold.'

'Her husband put up with this?' Laurent interrupted. 'In Chile, that sort of situation would end in tragedy.'

'Don't think this one didn't: apparently last year Shennan was driving out to Lignières every week, some fifteen miles away, just to buy bread. He claimed he was visiting an aristocrat who lived there, some odd duck he met on a hunting trip back in Argentina. By the third trip, that excuse no longer stuck, and each time he went to the bakery, the husband would watch from the window in the back room. He must have been apoplectic.'

Laurent couldn't believe his ears. He was no saint, far from it, but he felt openly taunting the husband was in very poor taste. 'I'd never have guessed Shennan was involved in something so tawdry.'

'Personally, I don't think he's a bad person,' replied Pierre. 'The contrary, in fact. But he seems to be the kind of man who can't disengage when there's a woman involved. He probably waits for the problems to solve themselves.

And of course, they never do. In this case it certainly didn't.'

'What happened?'

'The poor guy killed himself last September,' said Lilly. 'They found him dead in his garage. He downed a whole bottle of absinthe loaded with sleeping pills. His wife was devastated. She sold their business and their house for a pittance, and took her two kids to Haute-Savoie.'

'God, what a story. It's enough to give you indigestion,' said Hervé.

'Listen to you! If you've got indigestion it's because you gorged yourself, like you always do,' Lilly scolded, slapping him on the belly.

'It seems Shennan was pretty shaken,' said Pierre philosophically. 'But I'm sure soon enough the *châtelain* will find someone else to help him forget the whole business. He'll get back on that horse. Even if he wanted to change, I doubt he could. The spirit is willing, but the flesh is weak.'

'All right, let's pack up. Tomorrow we're taking a group from Paris out riding, and Pierre has a shift at the factory,' said Caroline, starting to clear the serving dishes.

Laurent turned to Yael, who had a pained look on her face.

'Are you not feeling well? If you like, I can give you a ride home, and tomorrow we'll come back to get your car.'

'Is that a genuine offer, or just another pick-up line?' asked Yael with a smile. 'Don't worry, I'm fine. These stories just turn my stomach. In the end, the bad guys always seem to get away. And anyway, I can drive myself. I'm sure we'll see each other around our little town. Maybe I'll even have you over for tea.'

'Now there's a thrilling prospect,' Laurent teased. 'However, I accept your offer and will see you around.' He tried not to let on how eager he was to see her again, the sooner the better.

They said farewell to Caroline and Pierre, and then to Lilly and Hervé. Laurent walked Yael to her car, an old, beat-up Citroën 2CV, and gallantly opened the door for her.

'To be honest, Laurent, I didn't think I'd like you. But that comparison to an engraving by Doré came as a surprise, and now you've got me curious. I hope we meet again.'

At this point Laurent wasn't about to let the opportunity slip away, so he made a suggestion.

'How about we get a drink tomorrow at around noon at La Cocadrille? We can have lunch there too.'

'That sounds wonderful. Of course, I'm sure all of Saint-Chartier will hear about it by the afternoon. See you tomorrow. Goodnight.'

Yael leant in to give Laurent a kiss goodbye, and her scent of musk and piquant spices lingered long in his mind.

IN THE GARDEN OF THE PRIEST

The day after the barbecue, with a bit of a hangover sapping his strength, Laurent sat down in his kitchen to have the strongest coffee of his life, a mixture of five shots of ristretto with a bit of honey and dark chocolate. He planned to follow it up with a cold shower. He wanted to be in top form. He intended to devote the morning to his new hobbies: tending to the garden and the chicken coop. He figured he could use some time to clarify his thoughts, and that a bit of physical exercise would make him fresh as a daisy for his date at noon.

To shake off the grogginess, he walked out into his small yard and sat down on the covered patio, still in pyjamas and a dressing gown. It was a crisp but beautiful day, and there, sitting on his plastic chaise longue, sipping his thick coffee, he began recalling the night's events as the caffeine slowly roused him.

Laurent was surprised: he'd had a delightful evening and couldn't wait for the hour of the aperitif to arrive so that he could see her again. In spite of or perhaps because of all the alcohol he'd consumed, he'd been prey to all sorts of lewd erotic dreams starring Yael. He blushed to recall he'd even fallen back on adolescent practices of self-love to calm the fires his lust had ignited.

He needed to see her right away. He wanted to get to know her better, learn everything about her – and yes, ask her why she was so hostile on the subject of Shennan. He hadn't failed to notice Yael's attitude, and that led him to wonder not only about her but also about the millionaire. How did he manage to stay on top of the chaos of the renovation, keep the Heritage Gestapo at bay and attend to his formidable wife, his three loving daughters in constant need of attention, his business – whatever that was – and a swarm of hot-tempered lovers to boot? He felt dizzy just imagining himself in Shennan's place!

The story about the woman with the bakery had left a bad taste in his mouth. He noticed that everyone tended to blame Shennan without stopping to think about her role, making him buy that baguette *chabanette* – which of course he had to try. He thought about it for a bit and decided he no longer envied Shennan but instead felt sorry him: poor man, such a slave to his appetites. Nothing's easier to manipulate than a man aroused.

'And what makes you think you're any different, you hypocrite?' he suddenly said aloud to himself. He gave himself a slap across the face.

Now a bit more clear-headed, he got up, washed the dishes and went to shower, trying not to think about Yael. He could only manage that by turning on the cold tap and standing under the bracing water. At last, renewed and ready to get started on his agricultural adventures, he set out for his tiny garden.

As noted, the vicarage came with the right to a small plot in a community garden behind the town's public wash house. Laurent made his first foray into gardening, taking any advice the other gardeners had to offer. From the start, he felt it was important to learn the local folk wisdom, hoping that when the time came he might harvest and eat something he'd grown himself.

First, though, his main concern had been to clear the brush, clean his plot and prepare the land. Later, after getting permission from the others, he bought and set up a small portable chicken coop in his section, where he planned to put a rooster and a few hens that would provide fresh eggs. He'd been persuaded to learn more about organic gardening after chatting with a couple of his neighbours, Jacquotte and Colette, whom he jokingly referred to as the Green Goddesses. The first and easiest step, he figured, would be to start raising hens with natural feed and scraps from his own kitchen. But his problems began as soon as he went to get hens at the market in Saint-Août. Laying hens, the kind he should have been interested in, were easy enough to buy, as Laurent learnt, but unfortunately he happened across a stall selling decidedly more unusual varieties. The vendor told him his birds would be constantly laying eggs, and Laurent believed him, happily walking off with three cardboard boxes with air holes. When he got back to his humble coop, he realised he was in over his head. The first rooster and hen he'd bought were of a breed called Frizzle

Cochin, and the hen, which he named Curler, turned out to be a feisty creature that constantly harassed all the others. The other rooster and hen were Crèvecoeurs, an adorable French breed with bluish tones and a V-shaped comb. He also purchased a pair of gorgeous Capuchine pigeons. Unfortunately, none of the three pairs managed to produce a single egg, and on top of that they required constant care, so much that their owner soon became the butt of all the other gardeners' mockery. One day a practical joker even left a rubber egg in the nest.

On this morning, he was cleaning the coop when he heard René say hello. Now René, it should be said, was quite a character: an early riser and great lover of Pernod, who saw to the opening and closing of the church. Laurent would often run into him in the garden or when out walking his dog. If anyone in Saint-Chartier was well informed, it was René, so Laurent turned away from his eggless chicken coop and walked straight over to talk to him, on the pretext of asking him which fertiliser he recommended for beets. Laurent hated beets with all his heart, but they were the first thing that came to mind.

René stood looking at him. 'I never would have thought someone like you would like beets. Personally I think they're a waste of soil.' He laughed, exhaling a cloud of anise-scented breath. 'By the way, how was your barbecue last night in La Berthenoux? I suppose you met our neighbour the potter.'

Laurent couldn't suppress a grimace. There was no one better than René to get the gossip from, even if the gossip was you. But he simply said, 'Monsieur René, how the devil do you know about that? Is there anything that escapes your notice in this town?'

'Monsieur Laurent, you attend a barbecue with two of the most attractive women for miles around, and you think people won't talk? Come now, be reasonable! But don't fret,' he went on, seeing the look on Laurent's face. 'I only know because I heard it from Mademoiselle Yael herself. I'm the one who supplies the firewood for her kiln. She's a very pleasant young woman and happened to mention she was headed for dinner at Caroline's house in La Berthenoux. And since you told me the same thing yesterday morning, I surmised that you'd see each other there. So you might say it's not that I'm nosy, it's that you two have a dreadful habit of telling me everything, imagining I take an interest in your lives.'

'When you put it that way, René, you're quite right. Rest assured, I'll try not to bore you any longer with my concerns.'

'Hold on now, I didn't say I minded, or that I'd rather not know. Besides, I'm fond of you. Did I ever tell you that when I was a boy, your grandfather gave me a pair of clogs, tailor-made, with my name carved in the wood? He was a good man. Pity he's no longer here to see your chickens,' he laughed.

'Yes, yes. So tell me, this Mademoiselle Yael isn't from around here. Has she lived in town for long?'

'No, from what she told me she's from Bordeaux, though her accent certainly doesn't sound like it. She rented her house just a few months after the Shennans arrived. A little while after that came the Pazhattes, who are from Brittany and live with their two kids near the school. Then came Thierry, the tree pruner (or *arboriste-grimpeur*, as he insists on being called), who moved in behind the Auges' farm, and then came you. We've never had so many newcomers in one year. Perhaps Monsieur Shennan will eventually manage to revitalise the town.'

Laurent wanted to know more. 'What about her ceramics? Are they nice? Because for some time now I've been wanting to buy a salad bowl, and it'd be nice if we could all support each other here in town,' he said, trying to appeal to René's sense of local pride.

'Sure,' René replied sarcastically. 'Buying a salad bowl is as good a way as any other to get a screw. You might even toss a salad.'

'Is it that obvious?'

'You're practically making me blush,' said René, aligning the rows for his tomato plants with a hoe.

Laurent thought for a moment.

'Well, since it's so obvious, and seeing as how we're neighbours, fellow gardeners and fans of Pernod, not to mention the fact that my grandfather once gave you a pair of clogs, why don't you drop the charade and tell me everything you know?'

'Who says I'm a fan of Pernod?' asked René, getting to his feet. He stuck his hoe in the earth, placed his foot on the top of the blade and studied Laurent carefully. 'Come now, don't tell me you're seriously interested in the potter!'

'I can't explain it without sounding like a schoolboy, but yes, I think I am,' said Laurent, stoically holding his gaze. 'I'm really taken with her.'

'You understand you're going to owe me several rounds at Le Juanch's tavern?'

'As many as it takes, and whenever you please, but spill it.'

'Let's sit down under the fig tree,' said René, pointing to a spot nearby. 'Our old priest, Father Jacob, used to teach the catechism there. It'll be quite pleasant, and we can also smoke one of those cigars of yours.'

Laurent took out two thin cigars from his jacket with religious care, and René began telling him what he knew.

'The truth is, Mademoiselle Yael is rather elusive and very rarely leaves her house. Most of what she eats she grows in the little garden in her yard or gets from the farms in town. Once a month she drives out of town, according to her to Blois, though personally I suspect that's not the case. At any rate, she always comes back with a lot of packages. She never has guests, though she's kind to everyone. Every morning at six on the dot, no matter the weather, she goes jogging with a little rucksack on her back. And can she run! She just zips along. Beyond that, I don't know what her house is like. I've never been inside past the living room or kitchen. Though one day the door was open, and I could see she had several screens and lots of books and things.'

'And the pottery?'

'Yes, there's also a wheel and things for the trade, and several pots, and bucket for shards. But I've never had the chance to see her work, and she doesn't sell what she makes in the markets nearby. I think she's here for the same reason you are, to try to find answers . . . Because that's why you're here, right?' René turned to look at him. 'I do hope you'll keep me posted on how things go with you two, but now, if you'll excuse me, I really must get back to work. I want to make it home on time – my wife's making a *tête de veau*, and it's always spectacular. One day we'll have to have you over to try it.'

With a handshake, Laurent left to meet Yael, stopping by the vicarage to change into more suitable attire. Then, with that pleasant feeling of having made good use of the morning, he left his house and headed to La Cocadrille, with no clear idea of what this date had in store.

THE ANGELUS AT LA COCADRILLE

The tavern was packed, as it usually was at this hour. Scanning the room, Laurent didn't see Yael. He'd arrived a little early, nervous before this first date.

Le Juanch called him over and, taking him by the shoulder, spoke into his ear.

'You're waiting for Mademoiselle Yael, I assume? I saved you a table in the back that looks out onto the garden. It's quite romantic. The only other people there are a few old ladies on the way to Nohant-Vic, and they're not from around here.' And in a more conspiratorial tone, he whispered, 'Good luck! I think you've got this in the bag.'

Laurent could feel a migraine coming on. The idea that everyone in the town was scrutinising him and trying to work their matchmaking arts put him in a bad mood. And he didn't think that Yael would be happy, either, if she knew everyone was cheering them on. As he walked through the main dining room toward his table, he could feel all eyes on him, along with some whispered comments that in all likelihood were about him.

'Gaston, bring me some of that beer you're trying to brew, on the double – in a pint glass, and make sure it's ice cold,' said Laurent, trying to gather his courage. 'And also a shot of that plum liqueur, the one I know you're bootlegging with the mayor.'

As Le Juanch brought a glass capped with a generous head of foam, the bar again went silent, and a thin voice could be heard very politely telling someone else where Laurent was. More silence, and then the sound of confident footsteps behind him. And as they drew closer, a rising murmur of voices followed in their wake.

'Your lady has arrived. *Bon courage*!' said Le Juanch, patting him on the shoulder. And referring to the beer, he added, 'Let me know what you think of the Carterius.' Then he turned and made his exit, bar towel draped over his shoulder. The tavern had become a stage, and the show about to begin promised to earn a standing ovation.

So it was that, lips and nose covered in beer foam, Laurent looked up and saw Yael standing before him, radiant enough to make a Greek statue sick with envy. She wore her thick tangle of curls pulled back behind her head, and now that he saw her face clearly, he found her even more beautiful than the night before. He also noticed different tones in her complexion in the daylight: it was desert-tanned skin, the colour of the Tamashek women in northern Mali, set off by her intoxicatingly bright, colourful eyes.

'Hello, Laurent. I can see you're already getting warmed up. Impressive, after the job you did last night,' said Yael. He made a gentlemanly motion to get up but she stopped him, placing her hand firmly on his shoulder.

At that very moment, as if to heighten his feelings of guilt, the church bells tolled the Angelus, the noontime prayers. Yael remarked she liked how they maintained that tradition. Laurent looked at her in surprise as Le Juanch set a pint of beer before her.

'Did you go to a Catholic school?' he asked. 'In Chile there's a large Jewish population, and many have no qualms about going to Catholic schools and universities,' he explained, this time taking a sip of the plum liqueur.

'I spent a few years living in the Old City in Jerusalem,' Yael explained. 'With all the convents inside the New Gate, I learnt the language of the bells. It was a way for me to keep myself entertained.'

'And from Jerusalem you moved to Saint-Chartier, of all places, where you're now living across the street from an international man of mystery. I hope you're not a Mossad agent!' Laurent joked.

Yael, who'd closed her eyes and taken a long draught, opened them again to look at him over the rim of the glass. Then she set the glass down again very calmly.

'What if I were? What would that change?'

'Well, to start with, I'd be scared to death. Mossad agents are famous for not messing around, and they don't give a damn about collateral damage,' Laurent defended himself.

'But you're not anti-Semitic. Or are you?' asked Yael, narrowing her eyes.

'If I were, I wouldn't be here.' Finally, Laurent was back on home turf. He needed to step up his game and stop acting like an amateur, he told himself.

The smile that spread across Yael's face seemed to augur a happy ending to the encounter, when a door slammed and a huge commotion arose the bar. They both leapt up to see what was going on.

One of the workers from the château had just rushed into the tavern and was trying to explain with frantic gestures what the shouting was all about. The man's atrocious French was peppered with an ill-treated Italian and something else that Laurent thought was Romanian. Still, Laurent could just about piece together that a fight had broken out in the château. Apparently one of the workers on the crew from Perpignan, who was Muslim, had started praying in the middle of the terrace just as the church bells tolled the Angelus. Shennan was inside the château, and when he saw him through the window, he bolted out to demand he stop. He tried to tell him, as politely as he could, that he wouldn't stand for public expressions of religion on his property. The worker ignored him and went on praying, and Shennan, not used to such stubborn disobedience, dragged him to the gate.

Even now the worker, a man from Mauritania named Ahmed El-Kubri, as Laurent later learnt, stood outside, red with anger, shouting through the railing in Arabic and French that he'd kill Shennan and his whole family. So the worker's boss, Monsieur Rataille, the contractor from Perpignan, had sent this Romanian to see if he could find any of the gendarmes who often stopped by the pub around lunchtime. As it happened, they weren't at their usual spot at the bar, and as Le Juanch went to call the station, the rest of the customers poured out to see for themselves the scene the Romanian had just described, since La Cocadrille was just a few yards from the château.

Yael didn't hang back and nervously pushed Laurent toward the street, where a crowd had quickly formed around the spectacle.

The worker, who turned out to be a brawny man much larger than Shennan, was in a sorry state. Just as the Romanian said, his face was a mess, and he was still rattling the heavy iron gate and shouting in Arabic. Shennan, on the other side of the bars, not two yards away from him, stood watching him in silence. Nothing in his immaculate clothes revealed that just a few minutes earlier he'd been in a scuffle. Some of the other workers looked on in astonishment behind him, while Monsieur Rataille, outside the gate, stood by the worker's side and tried in vain to calm him down.

Suddenly Shennan spoke in a powerful, clear voice, so that everyone could hear. 'This fellow was spoiling for a fight. I don't know his reasons, maybe he was trying to get money or cause trouble for me, but I don't give a damn: this is my house, and here no one's going to pray toward Mecca, Salt Lake City or anywhere else. Muslim prayers have five parts, and the Salat az-Zuhr doesn't start until after midday. But this bastard started praying while the church was ringing the Angelus, knowing full well that I could see him. He hasn't done it any other day, so it's clear his gesture was meant as a provocation to me. He can sue me if he wants. I have nothing against Muslims, and they have my respect, but I won't put up with radical Islamists. They're scum, and all they want is to kill us all off.'

And then, to everyone's amazement, he let loose a string of curses in Arabic. The worker froze, slowly pulled himself away from the gate, pushed aside the people around him and hurried away, fear written across his face.

After he left, Shennan stood silently for a moment and looked at the crowd gathered around him. Then he let out one of what Laurent later came to know as his disarming laughs.

'I beg your pardon for taking you away from such a pleasant establishment. Tell Le Juanch to cook up something good for me, I'll be right over for lunch. And tell him I want to try that new beer of his. A round on me for all the infidels.'

The crowd began to break up and return to the tavern, not without some murmuring.

'What the devil do you think he said to him?' asked Laurent, returning inside with Yael. 'And how on earth does Shennan know Arabic? Did you see how terrified the man looked when he left?'

Yael bit her upper lip before replying. 'He told him to bugger off and never threaten him again. And he said that if he so much as thought about reporting him to the police, Shennan would have someone cut off his balls and do the same to his two male sons, who live with his wife and parents in Kiffa.'

Laurent stopped. 'Seriously? Or are you kidding me?'

'I promise. Incidentally, Shennan's Arabic is pretty good,' she added without stopping.

Laurent jogged a few steps to catch up with her. 'Well now I know you're a Mossad agent.'

'Silly boy,' said Yael, elbowing him in the ribs. 'Don't forget I'm Yemeni, from the Arabian Peninsula. They speak Arabic there, and it's the language of my grandmother, who raised me.'

'I don't know,' protested Laurent. 'This is all very suspicious. And the fact that Shennan knows Arabic is very, very puzzling. The fact that you do, too, is a pretty unlikely coincidence.'

'Come on, Laurent, pull yourself together. I was looking forward to being romanced.'

'I know,' he insisted, 'but he even knew that the man has sons in . . . who knows where.'

'In Kiffa. That's east of Nouakchott,' said Yael. 'And it shows that Shennan, beyond that chatty, shallow demeanour, likes to keep all the variables around him under control.'

They went back into the bar, and from what they overheard the other patrons saying, they seemed uncertain what to make of the scene.

'Quite a commotion! Good thing I decided not to call the gendarmes,' whispered Le Juanch.

Laurent nodded and, taking Yael by the arm, led her back to their table, convinced that this woman had started to cast a spell over him. He got ready to use all the firepower at his disposal.

THE FINE

A few days after his encounter with Yael, Laurent awoke very tired. The previous afternoon he'd been helping Monsieur Roger with his horses and was worn out from the effort, with sore muscles in places he never suspected were part of his anatomy. He reluctantly looked at himself in the mirror and hardly recognised the man he saw. He made a solemn vow to get back into shape as soon as possible, since this easy life of eating well was wreaking havoc on his once enviable figure.

He made a few sad attempts at push-ups and sit-ups that only left him more depressed and then walked to the kitchen, head bowed, thinking he probably shouldn't touch the oversized brioche that the Green Goddesses had given him. Such a shame: there it sat, covered in a thin white cloth that he guiltily lifted up. Golden and dusted with powdered sugar, the brioche looked heavenly, with a crispy layer on top no doubt filled with fruit preserves that they themselves, experts as they were, had made by hand. He could already imagine cutting it up into hearty portions and generously spreading on butter from the Bodart farm, when the doorbell rang and pulled him out of his sweet reverie.

Before him stood the most eminent representative of the local gendarmerie, Sergeant and Station Chief Gilles Lafonnier, better known as 'Tartarin', because, like the famous character from Daudet's novels, he came from Provence and was fond of hunting – and because he too, according to local gossip, tended to exaggerate the number and quality of his kills. He often sported a triple-cartridge belt, like Pancho Villa, as if he thought he'd run out of ammunition for his double-barrel shotgun.

Laurent stood, mouth agape. The last thing he imagined was a visit from the local authorities. Tartarin raised his hand up to his *képi* in a military salute. It couldn't be anything serious, Laurent thought. But his mind wasn't running on all cylinders.

'What can I do for you?' he asked

'I'm afraid I don't come bearing good news,' the sergeant said. 'May I come in?'

'Of course. Would you like some coffee? I was just about to make some,' offered Laurent courteously, pointing the way to the kitchen.

Once inside, Laurent began fussing about with the coffee pot, and Tartarin said, 'That looks like one of those famous filled brioches that Jacquotte and Colette make. You do know, don't you, that you have to eat them within twenty-four hours, otherwise they go stale?'

'I didn't, but please cut a few pieces,' Laurent said,

happy to have found an excuse to try a bite. 'Sugar or acacia honey?'

Mouth stuffed with brioche, the sergeant spoke a few words in praise of the brioche as Laurent handed him a cup. He downed the coffee and shook his head vigorously.

'*Mon Dieu*, Monsieur de Rodergues! This coffee could rouse Tutankhamun from the dead!'

Then he took a notebook out from his chest pocket. 'Now let's see,' he said. 'I'm afraid it's an unpleasant matter, and the worst part is that I know it has nothing to do with you, even though it affects you directly. I suppose you're aware that your grandfather's house came with seven acres of pasture by the country road to Lourouer, off to the right from the cemetery.' When Laurent nodded he went on. 'How long has it been since you were last there?'

'Honestly, I only visited the fields the day after I arrived in town. Then I agreed to let Monsieur Salssart graze his cattle there on the condition that he take care of the land, along with the irrigation ditches, the hedges and the access gate. Has something happened to it?' he asked.

'It seems someone lit a bonfire on your property, and the wind spread the flames to the neighbouring hedges, leaving them a bit singed and frightening several cows, which tried to escape. As a result, this neighbour has filed a complaint asking for damages for negligence. On top of that, I'll have to fine you for setting the fire without permission from the municipality, even though I'm sure you had nothing to do with it. In any case, you shouldn't worry, it's not a steep fine, and you can contest it.'

'What? That's outrageous!' Laurent suddenly turned

livid. 'I had nothing to do with it! Anyone could have gone in and started that fire: hikers, children, whoever, but not me. I'm an upstanding citizen!'

Tartarin was surprised by his vehemence, but didn't let that stop him from helping himself to another slice of brioche.

'Monsieur de Rodergues, as I said, I have no doubts about your innocence, but unfortunately the field is in your name, and I've checked with Monsieur Salssart, who says that he also didn't light any fires. What's more – strange to say – he says he stopped by there late yesterday evening and didn't see any preparations for a bonfire, or anything of the sort. Whoever lit it did so after ten o'clock at night.'

Laurent remained silent for a moment. 'Which neighbour filed the complaint?' he asked.

'Tonton Boussard.'

'I haven't the slightest idea who that is. I don't know any Tonton Boussard.'

Clearing his throat, Sergeant Lafonnier contradicted him. 'I'm afraid you do. From what I've heard, you had a run-in with him a little over a month ago.'

'A month ago? But I've never had trouble with anyone. I certainly haven't quarrelled with any—' He stopped short. 'Hold on, you don't mean that fat, rude man who yelled at Madame Shennan and me in front of the city hall the day I met her and her daughters?'

'The very same.' The sergeant nodded. 'He's a difficult man, but all the same I have to admit he's a responsible citizen: he doesn't make trouble, he pays his debts on time, he works hard and he rarely speaks to anyone, as he's a natural loner. But when something does bother him, he'll find every legal trick in the book to blow it out of proportion. If it's any consolation, you may as well know that he's already filed four complaints against Shennan: one for the noise from the construction at the château, and another because he thought one of the workers didn't have the right permit for operating a crane – unfortunately he was right, much to Monsieur Shennan's chagrin. He also filed a complaint against the pair of Belgian retirees who live next to the fire station, because one day their dog got off its leash, and . . . anyway, I'm afraid the list goes from here to Narbonne. In the local police stations everyone knows him, and the annoying thing is he's always partly right. He's a professional nuisance, and with foreigners he's even worse. This week it's your turn.'

'Couldn't he have lit the fire himself?'

The sergeant smiled with a sad sympathy. 'I doubt it. He'd be stirring up trouble for himself, and that's not his style. In any event, there's no way to prove anything, and since you own the land, you're responsible for the fine, even if we indicate on the report that we're certain you had nothing to do with it. I do apologise, that's the most we can do. At the very least, you don't have to worry about the fine: your insurance company will pay for any damages, so it won't cost you a thing, except the time for the court appearance. As for Tonton . . . I think he's got it in for you because of your friendship with Shennan. He's waging an open war on them, and it's heating up.'

'I've had it up to here with my "friendship" with Shennan! How many times do I have to repeat that I've only ever spoken to his wife and daughters, and only on one occasion? With him I've never so much as exchanged a word!'

'Be that as it may, you seem to be the only person in town who's been invited over for tea,' Tartarin pointed out.

'To hell with that bloody tea! That was just because of the little incident we had with the dogs, nothing more!' Laurent was worked up.

'Now, don't get excited, parbleu! The fine is just a trifle. And now I must be off. Don't hesitate to call me should you need anything.' Tartarin got up, then added, 'One more thing – that brioche is divine. Would you mind if I took another slice?'

'Help yourself, Sergeant. If I can, I'll bring a whole one just for you when I go to the station to make my declaration. I want to state for the record that I came here to find peace and quiet, not to put up with any knuckle-dragging peasants. But I guess every village has its idiot who wants to fuck the sow.'

'A word of advice, if I may,' offered Tartarin. 'I know that overseas in the colonies, perhaps because of the sailors' tradition, people tend to employ a saltier vocabulary, but here, on the continent, it's rather frowned upon, and you in particular have a fondness for coarse language. Just a suggestion, and I'm only telling you because of some remarks I've heard from several ladies at the bakery.'

Laurent was beside himself with rage.

'Sergeant Lafonnier, I appreciate the lessons in urbanity, but I'm not from the French overseas colonies. I'm in my own house, so here at least I'll do and say whatever the hell I please. I say this with all due respect.'

Tartarin, unflappable, shook his hand and smiled, then again gave an official salute.

'I understand perfectly. Sometimes when I'm hunting, I can't help letting slip a few four-letter words myself. I'm just conveying the concern of a few ladies who otherwise find you quite charming.' He was on the bottom step when he suddenly turned around, as if he'd just remembered something. 'Say, you haven't seen Mademoiselle Yael, have you? I know what good friends you are, and we haven't seen her around town for a few days.'

'No, I haven't seen her. I know she went to Blois for a few weeks. And we're just acquaintances,' Laurent replied somewhat sharply.

'Just curious. A very interesting woman, that Mademoiselle Yael, wouldn't you agree?'

And without waiting for a reply, he carefully closed the verdigris gate.

Laurent walked straight to the kitchen, intending to pour himself a glass of the local liqueur and eat the rest of the brioche to calm down.

He placed an ashtray among the crumbs on the table and lit one of his Honduran cigars to think. He still hadn't met Shennan in person, and he'd already been drawn into his orbit. Even odder, every day he seemed to meet someone who adored him and someone else who regarded him with a sectarian hatred. He couldn't help thinking of Oscar Wilde's famous *bon mot*: 'The only thing worse than being talked about is not being talked about.'

He took a deep draw on his dark-leaf cigar and exhaled a giant cloud, hoping to see Yael's concerned face in the wisps of smoke, but his skills as a seer bore no fruit. And though he couldn't see the face of his lover in the smoke, he did suddenly recall the sergeant's last question, and he noticed now that he'd asked it in an unpleasantly official tone.

He put out the rest of the cigar in the ashtray with an advertisement for Ricard anise and headed to the shower.

SHENNAN AT THE GATE

Laurent was returning home from a long walk from the restaurant La Petite Fadette in Nohant-Vic, a place he went every Wednesday. The service was good, and so were the prices, and the dining room offered a warm and welcoming space with wainscoting, an oversized hearth and a window that looked out onto the small but distinctive church, the George Sand manor and the bust of Chopin on the corner. After a good meal, with his body warmed by a nice Armagnac and a sizeable *veguero* cigar that encircled him in a halo of smoke, the stroll back was an added treat. For Laurent, this cross-country promenade, with his grandfather's hand-carved boxwood walking stick, couldn't have been more pleasant.

When he reached the square in Saint-Chartier, from the pathway from the town of La Preugne that led past the washing house, he spotted someone leaning against the wall of his house with some grocery bags on the ground. He continued walking and studied the individual. Seeing how he moved, he felt certain it was none other than Shennan. His intuition was confirmed when the visitor, upon hearing his steps on the gravel, turned toward him, waved his hand and with a booming voice cried out, in Spanish, 'Don Laurent! It's about time we finally met!'

He had a peculiar way of talking and smiling at the same time that made it hard not to fall under his spell. Even Laurent, who was inclined to dislike him because of the melodrama in the bakery and the fire on his field, couldn't help but return the smile and spread his arms when Shennan, in the affable Argentine style, went to embrace him. Laurent had seen the world and wasn't easily fooled, and if even he had that reaction, what hope was there for unsuspecting women?

After embracing they shook hands vigorously, looking each other in the eyes, examining one another with curiosity and humour, like two wolves who cross paths in the woods. Once they determined they bore no animosity to each other, the Argentine spoke.

'Laurent, after the lives we've led, the fact that we both ended up in this tiny village in rural France can only mean that fate wants us to be friends.'

'What choice do we have? This isn't Patagonia, and it's impossible to live here without running into people at all hours of the day,' joked Laurent.

'Speaking of run-ins, I understand you had a memorable one with my wife and daughters. I brought you a few bottles from my cellar; they're from Chile and very good. I hope they're to your liking,' he said, pointing to the bags at his feet.

'Why don't we go inside and find out?' Laurent picked up one of the bags and noticed it was quite full.

Once inside, he invited Shennan to sit on one of the wing-back chairs and asked him to open whichever bottle he liked, while he went to light the hearth.

Shennan decided to play it safe and opened a Montes Alpha. Soon they were raising their glasses before the fire, searching for common ground in their past and sharing stories from the south.

'I should apologise on more than one account, Laurent. First for the construction noise – you must be at your wits' end – and then for not coming over to introduce myself sooner. And finally for all the gossip you've heard about us, which you must find a colossal bore. Besides, I understand that you ran into some trouble with one of your fields, and I suspect I'm to blame.'

'To answer in the same order, I can say the walls are thick, both inside and out, and I rarely hear any noise. As for your second point, it's equally true that I haven't introduced myself either, mostly because I assumed you were very busy with the construction, your family and your business. And as for the gossip, while I have heard a lot of things, perhaps you've heard some things about me as well, so we'll call it a tie – though I'm afraid what they say about me is much less interesting than what they say about you. And finally, I actually would appreciate some news about that trouble in the pasture, because it caused me a tremendous bother.'

'Yes, this business with the field is absurd, and it's all the fault of that insufferable farmer who's got some grudge against me – because I'm a foreigner, I suppose, and because I bought the château, and above all because I refused to sell him the fields next to his. When he wouldn't drop the matter, I told him that not only would I not sell them, but that you too would sell me yours before you leased them out to him. I know I had no right to say that, much less without having asked you, but you know how it is: sometimes in the heat of an argument one gets carried away, and my fiery Irish blood is always spoiling for a fight.'

'So that's all it was?' Laurent said. 'Regardless, even if you did say that, he has no right to raise such a fuss, especially one that's going to cost me time and money. I hope he gets kicked by a cow.'

'Don't worry,' Shennan reassured him. 'I've got it under control. As I understand it, he's going to withdraw the complaint, and then we'll all live happily ever after.'

'How do you know?' Laurent was astonished. 'Tartarin said that he had it in for you, that he was going to do everything in his power to make your life impossible.'

'That's right, but my lawyers in Paris are very resourceful and well connected.' Shennan's impish smile, accentuated by the play of light from the fireplace, gave his handsome face a slightly Satanic mien. 'And I can say, based on the information they've provided, that from now on Tonton will be downright chummy with us, because if he continues to raise a fuss, certain private affairs of his will come to light, and it seems they're quite scandalous.'

'I'm dying to ask what those "affairs" are, but I'd rather drink to having the matter settled. And thank you – on my behalf you needn't have bothered.'

'Not at all, Laurent. What he did to you was just the straw that broke the camel's back. I've always ignored Tonton to avoid trouble with the town,' Shennan confessed, frowning with a rather fierce expression, 'but when I saw he was starting to cause trouble for other people simply because they knew us, even tangentially, as in your case, I realised I had better put a stop to it now and teach him a lesson, give him something that'll sting for a bit. As for the other gossip, I assume it all has to do with women or with my business. You must have heard about the woman in Lignières, I suppose?'

'You have to admit, it's pretty bad.'

'See? Everyone wants to believe the version that makes me out to be the villain. For your information, Françoise, the baker, has been doing her own thing for years, and I was just one affair of many. I wasn't even the only one at the time, though I was perhaps the most conspicuous.'

'But is it true what they say about the baguette with horns?' asked Laurent, since that detail had been etched on his mind.

'You even heard about that stupid baguette? Good God!' Shennan moaned. But seeing Laurent's expectant look, he went on. 'Yes, it's true. When I'd go to the bakery she'd hand me the loaf over the counter and say, in front of the other customers, "Here's your bread, Monsieur Shennan, soft and warm just the way you like it." I'd die of embarrassment, but when I'd see that mischievous face of hers, her chest, her hips . . . What can I say? I couldn't control myself. She was worth it, no doubt about that, but you had to play by her rules. I'm not making excuses, please don't misunderstand me, but if you'd met her I'm sure you'd have ended up making a pilgrimage, too.'

'I don't doubt it. Of course, I'm in no position to judge, but what her husband did is really unfortunate,' countered Laurent.

'Of course, but how could I have imagined the guy would go off and do a thing like that? Françoise always said he didn't care what she did, and even if he did, he deserved whatever he got for something truly bad that he'd done in the past. And since the guy looked so meek and resigned, I chose to believe that there really wouldn't be any trouble.'

'And your wife never caught wind of it?'

'Oof, knock on wood,' said Shennan sheepishly. 'If Mayumi found out, the veil of the temple would be torn in two. Thankfully she's not very sociable, and with her aloofness, no one's going to run and fill her in. She's got quite a temper, but I imagine even if she did find out, her sense of decorum would prevail. She never lets herself lose control. Besides, in Japan, where she's from, no one expects model behaviour of the men, which is a plus. But even though I'm shameless, I love her and wouldn't want to offend her for the world.'

Laurent took a drink from his glass, thinking back to the conversation with Madame Mayumi and wondering about all the things Shennan knew about the world outside the wall of his fortress, and all the things he was unaware of within them. Still, he preferred to remain silent. This wasn't the first time he'd met a married playboy who made the mistake of thinking his excuses were airtight. Shennan brought him back out of his thoughts with another confession.

'As for the rest of the affairs chalked up to me, it's true I've had some, but not as many as I'd like, and almost never with the women I really want.' After this he settled into a mysterious silence, emerging a bit later to raise his glass in a toast. 'So that's me, Laurent. Please accept my welcome to Saint-Chartier, along with my invitation to have a drink in my home. I'd love to show you my collection of South American artefacts. I understand you're a marvellous rider, and a lot of what I have is equestrian gear.'

'I'd be delighted to, Carlos,' he replied, and seeing him get up, Laurent did the same, shaking his hand to show he did in fact accept Shennan's offer. Then, before his guest left, he remembered he wanted to ask him something. 'Your row with the worker the other day was quite something. How is it that you speak Arabic?'

'Oh, that,' he said, trying to look modest, but his eyes gave off sparks from his stoked ego. 'I had some business in that part of the world, and I've got a knack for languages. Though I don't remember seeing you in the crowd that day. I did notice a gorgeous woman with curly hair, however.' Noting Laurent's expression change, he continued. 'I see, you must have been the guy standing next to her. I confess, I didn't notice you then. She took up all my attention. Where did you meet her? Is she from around here?'

Laurent was surprised Shennan hadn't noticed Yael

in Saint-Chartier. He preferred not to go into detail and instead played coy.

'Not exactly. One day I'll tell you the story.'

Alone again, Laurent reflected on his first encounter with Shennan. He'd tried to resist, but he had to admit he'd been won over by the man's charm.

FLORA AND FAUN

A few days later Laurent visited a plant nursery in Châteauroux. After talking to the Green Goddesses one evening in their snug home, he'd gotten it into his head that he should plant some fruit trees on part of his land.

He was comparing possible trees when he happened upon the landscape gardener from the château. He caught sight of her from afar and confirmed his first impression: the young woman had an exceedingly romantic aura, as though she went through life on cottony clouds that let her float over the world without being tainted by it. Her eyes, almond-shaped with extremely long lashes, had an absent, melancholy look that made him think of those medieval poems that speak of a doe wounded by an arrow.

She stood inspecting the plants for a while, picking them up carefully and holding them in her hands, looking over the leaves and then delicately inhaling their fragrance.

Watching her work was like sitting in on a tea ceremony performed with soul-stirring meticulousness and care. This young lady was certainly beautiful, with an almost reed-like fragility that accentuated that ethereal quality she had; and yet, he reflected, she gave off an overly pure air, and besides, any sentimental predator could clearly see that in her heart she bore a heavy burden.

He walked over to say hello.

'*Bonjour*. I've seen you in Saint-Chartier working in the château gardens. My name is Laurent de Rodergues, and I live next door, in the old vicarage.'

She looked up in surprise from some saplings, as if she thought it strange that someone should remember her.

'Forgive me, I'm hopeless, and I didn't recognise you. When I pick out plants I'm so focused I don't notice anything else. I'm Solange Vartel, and as you might have guessed, I'm a landscape architect.'

'No apology needed. I can understand how you'd get lost among so many plants. I'm looking for some fruit trees myself, something to plant in a field I've got, and the choice isn't easy with everything on offer. I've seen your work, and let me say how impressed I was. It's astonishingly intricate.'

The mention of fruit trees seemed to excite her, and the praise lit up her face.

'I admire your initiative. I wish everyone would replant their abandoned fields. Have you thought about what you're going to buy? I love the fruit trees they grew in the Middle Ages. In fact, I'm trying to persuade Monsieur Shennan to plant several rows on the path to the old lazar house.'

Laurent noted with amusement that as she spoke of trees and species she became more animated, and he was interested in hearing her advice, even if he wasn't too

110

enthusiastic about some of the species she recommended, like the quince or the pomegranate. The colour seemed to return to her face, and her eyes no longer looked sad but shone with a reservoir of restrained longing, perhaps repressed, no doubt pained. *How many warm-hearted women must there be*, he wondered in silence, *who have been wounded for life by men's selfish, brutal banality?* He declined to reflect on his own missteps.

As she led him among the trees in search of the ones she recommended, Laurent fondly imagined her in a long white robe instead of the long black leather jacket she had on. He could easily picture her strolling over paths with a thick carpet of grass, as sparrows flitted about in song among the dense hedges.

Lost in his reverie of Flora, the goddess of flowering plants, Laurent suddenly heard a familiar voice calling out to her and, as if in a Greek drama, Pan appeared, in the person of Shennan, with a faun's mask of carnal lust painted across his face.

They were equally surprised.

'*Caramba*, Laurent, what are you doing here? I see you've met Solange, the genius behind the huge landscaping project we're trying to put together in the park around the château.'

Her face had suddenly lit up. She seemed elated when she turned to Shennan.

'Yes, Carlos, I've met your neighbour, and I'm helping him pick fruit trees for his pasture. Did you finish your important call?' Her use of 'Carlos' did not escape Laurent's notice. She was the second person working for him who allowed herself such a liberty.

'Yes,' replied Shennan simply, eyes fixed on Laurent.

The landscape architect, who apparently lived in her own naive world, seemed not to notice, but Laurent could see perfectly well that Shennan wasn't thrilled by this encounter. He'd puffed his chest up like a rooster. What would he do next – start roaring like a tiger and marking his territory?

Shennan's possessive attitude struck Laurent as ridiculous in the extreme, so he adopted a conciliatory air and began to explain to Solange that, in spite of what she'd said, he'd rather stick with more ordinary fruits, like pears, apples, cherries and peaches. Leaving to purchase the trees, he said goodbye to her and to Shennan, who had suddenly recovered his good humour and reiterated his promise to visit him soon.

The next day, while riding near the ruins of the old Chapel of Saint Joseph, a church that had been burnt to the ground during the revolution – nothing remained but the altar stone and a hollow where the altar itself once stood – Laurent saw a lorry with a load of plants sounding its horn outside the white wooden gate at the back side of the château. Out ran Solange to receive the plants, but she stopped short when she heard someone calling out from atop a tree.

'Hold on, Mademoiselle, I'll be right down,' that someone said. Less than a minute later, a figure wearing a helmet and earmuffs, in the distinctive outfit of a tree specialist, or rather an *arboriste-grimpeur*, stood at the foot of the lorry, ready to help her.

The man in question didn't look very tall, though Laurent could tell he was sinewy and muscular. When he took off the helmet, a luxuriant curly blonde mane spilt out onto his shoulders, and even from that distance, Laurent could tell that the deep-set eyes in that angular face were fixed longingly on Solange.

Laurent walked away laughing to himself: that love triangle was liable to turn into a comedy, with Shennan in the role of a satyr, outwitted by a squadron of Vestal Virgins.

THE *ARBORISTE-GRIMPEUR* AND THE SACRED BANYAN

Laurent was shaving with the scrupulous attention of thick-bearded men when he heard a knock at the door. This drove him mad, because a patio separated the front door from the street, and at the entrance to the patio stood a double wrought-iron gate with a lovely bell on a cord so that visitors could announce their presence, though no one seemed to pay it any heed.

'It's seven-thirty in the morning. Does no one in this town respect people's privacy? Does no one read the newspaper in peace before setting off to badger their neighbours?' he asked his foam-covered reflection in the mirror.

He poked his head out the window with only an undersized towel wrapped around his waist. At the door stood Tum, the Shennans' nanny, and another Asian woman with a plump, warm face, dressed entirely in Chinese garb and holding a package wrapped in aluminium foil. He asked them to wait a moment, forced himself into a pair of trousers and a T-shirt, and went to open the door.

Tum made the traditional Theravada gesture of peace, and the other woman bowed her head with a smile. Then, in her near-perfect English, the nanny explained the reason for their visit.

'Pardon us for bothering you, Monsieur Laurent. My companion, Yammei Bai, the Shennans' cook, has made one of her people's typical dishes, at the girls' request, and with Madame Mayumi's permission we've come to bring it to you.'

'Good heavens!' joked Laurent. 'What are those little devils plotting against me?'

Tum, horrified, appeared not to get the joke.

'No, Monsieur, they're not devils. They're good girls, but sometimes they're a bit . . . I can't recall the word, pardon me,' she said, ashamed.

'A bit precocious?' offered Laurent.

Tum's face lit up with one of the prettiest, most innocent smiles he'd ever seen, and the other woman smiled, too, not understanding a word. *It's a pity that some of the earth's peoples know how to smile almost without effort*, thought Laurent, *while others seem to be taught only to compose sour, standoffish faces*.

'I should warn you that while the dish is delicious, it's very spicy,' explained Tum, and then spoke a few words in a strange language to her companion, who nodded, handing the tray to Laurent.

'What language are you two speaking?' enquired Laurent, turning to Tum. 'I thought you were Burmese, but your companion is Chinese.'

'Yes, but she belongs to the Hani people, who live on the Burmese border. Ethnically, we both belong to the same

Sino-Burmese group, and our languages are similar. We've worked together for many years.'

Satisfied with this explanation, Laurent invited them in, led them to the kitchen, and lifted the aluminium foil to reveal a circular plate, deep and quite large, with food for half a dozen people, which gave off a sharp, pungent, yet delicious aroma.

Under a pyramid of violently red peppers lay pieces of chicken, cut and seasoned with herbs and aromatic Sichuan peppercorns. All this sat on a bed of julienned potatoes, stir-fried with fresh spring onions. The dish promised to be a strong sensation, especially so early in the morning.

The cook seemed to suddenly remember something, and from the ample sleeve of her garment she produced a pot full of still-warm rice, while she seemed to explain something, which Tum immediately translated.

'This is very high-quality Lijiang rice. Have a spoonful with each piece of chicken, and it will soften the heat.'

'This is far too much for me. You don't expect me to eat all this for breakfast?' complained Laurent.

'It's a dish served specifically at breakfast, so that you can start the day full of energy. In Yammei's land it's usually prepared on harvest days. Please, you'll see that it's not so much once you move aside the peppers. You'll need it to be in top shape for when you see the girls today. They're very excited about your visit,' Tum assured him. Laurent suspected she knew what he had in store and got a kick out of it.

'Is it really necessary for me to eat it right this minute?' insisted Laurent. 'I was just about to shave.'

116

'Yammei's gone to great lengths to make this dish, and she even slaughtered the chicken herself at five-thirty this morning. Please don't offend her,' said Tum, handing him a lovely pair of dark wooden chopsticks held together by a silver-plated chain. 'One last bit of advice: drink only hot water as you eat. It's better for retaining the flavour.'

'You've thought of everything. How can I say no?' He surrendered, sitting down at the table under the attentive gaze of the two women.

To his surprise, the meat was delicious. Crispy, tender, full of unknown flavours, hot but not overpowering, as heavily spiced foods often are. Everything was in balance and harmony.

The women, seeing that he ate with an appetite, took their leave with a bow, reminding him he was expected at four o'clock at the pergola in the park.

Despite his initial hesitation, Laurent ate the entire contents of the tray, and afterward he really did feel invigorated both inside and out. He needed to get the recipe from that cook Yammei.

After breakfast, he decided he'd enjoy his day until the appointed hour. He'd found that not using the internet or a mobile phone filled his day with more free time. Months earlier he'd come to the conclusion that technology was like tobacco: it seems indispensable until you free yourself from its thrall. He resolved to rediscover the value of the postal service and hand-written mail, and he thus spent a productive morning organising the cellar in the vicarage and putting onto shelves the many jars of preserves from his garden. He'd learnt to make them with the invaluable help of the Green Goddesses as well as René's wife, a woman with no ecological inclinations who nevertheless held onto ancestral family recipes that had provided Laurent with much joy and sustenance.

Next he ate a frugal lunch and headed to the château, whose main gate was unlocked. As soon as he entered, he sensed there was less commotion than before, and then he noticed that the façade work was already complete. The château's restoration, to a layman's eyes at least, seemed already quite far along. They'd even restored the old lightning rods, whose copper conduits ran into the ground next to each tower. Only in the gardens did he see work still to be done. Also in security, since not far away were parked several vans from an electricity company whose employees busied themselves with long rolls of cable that looked to him like the kind used in alarms.

The sound of paws running across the grass pulled him out of these observations, and he braced himself, hoping he wouldn't be knocked down again by the mastiff now racing toward him. An order from Madame Mayumi spared him – and not a second too late.

'Thanks. With the breakfast I've got in my stomach, I don't think I'm up for a roll in the grass,' joked Laurent, greeting his hostess.

'No, thank *you*, Monsieur de Rodergues. It's both kind and brave of you to accept the girls' invitation. They've spent all day preparing for the picnic. Unfortunately I won't be able to join you, as I have to pick out some fabric for the music room. My husband has finally agreed to put one

118

on the third floor. At least it's something, don't you think?'

He was about to reply when the girls arrived, their natural boisterousness accentuated by the barking of their hairless dog Barbie. When they reached Laurent, they each took his hand in turn and gave him a polite kiss on each cheek. Then, escorted by the two dogs, they surrounded him to lead him toward the pergola, waving goodbye to their mother with a simple 'Bye, Mum.'

Laurent, now captive, managed to half-turn to wave goodbye as well, but Madame Mayumi was already heading back toward the château with an anxious look on her face and didn't see him.

Tum was waiting for them at the entrance to the enormous wrought-iron pergola. As always, she looked beyond beautiful, with her skin tanned by the spring sun and hair woven into a braid that hung coquettishly over her shoulder, with a jade bracelet on her wrist. Yammei was inside, arranging plates and dishes on the table.

'Did you like Yammei's spicy chicken?' asked the oldest sister in quite passable Spanish.

'I didn't know you spoke Spanish. You have very good pronunciation,' said Laurent.

'Just a little, but my sisters know only a few words,' the girl bragged. 'If you want to win over Yammei, tell her the dish was *haochi*, which means "yummy" in Chinese.'

'Stop being so lovey-dovey in Spanish with Monsieur Laurent. It's rude if we can't understand you,' scolded the middle girl.

'I'm doing nothing of the sort,' said her sister, blushing

as the other two laughed, and Tum concealed a laugh of her own.

Laurent tried to calm them down. 'Now, let's not get upset. But what do we have here? This is a banquet fit for a king!' He marvelled at the table covered with a heavy embroidered tablecloth, delicate porcelain plates, stiff starched napkins bearing the family's monogram and glasses and cups that matched the gleaming sterling silverware. In the centre of the table awaiting the guests were all the delicacies of a proper afternoon tea: trays stacked three high with cucumber and ham sandwiches, macarons in every colour, tea biscuits, tarts with caramelised fruit and an enormous chocolate fondue surrounded by little trays, one of which only had flowers, which, they explained, were also edible and had been arranged according the instructions of Mademoiselle Vartel.

He still had the memory of the chicken fresh in his mind, but such a spread was unworthy of hesitation, so Laurent said without ceremony, 'Where do I sit? I want to eat it all!'

Laughing and shouting, they sat down to tuck into the feast. Not long after they started, the forester, the one Laurent had seen from afar alongside Solange, walked over. Once again he was wearing work clothes, but he looked more tanned, and had various scratches criss-crossing his face and arms. The girls welcomed him with cries of delight.

'Thierry, come sit with us. Everything is delicious!'

Thierry must have been used to dealing with children, because right away he did a simple magic trick that left them applauding with delight. But then he excused himself saying he needed someone who spoke English, because he'd run into a problem with the château gardener, who didn't speak a word of French.

'All of us here speak English, except for Yammei,' boasted the youngest.

'I know, my little mushroom queen,' he answered with a bow, 'but I need someone older, like this gentleman' – he pointed at Laurent – 'or Miss Tum.'

Laurent wiped his mouth and got up with Tum to go with Thierry, who explained the issue.

'There's a giant banyan in the back of the park, one of those trees that have huge branches and roots everywhere. It's not a local species – here we call it a Bengali ficus. Anyway, it's gigantic, and on the inside it's totally infested with stag beetles, a protected species, but one that's fatal for a tree like this. The banyan has been gnawed through, so a strong storm could bring it down, which would be a disaster and destroy a lot of the work being done in the garden.'

In the middle of these explanations, Solange joined the group.

'Thierry, don't you think we could prune away the sick branches and save the tree?' she asked. 'It's a beautiful specimen, and it's practically a miracle it was able to grow here at all.'

His expression showed he was tempted to grant her the wish. Yet his professional zeal outweighed his desire to please her.

'No, Mademoiselle Solange, it's hollowed out on the inside. In fact, it's so bad the gardener has his arms around it, crying like a baby.'

* * *

121

When they reached the spot, Laurent had to admit the tree was a natural work of art, with sinewy trunks everywhere that made up an intricate tangle, at once beautiful and fascinating. Solange explained that in 1878, the owner of the château, Madame Germaine, following the vogue in France at the time, brought all sorts of trees from the colonies. This one no doubt came from Chandernagore or Pondicherry, the two French settlements in India, or maybe from Madagascar. The sadness in her eyes at the thought that it would have to be cut down vouched for the uniqueness of this specimen.

'It's a pity,' she said. 'I planned to make a Siamese corner here, with red and black bamboo around the area. Monsieur Shennan had even had one of those beautiful "spirit houses" sent over from Thailand to decorate the site. He'll be crushed by the news.'

As the gardener clung to the tree, murmuring what appeared to be prayers, Thierry came over to show them an enormous beetle larva, thrashing about with remarkable energy on the palm of his hand.

Tum went to speak to the gardener, who was also Asian, and then translated the words he groaned and sighed.

'Khun Suan says this is the sacred tree of Hinduism, so it's also sacred for Theravada Buddhists. The leaves provided rest to Krishna, and it was under a banyan tree that the Buddha Gautama received enlightenment. He doesn't want us to cut it down – he says this kind of tree you have to let fall down by itself.'

Thierry and Solange had regret written on their faces. They understood the gardener's feelings, they said, but Thierry held firm.

'I don't like cutting down trees for no reason, and this one is spectacular, but if it falls down on top of someone it would be a tragedy. I'm sorry, I have to recommend we take it down,' he said. Laurent seized a moment when no one was looking and crushed the stag beetle larva under his foot. He didn't care how endangered it was – he liked the tree more.

Yammei, the cook, silently approached, walked over to Khun Suan and without a word began stroking his shoulder and whispering into his ear. Then she gently pulled him away from the tree, still stroking his shoulder, and took him back to the pergola. As he walked by the group he was still whimpering and sobbing. Tum suppressed a shiver and closed her eyes. Laurent noticed her trembling.

'What did he say? Whatever it was, it seems to have shaken you.'

Tum spoke with what seemed to be great effort.

'Khun Suan says it's never a good idea to cut down a banyan, but that doing so in springtime can only bring great misfortune on this house.'

'I can't think of any calamity worse than not having the garden in shape for the opening of the château on the date set by Monsieur Shennan,' Thierry said. 'I don't know about you, but I'd rather run the risk of offending the Thai gods than angering him.'

Solange nodded in agreement. Then Thierry asked them to leave, since they were going to start getting the tree ready right away and calculating how to angle the fall of the branches and trunks as they began sawing them off.

They glumly returned to the picnic, where the girls' joyful antics quickly helped Laurent forget the drama of the tree. The nanny tried to hide her distress, but it was obvious to Laurent that the gardener's words had made an impression on her.

That was Laurent's last visit to the château in those months. Spring was at its height, the weather had begun to improve, and with the landscape arrayed in all its splendour, he threw himself into long rides on horseback, hikes and trips to places of interest in the surrounding areas.

UNDER THE VAULT OF HEAVEN

On that June evening, Laurent had just come back from a hike with Chimay, who sat gnawing through a bone of prehistoric proportions that Roger had given him. In Saint-Chartier, the early summer sunlight lasts until quite late and fades into such a spectacular display one simply can't stay indoors. No sooner had he gotten home than he left the dog to enjoy his treat in the garden and set off on another walk, this time by himself.

Distracted by the profusion of wildflowers, he lingered alongside the road, gathering daffodils, nettles, bright gold buttercups, proud asphodels with white and yellow petals, speckled Mary's tears, stalks of loosestrife, wild thistles with lilac hues that the French, with their overly poetic imagination, call *cabaret des oiseaux* – birds' cabaret – along with many other specimens. Then he happened upon a cluster of wild asparagus, forgot about his floral rapture and single-mindedly set about digging them up.

An hour later, he'd filled up a knapsack and back-up

plastic bag with the asparagus and a type of wild garlic called bear leek – delicious in salads – along with cresses and the mythical mugwort, a herb indispensable for tenderising poultry. When he saw that night had started to fall, he turned to walk back to the town and, once there, headed toward the plaza, taking in the imposing view of the château towers, which always surprised him from that angle. By the time he reached the monument to wartime martyrs, it was already dark, but it was one of those June nights that are so clear that a careful observer could make out each and every star visible to the eye. Laurent always tried to identify them, but the sciences were not his strong suit, and he rarely got past Ursa Major.

A good friend of his in the Chilean navy, Germán, used to always go on about the Pleiades, reminiscing about his trips to Antarctica, but as these disquisitions about the stars typically followed an alcohol-soaked feast, Laurent always questioned the reliability of his friend's memory.

As he tried unsuccessfully to find Altair, someone called his name. His knees began to tremble, because he knew perfectly well who that voice belonged to. He turned around slowly, trying to think of what to say and not feeling especially witty. It had been weeks since he'd last seen her, and even though he thought about her every day, he'd chosen not to give in to weakness and fall in love with her, for he could tell such a love would be hard to tame, and if it bucked him he'd find no salve for his wounds.

Yael stood in her doorway, leaning against the wooden frame, unaware – or perhaps not – that the light from inside the house cast her body in silhouette and generously outlined the space between her legs. The curls on her shoulders seemed longer than Laurent remembered, her panther eyes gleamed teasingly, and around her neck hung a necklace with an enormous shell comfortably ensconced in her décolletage.

Laurent approached cautiously, hoping to appear more in control of himself than he felt. She gave him her hand and offered her cheek for a kiss. Obediently, he placed his lips on cheek, and as he did so he felt her curls caress his face and deeply inhaled her scent, losing all notion of time and space. The only thing real at that moment was the hand on the back of his neck and the moist, half-opened lips pressed against his.

The next morning, he awoke alone in his bed with no idea of what time it was, because he hadn't heard any of the insistent alarms that normally forced him out of bed at 6 a.m.

He saw he was wearing only his pyjama bottoms, which in itself was suspicious, since he normally slept without them. He sniffed the sheets and found they were clean, with none of the tell-tale marks or scents left behind by nights of frenzied lust. His head ached slightly, yet he didn't recall having drunk anything. As he stood up the headache climbed to his crown and became unspeakably intense. He leant against the wall, and the image of Yael, naked, came to his mind. He saw her from behind, with her straight, toned shoulders, her narrow waist, and her buttocks like two tan, rounded stones. He shook his head and the memories returned, this time bringing back the taste of her breasts to his mouth. He noticed an erection and felt an imperious desire to possess her, but he was alone and confused in his meticulously tidy room, with yesterday's clothes carefully folded on a chair, and his slippers, which he didn't often wear, arranged side by side in perfect symmetry under his nightstand.

Something didn't add up. He was certain he'd been with Yael, but he couldn't understand how he'd made it home back to his bed all alone. It was all very strange, so he threw himself into the bracing arms of an icy shower, then went straight to Yael's house in search of answers.

He knocked on her door, but no one answered. He checked and saw her car wasn't there, and he had no choice but to admit she was gone. Corroborating this conclusion was a piece of irrefutable evidence: a bag of rubbish tied to her garage door. The rubbish collectors came on Tuesday mornings, and it was now Tuesday afternoon, which meant she didn't intend to return until at least the following week – or who knew when.

He looked up and down the street, checking to make sure no one could see him, and took the bag of rubbish and began digging around in its contents. It was neither gentlemanly nor elegant, but he needed clues to find out why she had left, and he certainly had nothing better on hand.

He found several pieces of crumpled or ripped paper covered in scribbles and strange marks, a banana peel, more fruit scraps, coffee grounds, three empty tubes of ceramic paint – 'Maybe she really is a potter after all,' he muttered – two containers of high-fibre yoghurt, fabric cuttings, various advertising brochures and a series of cropped photos of the château and the people who lived or worked inside. This he found odd: the photos weren't artistic but rather professional, of the kind usually used in sociology or marketing studies . . . or investigations. He stuck the photos in his trouser pocket, retied the rubbish bag and put it back in its place, hanging on the door.

Lost, confused, feeling a bit like an abandoned puppy, he turned to head back. He couldn't understand how, after that night of love, Yael could disappear without at least leaving a note. That part especially stung.

He walked up the slight rise back to his house, and when he closed the gate behind him, he saw hanging on one of the spires of the gate his knapsack and the plastic bag full of asparagus. No doubt he'd left in a hurry and forgotten them.

With them was a note:

I found this next to my door, and I seem to remember seeing you once wearing this ratty old knapsack. Careful with the asparagus – they say it's an aphrodisiac.

He folded the note, grabbed the knapsack and the plastic bag, and walked up the stairs, singing at the top of his lungs, 'Y *si es delito el quererte, qué importa que me condenen a muerte en el tribunal de un beso.*' And if loving you is a crime, what does a death sentence matter in the courtroom of a kiss.

THE INVITATION

In Laurent's new routine, he took two trips a week to La Châtre, one on Wednesdays and one on Saturdays. The first was to go to the Crédit Agricole savings bank, stock up on minor provisions, poke around Monsieur Mercier's antique shop by the tower and along the way treat himself to a generous afternoon snack in a patisserie on the Rue Nationale. Nearly all of the patisseries were quite good, but this one had certain tarts that were dear to Laurent's heart. Afterward he'd take a short stroll to visit the book shops, the cultural centre and the library in search of literary novelties, though these were few and far between.

The other weekly outing, on Saturdays, took him to the morning street market. He enjoyed the hustle and bustle, and the fish stalls called to mind a view of the old port in Marseille. In the plaza he never failed to visit Rachid, an industrious Moroccan rogue who sold olives with various seasonings along with the vinegary hot peppers Laurent used when making stewed beans. Next, he'd head to his main objective, the stall that sold Corsican products, where he'd pick up his favourite sausage, the *figatellu*. He'd then return happy to Saint-Chartier, already imagining the sandwich he'd have on his patio.

One Saturday, as he walked from his car to his door, laden with shopping bags, he spotted the postwoman parking her own vehicle next to the western wall of the château, under the shade of a luxuriant lilac bush. She motioned to him, and once she'd killed the engine he walked over to her.

'Good thing I ran into you, Monsieur de Rodergues. I'm delivering Monsieur Shennan's invitations, and he's paid for receipt confirmation, so I need your signature.'

'Monsieur Shennan's invitations?' asked Laurent in surprise. 'To what?'

'To the inauguration of the château, on 15th July – I can't believe you haven't heard! Here's your invitation. Please sign on the line, where it says "received",' she said, handing him a notebook and confiding with pride, 'You know, even I've received an invitation.'

Laurent signed, and after the mail carrier left, he stood looking up at the château. It was true. He hadn't thought about it for some time, but in fact it had been days or even weeks since he'd seen lorries coming by or heard the noise of the cranes or the voices of the workers from the scaffolding.

At last Shennan has managed to his finish his château, he thought. *Bravo for him. It took willpower, muscle and nerve.*

Back in his kitchen, he cut open the envelope with a knife, while at the same time – unable to restrain himself – he cut himself a large chunk of sausage. As with everything Shennan did, both the envelope and the invitation itself showed the finest quality and design. Embossed into the paper was the emblem of the château, while the addressee's name had been handwritten by a professional calligrapher, with the capital letters decorated as in an illuminated manuscript. The card itself was staggeringly elegant, simple but overwhelming. Part of the point, Laurent felt sure, was to leave the guests' egos sizzling with delight simply that they were thought worthy of such a masterpiece of ornamentation. And of course Shennan had achieved that aim.

Yet the text had a roguish touch:

Château de Saint-Chartier
To celebrate the completion of the restoration work on our home, we are pleased to invite you to the festivities officially inaugurating the renovated Château de Saint-Chartier on 15th July 2009, at six o'clock in the evening.

With this event we wish to show our appreciation to all our friends and neighbours in Saint-Chartier whose assistance, encouragement and patience have made it possible to realise this shared dream. We look forward to seeing you there.

Formal summer attire requested.
Carlos Shennan and Mayumi Sayotaki

The line about 'formal summer attire' was sure to throw many people into confusion. Laurent smiled and opened a large bottle of ice-cold local beer.

THE CELEBRATION

On the afternoon of 15th July, Laurent set down the book he was reading and went to the kitchen to check the time: five o'clock. In just one hour the celebration at the château would begin. He went up to his room to shave, shower and choose his outfit. He hadn't decided what he would wear, but complying with the request of the invitation posed no difficulty for him.

One of the advantages of living in the vicarage was the amount of free space he had at his disposal. He had an entire dressing room all to himself where he kept everything: his suitcases, shoes, boots, coats, even his bedclothes and towels, and naturally his ironing board.

He looked out the window. The day was warm and bright, though of course it always cooled off after six. He had only three summer suits: one in dark blue alpaca, another in white linen and a third in seersucker with thick sky-blue pinstripes. This last one seemed like the best choice, because it would be different from the clothes he thought he'd see at the party.

To go along with it, he opted for a white linen shirt, and

instead of a tie, he thought it'd be good to catch people's eyes with a bow tie he'd had made with the same fabric as the suit but with the colours inverted. Shoes, socks and belt would be black, he decided, because after the bow tie he didn't dare do anything else too offbeat.

He was in no rush. He didn't really like massive parties like this, even though he recognised that the Shennans' restoration effort warranted his attendance. Besides, he knew he'd have fun seeing their daughters, and he was certain the event would be unsurpassed in both entertainment and catering. And finally, he thought as he drew the razor across his face, all of Saint-Chartier would be there, so he, as a member of the community, couldn't bow out.

He rubbed his jaw to check that he'd gotten a close shave, and it occurred to him how happy he'd be to run into the mysterious Yael at the party. What would she wear for the occasion? He hadn't seen her in weeks, not since that heated night of passion that seemed ever more distant and dreamlike. Still, he was entirely convinced that she wouldn't miss the inauguration of the château, even if he wasn't sure he wanted to know her real motives for going. He heard cars arriving and vans unloading the food that would be served in the reception. Suddenly, amidst the hubbub, he could make out musicians rehearsing, with bagpipes – hardly a common sound in Saint-Chartier – and other instruments that seemed almost to be vying to outdo each other. He peered out of the window and saw his fellow townspeople dressed to the nines, strolling about or talking in small groups to pass the time as they waited for the gates to open.

THE GIFT

That was when he realised he didn't have any kind of gift for the Shennans. Worse yet, finding something that would surprise them just half an hour before the reception would be a Herculean task. He thought about getting a bottle of wine from his personal collection, but he desisted before reaching the bottom step: compared to what Shennan had in his wine cellar, Laurent's bottles would be pure vinegar. Suddenly he grimaced, remembering that he did have something they'd love – but parting with it would be like shooting himself in the kneecap.

Reluctantly he went to the room he used as a study and took from his bookshelf a box wrapped in tissue paper. He carefully unfolded it and placed the contents on the table. There in all its splendour lay a small book, a work by Hector de Corlay on the town of Saint-Chartier that included historical details about the château.

No doubt Shennan already had this edition in his own well-stocked library, and in terms of paper and covers the original was nothing more than a simple booklet. But Laurent's version was different: it had undergone certain 'alterations' courtesy of Hernán Rubio, a Mexican painter and good friend of his. Months earlier, Laurent had asked him to bind the book in the finest leather and create a work of art on its cover, using a gouge and awl, based on the contents.

The results lay on the table, a bibliophile's delight for which he'd paid a fortune – though no doubt less than it was really worth, since clearly Eduardo had not skimped on the effort. He picked it up, gingerly opened it and lifted it up to his face to breathe in the aroma of tanned leather – cordovan on the cover with embossed *guadamecí* on the boards. The artist had chosen colours and materials to create striking chromatic compositions yet not detract from the seriousness of the contents. The Shennans couldn't help but be moved by such a gift. He wrapped it back up in the same tissue paper, carefully tucked it inside his jacket and left for the party.

THE GUESTS

As soon as he stepped out into the street, he began saying hello to people left and right. If success was to be measured by the number of townsfolk attending, the event was going to be a smash. People he almost never saw were making their way to the château. Farmers who hadn't taken a holiday since their wedding day, so as not to leave their cows and goats unmilked, came out of the woodwork and were now heading toward the château.

Laurent heard someone call out his name and, turning around, he practically collided with René and his wife. After exchanging the usual pleasantries, his wife went off to see a group of friends gathered by the remains of a stone baptismal font that stood in the plaza as a decoration. When he thought she was out of earshot, René gave Laurent a knowing look.

'We certainly won't be bored,' he said.

'What makes you say that? Do you know something I don't?'

'Look around you. When was the last time you saw so many people from the town in the same place? Everyone's here, even a few who swear they're bedridden with some terminal illness.'

René looked all around, nodding in the direction of various neighbours. 'That gentleman over there is Gérard, from the Fossat farm. I haven't seen him in twenty years. The couple over there are retirees who come every August, and we're still in July. Behind them is Pauline Bonpas, who holds a grudge against half of Saint-Chartier and thinks the other half is beneath her, and even she's come. Everyone's here, Monsieur Laurent . . . well, maybe not everyone: I haven't seen Mademoiselle Yael.'

'Mademoiselle Yael? You're taunting me, René!'

'Taunting? Come now, don't be silly. Let's enjoy the evening: the amount of food and drink awaiting us inside is going to make *La Grande Bouffe* look like a Sunday school special. Anyway, I'll leave you to it. I see my cousin Philippe coming down the way.'

The ancient and obese Madame Fraset rolled imperiously down the Rue des Luthiers. Two of her several grandchildren pushed her wheelchair, and their sweat-beaded faces didn't exactly show the affection and respect they ought to have felt for their grandmother. Next to them were the firefighters' squad, who were all in attendance wearing their finest. One of them, Michel, confided in Laurent that they intended to ask Shennan to help refurbish the fire station by donating the material left over from his renovation.

Farther off, various well-dressed officials from Châteauroux, the kind who must love working for people like

138

Shennan, stood smoking under the shade of the chestnut trees.

Laurent was watching it all when he noticed people begin to stir. Then a boy ran by his side and cried out, 'Grandma! They're opening the gates! Come on!'

Out of a sense of elegance, and to avoid shoving, Laurent opted to sit on a bench, enjoying his cigar and watching the people file past as he waved to the familiar faces from afar.

AT THE ENTRANCE

Once the crowd had died down, he unhurriedly walked up the main entrance. Directly beneath the stone arch a straightforward system for greeting guests and checking invitations had been set up. At least it looked straightforward, because it involved two young women taking the invitations, checking them against a list and handing the guests a programme and a coin with the logo of the château. Yet the simplicity of the procedure contrasted with its strict, martial efficiency, for despite their slender frame and beautiful features, they both had an unmistakably military air. Then Laurent noticed that both they and the other members of the security team stationed at the gate wore the insignia of the army on their lapels. Shennan had hired former members of an elite corps to handle his party. This struck Laurent as a bit excessive, but they were no doubt very competent. As he stepped inside, an individual looking like a gladiator who'd seen his share of arenas politely asked him if he wouldn't mind stepping through a metal detector.

'I don't mind at all,' Laurent replied. 'But I noticed you

didn't make the people ahead of me walk through it.'

The muscle-bound guard gave a good-natured smile as he proceeded to perform a discreet and extremely professional pat-down.

'Your observation shows my actions are warranted, Monsieur. As do your athletic build and your foreign air. Monsieur Shennan gave us instructions us to avoid using the metal detector or frisking guests unless they stood out. You did. Does that answer your question?'

'Perhaps. I suppose I should feel flattered. One question, though: have you taken similar measures with any women?'

One of the female security guards, who had caught Laurent's eye, was listening to the conversation and joined in.

'Yes, two in fact. I had to frisk them. Why do you ask?'

'Just curious. Was one of them by chance an athletic woman, Madame de Flalois, and the other a woman with dark features and long, curly hair?'

'Excellent deduction,' the agent said, smiling coquettishly.

'Thank you, Mademoiselle. Have a good evening.'

'Not at all, Monsieur. My name's Cathy. If you get bored, come back around and say hello.'

Laurent walked on, smiling on two counts: not only did this Mademoiselle Cathy clearly look hopeful about chatting some more, which flattered him, but he also had confirmation that Yael was indeed in attendance.

But on his way to the garden known as the rotunda, his happiness vanished as it occurred to him that Yael hadn't even bothered to stop by and say hello.

THE SHENNANS

Laurent figured it wouldn't be easy to talk to the Shennans. With all that crowd, they'd no doubt be occupied with the duties of being good hosts, which essentially consist of having enormous amounts of patience and finding a way to return the praise the guests believe they're obliged to heap on them.

They had sensibly positioned themselves on the grand terrace, and he decided to bide his time hovering about, devouring canapés and washing them down with glasses of champagne. After he'd waited for around half an hour, when at last there seemed to be fewer people around them, he decided his moment had arrived and walked over, intending to take up as little of their time as possible. They were just saying goodbye to a tall priest with the face of a rugby player – a traditionalist, no doubt, as he wore a cassock and sash. *Typical Carlos,* thought Laurent, *seeking refuge in the sacred from time to time, like a good Don Juan.*

When they saw Laurent, Madame Mayumi smiled warmly and Shennan went straight to embrace him.

'Laurent! It's about time you showed up. You certainly like to take your time. Apologies for the pat-down at the entrance. Forewarned is forearmed, you know.' Then he gestured to the priest. 'Allow me to introduce Father Gérard de Montfort, an old friend I like to argue about theology with. He was kind enough to bless the château and say a Mass in the private chapel.'

Laurent offered his hand to the priest, who grasped it firmly with an amiable smile. 'Shennan's told me about you,' said the priest. 'I hope we get the chance to talk sometime. He's quite discreet and wouldn't reveal whether or not should I be worried about the salvation of your soul.'

'Saint-Chartier is a very quiet place, Father, and God doesn't think me important enough to tempt,' Laurent laughed. 'Nothing would make me happier than to give you cause to worry.'

The priest burst into loud guffaws, then remarked to Shennan, 'I can smell a sinner from miles away, and I'm afraid we're going to have to meet with Monsieur Laurent in your cellar to bring him back to the right path.'

The Shennans and Laurent all laughed. Then the priest, looking at his watch, cut the conversation short. 'As much as I'd like to linger, I must be on my way. I'm giving a talk in Ardentes, and I ought to leave right now. Good evening to you, and again, it's truly a magnificent party.' And with a handshake for all, he trotted off down the stairs.

'What do you think of the party, Monsieur de

Rodergues?' Madame Mayumi then asked. 'As you can see, Carlos is immune to thrift and economy.'

What Shennan was immune to, it seemed, was his wife's sarcasm, for he smiled with real affection and embraced her, kissing her on the cheek.

'Well, just imagine what I'd be like if I didn't have Jiminy Cricket here always chirping on my shoulder.'

Laurent, in a show of male solidarity with his friend, turned to Mayumi and said, 'I sympathise with you, Madame, because I'm an admirer of your country, where even the simplest things can be elevated to the status of art. But I also sympathise with your husband, and in his position, I might well do the same. It's hard not to want to be surrounded by beautiful things, given the opportunity. But sharing them with others is pure generosity, and that pleasure, Madame, shouldn't be denied to him.'

'Spoken like a true friend!' Shennan patted him on the back enthusiastically, at which point Laurent bowed to Madame Mayumi.

'If I may, I have a gift here for you. It's very dear to me, but after the work you've done on the château, I think belongs to you. Please accept it,' he said, presenting his gift.

'But this should be for my husband. He's the one who's made this all possible, not me,' objected Madame Mayumi, confused.

'No, Madame. You've followed him and supported him in this adventure, so it should belong to you. Your husband has no need for gifts: the family he has is more than enough.'

'By God, Laurent, I'm touched!' Shennan exclaimed.

Gingerly Mayumi unwrapped the package. Her hands trembled as she looked at the book.

'Monsieur de Rodergues, this is too much. We can't accept it, please take it back,' she pleaded, looking suddenly shaken.

'My wife is right, Laurent. This book must have cost you a fortune. I've had books bound for my library, I know what they cost, and none of them is as beautiful as this. You've outdone yourself,' said Shennan, echoing his wife but still captivated by the covers of the book.

'Then let's speak no more of it. Your words do me honour, because they show you know the value of my gift, and that alone is enough. Madame, it's for you. I hope whenever you look at it you remember this good friend and neighbour of yours.'

She took his hands and, looking at him seriously, answered, 'Laurent, I assure you you're wrong. I don't deserve this gift. And even without it, know that we'd always remember you.'

Laurent kissed her hand, shook Shennan's, and took his leave, leaving them in the middle of the crowd that was forming around them. As he descended the stairs, he ran into Thierry, who was on his way up. They both stopped.

'Good evening,' said Laurent. 'What have you got there?' He saw Thierry was carrying a bush with tiny round berries.

'Mistletoe. Madame Shennan wanted me to bring some for the priest. And here I thought mistletoe was just for pagans.'

'Well, hurry up then. The priest is probably in the car park now. The Shennans, though, are here on the terrace.'

Thierry looked where Laurent pointed but shook his head. He noticeably gritted his teeth. 'No thanks. I have no desire to see Shennan. I'll just run to the car park. Catch you later.' And in a flash he leapt over the railing and onto the grass, and took off running.

Laurent watched him, impressed by Thierry's youthful agility, and also surprised by this newly revealed animosity toward the host.

IN THE CHÂTEAU PARK

Laurent couldn't help but be amazed by the festivities the
Shennans had arranged in the park around the château.
To his relief, they hadn't done anything so tacky as hire
mimes or magicians to chase after the guests, pestering
them for their attention. Quite the contrary. In honour
of his origins, Shennan had arranged for an Irish group
to play pub music on the violin, harp, mandolin, French
horn and bodhrán. A large crowd had gathered around the
circular stone platform that served as a stage. According
to the programme he'd been handed when he arrived, the
group came from Cork and the woman on the harp would
play Gaelic songs later on. The programme also mentioned
that an accordionist would be playing tangos, with dances
performed by three couples from the Argentine Society of
Paris. Laurent thought that sounded interesting and made
a note to watch their performance. But first he wanted to
take a look at the now-finished garden and see some of
the other attractions. What really caught his attention was

something described as a 'beer wagon under the supervision of Monsieur Gaston Le Juanch with a cask of Carterius', which, according to the programme, was located not far from the entrance to the garden.

He had no trouble finding it. It stood in the centre of an open space in the park, a huge old-fashioned caravan wagon hitched to two majestic Percheron horses peacefully grazing on the hay spread out before them. Le Juanch greeted him effusively, handing him a ceramic stein with his brand logo in relief.

'Wow, Gaston, your business has come a long way. The show you're putting on here is really something,' exclaimed Laurent. 'Where did you get that monster of a cask? I feel like a Lilliputian visiting Gulliver,' he added, pointing to the gigantic wooden barrel that served as a tap.

Le Juanch gave a laugh but didn't stop serving beers to the guests gathered round. 'The cask I had specially made, and yes, it's big, but not just to show off: inside it's got a whole refrigeration system. You like it?' he asked, looking like a child who's afraid of a negative response.

'The beer is fantastic. And the set-up is like something out of a movie. You're going to be rich,' he said between sips. 'What I'd really like is to take some of your beer home with me.'

'One step ahead of you. At the end of the summer we'll start bottling. It will all be artisanal, very high-end.'

'Sounds like quite an investment. You must be mortgaged to the hilt.'

Le Juanch sized him up, then discreetly leant over to speak more quietly.

'Actually, it was all Shennan. When he tried the beer that day after that dust-up with the construction worker, he offered to go in with me on the business. He's treated me very well, we're splitting it fifty-fifty, and he lets me do whatever I like, so long as he can handle the design and the publicity. And that suits me just fine, since I'd pay to not have to do that. But it's a secret.'

'Good move, accepting his offer. At the very worst, he'll just drink all your beer himself, being Irish. Congratulations again, and rest assured, I won't tell a soul.' Laurent patted him on the back and went on his way.

Gaston had a lot of people to attend to, and Laurent wanted to continue his tour. As he walked through the park, he thought about Shennan's almost magical ability to combine business and pleasure, as if he had one of those capes they tell of in Irish legends, thin enough to be invisible, but woven with a fibre made of steel.

THE ROASTING SPIT
AND THE ARCHITECT

An unmistakable scent rendered the map on his programme superfluous. Rather than follow it, he could now let himself be led by his nose to where meat was being roasted in the Argentine style. Several men dressed as gauchos were cooking chitterlings, sweetbreads, sirloin strips, skirt steaks, tenderloin and blood sausages over the coals spread out in various pits dug into the ground, while two other gauchos, with traditional *facón* and *verijero* knives at their waists, kept watch on a dozen thick iron spits stuck into the ground, each roasting a whole lamb. Behind them was a table piled with pyramids of Argentine empanadas, salad bowls in the purest *porteño* style, and sauce dishes brimming with chimichurri, all overseen by a gaucha. Also on offer were all kinds of *alfajores* and cakes made with dulce de leche.

The hosts, the programme explained, were devotees of French cuisine, but on this occasion, to introduce the townspeople to culinary traditions from other lands, they chose to feature products from two of the countries dearest to their hearts. Hence all the wine was Argentine and the whiskey Irish, something which seemed not to have offended the national pride of any of the locals. Even the Green Goddesses, who had stubbornly nationalist tastes, appeared quite happy enjoying empanadas and roast meat on a stone bench alongside their friends.

Chileans and Argentines will always have their differences, but that wasn't going to keep Laurent from a good Argentine steak. He walked up to the stand, asked for his medium rare and was already on his way with a beautiful piece of meat on his plate when he succumbed to the temptation to go back and add several empanadas and a roast potato covered in chimichurri. With all this and a good Malbec to boot, he looked for a place to sit down.

The only place he could find was a bench where, as luck would have it, Pia de La Tressondière sat by herself. For all her Parisian chic, the architect was literally stuffing her face with an empanada and didn't even notice that a stream of sauce was running down her wrist. Laurent sat down next to her and showed himself to be adept in the difficult art of managing a dish overladen with food and a full glass.

'Monsieur Laurent, what a pleasure running into you here.'

'The pleasure is all mine,' said Laurent, mouth filled with a heavenly bite of beef, giving the architect a look that made her blush.

After a pause she replied, 'You're more dangerous than you look at first glance. Pity I didn't meet you earlier. My work here is done, and I don't think I'll be back around these parts. Still, I'll give you my number in case you ever happen to come up to Paris.'

Laurent couldn't conceal his surprise. 'What do you mean, your work here is done? I assumed you'd handle Shennan's other projects in the area. You've done an impeccable job in Saint-Chartier, and people are falling over themselves in praise.'

'My experience with Monsieur Shennan has been draining, to say the least. He's very possessive and, with him, everything ends up getting too personal. Besides, he's the kind of difficult client who leaves hardly any room for creativity or ideas from the people around him. Believe me, it's for the best if I don't do any more projects with him.'

Laurent noticed that the architect had replaced her intimate, indiscriminate use of 'Carlos' with a strict use of 'Monsieur'. He didn't know what to say, so Pia, wiping her mouth, opened her miniature handbag and broke the silence by taking her leave.

'Well, Monsieur Laurent, here's my card, in case you're ever in Paris. I'll be on my way. Tomorrow morning first thing I have to visit a site in Orléans. Please say farewell to the Shennans for me. Each time I tried they were surrounded by guests.' Then she offered her hand, which Laurent shook warmly.

Pia was about to go when she seemed to remember something and turned back. Her eyes gleamed with fury when she spoke.

'I feel I should elaborate. Let me just say that working with a client as domineering as Shennan has been a unique experience, and I pray I'll never have to cross paths with him again. Maybe one day he'll run into someone with less patience than I, who can put him in his place.'

She took a breath and looked up at the château, relieved to have finally spoken freely. 'Luckily I had that,' she said, gesturing to the building. 'Seeing the château as it is now makes it all worth it. I wish you well, Monsieur.'

Laurent stood up to say goodbye, lingering on the sight of her perfect legs as she left. Then he put her card in the breast pocket of his jacket, sat down and continued eating and drinking without haste on his bench. He got up only to try the lamb and get another empanada and glass of Malbec. Afterward he went to the stand with *alfajores* and asked for two chocolate ones filled with coconut and dulce de leche. He wanted to savour them as he strolled, since he still intended to see the park in its entirety.

Everywhere people were milling about, some of them peacefully eating under the generous shade of the hundred-year-old trees, others, wine glass in hand, touring the park they'd heard so many stories about. A line of people waited outside the entrance to the old leprosarium, where Shennan had set up an exhibition of some of the more notable pieces in his collection of musical instruments. The gem of the collection was an enormous L-shaped structure made of decorated carved wooden poles holding a total of seventy-five bronze bells of varying shapes and weights. A guide explained that it was a faithful reproduction of an instrument from the fourth century BCE known as the Bells of Zeng Hou Yi, which had been found in an excavation in northern China. There was also an enormous Tibetan trumpet held aloft next to a box of disposable reeds that the brave could use to give it a blow. Concluding the exhibition were thirty different Asian and African drums that visitors could handle as they wished.

Yes, people were having a good time at the party, and Shennan's popularity could only keep climbing.

THE CYNIC'S DIVAN

What Laurent really wanted was to find Yael, so he quickened his pace when he finally spotted her, sitting on what the map identified as 'the Cynic's Divan'. This was a plain, circular stone bench lacking any carving or decoration that, because of its location on a slight rise in the terrain, provided a view onto the entire park and château.

She was engaged in a heated conversation with Monsieur Jancelle, the town's mayor, who stood up politely to greet him.

'*Bonsoir*, Monsieur de Rodergues. I was just telling our neighbour here that, as mayor, I'm exceedingly satisfied with the work the Shennans have done, and as a citizen I feel proud to have this renovated château.'

'Yes, I certainly can't find fault with his work,' conceded Yael with palpable coldness, 'if we're talking only about the restoration.'

The mayor shook his head. 'The young are never satisfied! I myself was wary and prejudiced when Monsieur

Shennan first arrived. But I can't lie. I have to swallow my earlier suspicions: neither he nor anyone who works for him has ever caused any trouble. They've made our château exceedingly beautiful, and they've helped several people in town boost our languishing local trade. Thanks to them we may even have a future we never thought possible as a tourist destination. Believe me, we have no cause for complaint.'

At this, Monsieur Jancelle, a sensible man, seeing that his two fellow guests desired a bit of privacy, claimed he had to go and say hello to a council member nearby and left them alone.

Laurent tried to break the ice with an ordinary topic of conversation. 'I suppose you've seen Le Juanch and his wagon?'

Yael was noticeably tense and had an absent look in her eyes. She gave a half-hearted reply. 'Yes, I'm happy for him. He's a good man.'

Seeing her lack of interest, Laurent, for better or worse, decided to go straight to a topic that would shake her out of her apathy.

'We certainly are lucky to have Shennan here.'

The expression 'fire in the eyes' was never more accurate. Yael looked up, and Laurent saw that her beautiful face had become the very essence of hatred and scorn. The intensity of her reaction surprised him, and he leant slowly back against the stone, fearful of that Pandora's box he seemed to have opened up.

'Shennan this, Shennan that . . . You're all a bunch of bloody fools!' cried Yael at last. 'You haven't the slightest idea who Carlos Shennan is, and you don't actually care, so long as he keeps your barn warm. You're like a herd of cattle, mooing and shitting in the fields, never giving a damn about anything but the grass you graze on.' She choked up, and a tear slipped down her cheek. Laurent was taken aback. He could almost see his reflection in the teardrop, wearing a dunce cap.

After that outburst, neither of them spoke for a long time. Then Yael's face began to relax, and sanity seemed about to return to her words. Her breast trembled slightly, and she took a deep breath before speaking again, much more calmly.

'Forgive me, Laurent; I had no right to say that to you, or to insult the people in the town, who have been nothing but kind to me. It's just that I can't stand to see how Shennan manipulates you all, and how happy you all seem to be hanging from his strings.'

'It's funny you should say that, because not long ago I had the unpleasant feeling that you were the one holding the puppet strings, yanking me out onstage only when called for by the script.' Laurent had kept that reproach in the larder of grudges.

'You're right, I didn't treat you very well. As you said in the tavern, in the end you were collateral damage.'

'Is that all I am to you?' He was genuinely hurt.

Yael started to get irritated. 'How can you care more about that than about me saying you're just Shennan's puppet?'

'Don't get upset, of course I care. But since I can never tell when you're coming or going, or what's going through your head . . .' He sensed he was going to lose the match and again end up in the dark.

157

'You really care what's going through my head? How touching. Sorry, Laurent, I like you a lot, you're fun, and in bed you really outdo yourself, but I've got more important things to do. Have fun with the toys Shennan's laid out for you all. And since you like to talk about puppets, remember the story of Pinocchio, especially the part when all the little boys end up with donkey ears.'

And before he could reply, she quickly got up and marched straight to the château. This reaction confused Laurent at first, but he quickly realised the reason for her sudden departure: Shennan, at the base of the steps, was speaking to a group of people who seemed to be on their way out. Yael had clearly been killing time, once again using him as a pawn in her complex game of chess.

Given her speed and look of determination as she walked up to Shennan, Laurent suddenly thought he should go after her – though whether to protect her from him or him from her, he wasn't sure.

Sure enough, the host was giving solemn handshakes and saying goodbye to a group of guests when Yael walked up to him and demanded, rather than requested, a few minutes alone. Shennan's instincts were sharp, and he knew he couldn't refuse, but at least he had the presence of mind to ask her to follow him to the other terrace, the one with the portico, on the excuse that he needed to oversee some aspect of the festivities there. Laurent followed them at a prudent distance, trying not to be seen, and just before he reached the terrace he took cover, hiding behind a large, late-nineteenth-century iron vase that stood on a pedestal. Shennan and Yael, meanwhile, were just a few yards away, face to face and hidden from all eyes except Laurent's. He couldn't make out what she was starting to say, but he could tell from her tone and posture that her words were hostile and contained an accusation.

Shennan looked increasingly upset as he listened to her. Standing with his hands open before him, he seemed powerless, as if he knew that any attempt to defend himself would be doomed. Clearly Yael was there to speak and not to listen. She launched into what appeared to be a long, furious tirade, repeatedly pointing an accusatory finger at Shennan's chest. Eventually she withdrew her hand, as if she'd finished her accusation, but then, with impressive speed, she delivered a resounding slap to his face. Then she turned and walked toward the front gate. She didn't look back.

Shennan stood there, watching her walk away. He covered his cheek with the palm of his hand and shook his head in obvious concern – and also, Laurent could have sworn, in sorrow.

Perhaps it was a certain compassion for his friend that led him to get up to leave. He suddenly felt guilty for witnessing the scene while crouching in the shadows. Yet just as he was about to go, Laurent looked up and saw in dismay that, standing in one of the upper windows, Madame Mayumi had witnessed the entire scene. Her face showed no emotion, but even so Laurent preferred not to imagine what was going through her head.

He crept a few steps away, deciding he'd finally go and try some of that Irish whiskey touted in the programme. He needed a drink. Then he noticed something else up ahead: half-hidden by the trunk of an ancient horse chestnut tree stood Tum, who from that position must have seen everything. While her boss could be elegantly inexpressive, the same could not be said of her. She clutched her arms as though trembling, and her face was a mask of despair, her fine features contorted in a bitter grimace.

That settled it: after what he'd just seen, he didn't need just one whiskey, but a whole row of doubles, even if it meant having to listen to the inevitable Gaelic strumming of the woman on the harp.

A COMMOTION

Torrents of beer gushed from the tap, Irish whiskey filled glass after glass, rivers of champagne flooded the terrace and discreetly generous pours of red wine washed down the lamb, beef and empanadas. Clearly, the party was getting lively.

Laurent, who could already feel himself trotting merrily down the path to Valley of the Woozy, was waiting for the tango show to begin when he spotted his archenemy, Tonton Boussard, waving at him with his cap in hand.

He walked over toward the farmer, astonished he had the brazenness to show up at the party, with his record of insulting both Shennan and him. He told himself he wouldn't put up with a single rude remark from that man.

But Tonton didn't make any. He extended his hand and said, 'Monsieur de Rodergues! I'm happy to see you, because I wanted to apologise. Your grandfather was an excellent man and wouldn't have forgiven me for my behaviour. I've acted like a fool with you and the Shennans, and I've had the chance to reflect. I've already withdrawn the complaint, so you don't have to worry about that, and as a peace offering I'd like to give you a calf.'

Laurent wasn't the kind of person to be stubborn when people showed penitence, and Tonton's tone seemed sincere. He didn't quite like him, but he shook his hand and assured him that all was forgotten, so long as he didn't require him to accept an entire calf. The farmer agreed and effusively took his leave, heading toward the beer. He'd already withdrawn his complaint – he couldn't be asked to try foreign products, too.

Laurent hurried back to the stage, where the accordion had already begun to play. Not far away he spotted the three Shennan girls, sitting in the first row with Thierry and Solange, who were looking very lovey-dovey. Odd that they were the ones taking care of them and not Tum, he thought, but she was probably helping Madame Mayumi or Yammei with some task or other.

A hearty round of applause welcomed the first couple that came onstage. They had the elegance of Buenos Aires written on their faces and slender bodies, and the audience grew as the duo glided back and forth, dousing a large part of those gathered round in their pheromones – including, to Laurent's surprise, Jean-Pierre Gimbault, who he spotted on the other side of the circular stage. Gimbault was of the earliest organisers of the Festival des Luthiers and possibly the one who had most vociferously attacked Shennan when the news went around that he'd bought the château. Laurent had heard from more than one neighbour about how, in interviews on

162

the radio and in the local press, Gimbault fulminated against Shennan's decision not to renew the festival's contract. Yet here he was, happy as a clam, enjoying the show with a glass of beer. Laurent studied him closely. He looked like a typical hard-nosed, strait-laced bureaucrat, the kind who collects inkpads and reads *Le Bulletin officiel* in the bathroom. So bland on the outside, but – who knew? – perhaps hot-blooded on the inside. Laurent was already imagining a whole series of perverse fetishes for him, when the object of his observation, presumably bored by all the tango, suddenly stepped out of the audience and left the show halfway through.

But Laurent didn't have time to be sad about the departure of this source of entertainment, because just then he felt someone quietly sidle up to him, standing closer to him than necessary, and whisper in his ear.

'You didn't stop by to say hello, so I wanted to personally make sure everything was going all right.' It was Mademoiselle Cathy, who wasn't the least bit shy and made her interest crystal clear.

'Am I now going to feel the weight of the law press down on me?' joked Laurent.

'I told you you looked suspicious from the moment I saw you.' She smiled.

'Good thing I'm not the only suspicious character.'

'Yes, but there are fewer of you left at the party. The woman with the curly hair who also caught our attention, the one you guessed we'd frisked, just left.'

'Well, it's a free country, isn't it?' answered Laurent, trying to play along but still thinking about Yael's strange attitude all night.

'My thoughts exactly,' purred Cathy, looking him squarely in the eyes. 'It's a free country, and you don't seem taken by anyone.'

Laurent cast about desperately for a response that was elegant, witty and suggestive, to let her know he was not only delighted with her insistence but would happily let himself be arrested whenever she pleased. But before he could speak, a voice on her walkie talkie suddenly monopolised her attention. Cathy excused herself with a motion of her hand and swiftly attended the call, which must have been important, because Laurent saw her clench her jaw as she listened, silently nodding at the orders he supposed she was receiving. When she put the radio back in her belt and turned again to Laurent, her eyes no longer showed any trace of desire. They had the cold, clinical, efficient look of a professional.

'I'm sorry,' she said. 'We'll have to continue this later. Come with me, please, and don't make a scene.'

Laurent hesitated. Was this a trick to take him to the garden? But his male ego suffered a serious reversal when she explained.

'Hurry up and act natural. Something's happened and we need your help. Madame Shennan herself asked us to tell you.'

Laurent felt a fist pushing against his stomach and couldn't breathe. Cathy wasn't making things up. It was true, something had happened, and as he followed along at a good clip, he remembered the shudder of foreboding he'd felt in the park.

They quickly reached the service entrance to the tower,

where they met up with the muscular agent who'd frisked him just a few hours earlier and another security agent who had Slavic features and light eyes. They heard the footsteps of someone racing down the stairs, and another of the agents appeared, looking flustered.

'Hurry, Madame Shennan's waiting for us in the library.'

They obeyed and ran up the staircase, pushing aside the poor gardener, who was coming down carrying a pot of orchids, and sat on the bottom step, muttering some Thai curse word full of the letter *k*.

The library, on the first floor of the north wing, was a room lined with deep beechwood bookshelves that must have held some ten thousand volumes. Under normal circumstances, it must have been an idyllic place to read, as it had excellent natural light and leather armchairs that spoke of comfort and good taste. Madame Shennan sat at a desk trying to make a call, but when she saw Cathy, she set down the phone, stood up and walked over to meet them. She got straight to the point.

'I appreciate your coming so quickly. I haven't seen my husband for around an hour and a half, and he's not answering his mobile phone,' she said. 'Believe me, I'm not an anxious person. But I know my husband and I know something's not right.'

'Could you tell us at exactly what time you last saw your husband? Do you remember where you were and who you were with?' This was the security guard who looked Slavic.

As Madame Shennan was about to reply, the other agent took out his pistol to examine it, presumably thinking he should have it ready in case he needed to use it. Madame Shennan looked at him coolly.

'Do you really think that's necessary? I don't want to frighten the visitors,' she said.

Cathy sought to reassure her. 'Don't be alarmed, Madame Shennan. It's best to be ready for any eventuality.'

The look in Madame Mayumi's eyes was unmistakably mocking. 'It takes more than a Heckler & Koch to alarm me, Mademoiselle. It just strikes me as somewhat premature to cock it.' Then, turning back to the Slavic agent, she calmly explained, 'I remember perfectly. It was seven-twenty, and we were standing on the large terrace talking to the local volunteer firefighters, who were asking Carlos for a small favour. He received a call on his mobile, and after promising to help them, said farewell and told me he had to step into his office for a minute to attend to an urgent matter.'

'I suppose you've already checked your husband's office,' said the agent, jotting down all the information in his notebook.

Just then her mobile rang. Everyone held their breath, except Madame Shennan, who quickly answered. A man's voice could be heard on the other end. She answered in Japanese, with short, sharp sentences that sounded like orders. She immediately hung up and explained, 'Pardon me, that was my brother calling from Nagoya. I told him to call me later.' Then she thought for a minute before answering the agent. 'Yes, I went to the office, and once I saw Carlos hadn't gone inside, I decided to call you.'

'What led you to conclude that your husband hadn't gone into the office?'

166

'His office and the hunting room are the only places where smoking is permitted inside the château. As a result, both rooms usually reek of tobacco, because the first thing Carlos does when he steps inside is light a cigarette. His office didn't smell of recent smoke, and the ashtray was empty, two details which, had he been there, would have been inconceivable. So I knew my husband hadn't gone into his office.'

'I see. That's all we need,' concluded the Slav. 'We'll spread out through the château to look for Monsieur Shennan. You, Madame, stay on this floor, in case he shows up or calls. And don't worry, it's probably a false alarm.' Then, turning to the other agents, he said, 'All right. The château has four floors, not counting the basement service floor. Madame Shennan can take a look at the rooms on this floor, and each of us will take one of the others. Any questions before we split up?' He looked at everyone in turn. 'Cathy, what's on your mind? If there's something you want to say, say it now.'

'No offence or disrespect, Madame Shennan, but your husband does have a certain reputation,' said Cathy somewhat reluctantly. 'Are you sure he's not gone voluntarily missing . . . with someone else?'

Madame Shennan studied her with great interest but looked unmoved by this blunt allusion to her husband's proclivities. Fearing her response, Laurent couldn't help tensing up when he saw she was about to speak.

'No offence taken, Mademoiselle. On the contrary, I applaud you for being the only one here with enough nerve to ask the question I'm sure it was on all your colleagues' minds. That shows me you're the most professional.' Then, stroking the cuff of her silk sleeve, she stopped to look at a portrait of her husband hanging in a corner of the room and began to explain. 'I'm aware of both my husband's reputation and his behaviour, but I can assure you that with his Irish Catholic scruples it's inconceivable he'd use our home as a place to indulge his sexual desires with any woman other than me.'

Laurent was impressed by her sangfroid but not terribly convinced by her argument.

And then, after a long pause, Madame Shennan looked each one in the eyes and offered another reason that seemed more plausible.

'Carlos has extramarital affairs, I know. But he's never allowed that to jeopardise our family life, nor has he been so vulgar as to let his affairs become anything other than fleeting. For all his flaws and shortcomings, he's still a good father and a good husband, and—'

'Madame, you don't owe us any explanations. This is your home and we're here to serve you,' Cathy cut in respectfully. 'Let's not waste time and split up.'

The agents left, but Laurent, at Madame Shennan's request, stayed back for a moment with her. She looked at him sadly.

'I'm sorry to get you mixed up in this, Monsieur de Rodergues, but among all the guests at the château today you're perhaps the person who knows Carlos best.'

Laurent placed his hand on her forearm.

'Not at all. It's an honour to be thought worthy of your trust. But I should go straight to the floor I've been assigned without wasting another second. The sooner we find him and get this over with, the better.'

'Wait,' Madame Shennan pleaded, 'let me have Xiao Li go with you. She knows every nook and cranny of the château, because she was at Carlos's side during the renovation work, and she's got a master key to all the doors.' As she spoke, she dialled a number on her phone, which was answered immediately. Within just a few minutes, Shennan's assistant was standing before them, though she didn't look like the same person Laurent had met. Had he not known it was her, a woman impervious to temptation and incapable of letting her guard down, he would have sworn she'd had a few drinks, since her face was flushed and the look in her eyes lacked the usual unfaltering disdain.

Madame Shennan briefly filled her in on the problem and what was required of her. Xiao Li, with an incredulous expression, took out a mobile from her jacket pocket.

'That's odd, I just got a message from Shennan about half an hour ago, asking me for the number of a client of his. Let me try to call him on his other phone.'

'What "other phone"?' Now Madame Shennan really was surprised. 'I didn't know Carlos had two phones.'

The secretary remained silent, and for a few seconds she seemed to be looking for an adequate response that wouldn't violate the confidentiality she owed her boss. But Madame Mayumi was in no mood for games and, seeing the doubtful look Xiao Li gave Laurent, pressed her to explain.

'Monsieur de Rodergues is a trusted friend. Say whatever you have to say, and quickly.'

The secretary, used to obeying the chain of command, finally spoke.

'Madame, you're well aware of the complex nature of your husband's business. For the sake of security and discretion, the phone is only for communication between the two of us – no one else. We use it for certain transactions that require involving as few people as possible.'

As she spoke she tapped a number on the miniature keypad and lifted it up so Madame Shennan could hear that it was ringing with no answer. Then Xiao Li became alarmed.

'This is very strange. He always keeps this phone at his side, and I can't recall him ever not picking up, no matter how awkward the situation. Come with me, Monsieur. We'll look together. I'll open any doors you wish.'

Apparently having recovered her efficiency, the secretary marched out of the library without another a word to Madame Shennan. Laurent could only follow her to the second floor, the one he'd been assigned.

THE SECOND FLOOR

The château's second floor was divided into two wings connected by a central tower that rose from the grand terrace to the attic, which in turn gave access to an upper terrace. Laurent and Xiao Li began to look through the south wing, which contained two large rooms. The first, an open space with leather recliners and decorated like an art deco cinema, they used as a home theatre. Neither here nor in the matching half-bath was there any sign of Shennan. The other room was a guest bedroom, with a bathroom decorated entirely in cream-coloured marble with blue veins that reminded Laurent of lapis lazuli. Completing the room was a separate small sitting room with a chaise longue, a large plasma-screen television, a sound system, a desk and chair and a small bookcase full of mystery novels. They didn't find the slightest indication that Shennan had been here, either, so they walked back to the landing dividing the two areas on that level, which Laurent recognised as the place where he'd run into Pia de La Tressondière on his first visit to the château.

The north wing contained only the oversized bedroom for special guests where Laurent had changed clothes after the incident with the dog. It looked even larger than he remembered, and even less welcoming, perhaps because there was no fire in the fireplace, or perhaps because of the ominous situation that brought him here. Whatever the reason, it now lacked the charm he'd felt on that first occasion.

He and Xiao Li inspected it with painstaking thoroughness, even looking under the bed, in the bathroom and inside the study-alcove inside the adjoining tower that offered an imposing view over the park.

Xiao Li had begun throwing open the doors of the large Breton armoires when Laurent noticed something dark, a stain at the foot of the processional lantern that stood by the wall. Without a word, he walked over to make sure his eyes weren't playing tricks on him and the stain wasn't maybe a shadow cast by the lantern. He knelt down and saw that there was indeed something running along the baseboard – in fact, it seemed to be coming from underneath it. The dark parquet floor didn't provide the best background for distinguishing colours, but what from far away seemed blackish now looked unmistakably like blood. Almost paralysed by fear, Laurent touched the stain with his finger, and the sticky wet feeling removed all doubt.

He quickly overcame his fright and swung into action. Just behind that wall was the secret passageway that the girls had shown him. Determined not to waste time, he took from his pocket the business card Pia had given him and slid it under the baseboard, pushing it in. The edge of

172

the card slid smoothly and came out stained with blood. Laurent knew then that what he'd find behind the panel would be unpleasant, and his sixth sense warned him like an urgent, pounding alarm, that a long list of troubles was soon to follow.

Nevertheless, he got up and knocked on the panel, remembering what Shennan's daughters had said about how to open it. Before sliding it back, he called over Xiao Li, who was again on her mobile, looking out of the window in the hopes that her boss might appear among the guests.

Then, unexpectedly, he heard a mobile phone ringing from behind the panel, and he was overcome by an almost magical sense of calm and certainty.

'Don't bother, and come over here. I think I've found him.'

Xiao Li looked confused. She walked over with her phone still ringing, and when she stood next to Laurent she could hear the sound from the other side of the panel. Terror-stricken, she switched off her phone, and immediately the passageway went silent. That's when she noticed the blood on the floor and the card stained a bright red in Laurent's hands.

Seized by terror, Xiao Li went pale, but even so, she didn't lose her self-control.

'We have to call Madame Shennan and the security agents,' she said.

'Better call the agents first. You do that while I move the panel.'

'How did you know the panel was movable?' she asked suspiciously.

'The girls showed me,' said Laurent. Suddenly he felt

irritated. 'Do you think that if I had something to do with this I'd come here to be the one to find the crime scene, or whatever's behind this panel?'

Xiao Li looked at him intently, then immediately called the security team and her boss. Laurent didn't give a damn whether or not she believed him, or whether or not she called Madame Mayumi. She could do whatever the hell she wanted. She tapped desperately on her phone while he continued to feel the panel until he found the inner latch and released it.

As he slid it back, he heard the sound of footsteps rushing down the stairs and into the bedroom behind him. They were too late. Before them lay the lifeless body of Carlos Shennan.

At that point everything happened in a flash. Xiao Li succumbed to a fit of hysteria and started shrieking with high-pitched wails, almost howls. Fearing her screams would alert Madame Shennan, Laurent could only think to put his arms around her to try to calm her down. Meanwhile, the security agents poured into the tower, guns drawn, only to stop frozen and speechless at the scene before them.

Laurent assumed they'd be no stranger to dead bodies, yet they seemed hypnotised by the sight of Shennan, smashed and covered in blood, splayed out head-first, torso slightly bent, matching the angle of the wall in the narrow passageway, with a rivulet of blood dribbling down from step to step toward them.

As he held the diminutive body of the secretary, still

heaving and sobbing, Laurent realised in a flash of clarity that the girls and Tum weren't the only ones who knew about that secret passage. Clearly so did their father, and he suspected a few other people did, too. He looked at his lifeless friend, and with the same clarity wondered how someone could take such a dramatic fall in such a small staircase.

'We have to call the police, right now,' the Slavic agent said, and began giving precise orders to the rest. 'Bertrand, I don't think anyone at the party has noticed anything, but just in case, close the outer gate and check that all the others are closed too: the one in the garden, the one that goes to the cemetery, and one by the main entrance. Make sure people don't start panicking inside the park, and if someone wants to get inside, find some excuse or other to stop them. If anyone tries to leave, tell them they can't, because there's a surprise in the programme, or whatever believable story pops into your head. As for Madame Shennan, we need to call her and—'

'No need to call me, I'm right here.' Her voice was calm. 'I heard Xiao Li's screams and came straight away, just after all of you.'

Everyone turned at once, stepping back to clear a path to the passageway. Xiao Li, in a surprising gesture, broke away from Laurent and ran to Madame Mayumi, taking her by the hand and looking her in the eyes with tears and sobs. No words were needed. Madame Shennan looked back at her full of sadness, gently brushed her black hair and moved her aside to step toward Laurent, who was standing between her and the opening to the passageway.

'Madame, I don't think you should see your husband like this,' he implored.

But she took a step forward and serenely replied, 'Thank you, Laurent, but for some time now I've had the darkest premonitions.'

THE GENDARMES

For all their experience and all their efforts, the security agents couldn't keep the guests from growing nervous and eventually panicking. That idyllic summer party in a lovely park with lively music and endless food and drink had become a scene of chaos as soon as the gates were closed to the public. A few minutes later, the sirens of the ambulance and the police pierced the air, an extraordinarily rare sound in a small rural town in central France like Saint-Chartier, where life was quiet and absolutely nothing ever happened.

The authorities arrived to find a situation bordering on anarchy. Trying to flee what they assumed was some catastrophe, some guests started clambering over the lower walls, while others argued with the security agents or pressed against the gate, making it impossible for the police and the ambulance to get inside the park.

The gendarmes had to get out megaphones to ask people to clear a path for the ambulance. They spread out and closed off vehicular traffic to allow the thousand or so people at the party to leave. The insufficient number of officers made it impossible to search the guests, who, once the gates finally opened, poured out, increasing the risk of accidents or stampedes.

Sergeant Lafonnier, accompanied by the police chief from La Châtre, took around twenty minutes to reach the place where the body of Carlos Shennan had been found. Unfortunately, the media were also on the way to the château, since many guests had begun calling friends and relatives, multiplying the spread of the news. The investigation required utmost discretion and stealth, two things that were now entirely impossible.

As soon as he entered the guest room, Sergeant Lafonnier introduced the chief to Madame Mayumi and asked everyone else to introduce themselves, except Laurent and Mademoiselle Xiao Li, whose identities he corroborated himself. The chief asked to see the body of the victim, and perhaps because he'd been stationed in Marseille, where he'd no doubt been exposed to grimmer scenarios, he didn't show any surprise at Shennan's body. Calmly, he asked the sergeant to call the coroner in Châteauroux, ordered an officer to stand guard and asked to be taken to a room where he could speak to everyone who had witnessed the discovery of the body.

Madame Shennan proposed they retire to the parlour next to the library, and they went there to give the first statements.

THE FOLLOWING WEEK

If Laurent de Rodergues ever made up his mind to write his memoirs, no doubt he'd describe the week following the death of Carlos Shennan as one of the most unpleasant and unsettling experiences of his life.

Emotional considerations aside, Shennan's passing marked the beginning of Laurent's suffering, for he was subjected to the traumatic experience of being the prime suspect in the investigation into the death. Not only had he found Shennan's body, he also knew about the secret passage, something that apparently no one else but Shennan's daughters and their nanny was aware of.

To anyone leading an investigation, Laurent was a natural suspect: he was a foreigner and a family friend with no job or known source of income. He wasn't detained overnight, but his passport was confiscated, and he was told not very subtly that if he felt the need for a change of airs, he should refrain and instead actively cooperate on solving the case. He had to repeat his statement over and over again, so as not to jeopardise his presumption of innocence. He even began to fear he'd wind up in prison.

Fortunately, the other people questioned had only words of praise for him. Of these, Madame Shennan's defence carried the most weight, yet oddly enough, it was the statement from the security agent, Cathy Barnaud, that ultimately exonerated him. She went on record saying she'd found Laurent de Rodergues suspicious from the moment he arrived and therefore hadn't let him out of her sight all evening, making it impossible for him to commit a crime.

The general insistence on his innocence, the lack of fingerprints or witnesses against him, the absence of any motive or justification and the results of the coroner's reports, which conclusively stated that there was no indication that a third party had been involved, ultimately dampened the police's initial enthusiasm and freed Laurent from suspicion or blame.

In the end, the theory of an accidental death won out:

For reasons unknown, the deceased had cause to use the secret passage, which lacked interior lighting.

The deceased was known to race up and down stairs and habitually rush about, and to have a certain propensity to danger. On the night in question, in the course of the celebrations taking place at his home, he had ingested a considerable quantity of alcohol, which had likely dulled his reflexes and his vision.

The passageway was constructed in the fifteenth century, a time when the average man was noticeably shorter than today. At a height of 1.81 metres, the deceased was taller than today's national average, while the passageway, due to the nature of its construction, varies in height and width, reaching 1.73 metres at its highest point.

It has an irregular ceiling, with stones protruding in various places. On one of these stones, which comes to a point, remains of the victim's scalp and blood were found. The investigation has concluded that, by moving quickly and with only the dim light of his mobile phone, presumably used to light the steps, the deceased struck his head on the protruding stone.

Following this impact there are two possibilities:

that the deceased lost consciousness, fell forward down the stairs and broke his neck, which the autopsy identified as the cause of death;

that the deceased lost his balance without losing consciousness, resulting in the same outcome.

Yet what still had no reasonable explanation was Carlos Shennan's presence in the passageway in the first place. The police opted to conclude that he knew of its existence in advance, and for whatever reason, perhaps out of his well-known predilection for jokes and secrets, had decided not to tell anyone about it.

Laurent, much to his relief, was freed from suspicion, and the police apologised for the inconvenience the investigation had caused. That same night his friends took him out to celebrate in La Cocadrille, where everyone, especially Le Juanch, raised several glasses in camaraderie and friendship to the memory of Carlos Shennan.

Once the investigation had concluded, a massive funeral was held and Shennan was buried in the town cemetery, in the stately mausoleum of sculpted porphyry that he himself, with considerable foresight, had arranged to have built by the workers who had carried out the restoration of the château.

A few days later, without a word to anyone, Madame Shennan, her daughters, the nanny and Xiao Li left for Asia. The château was entrusted to the care of Khun Suan, the Thai gardener, and Yammei, the cook, who seemed to have found common causes for meeting.

Sooner or later all mortal things are forgotten, and the fleeting glory of the restoration gave way once more to the silence that had long reined in the château. Still, the renovations would captivate tourists and wanderers for years to come, and for some time that mysterious death regularly came up in every conversation anyone had about the town. No doubt Shennan, from the next world, was delighted to see himself become one more figure in the local Berry legends.

SECOND CHORD

ON THE CHURCH STEPS

Laurent extinguished his cigarette on the stone steps and got up to toss the butt in the rubbish bin. He wanted to stop by Isabelle and Roger's farm and pick up milk, butter and fresh cheese. The local cheese, called Valençay, is moulded into a truncated pyramid, and tradition holds that it owes its shape to Napoleon, who was presented with a pyramid of cheese in memory of his expedition to Egypt; yet the emperor had unpleasant memories of that adventure and lopped off the top with his sabre. As the Italians say, *se non è vero, è ben trovato* – it's a good story, even if it's not true. In any case, Isabelle and Roger made an outstanding cheese.

The news from the lawyer, the unexpected inheritance from Shennan, the fact that he'd been included in his will and everything else had plunged Laurent into feverish thoughts, and after recalling all the details of his friend's death, he realised that, as much as he wanted to believe the conclusions of the police investigation, deep down he had never been convinced.

Nothing gives you a new perspective on things like a bit of distance. Laurent, because of the painful ordeal he'd undergone as a result of Shennan's death, had tried to put the entire sorry incident out of his mind, but looking back now over his memories and the circumstances of those distant summer days, he rediscovered the doubts and questions that beset him when he'd first found Shennan's body. His sixth sense, his intuition, his nose – call it what you will – told him, shouted at him even, that his death was premeditated, though cleverly camouflaged to look like an accident. And if there was anything Laurent had in abundance, it was time, peace and quiet, three things that are indispensable when searching for answers. And answers were what he needed.

On his way back home, with a bag full of farm products, he made up his mind to investigate everything that had occurred during the celebration at the château. Laurent felt he owed Carlos this last attempt to clear up the mystery surrounding his death.

THE AMATEUR'S LIST

Using what he'd read and seen in crime novels and films, Laurent devised his own method of investigation. The first thing he did was to get a notepad and write down everything he remembered; next he drew up lists of the people he knew who might be involved in the case, no matter how tangentially; and last, he wrote down a brief description of each of those people. Then he reviewed his list again and again, and slowly he worked out a chart showing everyone's potential connections to Carlos Shennan and to each other. The hardest part of the entire process was establishing what motives everyone might have had for wanting Shennan dead, or how they would benefit from his death, and then to determine where they were at the time of death, according to the coroner.

In Berry, the weather in October tends to be gentle, and making use of his good relationship to Khun Suan, who allowed him onto the grounds, he would often stroll around the château park. He always wound up on the Cynic's Divan, where he'd sit and think, trying not to recall his bitter final encounter with Yael. From there his gaze would linger on the proud shape of the medieval fortress, and he longed for it to unveil the secrets it had accumulated over the centuries. In particular, he wished the château could reveal what had taken place in the secret passage on 15th July.

Even with the good weather, the day was drawing to a close, and Laurent's stone bench was gradually getting colder. But Laurent hadn't finished studying his notes. From the pocket of his pea coat he took out a flask of cherry brandy, just to warm himself up a bit from his throat to his tail, since he'd resolved not to get up until he had a concrete plan. Again he looked at his notes and glanced over the list, with the addresses and contact information of everyone on it. He'd decided to visit them and interview them each in turn, and if their explanations seemed convincing, he'd cross them off the list. The only thing he needed to do now was decide on the order he'd approach them in – though Laurent knew perfectly well who he'd leave for last.

He glanced at his watch and saw it was almost dinner time. He got up, mechanically brushing off the seat of his trousers, gathered up his notes and crossed the park to head back to his place. Along one of the paths he noticed phrases in Latin carved into the side of one of the flower beds. Most of them didn't look familiar. Laurent lingered reading them before finally continuing on his way, smiling as he thought about Shennan's complicated, eclectic personality. No doubt the idea for the wall was his, and had given rise to lengthy arguments with his Parisian architect.

One of the Latin maxims that Laurent didn't notice would

have been especially relevant: *stare decisis et non quieta movere*, stir not what is still. Wise counsel which humankind stubbornly ignores, and which Laurent would have done well to heed – though in his defence, it was a line he'd never heard.

As he descended the steps that surrounded the fountain in the park, he saw Khun Suan on one of the side paths, pushing a wheelbarrow full of dead leaves. At his side, beaming with love, walked Yammei, the Chinese cook, cradling a tiny white kitten in her arms. They waved from afar and Laurent waved back, thinking that the château had dealt its dwellers quite different lots, and clearly the gardener and the cook were among the most fortunate.

Back home at the vicarage, as his oxtail pot-au-feu with potatoes and carrots simmered in the kitchen, Laurent reviewed his list over a glass of wine. This wasn't the list on his notepad but one on a cork bulletin board he'd set up in the middle of his living room, which doubled as a study. On it he'd pinned all the photos and blueprints he had of the château, along with the photos he'd acquired through various means of the people on his list. Forced to set aside his technological prejudices, he'd set up an enormous printer, a scanner and a large computer screen and keyboard on a side table. He'd used the computer to expand his network of information, and through it he'd uncovered a lot of material on all the names on his list – all except one, though that fact didn't surprise him. He gave it some thought, and the order he should follow became clear. He proceeded to read the list aloud as the aroma from the cast-iron pot wafted into the living room. Only God knows what the future will hold, but one thing was clear: tonight Monsieur Laurent de Rodergues was going to dine splendidly.

His plan of action was to visit the following people:

- Sergeant Gilles Lafonnier, at the police station in La Châtre. Laurent needed to ascertain details about the case that weren't released to the press and hear first-hand the sergeant's thoughts about Shennan's death and the people on the list.
- Jean-Pierre Gimbault, head of the Association of Friends of the Festival des Luthiers. He was one of Shennan's detractors, but he'd attended the party and disappeared during the range of time when Shennan was determined to have died. Laurent arranged to meet him the day after his meeting with Sergeant Lafonnier.
- Jeannette and Claude Monatti. He'd visit them at their house in Montgivray. Shortly before the Shennans' party, the newsletter they wrote and published had lowered its level of vitriol, but they didn't attend the celebration and hadn't been seen in the vicinity. Nevertheless, the fact that on the day of the event several leaflets and fliers had appeared in Saint-Chartier and La Châtre signed by *La Cordophonie*, the name of the Monattis' newsletter, made a trip to their home essential.
- Thierry Chanteau, Lignières. Just one day before the festivities at the château, Laurent would readily have vouched for the *arboriste-grimpeur* – he'd have sworn an oath in front of anyone. Thierry

190

had a face that radiated idealism and integrity, and Laurent didn't think he was a good enough actor to fake those values with such perfection. Still, he recalled the scene on the staircase, and the way Thierry had grimaced when Laurent suggested he talk to Shennan. It was that memory that made a chat with the forester necessary. After doing a little digging, Laurent learnt that Thierry was now in Lignières, near the racetrack, where the Cirque Bidon was camped out. The circus was a quirky show that every summer toured around the towns in the area in caravans pulled by Frisian horses. It blended acrobatics and humour with an environmental message and a certain social critique in a setting that called to mind a more romantic past. Thierry had once been a member of the troupe and had a good relationship with the owner, and was probably helping out with maintaining the props, equipment and caravans in the off-season.

- Solange Vartel, Saint-Août. The landscape architect was the very embodiment of pacifist principles, and Laurent thought her incapable of anything even remotely violent. Yet given her close friendship with Thierry, she perhaps knew something about the source of his apparent hatred for Shennan. Solange was now working on an urban landscaping project in Saint-Août, a town just five miles from Saint-Chartier, and Laurent had heard from her parents that she'd be delighted to see him.

- Tonton Boussard, La Preugne. This was the interview he most dreaded, but given their past there was no way around it. Tonton had of course apologised to him at the party, and he'd even spoken highly of Shennan, but that might have all been a ruse. Laurent arranged to see him on his own farm, where he lived alone with his dogs, his cows, and – inconceivable as it seemed for someone like him – a pet cassowary, a large flightless bird similar to an emu.

- Yves Rataille, Châteauroux. In theory, the cordial, affable man had nothing to do with the object of his investigation. But the pugnacious Ahmed El-Kubri, the Mauritanian worker with whom Shennan had gotten in a fight, was one of his employees, and Laurent hadn't managed to contact him directly or determine where he was. When Laurent phoned, Yves told him that from his work on the château he'd landed a project with the Châteauroux prefecture government, so they made an appointment to meet at his office on the new construction site.

- Pia de La Tressondière, Paris, 13th arrondissement. The architect had agreed to meet him, though she had warned him she couldn't spare much time. When Laurent explained why he was interested in talking to her, she seemed reluctant, and her nervousness was palpable even over the telephone. Laurent couldn't quite believe she had anything to do with the case, but the rage and indignation she'd shown Shennan on the day he died were grounds for a closer look. Clearly she was a woman scorned, and Laurent knew from his own experience that hell hath no equal fury. The memory of her steely blue eyes sent a shiver down his spine.

- Yael Golani, Paris, Le Marais. The scene Yael had caused just moments before Shennan's death, her sudden departure from the party and her haste in cancelling her lease in Saint-Chartier gave her the honour of topping the list of likely suspects. Besides, Laurent felt he'd been treated unfairly and deserved an explanation, because – and this is what hurt the most – he hadn't gotten over her. Far from it. Tracking her down been a Herculean task, and he'd managed to do so more by chance than by tenacity: when his perseverance in the search had begun to flag, to distract himself from his pessimistic thoughts he'd gone to take a stroll around the market at Thevet-Saint-Julien. There, browsing the old junk and used books, he ran into Hervé, Lilly's partner, whom he'd met at Caroline and Pierre's house the same day he'd met Yael. They exchanged pleasantries and news, and Hervé asked teasingly whether Laurent was still in touch with her. He said he wasn't, and Hervé, with an impish grin, told him he'd recently been distributing goods in the old Jewish quarter of Paris, Le Marais, and there, from his lorry, he thought he spotted Yael through the window of a shop that sold religious objects. She seemed to work there.

After this review of his line-up and a lavish dinner, Laurent closed the folder and headed to his bedroom. Even as he lay in bed, he couldn't stop thinking about how best to approach each suspect.

AT THE POLICE STATION

Sergeant Lafonnier was an honest, endearing man – a true agent of the law, fully committed to safeguarding the public order and protecting the upstanding citizens from the unscrupulous ones. These were his positive traits, and they were only partly offset by his total lack of imagination and his absolute faith in the rules, with which he identified so thoroughly that he was unable to skirt their provisions even in the most intimate moments. Laurent intended to extract as much information as possible from him, so he had no choice but to have a long conversation.

The place they'd arranged to meet at was the new police station, a building entirely devoid of charm, with a dour modern aesthetic seemingly dreamt up by state architects of the Pyongyang regime. The sergeant stood waiting at the door, and after they exchanged the usual pleasantries, he led Laurent to a conference room and poured him a cup of fairly decent coffee. On the table sat an enormous file folder, which he said contained all the information about the Shennan case.

Laurent wanted to pounce on it, but Tartarin stopped him. He would be the one to consult it and decide which responses to give him, since certain pages were marked as confidential.

'How can the report be confidential if you determined that Shennan's death was an accident?' Laurent asked with irritation.

The sergeant nodded slowly, calibrating his response.

'That is indeed what we determined,' he replied, 'but the information marked confidential has to do with Shennan's business dealings or private life, not his death. Let's get right down to it: tell me what you want to know and I'll do what I can to answer in as much detail as possible. I'll have to request that you not ask too much, as I'm doing this without consulting my superiors, and I can't overstep my authority.'

Embarrassed for his impulsiveness, Laurent apologised and took out his notepad, where he'd written down a long list of items he wanted to clarify or ask. Tartarin couldn't help laughing, and looked at him with a certain compassion.

'Monsieur Laurent, you're taking this very seriously, and while I value your zeal as a citizen, I'm sorry to see you wasting so much time on this. I myself was fond of Monsieur Shennan, and I admire what he did with the château, so I personally took an exceptional interest in the investigation, and believe me, there were no third parties involved, I promise you.'

'Sergeant, I hold you in the highest regard, and I'm certain you did everything you could, but I also know that you have other cases and matters occupying your schedule. As an individual with time on his hands, and a witness to the events, I've gone over everything I know about the case and have reached the conclusion that there are factors worth reconsidering. That's why I asked for this meeting: no doubt one or several of my assumptions are mistaken, and my suspicions have logical, coherent explanations that I haven't taken into account. With your help, I'm hoping to dispel them.'

'Understood. Then let's begin,' said the sergeant, cutting him off.

Pencil and pad in hand, Laurent let loose a volley of questions.

'For starters, did you ever find out what the devil Shennan was doing in that passageway that no one else except his daughters and Mademoiselle Tum knew about?'

Sergeant Lafonnier seemed to have given the matter a considerable amount of thought.

'That was a question that kept coming up again throughout the investigation. And to date no one's managed to provide a logical or convincing answer. There's one detail that could explain his presence there, but it cancels itself out, so to speak, given the position of his body.'

Laurent gave a start. 'A detail? What do you mean?'

Tartarin was clearly delighted to take the lead in the conversation, and he paused dramatically before replying. 'Inside Monsieur Shennan's jacket pocket we found three tiny leather pouches, each containing a gold bangle inscribed with the name of one of his daughters.'

'I didn't know that, but it doesn't strike me as the least bit strange,' Laurent countered. 'Shennan doted on his daughters and probably wanted to surprise them with a gift. He loved that sort of thing.'

'Yes, of course,' Tartarin confirmed. 'But if he wanted to surprise them, he didn't need to go through the passageway, since there was no one in the girls' room, and he could have easily used the door. And that's not even the oddest thing. Think about it: he died falling down the stairs, when logically he should have left the gifts in his daughters' room, not still have them on him.'

'I see. You're right – either he'd be going up the stairs with the gifts or coming down without them. It wouldn't make sense for him to have the bracelets on the way back down. Funny, here I come looking for answers, and you start by raising another question. Wonderful.'

Tartarin couldn't help giving a mischievous laugh. 'Well, Monsieur Laurent, I just want you to understand how difficult this job is.'

'So what does it mean, Lafonnier? Give me your version. Your own, not the department's.'

'Honestly, Monsieur de Rodergues, I'm sorry to disappoint you, but I think the official version is correct,' he replied after a moment's thought. 'I admit, with Shennan's turbulent private and professional life, we were all predisposed to think his death was a homicide, but there was nothing, not the slightest sign, indicating anything other than the official conclusion.'

'At no time did you ever doubt the cause of death?' insisted Laurent, not willing to give up.

'The theory that Shennan was murdered had a lot going for it: the controversies around the closing of the festival, the anonymous letters, his love affairs – after all, he left his feathers in every henhouse in the area . . . It's true, for a long time I had my doubts, but I didn't find anything to back them up, and if he really was murdered, you have to admit, he died one of the most bizarre deaths in the history of crime. He barely even fitted in that passageway.'

Laurent saw that the clock was ticking and he was getting nowhere, so he decided to be more direct.

'I've taken the liberty of drawing up a list of people who caught my attention. One them is Mademoiselle Yael. You asked me about her once. Do you remember her?'

'Well, well, I was wondering how long it would take you to bring her up. Actually she had us stumped even before the accident. Have you heard from her again?'

'In fact that's one of the reasons I'm here. I've located everyone on my list except her,' he lied.

'Why don't we go to the courtyard? We can smoke a cigarette there.'

Laurent understood the sergeant was about to reveal a secret.

The courtyard behind the station was as dull as the inside of the building, but at least smoking was allowed there. Tartarin offered him one of his Gitanes Maïs, and Laurent, more out of politeness than desire, took one from the pack, letting Tartarin light it for him.

The sergeant blew a cloud of smoke.

'I buy them for tradition's sake. It's sad to see something that's been a part of us for so long get legislated out of existence. It's one of my little crusades. How many suspects are on your list, Monsieur?' he asked.

'I wouldn't call them suspects,' said Laurent, coughing from the cigarette, which was too strong for him. 'They're just people I'm curious about. There are a total of nine people on my list, but I don't have the least bit of evidence against any of them. They simply had their differences with Shennan.'

Tartarin laughed again.

'They had their differences? Only nine? Clearly you're limiting your investigation to the immediate area. Shennan had a long list of enemies scattered around the world. In business he had an iron fist, from what we learnt.'

'Do you mean he was mixed up in illegal activities? I've heard rumours, but nothing specific, just the odd remark here and there.'

Tartarin took another drag on his Gitanes.

'Illegal? Well . . . there was actually nothing that could be proved, and he was never charged with anything. Monsieur Shennan had small industrial labs in various countries, and individually none of them produced anything dangerous. However, as we heard from a special agent from the national security services, Shennan's name was linked to the production of chemical weapons. The unproven theory was that while each factory's product was innocuous on its own, through his network he could supply all the components needed for chemical weapons. You can imagine the enormous interest such a supply could arouse in certain powers subject to international constraints. That's why the US and Israeli intelligence agencies took an interest in Shennan's move to Saint-Chartier. They even requested reports on his activities. Now, as I said, nothing was ever proved, and Shennan's behaviour here, dalliances aside, was nothing short of exemplary, so over time these agencies began to lose interest.'

'And what does this have to do with Yael?'

'Her presence didn't escape our notice, of course, especially since Shennan himself told us that the mademoiselle in question carried an Israeli passport.'

Laurent couldn't hide his surprise. 'Shennan talked to you about Yael? When was that? I thought they didn't know each other.'

The officer answered readily. 'I remember it perfectly. It was just after the incident with the worker from Mauritania. Shennan came by to reassure us about the episode, and in the course of the conversation, he jokingly brought up Mademoiselle Yael's nationality. It was his enigmatic way of informing us. How did he know? I couldn't say, but he always knew everything. Personally I think he had contacts at our head office. Based on that information, we briefly tailed her, but she rarely left home, and when she did it was to go to Bourges, where she'd meet with an older man in a cafe. You might even say she was boring, though on the other hand I should note that we never figured out what really brought her to Saint-Chartier.'

'And doesn't it seem odd to you that she claimed to be a potter, but no one ever saw her work, and she didn't sell in any local markets or shops? Don't you think her job was an excuse, a screen?'

'Perhaps. As you know better than anyone, Laurent, life in Saint-Chartier is so monotonous that anyone whose head is filled with crime novels and cop shows can let their imagination run wild and start suspecting any of their neighbours' actions.

It's understandable that you'd want to try your hand at being a detective,' added the sergeant condescendingly, 'but that's what we're here for. We didn't find anything to indicate Shennan's death was a homicide, just like we didn't find anything criminal in Mademoiselle Yael's behaviour, no matter how suspicious it appeared. And that's all there is. Honestly, I'm quite fond of you, but you should really give up your investigation. You'll just end up wasting your time.'

Lafonnier had finished his cigarette, and Laurent took the hint and put his out too, flicking it into a nearby rubbish bin.

Tartarin spoke again. 'Well, Monsieur de Rodergues, I think we'll have to stop here. Even though I stand by the official theory and don't think Monsieur Shennan's unfortunate end was premeditated, or involved anyone else, I hope I've been of service to you.'

Laurent held out his hand. 'I appreciate your time, Sergeant. You've been very helpful, and I'll keep you posted if I reach any conclusions. Hope to see you around Saint-Chartier soon. As you know, Monsieur Charbonnier is organising a Town Preservation and Promotion Society, and the first meeting will be at La Cocadrille. Hope you can make it.'

'It would be an honour,' replied the sergeant, shaking Laurent's hand. 'Besides, now with that Carterius beer, there's all the more reason to stop by more often. Tell them they can count me in.'

FATHER GÉRARD DE MONFORT

Laurent found moving about to be a bother. He didn't especially like having to leave his home terrain, and he usually tried to condense all the errands he had to run into a single morning. That day was no exception. His conversation with the sergeant had lasted longer than expected, so he decided to stay and have lunch in La Châtre, a pretty town of around five thousand inhabitants that had just about everything, including a cinema inside the old chapel of the Carmelite convent.

Whenever he found himself in those parts, Laurent headed to the Lion d'Argent, a hotel and restaurant at the roundabout on the road to Montluçon. He was in search of the Rue Nationale when he caught sight of a familiar figure coming out of one of the beautiful bourgeois houses that lined the street down from the church. It was Father Gérard de Montfort: his stout frame, cassock and black beret were unmistakable.

Laurent didn't take such coincidences lightly. He was investigating the death of Shennan, and now providence had placed before him one of the last people to speak to him. It was too much of a coincidence not to take advantage of it. He quickened his pace and called out to the priest by name, who turned around and smiled in recognition.

'Monsieur de Rodergues, what a pleasant surprise!'

As they shook hands, the worldly priest sensed that Laurent sought something more than a simple conversation in the street.

'I get the impression you want to talk about something specific and in private, so why don't we step into the church? It's very spacious, and I don't think we'll run into many parishioners. We can chat in peace there.'

Once inside, they chose to sit at the end of the nave, under the organ, since it was a weekday and the main entrance was closed. They sat down on the pew, and the priest cut to the chase.

'I don't suppose you've committed any sins you need to confess, so there's no need to beat around the bush. Ask me whatever you like. I'm not easily scandalised.'

Laurent smiled, remembering his childhood years at a Jesuit school. 'Father, as I told you at the party, Saint-Chartier is such a quiet place that my greatest sins are sins of thought.'

The priest studied him as the light from the stained-glass windows danced on their faces in multicoloured flickers. Finally he spoke.

'I fear you want to speak to me about Carlos Shennan, God rest his soul.'

This surprised Laurent. 'How did you guess? In any case, if you're uncomfortable talking about him . . .'

'Not at all,' the chaplain said. 'I've thought about that

day often, and perhaps it would do me well to talk about his tragic death, too.'

Laurent told him everything he'd been thinking recently, as well as the investigation he was carrying out of his own accord, up to his meeting a few hours before at the police station. Father Gérard listened without interrupting, nodding, at times showing surprise and at other times smiling.

When he'd finished, Laurent said, 'You must think I've lost it.'

'Quite the contrary.' Father Gérard gave him a sympathetic look. 'I believe everything you've said, and I agree that certain circumstances about Monsieur Shennan's death do make it look suspicious. I'm happy to assist you, provided we don't violate the seal of the confessional.'

Laurent stifled a laugh. 'Don't tell me you're hearing confession from someone on my list . . .'

'You're right, almost no one goes to confession nowadays, but you're not considering the possibility that people who aren't on your list may have seen or heard things you don't know about.'

'Does this mean that you know something I don't?' asked Laurent with excitement.

'Don't get excited,' said the priest. 'Nothing I know is important enough to solve the mystery. Keep in mind, priests don't just hear confession, we also have to put up with parishioners' long, boring stories, and we get a fair amount of gossip passed off under the dubious pretext of "good intentions". We specialise in determining how good those intentions are, or whether it's really just an excuse to badmouth dressed up as casual conversation. You can't imagine the kinds of nasty remarks people slide into their confessions. In Monsieur Shennan's case, obviously I heard a lot of stories, almost always about his love affairs, and I must admit, moral considerations aside, I marvel at his ability, because I can't understand how he managed to juggle so many.'

Laurent couldn't help chuckling. 'Honestly, Father, I still wonder how he did it. Carlos had more active fronts than the Wehrmacht.'

'Indeed,' said the priest. 'Oddly, though, almost no one was ever critical of him. People found it normal for a man like him to stand above good and evil, and they told me about his exploits as if he were some sort of sexual Robin Hood. I brought it up with him, of course, and not because I was his guardian angel, but because of his family, and above all his wife – a remarkable woman. And because I thought in the end it would all blow up in his face.'

Laurent struggled to get comfortable on the hard pew and with a look asked him to continue. The priest sized him up, then seemed to make up his mind.

'I see you really were fond of Carlos,' he said. 'And I can trust you. That's why I'm going to tell you something. I think I ought to tell you, and in any case, what I'm about to say wasn't told to me in confession, and I wasn't asked to keep it to myself.' He closed his eyes to gather his memories, and began his tale.

'About five months before the inauguration, I met Monsieur Shennan at a lecture after a traditionalist Mass we held in Niherne. One of the people attending was an aristocrat from Lignières who I'm very friendly with. He came over to me with Monsieur Shennan and introduced us. You know what he was like, it was impossible not to be charmed. But much to my surprise, he also turned out to be quite an expert in theological matters. He had bold but intriguing ideas – he told me he'd worked out a theory for setting up traditionalist rural collectives that would be like a cross between an Israeli kibbutz and an Amish community. He was even willing to provide us with an estate in Argentina to carry out his idea, if we were interested.'

'I'd never have imagined Carlos would take an interest in such things, much less want to get involved as a kind of patron,' Laurent remarked.

'You ought not to be surprised. Monsieur Shennan was a very complicated man, and I can assure you he had a rich inner life. He was tormented and suffered horribly on the inside, though he took pains not to let it show,' said the Father, seeing Laurent's scepticism. 'Though perhaps in order to understand this, you should know that in one of our conversations, Shennan revealed to me that he was gravely ill.'

'What do you mean? He was the very picture of health!'

'Apparently he'd contracted some rare disease on one of his trips. He didn't explain in detail or tell me the name of his illness, but his hints made it abundantly clear this was so. I think that's why he was so worried about making adequate provisions for his family's future. I got the impression he wanted to do so before his health deteriorated.'

'His daughters are certainly quite young. But Madame Mayumi would be able to manage . . .'

'She's a very intelligent woman, but apparently she wasn't up to speed on his business. It seems it was the sort of thing that's not easy to explain or pass on to someone else. You have to understand the nature of our conversations,' he went on. 'She was dead-set against the idea of the château, and especially against taking their family to France. Carlos, who adored her, felt he couldn't open up to her about his dreams or his anxieties. That's why he came to me so often, and how I came to learn so much about him, and about his problems.'

Laurent sat for a moment in thought, digesting everything the priest had told him.

'I understand, Father, but I must say I'm a bit stunned: Carlos never struck me as a man who was ill or worried about communication problems with his wife. Just the opposite: he seemed thirsty for life and action.'

'Didn't it ever occur to you he was burning his candle at both ends? That he was living on the edge because he knew his life was ending?' asked the priest. 'Besides, you know Carlos wasn't the kind of person who wanted people to feel sorry for him.'

'Perhaps, but I'm still surprised I never sensed his inner struggle.'

'He was definitely a bon vivant,' the priest went on. 'He was like a gladiator: he knew his life lay in the colosseum, but he knew well he'd die there too. That's why he didn't keep himself from doing anything he liked. And yet, I assure you, he was painfully aware of everything he did wrong. And unable to stop himself. In his last days he spent a long time thinking about everyone he'd hurt, and he even asked me to help him figure out how he could be forgiven by them, or partly alleviate the damage he'd done.'

'And what did the two of you decide?'

'That's the sad thing,' said the Father. 'We spoke the day of the party and made plans to discuss the matter the following week, but as you know, it was not to be . . .'

Laurent looked at his watch, well aware that he couldn't keep taking up the priest's time. However, everything he'd told him was so new, so unexpected, that it left his head spinning with new questions.

'I'm more confused now than when I walked in, Father,' he confessed. 'Next you'll tell me Carlos didn't even like chasing after women.'

'That's another matter entirely. His love of women was part of his very essence, and there was nothing he could do to change. Even after he found out he was dying – or perhaps because he found out – he fell madly in love with someone, adding yet another problem to the ones he already had.'

'I don't see how one more dalliance would have been a problem for Carlos . . .'

'He told me his meaningless affairs had led him to do many foolish things, but his family was fundamental to him, and until then he'd never done anything to jeopardise it. Perhaps for the first time in his life, Carlos was willing to do anything for love. He was anxious, confused; he didn't know where to turn. What I'm saying, Laurent, is that you should consider adding the name of Carlos Shennan to your list.'

As Laurent sat with a stunned look on his face, still processing what he'd just heard, the priest got up. At the church door, they shook hands.

'Father, I'm immensely grateful for everything you've told me. And yet, the way Carlos died didn't look like a suicide, if that's what you were insinuating. The position of the body, the location . . . It just doesn't seem possible.'

'My good man,' said the priest with a smile, 'if anyone could contrive some thoroughly implausible set-up, it was Carlos Shennan.'

Laurent watched him walk off toward the City Hall, where he'd presumably parked his car. Waving once more, he turned toward the restaurant, meditating on the bundle of contradictions that was Carlos Shennan: an amateur theologian of the traditionalist school, and a radical anarchist in morals and customs; a playboy and seducer, but an obsessive family man; a businessman with 'unusual' dealings who nevertheless kept himself within legal bounds; a man who made enemies as easily as friends, who was afflicted with a mysterious illness yet as lovesick as a teenager.

He'd originally planned to get the lightest set menu, but circumstances forced him to abandon his scruples and order à la carte.

JEAN-PIERRE GIMBAULT

The meal was sumptuous, but later on Laurent concluded it may not have been a good idea to finish off an entire bottle of wine. His initial plan was to appear shrewd and persuasive with Gimbault, but his capacities had been somewhat depleted by the meal.

They'd agreed to meet in Gimbault's house, near the stone-carving school by the riverside. He had no trouble finding it because Gimbault himself was in the yard out front, retying some rose bushes that had come undone. Apparently, the night before, there had been strong winds.

He looked very focused on his work, and when he heard his name he turned with a start. Laurent knew it wouldn't be easy to get him to talk: from first glance he could tell he was the kind of person who rarely said any more than necessary, a typical trait among career bureaucrats, where discretion is at times a path to promotions, or at least keeps one from falling from grace in the purges that inevitably follow political changes.

Gimbault took off his gardening gloves and motioned him to come inside, studying him carefully as he walked down the noisy gravel path. Laurent shook his hand. He always paid attention to handshakes, and this time he noticed that the bureaucrat was a true local: in Berry even the women shook firmly, usually with hard, callused palms. Gimbault was no exception, and though one might not expect this of a man who worked in an office, he had an iron grip. His eyes showed a cold self-control, which seemed to confirm his first impressions from the party.

The inside of his house also surprised Laurent, because it was clearly the home of a music lover: on the walls hung instruments and posters from music festivals from around the world, while in the background hummed the chords of a cello from a professional record player sitting atop a cabinet.

'Have a seat, Monsieur de Rodergues, and tell me what I can do for you. On the phone you weren't very explicit.'

'You're right, and the reason is, I was afraid you'd refuse to see me,' Laurent confessed.

'You needn't have worried about that. I'll tell you right now that if I don't feel comfortable with your questions, I won't hesitate to ask you to leave.'

Laurent knew that Gimbault wasn't joking – humour didn't seem to be his strong suit –so he sought to be agreeable and create a friendly atmosphere for conversation. On the wall behind the sofa he noticed a vielle, an instrument used in local folk music that's very expensive and very difficult to make, typically with a neck of finely carved wood. This one had a bust of George Sand.

'Don't tell me you play the vielle? I hear it's exceedingly difficult.'

'I've played since I was a child. I learnt from Les Gâs du Berry. My father and grandfather also played. It's a pity that none of my children have taken an interest in it.' He allowed himself a sigh. 'It's so hard to keep up traditions in today's world.'

Laurent saw that the question relaxed his host, and immediately knew how to steer the conversation.

'As a matter of fact, I'm here to talk about the festival. I live in Saint-Chartier, as I mentioned, just across from the château. You probably don't remember me, but we saw each other at the opening celebration: I was watching the tango show and you were enjoying a beer.'

'No, I didn't see you, but I have to say, ever since then I've become quite fond of that beer. I think it was a great idea for Shennan to support Le Juanch. He wasn't a bad fellow. It's a shame he died – I think he would have done good things for the region.' He appeared to be sincere, and that left Laurent flummoxed, since he was prepared for scathing words about Shennan.

'Do you really mean that? I thought you couldn't stand him, or at least that's what I understood when I heard you on the radio.'

'You're right, at first I acted like a fool. You have to understand, the festival is my life. I've been involved since I was a child, and for me it and the Château de Saint-Chartier are inseparable. When I heard Shennan wasn't going to renew the contract, I flew into a rage. I lost my cool, something I very rarely do, though if you knew me, you'd understand how important the festival is to me. Forgive me, I haven't offered you anything. Would you like some coffee?'

Laurent considered this. He'd had two coffees already, but one more would be a great help in fighting against the sleepiness barrelling down on him like an alpine avalanche.

'Yes, please. Strong, if you don't mind.'

'The local life and the local food make one a bit lethargic, don't they?' laughed Gimbault.

'Lethargic? I've spent my entire life in South America, and I never took a siesta, whereas here every day after lunch it's all I can do not to collapse.'

'I know exactly what you mean.' Gimbault walked to the kitchen, and by the time he came back with the coffee, Laurent had already decided he wasn't guilty of anything. Yet he was still curious about his change of heart about Shennan, so he resumed the conversation, taking a more direct tack.

'I don't want to deceive you, Monsieur. Shennan's death left me rattled, and as you probably know, for a time I was considered a suspect. I can't explain why, but I'm curious about everything that took place at the celebration, and I was surprised to see you there.'

Gimbault held his cup as he listened, and didn't seem disturbed by his words.

'Rest assured, you weren't the only one surprised. And if it's any consolation, the police paid me a visit, too. As I said, I was no fan of Shennan – I'd practically declared war on him. I thought it was a mistake to move the festival, and I told him so directly and indirectly, in every forum and using every means at my disposal. But in February Shennan appeared on my doorstep unannounced and said there was something he wanted to show me. At first I was reluctant. I was even afraid he was going to beat me up – you've no doubt heard the rumours about him. I told him to leave me alone and go to hell, but he didn't react. He insisted, and was very persuasive: leaning over the wall in the garden, he began to talk about music, and we found common ground. Ten minutes later, I was grabbing my coat and hat and getting in his car to go to the château.

'On the way, he told me he completely understood, and that in my place he would have reacted the same way. That's why he wanted me to see the work being done, to show me that it wouldn't have been possible to hold the festival in the château. I didn't want to believe him, but I was already in the car, and like everyone else, I couldn't help feeling a bit curious about the château and the restoration work.

'Once inside, Shennan began showing me all the sections on the verge of collapse, and there were quite a few of them. He even showed me a certificate from the Department of Historic Monuments indicating that it didn't recommend the château for large-scale events. The truth is, the terrace was crumbling, a wall had collapsed, a lot of the earthenware tiling was barely hanging on. Thirty trees that were totally rotten on the inside had to be cut down, otherwise they could have caused an accident. In short, I realised it was true that without Shennan, the château's days were numbered.

'On the other hand, he also said he wanted the festival to regain its initial spirit, when the audience was smaller and more select, and he assured me he was willing to work with me to study how best to gradually hold festival activities in Saint-Chartier, in the château. Honestly, I don't think he was lying, and in case I had any doubts, he made sure to show me his collection of exotic instruments, which he planned to open to the public.

'When he brought me back home, I still hadn't gotten over my shock. He explained that he preferred to find what united us than dwell on what divided us. And from that moment on I decided he deserved a chance, and I stopped attacking him.'

Laurent set his cup on the table. 'I'm not surprised by what you say. Shennan liked to grab the bull by its horns. I don't think he was lying when he said he wanted to work with you. He was restoring a historical monument, and he wouldn't shy away from his duty to restore the festival, too, at least in part. I hope someone does in the future. Anyway, I appreciate your taking the time, and thanks especially for the coffee. If you're in Saint-Chartier, you know where to find me.'

Gimbault, now totally at ease, promised to keep Laurent posted about the events held throughout the year. Back in his car, Laurent scratched him off his list, and decided that, once he got home, he would take a siesta after all, and that he'd put on some music by Eartha Kitt to fall asleep to.

JEANNETTE AND CLAUDE MONATTI

Laurent was rereading his notes, sitting in the park outside the small château in Montgivray. It was a nice afternoon, and he'd always liked that town, especially the path along the stream to La Châtre.

He was killing time, because he'd decided to approach the Monattis. They hadn't responded to the note he'd sent them by mail a few days earlier; perhaps it had gone straight to the rubbish bin, or maybe they'd simply chosen to ignore it.

After deciding on the steps he'd take that morning, he got up from the bench and headed to the cafe opposite the château. It wasn't the first time he'd been there, and he had to admit its somewhat bohemian atmosphere had its charm. He sat down at the bar and ordered an espresso with a dash of Ricard.

The waitress had a chatty air as she brought him his coffee, and Laurent tried to strike up a conversation.

'I'm on my way to see Madame and Monsieur Monatti. Do you know them? I'm told they live in the old mill.'

'Are you a relative or friend of theirs?' the waitress asked.

The fact that Laurent was neither of those things made her very talkative.

'Oof. Well, good luck, they're a piece of work. Insufferable radicals, those two.'

'I can see you're very fond of them,' Laurent laughed. 'Now I definitely want to meet them. What makes you say they're radical? That strikes me as a pretty strong word for people in the music profession.'

The waitress gave him a hostile look. 'I call them that because they're extremely arrogant. The Monattis are the kind of people who see everything in absolutes: either you're with them or you're against them. And they go on all day as if traditional folk music were the only kind of music. In any case you'll meet them soon enough; they're not especially likable. And if you think I'm wrong, stop by afterwards, and your next drink is on the house.'

'I will, but first tell me how to get to the mill,' insisted Laurent.

'There are two mills here,' the young woman explained. 'They live in the one off the road to the right, on the path that goes behind the cemetery. It's the last house, in a beautiful setting. They say the trail there used to be one of the paths pilgrims took on the Camino de Santiago. Head out that way until you get to a small bridge. There's a beautiful view of the mill there. A lot of newly-weds go there to take wedding photos.'

Laurent paid and thanked her. He decided to walk out to the Monattis' house.

The path alongside the river out to the mill was worth

it, especially since there were no cars. Really, the whole landscape was worthy of the Musée d'Orsay, with terraced stone pools covered in lotuses and yellow water lilies leading up to the waterwheel. The house, with its large, stone-framed windows and various species of ivy climbing the walls, had been tastefully restored, and the surrounding garden was enlivened by all kinds of colourful bushes. Laurent walked once around the house and had to agree with the waitress: it really was idyllic. Retracing his steps, he found a very short woman of around fifty, in an odd get-up of purple stockings and pointed gold slippers, engaged in some sort of work around a hole in the ground.

Right away Laurent could tell she was preparing a *méchoui*, a North African roast lamb, and seeing a table set out not far away, under an arbour, he mused that feasting on a succulent lamb in such a beautifully manicured garden must be an unforgettable experience. Yet dining al fresco with the Monattis was not on his wish list.

Laurent addressed the woman. 'Excuse me, I'm looking for Jeannette Monatti and her husband.'

The woman looked him up and down rather brazenly. 'You're the South American who lives in Saint-Chartier, aren't you?'

'How did you know?' asked Laurent, taken aback.

The woman saw his surprise, and Laurent in turn saw how delighted she was to have caught him with his guard down. It looked like the interview wasn't going to be easy.

'You were pointed out to me a while back, at the flea market in Thevet-Saint-Julien. We don't get a lot of new people here and, naturally, for a time they become a topic of conversation.

219

We're from Clermont-Ferrand, and when we moved into the mill people spent a season gossiping about us. Maybe the things we do still give people something to talk about.'

The woman continued her work without inviting Laurent in, and the conversation, maintained over a boxwood hedge while he stood in wet grass, wasn't ideal for his plans. He decided to remedy that situation, extending his hand over the hedge.

'Well, as I suppose you know already, my name is Laurent de Rodergues.'

The woman gave an impish, girlish laugh. 'Yes, I know. Just as you know who we are. I'm sorry I can't invite you in, but my husband's gone to the bakery, and a handsome man like you in the home of a woman like me, all by herself, could only give rise to rumours.'

Laurent looked at her, trying to determine whether or not she was joking. Madame Monatti could no doubt be many things, but she was in no way an object of desire for him. Covered in beads and baubles and rings, and draped in a kaftan so large it made her body look misshapen, the diminutive woman wore spectacles as thick as a pirate's spyglass and had a headful of frizzy hair tied up by a scarf that looked dirty. Least appealing of all was her excessively generous neckline, which revealed two breasts tattooed with a motley thicket of flowers that could well have been a source of inspiration for Baudelaire. To his horror, he realised she was speaking entirely in earnest. He decided to respond in jest.

'My goodness, Madame Monatti, reading your newsletter, and seeing your modern and uninhibited sense of style, I'd never have thought you cared about what people said.'

A coquettish glance flashed under her heavy eyelids.

'Aren't you a devil, Laurent? See why we can't be alone inside? You're undressing me with your eyes, and I admit I'm not immune to your manly aura. Don't give me that look; you're a dyed in the wool Casanova.'

Laurent, totally petrified, didn't know what to say. If this was how she reacted ten minutes after meeting, with a hedge in between them, in a more intimate setting she must metamorphose into a fearsome Hydra. He spared a thought for poor Monsieur Monatti, who must have been inventing endlessly long lines at the bakery to delay his return.

For his part, Laurent decided that his best course of action would probably be to accept the cold that the wet grass was going to give him.

'You're right, Madame. It's better for both of us to continue talking like this. I wouldn't for all the world want to sully your good name.'

'I agree, Laurent. It's best if we leave our mutual attraction in the hands of fate. Besides, my husband will be back any minute, and he's terribly jealous.'

Just then Laurent heard wheels rolling up on the gravel path that led to the front door of the house.

'That'll be Claude. Go around to the front and ask for us as if you hadn't just spoken to me,' she commanded, blowing him a twilight kiss.

Glad to have escaped unscathed from such a predicament, Laurent walked around to the entrance to the house.

Laurent didn't need to be a psychic to know that the man getting out of the white Peugeot was the male version of

221

Madame Monatti. He was nearly bald and determined to wear the few remaining strands of hair he had left in a straggly ponytail. Pretending to arrive by the footpath, Laurent watched as Claude looked himself over in the rear-view mirror and gave himself a wink of approval. He couldn't help finding that gesture of self-admiration endearing.

He said hello and introduced himself while Madame Monatti made her entrance, acting out the most innocent surprise; she opened her arms and rushed to Laurent, imprinting two loud, sticky kisses on his cheeks, which made him feel like a baby unable to free himself from some especially irksome relative.

As soon as Laurent managed to extricate himself, the husband, who seemed to be the more easy-going of the two, invited him into the house, which was tropically warm. They told him to have a seat, and as he did so, the wife, claiming to be hot, removed her jacket, revealing only a sheer camisole that showed off the lush vegetation on her breasts and almost made Laurent forget about the investigation and take flight.

Luckily he repressed his impulses and started up a friendly conversation with her husband, while she brewed a concoction of exotic herbs whose emanations led Laurent to wonder if they weren't narcotic.

Back on the sofa, she began constantly winking and grinning and making various faces at him behind her husband's back, adding an occasional foot caress under the table. Laurent was completely overwhelmed. Perhaps taking pity on him, Claude Monatti got straight to the point.

'And what can we do for you, Laurent? We got your note,

but we figured that not responding would be the best way to get you to come.' They both burst out laughing, slapping their thighs, as if this confession were a hilarious punchline.

Laurent decided on a broad, polite Cheshire grin, while calculating how much wax he'd need to make voodoo figurines of them both.

'I guess I was worth the wait,' he replied.

Monsieur Monatti gave him a mistrustful look.

'Worth the wait . . . What's that supposed to mean? Are you trying to make fools of us by showing us that you're a man of the world? Or are you trying to impress my wife so you can seduce her?' This unexpected reaction plunged Laurent in total confusion.

'I assure you, you've misunderstood me. It's just a saying, and—'

The Monattis laughed again, clutching their sides.

'My God, Laurent!' Monsieur Monatti exclaimed, choking with laughter. 'Can't you tell we're joking? I can't believe you fell for that!'

'Yes, we like to tease our new friends,' said his wife. 'But I think we should let Monsieur de Rodergues talk.'

'Of course, love. Forgive us and tell us what you'd like,' said her husband, noisily blowing his nose. Trying to regain what was left of his composure, Laurent began telling them of his curiosity about the way Shennan had died.

'Since you didn't go to the party, there's no harm in talking about it,' he remarked, but his words were interrupted by Madame Monatti.

'But we did go to the party.'

'You two are incorrigible,' laughed Laurent, thinking

this was another of their jokes. 'Anyway, as I was saying—'

'No, I'm not joking,' she cut in again. 'We were at the party when Shennan died.'

'But your names weren't on the guest list, and I didn't see you anywhere,' countered Laurent, a bit irked.

The Monattis gave each other a knowing look and laughed again. Laurent felt a strong desire to give these two imbeciles a thrashing. Finally Monsieur Monatti spoke.

'We weren't invited, it's true, and in fact we'd even distributed fliers denouncing Shennan, but we snuck into the cemetery to have a look. If you climb up onto the stones against the wall of the château garden, the view is phenomenal. Once there, we caught a whiff of the roast lamb, and saw the wine and beer, and we told ourselves that for all of our consciousness-raising efforts we deserved a drink and a bite to eat.'

'That's right. Once inside we had a delightful time, and though you didn't see us, we saw you, several times,' Madame Monatti said in a mysterious tone that unsettled Laurent.

Her husband took over.

'The thing is, you caught my wife's eye. We're a free-thinking couple, and she wanted to meet you. We were following you for a bit, until at one point you jumped behind a tree to hide, and we had to do the same thing, behind a large bush. Then we saw Carlos Shennan go to the little arched terrace with a very beautiful girl. We saw her start shouting at him and give him a wallop he wouldn't soon forget, and then finally leave in tears. The look of distress on Monsieur Shennan's face was something else, but if you'd seen the look on *your* face . . .'

Laurent couldn't believe his ears. 'But why didn't you say anything to the police?'

'Laurent, please. We're hippies, not idiots. The whole town was covered in fliers denouncing Shennan with our newsletter's name on them. We were always attacking him, we'd crashed his party, and to top it all off he turns up dead. As you can imagine, we had a panic attack.'

'Yes, I can see why you wouldn't have wanted to have to explain yourselves. But why did you hate him so much?'

'We didn't hate him at all,' explained Madame Monatti, pouring more tea into Laurent's cup. 'But he was a very convenient character for our publication: a capitalist who brought foreign workers into town, cancelled an important musical event, chased women . . . Shennan was our little gold mine. Thanks to him, we made a lot of money with our articles, and most of all, he helped us make ourselves known and get more work. Remember, we make instruments. Maybe we're not as famous or professional as that duo in Saint-Chartier, but we have a significant client base thanks to our newsletter. Believe us, Shennan's death has been a disaster for us: now we have to look for another scapegoat.'

'I suppose that makes sense,' Laurent conceded, 'but how did you slip through the security checkpoint?'

'We left before the commotion started. After seeing Shennan get slapped, we went off to try the beer and empanadas, and jumped over the cemetery wall again, though it took more effort, because on the garden side there aren't any tombstones.'

Laurent had trouble imagining them clambering up the wall, bellies full of lamb, empanadas and alfajores. He'd dug up all that he could, and wanted to get out of there as quickly as possible. Getting to his feet, he said, 'Once again, thanks for this interesting little talk, but I'm afraid I must be on my way back to Saint-Chartier, or I'll be late for my next meeting.'

'Not at all, Laurent.' The unexpectedly nimble Madame Monatti was now at his side, grabbing his arm with one hand and holding up a pencil and sheet of paper in the other. 'Don't worry, Claude, I'll walk him out. But first I'm sure Monsieur de Rodergues will be kind enough to give us his address, isn't that right?'

'With . . . pleasure.' Laurent grimaced, knowing that this could lead nowhere good.

On the way out, when her husband wasn't looking, Madame Monatti whispered, 'I'll write to you, Laurent, and we'll meet as soon as possible. You've got me going mad. Off you go, or I won't be able to contain myself.'

Once outside, Laurent fled at a good clip in search of his car. The Monattis almost certainly had nothing to do with Shennan's death, but his visit had raised two new causes for concern:

1. What if the police found out what took place between Yael and Shennan?
2. What if Jeannette Monatti really did show up one day at the vicarage?

His soul shaken by this second possibility, he started his car, telling himself that only in La Cocadrille could he find the peace and tranquillity he so desperately needed.

TAVERN OR TABERNACLE?

On his way back to La Cocadrille, Laurent started thinking about the information he'd uncovered in his investigation, which was becoming more and more labyrinthine. The Monattis had crashed the party, watched Shennan get slapped, seen him hiding behind a tree: none of this comforted him. He just wanted to get to the tavern. Stepping inside would be like submerging himself in one of those ritual baths, a sort of purifying font where he could wash away the sin and scourges of the world

When he arrived, he saw half a dozen horses tied to the fence outside, as though La Cocadrille were a Wild West saloon. One of them he immediately recognised as Calypso, the horse Caroline de Flalois rode. He then recalled that on weekdays she often hosted groups from Paris, and one of her *routes de balade* came through Saint-Chartier.

As soon as he entered his temple of tranquillity, he practically collided with Le Juanch, who greeted him with an embrace.

'Laurent, you haven't been coming by lately. I hope you're not cheating on us at other restaurants. No one else is going to treat you like we do.'

'I know, Gaston, and I'd never so much as think of being unfaithful. It's just that I've been working a bit. Get me a beer and something to eat. I need to relax my spirits,' Laurent pleaded.

'What's wrong?' asked Le Juanch, taking him by the arm to a table.

'Do you know Madame Monatti?'

'Oh God, say no more. That woman could break sea ice in Antarctica. I'll get you a Carterius right away, and some stuffed pig's trotters au gratin with a garlic mousseline that will lift your spirits,' said Le Juanch, running off to the kitchen. 'On the house.'

Laurent took a seat, reflecting on the importance of camaraderie and solidarity among men. Suddenly a strong, feminine hand touched him on the shoulder.

'Laurent, you don't even say hello any more?' It was Caroline, decked out like an Amazon, in black riding boots instead of the gaiters she usually wore, possibly to match the Parisians. 'Don't you want to sit with us? We're a table full of beautiful women.'

'I appreciate the invitation, but I have to leave soon,' he replied. 'Do you remember Thierry, the forester? I'm going to go see him in Lignières. Besides, Gaston is bringing me some pig's trotters au gratin, and I'm afraid that the spectacle of me wolfing them down would scare off your friends.' After this excuse he added, 'By the way, Caroline, have you heard from Yael?'

'I wanted to ask you the same question.' She frowned. 'I haven't seen her since the day of the party in the château, and that was a long time ago. She hasn't even called. Though I assumed you two would have stayed in contact. Anyway, why do you want to see Thierry? I didn't know you were friends.'

Laurent shrugged. 'Actually we barely know each other, we just crossed paths two or three times at the Shennans' house. But I wanted to ask him something about Carlos, something that's got me puzzled.'

Caroline looked at him slowly, gauging what he knew or didn't know, then gave him a warning.

'Be careful, Shennan's a touchy subject for Thierry. To be honest, I never understood how he could work for him after what happened.'

'I don't follow. What do you mean?'

'I thought you knew,' whispered Caroline, looking around to make sure no one else could hear. 'Do you remember the day you met Yael, when we talked about the scandal with Shennan and the woman from Lignières, whose husband committed suicide?'

'I remember perfectly, but I don't see what it has to do with Thierry.'

'Her husband was Thierry's brother.' Just then a gorgeous woman walked over, also in riding gear, but wearing a spectacular pistachio tweed jacket, leather vest and white silk blouse with matching bow tie.

'Caroline, your food's here. Are you coming?' she asked.

'Yes, of course. This is Laurent de Rodergues, an old friend and excellent rider.'

Laurent stood up politely to greet her. The Parisian quickly assessed him, then smiled and said, '*Enchantée*, Laurent. I hope the next time we're out here you can join us.'

Caroline gave Laurent a wink goodbye. 'I'll try to convince him. See you later, Laurent.'

With a polite nod in response, Laurent collapsed into his chair. The news Caroline had just delivered had knocked him for a loop.

Fortunately, Le Juanch was on his way over with a glass of beer in one hand and a steaming tray in the other. Before plunging into the whirlwind of his preoccupations, he needed to restore his strength.

THIERRY CHANTEAU

The road to Lignières was practically empty, and Laurent arrived early for his afternoon meeting with Thierry, but he didn't mind. It was a pretty town with plenty of charm. First he decided to take a stroll through the centre, and then couldn't decide whether to get a coffee at the bistro next to the château or to give in to gluttony and dive headlong into the Breton crêperie. Luckily, the crêperie was closed.

The cafe in the plaza was itself nothing special, but Laurent liked to go once in a while. All kinds of ultramontane royalists from all over Europe would converge on the cafe to call on His Royal Highness Sixtus Henry of Bourbon-Parma, the ageing son of a pretender to the Spanish throne. He was known as 'the Standard-Bearer of Tradition', though on one occasion Laurent had heard the more pompous title of 'Rightful Heir in Exile', which no doubt had more dramatic force. Laurent loved to sit at the bar and listen to conversations that took place there, because, politics aside, they had an elegant, nineteenth-century tone worthy of the noblest aristocrats. The place never disappointed, and that day he happened upon a group of Corsican traditionalists and a duo from Albania who supported the return of the monarchy with the son of the late Crown Prince Leka as king.

After he left, he ventured over to the palace of Prince Sixtus Henry; if he had visitors, the outer gate would no doubt be open, and he could walk along the moat, enjoying the view of the unkempt gardens, neglected for years. Arriving at the area behind the church, he heard chanting in Latin, and he thought of Father Gérard, who'd mentioned he had met Shennan in this very château, and it occurred to him he could visit him to talk about the story with the baker. He checked his watch, and seeing that it was almost time for his appointment, went back toward his car the way he'd come.

The racecourse in Lignières not only put on horse races and sulky races, it also hosted the equestrian fair and had a stable for raising and mating horses. Camped out temporarily on its grounds was the Cirque Bidon, on holiday from its exhausting summer tours. They spent the off season repairing rickety caravans, checking over tools of their trade and the sets for their shows, and rehearsing new tricks and routines.

Laurent walked through the circus camp, admiring the dozen old-fashioned painted caravans and the Percheron horses that stood nearby, tethered to wooden stakes hammered into the ground. He saw artists painting their juggling pins or repairing their equipment, and he could tell from the way they dressed and behaved they had an undeniable attachment to the past. He couldn't help giving a smile, thinking these performers weren't so different from the royalists in the cafe. After all, they were all just romantics who longed to bring back the customs of better, bygone days.

He saw a young woman dressed as a can-can dancer strutting around with a chicken on her head, which Laurent mistook from afar for a feather hat. She turned out to be a very friendly Italian lady, who told him Thierry was doing some repairs on the inside of a green caravan with gold trimmings and a red door.

He had no trouble finding it. Under the cart he saw what were clearly chamber pots, and it occurred to him that the caravans were flawless not only in their beauty but also in their historical accuracy, and that a nostalgic aesthetic is hard to revive when one's body has grown accustomed to certain creature comforts, such as a modern toilet. He imagined having to step out of the cart on a cold, rainy night, and that put an end to the reverie of living in a caravan alongside a gypsy with gleaming eyes and an unfastened bodice.

There was Thierry, on his knees with his back turned to him as he varnished the bottom bedframe.

'Hello, Laurent. Give me just a moment,' he said, not turning around.

'How do you know it was me?' asked Laurent, surprised he'd been recognised even before he spoke.

'Your aftershave is unmistakable, and since in the circus we shower at night, in the morning we don't smell so nice. Hold on a second, I'm almost done. This is the ringmaster's bed, and she's very demanding.'

'To hear you tell it, you'd think I'm some sort of flamboyant playboy.'

'Oh, please. Solange always said your cologne had a very pleasant, masculine scent.' Thierry finished his task, wiped his hand on his trousers and shook Laurent's. 'Let me put away the varnish and clean the brush, then we can go for a walk and talk in peace.'

They walked past the horse-training field, where a group of elementary-school Amazons were practising jumping. Thierry was the first to open fire.

'I have to admit, I was surprised by your call and your eagerness to see me, especially when you told me it had to do with Monsieur Shennan's death. I'd also like to take this chance to apologise. When they were questioning you and rumour had it that you were the suspect, I didn't do anything to help, even though there was no doubt in my mind that you had nothing to do with it.'

Laurent didn't know what to say. If Thierry really did have something to do with Shennan's death, then of course he'd have acted the way he did, letting events play out and not doing anything. But he also had to consider that if Thierry was innocent, he logically wouldn't have known anything and therefore couldn't have done anything to help his case. He decided to say exactly what he had just thought.

'Don't worry, I don't see what you could have done, unless of course you had some information about Shennan's death. But that would mean that you were involved, in which case it'd be in your interest to keep quiet and protect yourself.'

Thierry opened his eyes inordinately wide. 'You can't be serious. I had nothing to do with it. Besides, I don't believe in violence.'

'Come on, Thierry,' Laurent said. 'Coming from a woodman, that sounds like something you'd say at a Boy Scout bonfire.'

'I'm not a woodman, I'm an *arboriste-grimpeur*,' countered Thierry in his defence.

'That sounds even worse. Don't dig yourself in deeper,' advised Laurent patiently. 'And yes, the days I spent being interrogated as a suspect gave me a lot to think about, and that's why I've taken it upon myself to go back over everything that happened.'

'But Laurent, that was months ago. Why now?'

Laurent didn't think it appropriate to tell him about the inheritance he'd received from Shennan, so he just said, 'Because ever since then I've been thinking about the case.'

'Well, I think it's a waste of time, but I'll try to help. What do you want to know? Or better yet, what do you think I can tell you?' He seemed sincere in his desire to help.

'Actually, I came with just one question, but a few hours ago another one came up,' Laurent said. 'I'll be brief, Thierry. Tell me, do you remember the day of the celebration clearly?'

'I remember it perfectly.'

'So you'll recall that, shortly before Shennan disappeared, you came over to the terrace with some mistletoe for Madame Mayumi. When I told you I'd been talking to her husband, you made a face and said you had, and I quote, "no desire to see him". That came as quite a surprise, since you've always been quite friendly with everyone.' Laurent gave him a prosecutorial look.

Thierry relaxed and smiled, then asked, 'OK. And the second question?'

'Just today I learnt that the husband of the woman from the bakery in Lignières was your brother.'

Thierry let out a grunt. 'It's funny, everyone refers to her like a character from a novel, "the woman from Lignières", as if there weren't other women or other bakers in town. Yes, he was my brother, but that has nothing to do with your question about Shennan. Or do you think they're somehow related?' he asked with sarcasm.

'I don't know, what do you think? Your brother commits suicide, you start working for the man who led him to do so, and before long he shows up dead under mysterious circumstances. And to top it off, just a few hours before that happens you say you can't stand the man. How does it look to you?' asked Laurent, holding his hands up.

Thierry smiled again. He had one of those toothy grins somewhere between sad and melancholy that must have paid off handsomely for him in the romantic realm.

'Yes, fine, when you put it that way, it does sound obscenely bad, I admit.'

'So let's hear what you have to say. I want to cross you off my list.'

'Wow, so there's a list? How many others do I share the honour with?' he asked, clearly mocking him.

Laurent, not always terribly perceptive, didn't catch the sarcasm. 'Nine, but I've already crossed a few off.'

'First I'll answer your second question. Neither Shennan,

nor any of my sister-in-law's many other lovers, is the least bit responsible for the fact that my brother hanged himself. You're a gentleman, and I know what I tell you will stay between us.' Thierry didn't wait for Laurent to agree before he explained.

'My brother and his wife knew each other since they were kids, and by age fifteen they were already a couple. He was a great person, and so was she. When they got married, my sister-in-law had a rough go of it, because her family, farmers with quite a lot of money and land, didn't look well on the marriage. Besides, my brother was only a baker's assistant; he didn't even have a baking certificate. She stood up to everyone, she even asked for her inheritance early so she could pay for both of them to get certified, as well as to rent the space and equipment.

'Everything seemed to be going well. They worked hard, and before long they had two beautiful children. And my sister-in-law was very happy, because my brother really was a wonderful person, kind and not afraid of work. Anyway, as you know, bakers work very early in the morning, something that my brother usually did with his assistant, a young guy from Orléans. And one day my sister-in-law couldn't sleep and decided to get up and take them some breakfast, thinking it would brighten their day.' Thierry closed his eyes and paused for a moment. 'Since she had a set of keys, she walked straight in without knocking and found my brother and his assistant on top of the kneading table, buck naked, lips locked . . . and you can imagine the rest.'

Laurent wasn't at his most empathetic that day, and he cut in, 'Just like in *The Postman Always Rings Twice*, that's a terrific scene.'

Thierry, a saint, didn't bat an eye. 'Yes, sure, but my sister-in-law wasn't at the movies, and the actor was the father of her children. Understandably, she was furious. The first thing she tried to do was fire the assistant, but then my brother started acting like an idiot: he admitted he'd known he was gay for years, but said he'd always controlled himself, except on occasional hook-ups when he'd had to travel to Paris or other provinces for business. She begged him to make an effort, and she tried to be understanding, but the fool said he'd fallen in love with the assistant, and they ran off, leaving her with the children.'

Laurent's mouth hung open in surprise. 'That's some story, Thierry. Sleepy rural France is a lot seamier than I thought.'

'Mind you, the story doesn't end there: a few months later my brother showed up out of the blue. Apparently the assistant had found someone with a tastier baguette, so to speak. Back home, meanwhile, no one knew a thing, because we're from Normandy, and my sister-in-law had explained my brother's disappearance by saying he'd gone to take care of our mother. In short, she allowed him to come back home, in memory of better times, but she told him that just as he'd shown no respect for her, she'd show no respect for him. So she went ahead and shagged any guy she wanted. One of them was Carlos Shennan. Over time, my brother grew bitter, because my sister-in-law treated him with open scorn, and in the end he took his own life. Then she lived unhappily ever after, the end. As you can see, I don't blame Shennan for anything. My brother was responsible for his own fate and his own mistakes. Does that answer your question?' Thierry asked, hands on his hips.

'Yes,' Laurent conceded, 'that more than answers it. I'm sure your sister-in-law must feel horribly guilty. Such a sad story.'

'Don't worry, she's strong. Now for the first question,' he pressed on, 'I only have twenty more minutes.'

But before Laurent could say anything, Thierry launched into another tale.

'As you know, I'm quite fond of Solange, the landscape architect. In fact, ever since the first day I saw her in the park in Saint-Chartier, I've been mad about her. And while she liked me, I'm sure you can guess that she was fascinated by Shennan's reputation: he was educated, attractive and what's more, he'd just placed a blind confidence in her for the landscaping project. Understandably, she felt flattered, and was always going on about Monsieur Shennan this and Monsieur Shennan that. You can imagine how nice that feels, when you're in the middle of trying to win someone's heart. Frankly I was sick of hearing about him.'

Laurent tried to reassure him. 'But she doesn't fit the type of women that Shennan liked. She's too young and fragile.' Though as he said this he recalled the scene in the nursery, and Shennan's face when he saw Laurent talking to Solange about which fruit trees he wanted to plant.

'I don't know, Laurent. The fact is, she loved to go off talking about plants with Shennan, and he was a born seducer, and a tireless one. I think that, even though she wasn't his type, he wouldn't have turned her down, if only to add another notch to his bedpost. Honestly, at the time I thought anything was possible. In fact, the day of the party he'd been very attentive, introducing her to everyone as "the genius responsible for the park" and taking her by the arm to talk with his guests.

That's why I was so upset when you saw me. Still, you have my word that after I delivered the mistletoe I spent the whole time with Solange, walking around the gardens, and that later on we met up with a group of young musicians she knows. So I've got an alibi and everything.'

Now it was Laurent's turn to feel uncomfortable. 'I apologise for wasting your time, Thierry. And for putting you on the list. You don't deserve to have me come and harass you with these questions. I won't keep you any longer. Hopefully one day we can get together in more pleasant circumstances. In fact, tomorrow I'll see Solange, and I'll suggest we get together for a barbecue or something.'

Thierry looked up, and Laurent saw in his eyes an expression that reminded him of a puma cornered against a rock wall.

'Why are you going to see Solange?' Thierry protested. 'You can't possibly think she had anything to do with this. Besides, you have my word she was with me the whole time.'

'I can see she's a sensitive topic, Thierry. She's not on my list,' he lied, well aware that, given their relationship, they might well cover for each other with mutually reinforcing alibis. 'I just want to find out if Shennan ever told her anything that might have to do with his death. As far as I'm concerned, she's as harmless as the saint she's named after.'

That seemed to reassure Thierry, and he offered Laurent his hand.

'That's good. Now I won't have to worry. Thanks for understanding, and yes, let's get together once you're finished playing Poirot.'

* * *

Back in his car, Laurent thought that his list was turning out to be a disaster, since no one really seemed suspicious. Perhaps the weakest position at the moment was Thierry's, though his instinct told him that the tree trimmer, or rather *arboriste-grimpeur*, had nothing to do with Shennan's death.

SOLANGE VARTEL

Solange had arranged to meet him on a Tuesday, the day of the market at Saint-Août. Laurent thought they could take a walk around the main street, something he always liked, because he enjoyed seeing the stalls selling animals. He'd order a suckling pig from Monsieur Fiett, and then they'd eat at Chez Sandrine Jamet, a surprisingly good eatery.

They'd arranged to meet in the plaza in front of the church, and since he arrived a bit early, he decided to poke around inside. The church boasted a spectacular wooden baldachin originally made in the Franciscan convent in Châteauroux, and apparently dismantled and hidden in this church by a group of the faithful during the Revolution. Laurent found it perhaps a bit out of proportion for a parish church, but it was still impressive, as was the fact that it had been spared the revolutionary flames.

When he stepped outside again he saw Solange. When she wasn't mucking around in flower beds she had an amusing style of dress that always reminded him of Mary

Poppins. Black was the essential element in all her outfits, which usually consisted of tall laced boots, hats topped with feathers and beads, flowing skirts with frills and embroidery and delicate lace, frock coats whose wide lapels were always graced with a cameo brooch of agate or ivory, and finally, to tie it all together, an old-fashioned umbrella with an impossibly intricate handle. Anyone else would have looked outlandish in such a get-up, but on Solange the clothes came together in a coherent ensemble that didn't strike anyone as odd. The fact is, in spite of her fragile appearance, she was a woman who inspired respect. Nothing about her suggested weakness – quite the contrary.

Perhaps because it was a market day, that morning Solange had chosen an audacious hat with golden pheasant plumes that elicited crows of approval from the roosters in their cages, like catcalls from rowdy inmates.

'Good morning,' Laurent said. 'Your hats never disappoint.'

Solange was one of those women who rarely laughed, but she knew how to give a warm embrace of a smile.

'Thank you. Every day I wonder if my hats are the only thing you like about me.'

Laurent gave a hearty laugh. 'Be good now, don't get me going. We don't want your prince charming, the *arboriste-grimpeur*, drowning us in the ocean of his jealousy.'

Solange had a knack for comedy, and feigned a look of surprise.

'Thierry? Poor thing! You don't think he's jealous, do you?' And for the first time since he'd met her, he witnessed the miracle of her laughing at her own joke. Then she said, 'Shall we look around the market before they take down the stalls?'

That Tuesday the market was packed, and they spent a lot of time greeting people they knew. Solange, to his surprise, stopped by a sausage-maker's stand to buy an enormous blood pudding and a breaded pig's trotter.

'I'd never have imagined you'd buy such a thing. You don't seem like the kind of person who likes *cuisine canaille*.'

Solange corrected him at once. 'Laurent, *cuisine canaille* refers to tripe and offal. Totally different from this fresh *boudin*. And just because I'm skinny doesn't mean I don't like to eat. I just don't stuff myself, unlike some others I know, who have noticeably put on weight since they moved to France.'

Laurent felt attacked.

'True, I have put on weight,' he admitted. 'I don't know whether it's the peacefulness or the scenery, but I've always got an appetite.'

A good while later they went to Sandrine Jamet's, a restaurant whose delightful owner ran the place with her parents. Laurent always admired her conscientiousness and diligence, along with her unfailing kindness. Sitting at the table, Solange looked at Laurent and revealed, 'You know, Thierry called and told me why you wanted to see me.'

Now it was Laurent's turn to feign shock. 'I can't believe my ears! Why would he do such a thing? Please, Solange, I'm not the sharpest knife in the drawer, but I'm also not the dullest. I knew from the start that he'd call you.'

'In that case, since I know why you're here, and since Carlos's death also left me with a bad feeling in my bones, why beat around the bush? Ask away.'

The way she spoke roused Laurent's curiosity. 'What do you mean?'

'Well, ever since I learnt he was dead, I was certain it wasn't just an accident. Everything felt too strange, almost unreal: the inauguration of the château, all those guests, the gauchos roasting meat, the music group, the security detail that looked like something out of an action film . . . even the fact that they held you as a suspect itself struck me as suspicious.'

'I see,' said Laurent. 'Though the fact that I could have been found guilty didn't seem to cause you much distress.'

'Don't say that; I was always certain you had nothing to do with it, and that they wouldn't end up arresting you, which they didn't. Though I might also point out I was more convinced of your innocence than you are of Thierry's or mine,' said Solange with a teasing glance. He replied with an amusing expression.

Sandrine placed two plates of duck gizzard salad before them.

Solange speared a piece of the salad and added in a low voice, 'Besides, I think I know what you want to ask me. You want to know exactly what kind of relationship I had with Carlos Shennan, isn't that right?'

'Not only that. Since you've given the matter some thought, I'd also very much like to hear what theories you have.'

Solange nodded. 'My relationship with Carlos was strictly professional at first, but I won't deny that the man had many charms, and once when we were visiting greenhouses up north, we had a one-night stand. The problems is, I took it to be a one-off, whereas Shennan chose to take it more seriously, which led to some misunderstandings between us.'

Laurent shook his head. 'Goddamn Carlos. Never in my life have I met someone who had so much trouble keeping it in his pants.'

'Please, Laurent, we're both grown-ups. Besides, I was the one who put the moves on him. One of the things I liked most about him at first was that, despite being a professional seducer, with me he acted totally differently – he showed me a sort of reverential respect. The night we spent together was one of the best experiences I've ever had, sexually speaking, and the way he acted . . . let's just say that had he not been married with children, I wouldn't have let him get away.'

When he heard her speak, Laurent recalled the words of Father Gérard and wondered whether she might not be the woman Shennan had fallen head over heels for.

'Who'd have thought? Poor Carlos,' said Laurent playfully. 'In the end, at least as far as you were concerned, he ended up being "the hunter hunted".'

Solange made an exasperated face. 'What makes you say that? Do you think I'm unable to seduce a man or take the initiative in a relationship? Ever since I was a kid, people have insisted on seeing me as some sort of character from *Jane Eyre*. It's the story of my life. Sorry to disappoint you, but it's not true. I can't stand how everyone thinks they have a duty to protect me. I'm not some porcelain figurine, nor am I a saint. If someone tried to hurt me, I guarantee I'd know how to defend myself, and even how to punish them, should it come to that.'

A new Solange appeared before his eyes. And he couldn't help feeling presumptuous – foolish, even. Ever since the moment he'd met her, he too had felt inclined to protect her.

'I'm glad to know you're such a tiger,' he joked, mostly to make her forget her anger. 'That's a real weight off my shoulders. Now I won't feel guilty when I put the moves on you.'

She burst out laughing.

'You're just like Carlos, Laurent,' she said finally. 'You both know how to make a woman laugh, and that's a gift that opens many doors.'

'I appreciate the compliment, Solange, but there's one thing I still don't understand. If you liked Carlos so much, why didn't you continue the affair?'

'Basically for two reasons: first, I'm more practical than I seem, and my job is sacred to me. What I was doing for Shennan was a project that totally absorbed me, and I wasn't about to lose my head over some silly infatuation. And second, because I'm not a bad person. I like Carlos's wife and daughters, and I was always clear that I was there to design a park, not to wreck a home. Besides, once Carlos started playing the submissive lover, he lost some of his appeal.'

'And Thierry? What part does he play in this whole drama?'

Sandrine came by to take away the plates, and they both sat in silence for a moment. That was when Laurent saw that Solange's eyes were gleaming with delight. She was having a ball.

'As in any good movie, you need a knight in shining armour, and Thierry came along with his curly golden locks at just the right time. He's a good man, he's sweet, and he's gorgeous too. Besides, his job is related to what I do. He's someone who needs to love, and he has the added appeal of not having a family – a perfect equation. I appreciate how we haven't been clingy or cloying in our relationship, except of course when he starts acting like the defender of my honour. When he does, I make fun of him and call him "the Guardian of the Sublime Porte".'

'So he's got no idea about what happened between you and Shennan.'

'Exactly. And I intend to keep it that way.'

'But if he doesn't know anything, why did he show such spite for Shennan when I ran into him at the party?' He proceeded to tell her the details of that encounter.

'Like I said, Thierry was morbidly jealous of Shennan, despite the fact that he had no idea what happened between us. Carlos, the whole time, in public and in private, always flattered me and showed me exaggerated attention. In fact, I'm sure Madame Mayumi got a whiff of it, but she's every inch a lady, and she never treated me with anything other than kindness and respect. The day of the party, Carlos was so proud with how good the park looked that he spent the evening introducing me to people, smothering me with compliments and praise, and that made Thierry hit the roof. In any case, Thierry never did more than throw the occasional tantrum. He wouldn't have been capable of killing Carlos. He doesn't have the imagination to plan anything as intricate as a murder in a secret passageway. If they'd ever had it out, it would have been with fists. Besides, one thing you may not know is that Thierry has never set foot inside the château.'

'You make a convincing case, and I have nothing to counter your arguments with, so I have just one question left. Do you have any idea what could have happened? Did you ever see Shennan argue with anyone unusual?'

'Laurent, did you not know him? Shennan was the king of arguments! He'd always get business calls, and he'd lose his temper at the drop of a hat. You can't imagine how many languages he knows how to curse people out in over the phone. On a few occasions I heard him dictate what seemed like battle orders to that dreadful bulldog of a secretary. Speaking of which,' said Solange, looking at him with a feline smile, 'have you put her on your list? She had a visceral hatred for any woman who came close to her dear boss, and I get the impression she's a force to be reckoned with. Besides, if the butler is always a suspect in crime novels, I don't see why she can't be one too.'

Laurent felt like an idiot. Solange was completely right, and it hadn't even occurred to him to put Xiao Li on his list. Still, he didn't like looking like a fool in front of her, so he tried to defend himself with an argument that sounded plausible.

'I don't think it was her. She was with me when we discovered Shennan's body, and I don't think anyone could fake a look of horror like that.'

Solange rolled her eyes theatrically and shot down his theory.

'Men are very gullible. For how many thousands of years have you been believing our orgasms are real?'

'There's nothing like talking to an intelligent woman to shatter the male ego. I'll spend this very evening thinking about how many women have lied to me about that. But honestly now, you don't remember anything that stood out about his death, or in the days running up to it?'

She seemed to think, and finally shook her head.

'Honestly, I don't remember anything, but I'll try to think back, and if I come up with anything I promise to let you know right away. But let's get going. I've got a meeting with the town planning councillor.'

Laurent, thanking her for the pleasant meal, called Sandrine for the check. A bit later, as they were putting on their jackets, Solange asked, 'I know it's none of my business, but have you ever thought of fixing up the garden in the vicarage? It's really in a sad state.'

'I'd like to,' sighed Laurent. 'I'd love to have you come and take a look. As long as Thierry approves, of course.'

'That's impossible, Thierry can smell a rival miles away,' joked Solange, and gave him a delightful kiss on the cheek goodbye.

Laurent watched her walk off with her Victorian air, and in the wake of all the surprising revelations during the meal, he wondered, not without a certain envy for Thierry, what she'd be like in a more intimate setting.

TONTON BOUSSARD

The next day, as he ate breakfast in the kitchen in the vicarage, Laurent mentally reviewed the details of his conversation with Solange. He was happy to cross both her and Thierry off his list, but that meant he was running out of possible culprits. The prospect of having to admit Sergeant Lafonnier was right was galling.

This thought led him to reconsider the figure of Xiao Li, Carlos Shennan's loyal, efficient, self-sacrificing secretary, yet he dismissed the idea almost out of hand. No one could feign the tears and immense grief he'd witnessed when they'd discovered the body together.

On his schedule that day he had a formidable interview, one of the ones he looked forward to the least: his dear enemy Tonton Boussard. Deep down, Laurent wanted the farmer to have something to do with Shennan's death, although he thought it entirely impossible that he could have woven such a complicated plan to murder him. He could more easily imagine

Tonton showing up one afternoon in the château with a loaded shotgun ready to pump Shennan full of lead, or better yet, running him down with a tractor in the rows of colza, backing up over him again and again with diabolical savagery.

Tonton's farmhouse in La Preugne, like most in the area, had an enormous barn on the side for storing hay and a smaller structure for the cows. All the roofs were covered in Verneuil tiles. When he reached it, Laurent dreaded running into the cassowary he'd heard about. Hopefully it was just a rural legend – maybe what some fool took to be a cassowary was actually just a wild turkey, since after all they were both birds from distant lands. Now that he thought of it, though, such an animal would make an extremely effective watchdog, or he supposed watchbird, given that one peck of its beak could easily split any thief's head open, and the noise they make when irritated is deafening. Maybe Tonton knew what he was doing and wasn't such a fool after all.

When he looked out over the Vallée Noire, it was like a postcard scene, and everything seemed tidy and in its proper place. For now, he couldn't hear the Jurassic squawking of any cassowaries, nor even any barking or lowing. A deep silence hung over the whole area. Suddenly a shot rang out among the trees, and all at once the racket that must be the norm returned as the farm snapped out of its torpor. Laurent even thought he could hear the broad strides of a large, flightless bird. Just in case, he stood by one of the buildings where he could take refuge if necessary.

From there he saw Tonton making his way up a path between elm trees. He carried his shotgun over his shoulder, and he was dragging by the tail a sort of gigantic mutant rat, with terrifying, violently orange incisors. Tonton walked up to Laurent and pointed to a stone bench.

'Have a seat, Monsieur, and while we talk I'll skin this coypu, which must weigh a good twelve kilos.'

'Is this your way of getting me to leave early?' joked Laurent, trying to hide the disgust he felt at the sight of that giant rodent. And since Boussard didn't reply, he asked again, 'Is this that species of beaver they say lives here in Verneuil-sur-Igneraie?'

'That's right,' replied the farmer, hanging the rodent from a hook and taking a rhomboid-shaped hunting knife from his belt. 'They're a real plague. They brought them from Patagonia for their hides, and they couldn't adapt to captivity. Then someone had the brilliant idea of setting them free, and now all the riverbanks are crawling with them. And the worst part is, they're protected. I wish the people who made laws in the cities lived in the countryside. There's a stream down there that runs through my fields, and the habitats these creatures build are almost ten square feet each. You can imagine what kind of erosion they cause when there's a whole colony. I reckon that on my land alone there must be around eighty.'

The farmer, like all those of his profession, was accustomed to talking without stopping working. Judging by the swift, clean way he skinned the animal, Laurent had to admit that Tonton was no doubt an expert hunter. With just two more strokes of his knife, he gutted the animal and cut off its head.

'What are you going to do with that?' asked Laurent. 'You're not going to eat it, are you?'

'Of course I am. Their meat is much better than pork. It's

a herbivore that lives in unpolluted rivers. I'd like to see what conditions many of the chickens they sell in the supermarket live in. The taste is a bit stronger than rabbit, but in a terrine it's delicious. I make it by soaking the meat in Armagnac and blending it with a cream of carrot, pumpkin and chive.'

'And the hide? You're also going to keep that?'

'It's fabulous, even better than otter fur. With the ones I've hunted I've already made a bedspread, and now I want to make a lining for my work jacket.'

Tonton wiped his hands on a rag and, holding the knife and the body of the victim, he invited Laurent to step inside the farmhouse, where he went straight to the kitchen sink to wash his hands and the knife.

Laurent took the opportunity to look around. The house was immaculate and decorated pleasantly but simply, with no photos or family souvenirs on display. He noticed that Tonton, who stood with his back to him, bore a resemblance to his home: he must be around seventy, but he kept himself perfectly fit, and radiated solidity and physical vigour, with a blacksmith's wrists and hands as big as loaves of bread.

'Make yourself at home, Monsieur de Rodergues. I'll be right with you.'

Before Laurent had a chance to sit down Tonton was already at his side with a bottle and two glasses.

'This cherry liqueur I distil myself – illegally, but it tastes better that way. If it went through the public distillery, the flavour would be very different, I can assure you. Too many laws and regulations kill the spirit.' He served them each a glass, then got up as if he'd forgotten something. A few minutes later he returned with a sort of pâté spread on toast.

'Don't tell me that's a cousin of the one you just killed.'

Laurent knew that this was price of entry, so he picked up the toast and took a healthy bite. He wouldn't be daunted by a little rodent canapé. Each one had a thin slice of gherkin and two capers, and the flavour wasn't bad: if he'd been told it was rabbit or wild boar he would have believed it. He felt obliged to give the farmer some well-deserved praise.

'Honestly, it's very good. The flavour is much more delicate than I expected, and the liqueur is excellent. I never imagined you'd be so domestic.'

'What did you expect me to be like? I bet if you told me the truth, it wouldn't be very pleasant. Though perhaps I deserve that.'

It was the second time Tonton's words had disarmed Laurent's initial animosity, the first being at the party, when he'd apologised.

'You're partly right, but I had good reason: the first time we saw each other, you began ranting at me, and then you filed a complaint against me for something that I didn't do.'

'You're right about the first occasion,' the farmer replied, 'but not about the second, because, by law, unless a third party was seen carrying out the action in question, complaints always fall back on the owner of the land. Unfortunately that owner was you, but I promise there was no express intention on my part, and honestly, I didn't remember that the field belonged to your grandfather.'

Laurent realised that Tonton wanted to talk or open up to someone. Rural life can be very lonely if you live on an isolated farm like this one.

'Tell me what brings you here, Monsieur. If I understood you correctly over the telephone, you want to talk about the death of Monsieur Shennan. I have no objection, though I should tell you I don't see how my opinions could be of interest.'

Laurent didn't know how to broach the subject without showing his hand, so he opted to take it head-on, and to gather his courage, he downed the rest of the liqueur.

'Well, Monsieur Boussard,' he began, 'I really don't see how I can play games with you, so I think it's best if I get straight to the point and tell you what I'm after, even at the risk of offending you and getting run off your property.'

'Let's hear it, then. Tell me what you want, and I'll decide whether or not to unleash the cassowary on you.'

'Do you really have a cassowary running around on your land?' he asked in an almost childlike tone, which brought a faint hint of a smile to Tonton's face.

'Yes, it's a long and unbelievable story, but I do have one. I'll show it to you later. Now get to the point.'

'I'm trying to determine what several people were doing at the time of Monsieur Shennan's death.'

'In other words, there's a series of people you think have something to do with Shennan, and you want to know if any of them were involved in his death. And I have the singular privilege of being on this list,' said Tonton, not even looking up from the table. 'And therefore you're here to interrogate me, more or less. Have I got that right?'

Laurent had to admit, the farmer couldn't have summed it up any better. 'Yes, exactly, you've got it perfectly right. If it's any consolation, I can tell you I'm interviewing around ten people. You're not the only one.'

Tonton didn't seem offended by Laurent's insinuation but looked genuinely interested in hearing his questions about the day Shennan died. So Laurent decided to confront the awkwardness head on and started with his questions.

'If you recall, Monsieur Boussard, we had a conversation in the park shortly before Shennan died.'

'Of course. I said hello, apologised for the day I was a bit rude with you and Madame Shennan, and I apologised for the complaint as well, saying I'd withdrawn it and wanted to give you a calf as a peace offering – a gift you rejected, saying it was all in the past.'

The innocent face of the farmer didn't fool Laurent, who knew he was being mocked with that cheek that often farmers have, no matter where they're from. Tonton was a sly one, and he almost managed to make him feel guilty. Laurent opted for a tactical retreat to gather his troops for the next charge.

'Yes, that was quite gentlemanly of you, and I appreciate it. As for the calf, please understand that I live alone and have a very small freezer, and can't really store seventy kilos of anything, no matter how delicious. But as you can see, I didn't turn my nose up at your river rat pâté.'

'Eighty-eight, the calf weighed eighty-eight kilos, really fantastic meat, but don't worry about it,' said Tonton. 'Shall we continue?'

If his goal was to confuse his guest, he was succeeding, because for a moment Laurent didn't know what to do next.

'As you'll recall,' he finally said, 'after we spoke I didn't see you again. Do you remember what you did, or whether you saw anything that caught your attention?'

'Yes.'

To call Tonton's response laconic would be an understatement.

'Yes to which part?' Laurent was starting to get agitated.

'Just that I remember what I did, and I did see things that caught my attention.'

Laurent couldn't sit still. 'Please elaborate.'

The farmer got up slowly from his chair, and Laurent couldn't contain his exasperation.

'But for God's sake, where on earth are you going?'

'Where do you think? To milk the cows. It's time. Come along and we'll keep talking. Unless you're afraid of them . . .'

Laurent let his head drop.

Perhaps Interpol has agents who specialise in interrogating farmers. As for him, he was about to throw in the towel, along with the sponge and the bucket for good measure. But he had no choice but to follow him obediently to the cowshed.

When they got there, without a word the farmer handed him a short three-legged wooden stool and a tin bucket.

'Most farmers have milking machines, and probably have more cows, too. I just have eight Normandy cows, and I don't like to be in a hurry. We can sit back to back and continue talking.'

Laurent had milked a cow on more than one occasion in the south, but he wasn't dressed appropriately, nor was this the purpose of his visit. Even so, he made an effort and got down to work.

After a few minutes of silence, he had to admit that it was a very relaxing chore. The stable was clean, as were the cows, and there was something intoxicatingly bucolic about the smell of hay and manure. No doubt George Sand would have put something like this in one of her novels. The spurts of hot milk, the steam rising from the tin bucket, the whorls of foam forming on the surface – it was also terribly absorbing, and it distracted him from his initial desire to give Tonton a whack in the head with the stool.

Tonton chose the moment when Laurent was most thoroughly absorbed and carefree to speak.

'I didn't do anything in particular. I wandered around the park, looked at the garden, tried the food, listened to the music, and that's where I was when the gendarmes came. Most likely you can corroborate this with the list they made as they tried to get us to leave in an orderly fashion.'

'You didn't speak to anyone? There's no one who can vouch for where you were at the time?'

'Hmm, I don't know. I said hello to a lot of people, but just in passing. I didn't spend long talking to anyone. I'm not very sociable.'

'You don't say. I never would have guessed. And what did you see that surprised you?'

'Oh, that.' And he fell back into silence.

Laurent was at his wits' end. 'Yes, that. Out with it, because if that cow there doesn't give you a kick in the head I'll give you one myself. I've had it up to here with the getting the run-around.'

The farmer turned on his stool, guffawing, and even slapped his thigh.

'Now this I like. Just now you reminded me of your grandfather. He was a good person, but he had a terrible temper whenever someone wouldn't get to the point. Sorry, but today I'm in a good mood and feeling playful. But don't get upset, I'm getting to it.' Then he turned back around to continue milking Josephine, which was the name of the

259

cow. After a few minutes he started to speak again.

'Well, the first thing that surprised me was that after hearing all the talk about the Patagonian lamb, about how amazing it was, I didn't think it was any better than the ones my cousin raises in Montipouret. And don't give me that look. I know you don't raise animals, so you don't care about such things, but I do. What you will care about is the other thing I saw, something that really did catch my attention: not long after I spoke with you, I saw that couple from Montgivray, the chubby ones who dress like hippies and are always stirring up trouble. You know the ones I mean?'

Laurent wiped his hand over his face, and without realising it covered himself in milk and udder grease.

'The Monattis. What about them?'

'Well, I saw them slip right into the house from the side of the tower that goes up to the rooms, and I got the impression they did so *surreptitiously*.'

Laurent tried to downplay the excitement this information caused.

'And I get the impression that you don't often use the word "surreptitiously". If I were the suspicious type, I'd say you'd rehearsed it for the occasion. You didn't see them leave?'

'Yes, it's true, I saw the word in the local paper, but I swear I didn't see the hippies again, and honestly I didn't give them much thought until just now, when you asked if I saw anything unusual.'

Laurent got up. 'You're right, I do care about what you've just told me, so I don't think I'll be able to keep helping you milk. I've got to go and check on a few things.'

'I see. Don't worry, do what you have to do, and thanks

for the help. But can I ask a question before you go?'

'Of course, whatever you like,' said Laurent obligingly.

'There were a lot of versions of the story, and not even the papers were very clear. Where exactly did Shennan's body turn up? Some said in the cellar, others said in the stairs to the tower . . .'

Laurent was puzzled.

'The papers didn't say? Well, all right, I found Shennan myself in a secret passageway on the second floor.'

The farmer looked up in surprise.

'In a secret passageway? When I was little, people talked about those passageways, but no one in the town ever saw one. Apparently Madame Germaine, the woman who restored the château in 1878, walled up all the entrances.'

'Well, now you know. Turns out there were secret passageways after all.' Shaking Tonton's hand, Laurent bid him farewell, and then turned back around. 'I don't suppose the cassowary's running loose around here?'

'How could you believe I'd have a bird like that running around the garden? The only cassowary here is stuffed. I bought it at an antique fair in Issoudun, and I keep it in the living room. Some kid must have seen it through the window when I had a fire going in the fireplace. In the light of the flames the feathers glint like it's alive, and its head is turned toward the window, so maybe that's where the legend comes from. Anyway, you'd best be on your way. I've still got six cows to go and can't spend all day talking.'

BETWEEN MEETINGS, A MEMORY

Laurent spent the days following his meeting with Tonton Boussard holed up in the vicarage, reviewing notes and drawing up charts of possibilities. The farmer's revelation about the Monattis had given him a boost of optimism, but the more he analysed the case the less sense it made that they would have had something to do with the crime. In his eyes, they were nothing more than a couple of run-of-the-mill opportunists – shameless but harmless. Annoying, certainly, ridiculous and somewhat parasitical too, but ultimately cowards. Over the course of his life, Laurent had run into many individuals of that sort, and he know how to spot them at first glance.

Finally, on the morning of his appointment with Monsieur Rataille, the businessman who'd overseen the construction on the château, he decided to set aside his charts, at least until he could see things more clearly. They'd arranged to meet in Châteauroux, and he had to leave no later than ten, or he wouldn't arrive on time.

He left his lists on the table and, seeing the overcast sky, he armed himself with an umbrella and a military raincoat, which he always thought provided the best protection from the water.

On the way to his car, he thought it might be a good idea to call Cathy Barnaud, the woman from the security agency who'd helped out in the search for Shennan. Maybe she knew something about the Monattis' party crashing or their mischief inside the château. Suddenly he slapped himself on the forehead: she was the one who, with her statement, had cleared his name during the investigation. Laurent was well aware of what she'd done, and he'd planned to send her a gift or call her, but as the days had gone by he'd gradually forgotten. Now he suddenly felt guilty. It hadn't occurred to him that by testifying that they'd been together the whole time, she'd lied, and that, perhaps out of a sense of loyalty, none of her colleagues had ratted her out. And despite all that, he still hadn't even thanked her. He was a disgrace. His mind suddenly made up, he got out of his car and walked back to the house. He went straight to the telephone, looked up her number and without giving it a second thought called her.

The other end of the line picked up right away.

'Hello, Laurent,' said Cathy in a husky voice.

Laurent, taken aback, looked at his phone. 'How on earth did you know it was me? I'm impressed. I feel like I'm in a spy movie.'

'It's really nice to hear from you,' she went on saying, as if she hadn't heard his question. 'I wanted to call, but I felt a little strange doing so after everything that happened. And since you never contacted me . . .'

'Stop playing around and tell me how you knew it was me.' Laurent didn't like being surprised like that. He wanted to hold onto a sense of freedom – he didn't enjoy feeling as though he was being controlled. 'Do you guys have a satellite in your office?'

Cathy burst out laughing. 'Aren't you adorable? There's no secret: I've got an ordinary, everyday phone, I've just activated a few extra functions. Anyone can get them, if they pay for them. One of them is a caller ID that gives you the caller's postal code. That's how I knew it was someone from Saint-Chartier, and the only person I wanted to talk to from there is you. Happy now?'

Laurent felt somewhat stupid for his reaction, and even guiltier than before.

'I'm calling to apologise, but now I have to apologise on two counts, first for being so stupid just now, and second for not having thanked you as I ought to have for everything you did for me during the investigation into Shennan's death. Only you and Madame Mayumi intervened on my behalf.'

'That's very thoughtful of you. When I saw it was you, I thought you'd be calling to ask for a favour, and I almost didn't pick up . . .'

Now Laurent didn't feel guilty but crass. 'I'm actually just leaving to go to a meeting in Châteauroux, but I'll be free in the afternoon. Would you like to get together?'

'You're in luck. For three weeks I've been working on a complicated case, but as of this afternoon I'm back and not too busy. If you like, I can come by Châteauroux. I imagine there must be someplace nice there where we can meet.'

'Say no more. I'll find someplace interesting. Let me know when you're on your way. Thanks again for everything. You can't imagine much I've wanted to see you so I could thank you in person.'

He hung up, and as he walked back to his car, he realised that the last thing he'd said, though improvised, was more than just a little white lie to excuse his long silence. He really did want to see Cathy, and not just so he could ask her about Shennan's death. She was attractive, fun and devilishly sexy.

He started the car, put on some colonial baroque music and headed out to his meeting with Monsieur Rataille. They'd only met in passing through the restoration work on the château, but he'd made a good impression on him: he seemed like a sterling man, the kind whose greatest ambition was to retire as early as possible and devote himself to fishing.

YVES RATAILLE

He'd arranged to meet Monsieur Rataille at the construction site where he was working, in one of those office trailers typically used on large projects. Apparently Rataille had made the most of the job at the Château de Saint-Chartier, becoming an effective salesman in his off hours, and had landed several contracts. The work he was doing in Châteauroux consisted of the complete restoration of an elegant bourgeois mansion located between the house of Grand Marshal Bertrand and the old Cordeliers Convent.

The businessman stood waiting for him at the entrance to the property, a majestic stone gate with a wooden double door adorned with tin rosettes.

'Good morning, Monsieur de Rodergues,' he said. 'Step into my office. I've got hot coffee and chocolate croissants.'

Monsieur Rataille originally hailed from Roussillon, and he struck Laurent as a classic exemplar of that land. Like many from that part of southern France, he could get by well in Spanish, as his native language was Catalan. His friendly air was heightened by the fact that he was one of those people who have the rare fortune of always looking impeccably clean.

This was something Laurent had learnt in Chile as a child: there are those who know how to receive a guest and those who don't. Rataille belonged to the former group, and he kept his office in a military order: the project blueprints were displayed on one of the walls, while on a draughting table he had laid out in perfect condition all the tools of that noble profession, which is never given the attention it deserves.

Rataille served the coffee, set the plate of croissants in the centre of the table and invited Laurent to take a seat in the chair opposite his.

'So, what brings you to Châteauroux? Don't tell me you're looking for a house, because the one you have in that vicarage is marvellous. If you're thinking of selling, don't hesitate to give me a call. I've had my eye on it for a long time.'

Mouth full of the flaky croissant, Laurent could only shake his head, and once he'd managed to swallow, replied, 'Thanks for the offer. I'm quite happy in the vicarage, but rest assured that if I ever decide to move, you're the one I'll call. I know you'd work wonders on it. However, I'm here to see you for another reason that has to do with the death of your former client.'

'You mean poor Monsieur Shennan, of course. I'll do whatever I can. He was a good client – a bit of a micromanager during construction, but I should say in his defence that most of his opinions were well-founded.

I must admit, I liked watching his never-ending spats with the architect.'

'Madame Pia de La Tressondière seems quite inflexible and sure of herself,' replied Laurent in an attempt to get him to open up.

Rataille, the sharpest of the sharp, didn't take the bait, giving instead a diplomatic response. 'She's meticulous, and she knows her job very well, but you're right that she was too inflexible. Draughting plans is one thing, and reality is quite another. The château renovation was an especially complicated project, and a lot of unexpected problems cropped up. That's why it's best not to be tied to the original plans without taking into account the imponderables that any restoration project will inevitably entail. For example, on the third floor, when everything was finished and even plastered over, we heard an enormous crash and had to open up the wall again. Inside, a metre deep, we found a huge beam that had rotted through. You can't imagine how much it took to tear down that wall, prop everything up, remove the beam, chop it up and fill everything back in with stone.'

'No doubt,' Laurent interrupted, fearing that Rataille would launch into a dissertation on the minutiae of the construction project. 'As you'll recall, I had the misfortune of finding Monsieur Shennan's body in a passageway.'

'Yes, I remember that secret passage, which goes from the guest room to the girls' room. After we discovered it, I always liked to think it had been put to some mischief in its day,' said Rataille with a wink.

Laurent practically choked and spilt his coffee. 'You knew about that secret passage? I thought it was something no one but the girls knew about, not even Shennan.'

'Please, Monsieur. I'm a professional! How could we miss a thing like that? I was the one who suggested there was a false wall there after I looked over the blueprints. Madame the architect, with all her degrees from the Sorbonne, hadn't noticed. When we opened it up in front of her, she tried to wave it off, saying we should seal it up again so we didn't have to redo the wiring and the heating.'

For a second Laurent practically thought he'd have a heart attack. Apparently the secret passage was a public thoroughfare: all it was missing was a newspaper kiosk and a soda fountain! He couldn't contain himself.

'This is outrageous! The police gave me the third degree over how I knew about that passageway, but it seems its existence was common knowledge. Why didn't you tell anyone you knew about it?'

Poor Rataille appeared at a loss. 'I had no clue that's why they detained you. Had I known, I would have easily cleared up the matter, but at no point did the police ask me about the passageway, nor about my whereabouts during the party. Believe me, I'm very sorry.'

Laurent realised he'd gotten upset over nothing, and immediately apologised. 'Forgive the sudden outburst, it's just that the more I learn, the less I understand why I was the only one questioned about that blasted passageway.'

'Not at all, you have plenty of reason to get angry,' Rataille agreed. 'And if they'd suspected everyone who knew about it, they would have had to interrogate everyone who was there when we tore down the false wall.'

'Would you mind telling me who was with you then?'

'I remember perfectly. There were only four of us. I felt that would be for the best, because if we discovered something interesting and word got out, the site would turn into a piece of Swiss cheese, with all the employees carrying out excavations of their own in search of a bit of treasure for themselves. That's why it was only Monsieur Shennan, Madame the architect, the worker who tore down the wall, and myself.'

'A worker? Which one?'

'Actually, it was Ahmed. I don't know how that didn't occur to me until just now,' said Rataille in surprise. 'I didn't want to let any other employees in, and after he found the passageway he promised not to tell anyone else. He took care of everything. He tore down the wall, got the passageway into decent shape, cleaned it up and repaired what needed fixing. All by himself he plastered and painted the room and strung a wire from the next room for lighting. We didn't even put heating inside. Shennan's idea was for it to be a secret nook inside the girls' playroom. If you recall, the door to the passage was a mirror with a magnet. He did it so that they could play and amaze their friends. And since they slept with their nanny, there was no danger that they'd use it unsupervised.'

'When you say Ahmed, do you mean that worker who Shennan got in a fight with?' Laurent was beside himself with delight. 'Monsieur Rataille, this is quite a coincidence. I came here to ask you about him, and even before I've said anything you go and bring him up. I'm trying to piece together a theory about Shennan's death. I'm doing it as a pastime that might turn into a book.' Barely realising it, Laurent was lying more and more smoothly and confidently.

'It was very sad, what happened to him,' sighed Monsieur

Rataille at length. 'He was a fantastic worker, and I had no complaints. In Perpignan there's a large North African population that goes back to colonial times. A lot of them have wives and children back home, and because they're lonely, they're an easy target for those Salafist preachers that keep turning up everywhere. First they offer friendship, they help them out with everyday tasks, they even lend them money. Then they find excuses to bring them to the mosque, at first for social events, like a lamb roast in honour of some religious festival, and gradually they snare them, until they end up brainwashing them.

'Ahmed is a typical case. He was an open-minded, unfastidious Muslim, like everyone in that area. Many of them would go out for a beer on Fridays with the rest of the group. If there was ham in the stew at the company cafeteria, they'd eat it without a fuss, and the practising Muslims didn't harass them. The trouble started when I hired a young man from Ouarzazate, Ibrahim, an individual who made me a very good first impression: clean, dressed in modern clothes, polite and very hardworking. You could tell he'd been to school. Six months after he came to work for us he started chipping away at the foundations. I always had a lot of North Africans and rarely had trouble, but once that Ibrahim showed up things went south: they wanted changes in the cafeteria menu, breaks for prayer, a space to pray . . . then they started growing beards, then wearing *chéchias* – those fez-like caps – and then things took a turn for the worst. There were fights with other workers, and some Algerian employees even got beaten up after being accused of being lax in their faith. People stopped showing up, had to be fired and so on. The only worker left from that time was Ahmed, and the funny thing is that down in Saint-Chartier everything seemed to be returning to normal. I even thought he'd voluntarily asked to work on this project to get out of the oppressive, cult-like atmosphere. As I imagine you know, I put everyone up in two rented houses in La Châtre. Well, one day one of those bearded zealots knocked on the door looking for Ahmed, and I told him he wasn't there. But somehow the man knew we were working in Saint-Chartier, and a few days later, when we were leaving the château, he walked up to Ahmed and berated him in Arabic. It was like a teacher scolding a schoolboy. Ahmed has a bad temper, and I expected the worst, but he took the chiding with a demoralised, ashamed look on his face. Then he told us the man was a relative of his who lived in Châteauroux who was very angry because he hadn't gone to pay them a visit, but I could smell a lie. From that point on his attitude got progressively worse, until the day he had the altercation with Shennan. And as far as that goes, I can assure you it was a full-blown provocation. There had never been a problem before, and he never prayed anywhere, and Monsieur Shennan was especially nice to him, to such an extent that Ahmed even said, in awe, that he was impressed by Monsieur Shennan's knowledge of Islam, which makes what happened later even more incomprehensible.'

'That's too bad,' agreed Laurent. 'And I suppose Ahmed no longer works for you. Even so, do you by chance know where he is now?'

'No, I have no idea.' Rataille had the habit of doodling animals while he spoke, and he wasn't a bad artist: the paper before him was now a veritable ark. 'After the incident with Shennan I had a talk with him. He told me I was a good boss and he respected me, but he had a mission, and his duty was to help his oppressed Muslim brothers in France and around the world. Of course, I gladly shunned those who gladly fled from me, as they say. I paid him his severance, and goodbye and good riddance.'

'That was the end of it? You had no contact after that?'

Rataille seemed distracted for a moment, but in fact he was thinking.

'You're right, there is a sort of epilogue to the story. Months later, I was visited by the gendarmes, along with a plainclothes officer who you could tell from miles away worked for the national police. They wanted to see my files on Ahmed, Ibrahim and everyone else who fraternised with them. Apparently Ahmed had joined a very violent Salafist cell.'

'Do you think he could have had something to do with Shennan's death?'

'I must admit, when I heard of his death, the first name that came to mind was Ahmed's, but based on what I learnt later, there's no way he had anything to do with it. He would have filled his pockets with explosives and blown himself up in that passageway, killing everyone around. As you know, sophistication isn't those bastards' MO.'

'I've never heard you say a coarse word,' said Laurent, astonished.

'You'd be surprised. A curse once in a while does a world of good.' Rataille smiled. 'Is there anything else I can do for you? I hope you don't give me an unflattering portrait in your novel. And of course, I hope you'll sign my copy when it goes on sale.'

'I assure you I portray you as the gentleman you are.' Laurent got up from his chair. 'Though for that to happen, I'd have to find a publishing house willing to publish it, which at the moment looks unlikely.'

After this they shook hands and Rataille returned to his blueprints and work plans, while Laurent stepped outside.

No sooner had he done so than he called Cathy. He hadn't forgotten their date and wanted to know at what time she'd arrive. But she surprised him with a new request.

'I'm behind schedule, and I'm afraid I'd be making you wait too long in Châteauroux. If it's all right with you, why don't I just come to your place? I'll arrive around eight thirty, I think. Don't go to any trouble, something simple is fine, really.'

Laurent didn't believe the story: Cathy asked for simplicity, but her voice revealed excitement and a certain nervousness. He could tell without a shadow of a doubt that he'd have to go to some trouble – not only because he wanted to, but because she deserved nothing less. He wanted to put together an unforgettable dinner, with good wines and cold champagne, and while he was at it, a linen tablecloth, flowers, candles and music. For the first time in months, ever since that distant encounter with Yael, he discovered he was excited, afraid of disappointing someone and, why not admit it, a bit anxious. He stroked his chin in thought and noticed he had a six-day beard. Good Lord, he'd fallen out of practice! He'd nearly forgotten how to wine and dine a woman! And he'd forgotten how anxious he always got about everything turning out all right.

He spent a good portion of the afternoon inspecting the offerings of the local chefs, and before he knew it he found himself laden with bags, heading to his car and talking aloud to himself, something he only did when he was nervous and had a lot of chores ahead.

IN THE RINGS OF
THE CIRCUS OF EROS

Laurent arrived at the vicarage laden with all kinds of packages. And as bad luck would have it, he ran into René, who was closing the church door and talking to Madame Fanchier, the elderly woman who had welcomed him to the town with croissants and a pitcher of milk.

'Good afternoon, Monsieur de Rodergues,' they said in unison, inspecting his packages.

'You shouldn't have gone to the trouble, bringing us all these gifts,' laughed Madame Fanchier.

Laurent hoped she was kidding. Since he didn't know how to hide the apprehensive look on his face, René intervened.

'Madame Fanchier is joking, but it'd be nice if you had us over for an aperitif one day, so we could tell you about your grandfather. She's got a lot of photos from that time.'

'Of course. By next week I hope to be more free, and it would be an honour to have you over to my house. I can't today because I'm expecting some friends.'

Madame, who was no fool, asked, 'You must be

expecting a woman, Laurent? That rosé champagne you've got doesn't look like it's for gentlemen, and the flowers even less: those lilies must have cost an arm and a leg.'

'The CIA and FBI don't know what they're missing by not hiring you as agents. You're a bit frightening, to tell the truth. And now that I've been discovered, you'll have to excuse me, because I have to get everything ready.'

With a bow of his head, he turned toward his house.

'Is it anyone we know? Not Mademoiselle Yael?' René called after him.

'No one you know!' Laurent called back.

Once inside, he decided to sweep and change the sheets. Most men who live alone seem to think that every three weeks or once a month is plenty, but Laurent knew women had very extravagant opinions on the matter. Then he went to set the table, since the dinner would consist of prepared dishes he'd bought in various speciality shops in Châteauroux. The champagne was in the refrigerator and the flowers in a vase; all he had to do was shower and shave.

As he did he recalled how, on the day of Shennan's party, Cathy had walked up to him and spoken to him over his shoulder. Their subtle flirtation had been cut short when the host disappeared. Everything was turned upside down so quickly: in one evening, so many people's plans and expectations had come to nothing, and all that would remain, besides the magnificently restored château, was the Carterius beer.

He pulled on his trousers as best he could – nothing fit any more as it did when he first arrived – and as he walked downstairs to put on music, he heard a screech of tyres that could only be Cathy's car. She'd probably taken classes in defensive driving and the like. He ought to bring up the subject and have her teach him some of those manoeuvres. If nothing else, it'd be a good way to escape from Jeannette Monatti's advances.

He heard her trotting down on the gravel path and up the stairs, and then knocking on the door. He wasn't sure this date was a good idea. The last woman he'd had over was Yael, and she'd brought him nothing but misery and woe . . . And suddenly, and with a diaphanous clarity, he understood something: both women were intelligent and attractive, but Yael lived in mystery and denial, while Cathy was open and direct. He put away his doubts and opened the door.

There she stood, in boots that came halfway up her thighs, black tights with intricate lace arabesques, a dizzying black leather miniskirt and a black leather jacket that she wore very tight, with the mink collar turned up. She'd changed her hairstyle and now wore it in natural, copper-blonde curls that highlighted her sea-green eyes and accentuated the contrast between her athletic body and her feminine curves. Cathy held out a gift-wrapped package to Laurent.

'You look like you're in a daze, but if I were you I'd think about opening the gift.' And without waiting for an invitation, she stepped inside and headed to the living room, unbuttoning her jacket as she went.

Laurent stood in the entryway, holding the package, unsure of what to say. His jaw was practically on the floor. At the party he'd found Cathy attractive, but he didn't remember her looking this stunning. When he'd opened the door to her, he'd let in an avalanche of sensuality that swallowed him whole. He watched her moving about the house and taking off her jacket, and he let his eyes linger on her square shoulders, her tanned skin, her small breasts showing impudently through her satin blouse . . . And then he felt certain the night would end up in a tangle of limbs, and he thought once more how lucky he'd been to meet Cathy, with all her outstanding qualities: everything in her was true, sincere, direct, straightforward.

'I'm speechless,' he said at last. 'You look stunning. I'm afraid what I've prepared won't cut it. And please, make yourself comfortable. I can see you're already at home here, like you've been here before.'

'But I have, Laurent,' she said with a mischievous grin. 'When they hauled you off to the station, I snuck inside to make sure you hadn't left anything compromising lying around. Sometimes you're so naive . . .'

'You've been here before? But you don't have a key.'

Cathy gave him a look that seemed to say, *You must have been born yesterday.*

'And if you really had found something compromising,' Laurent went on, 'what would you have done? Hidden it? That's a crime! "Tampering with evidence", I think they call it. Some officer of the law you are . . .'

'Silly boy,' said Cathy. 'In the first place, I'm not an officer of any law. I work for a private security company, and yes, if I had found anything I would have hidden it, since I was trying to help you. Now stop worrying about things that don't matter' – she changed topics – 'and let's go to the living room so you can open my present.'

Obediently, Laurent followed. He couldn't take his eyes off her.

Cathy sat down and placed her toned arms on the back of the sofa. She crossed her legs and revealed a seductive pair of thighs, as Laurent went to fetch the champagne.

He poured two glasses and raised his in a solemn toast. 'Here's to you, because in the midst of all my trouble, you stood up for me. And here's to the hope that you'll forgive me for not thanking you at the time. Cheers.'

Cathy graciously bowed her head, accepting his words, and brought the glass up to her lips and took a long sip. Laurent was about to sit down on the chair facing her, thinking with typical male cluelessness that he should take things slowly, when Cathy spoke up. 'Come over here, Laurent. Sit next to me, will you? It's like you're afraid of me or something.'

Laurent sat down beside her, and before he could react, Cathy put her arm around him with lightning speed. Then she grabbed him by the neck with her strong hand and long fingers and pulled him toward her, and he found his lips locked to hers in a warm, passionate kiss. He wasn't used to being manhandled – womanhandled? – like this, but he didn't object to the novelty. In fact, it exhilarated him, and when they finally stood up he found himself wanting more.

Dinner was relaxed and unhurried. Both of them seemed to be hungry, and Laurent was surprised by Cathy's appetite. Feeling his eyes on her, she explained.

'In survival training in the army, they taught us when there's food you have to eat it, even if you're not hungry.

Besides, today I am hungry, maybe because you've whetted my appetite . . . But tell me, what are you up to these days? What have you been doing since you cleared your name in the Shennan case?'

Downing his wine, Laurent said his life had been quiet up to the day that Jablard, the attorney, had visited to tell him about the inheritance. At that point Cathy set her glass down on the table, a bit piqued.

'Don't tell me that aside from that Israeli girl, you were screwing Madame Shennan too.'

Laurent, flattered by this attack of jealousy that Cathy hadn't been able to repress, wiped his lips on his napkin before replying.

'How could you think that? Shennan was my friend, and I'm not the type. Besides, that woman is a lady from head to toe. And even though she's very beautiful, there's something about her I can't explain but which makes her not at all desirable. I don't think I could feel comfortable with her in an intimate setting. In any case, I don't recall ever telling you about Yael.'

'I know what you mean, I feel the same way. I found Mayumi very attractive but never would have gone to bed with her.'

Laurent choked on his drink. After all, he was a rather traditional man.

Cathy saw his shock and had no qualms about telling him, 'I don't know why you're so surprised. It's like I was saying a moment ago about the food: it's a dish I've tried several times and didn't dislike. I like men, but interesting, worthwhile ones seem to be an endangered species, and I'm a practical girl.'

Laurent chewed in silence for a while, taking in this information, but Cathy didn't remain silent.

'Does it really bother you that I'm so upfront? Would you rather the women I've had sex with were men? Or even better, that I just hadn't said anything?'

Cathy's reasoning caught him off guard. 'I'd rather you be upfront,' he was forced to admit.

Cathy looked at him, pleased. 'I think we'll get along after all. Anyway, you still haven't told me what's going on with you. Take your time.'

Laurent told her everything from when the police stopped harassing him to when the lawyer showed up on his doorstep, which sparked his interest in going back over the case. Cathy practically died of laughter when he told her he had a list of suspects that he was going through one by one.

'I can provide you with sophisticated listening equipment, and if you ever need to tail someone, or obtain hard-to-access information, don't hesitate to ask.'

'Thanks very much, though I hope it won't come to that. Though I'll let you know once I've interviewed the last two people on my list, and if the conclusions warrant it.'

'Who's left on the list?' Cathy wanted to know.

'The architect from Paris and Yael, "that Israeli girl", as you insist on calling her.'

'Some duo! My money's on the Israeli girl: she's got the mental and physical preparation to carry out whatever she wants. And believe me, it takes a wolf to know a wolf.'

'What's that, some Siberian proverb?' Laurent teased.

'Come on, little Sherlock,' replied Cathy in the same tone. 'How's the investigation coming along?'

One by one, Laurent described his interviews, highlighting his discovery that the Monattis had snuck into the château, patently contradicting the story they'd told him.

'I know who you mean – the couple that look like they stepped out of a Tolkien novel. What do they call those short little things with the big feet? Hobbits, that's right. Those idiots went into the house and walked out with one of Monsieur Shennan's antique instruments without even bothering to check whether there were cameras. Before they got outside, we were onto them and stopped them on the ground floor. They had the nerve to say they were playing a joke on Shennan. We wanted to give them more of a fright, but it was their lucky day: Shennan told us over the phone to let them go as soon as we'd recovered the instrument.

'The truth is, Laurent, everything in that château was a bit surreal: the Chinese secretary shouting the whole time, Madame Shennan roving about like a ghost in search of someone, Carlos smiling and flirting with everyone around . . .' Cathy caught Laurent's glance. 'That's right, honey, you guessed it. He also flirted with my co-worker and me, and I must confess on behalf of both of us that he didn't lack charm. Then that forester guy showed up, looking like the pageboy in a Botticelli painting, and the landscape architect with that innocent schoolgirl routine that didn't fool me. And the architect throwing barbs left and right, the nanny or whatever she is running through the rooms looking for who knows who, the gardener and the cook screwing in the pantry like it was going out of style . . . had it not been for Shennan's unfortunate demise, which damaged our image as a company, it would have been one of the most entertaining assignments of my life.'

Laurent could hardly believe his ears. 'How do you know all this? Did Shennan have the château chock-full of cameras and microphones?'

'Yes, of course, he had cameras anywhere there was anything of value, and on the entryways as well. And we installed some mini cameras of our own without his permission. It's a typical practice that gives good results. Besides, we were spread out around the premises, walking around in endless circles, and one way to deal with the boredom is to talk about what's going on or provide constant updates. For example, it was one of my colleagues who told me you were watching the show. When you came through the front gate, I gave everyone your description and asked them to keep me informed of your whereabouts. But don't go thinking you're something special. You were just an oddity, something exotic.'

'Very funny. Are you sure you didn't see anything that might be important for my investigation?'

'Honestly, no. It was a great party, except for what I just said. Everyone was delightful, and delightfully rural. If one thing stood out as unusual, it was Monsieur Shennan himself. But don't take that literally, it's just an impression I had.'

'What makes you say that? It may have been just an impression, but you're obviously very observant, and your line of work has honed your intuition.'

'Something was wrong with him. On the outside he was an utterly convincing actor, a man who'd been around the block and could handle anything you threw at him. But I could have sworn that on the inside he was deeply shaken. I can't prove anything, and I didn't give it the attention it maybe warranted, but at several points he looked tense, like he was waiting for something, or like he was scared. Or maybe both.'

Laurent poured two generous glasses of Burgundy. 'It's funny you say that, because if he was afraid of something, clearly his fears were founded, considering what happened later. And if he was tense, waiting for someone . . . I don't know, perhaps those two feelings were related, both to each other and to what eventually occurred.'

'I'll talk to my colleagues. This Sunday we've got shooting practice and are going out to dinner afterward. If they noticed anything, I'll let you know right away.' Then she moved closer. 'And now that I know what a good host you are, I just may come back soon for another visit.'

Laurent felt Cathy's body heat next to him and didn't wait to be asked. He knew perfectly well what she was insinuating: he'd been wanting her since the moment she stepped inside his door. He took her in his arms and led her upstairs. Before she'd arrived, in a fit of hope and optimism, he'd left a few multicoloured candles burning in his room, a detail that brought out a laugh from Cathy. Then she started nibbling on his neck with real gusto.

L'ANCIEN CHÂTELAIN

Three days had gone by since Cathy's taxing visit, which lasted 'only' twelve hours and thirty-seven minutes. Physical fatigue aside, the experience was extremely satisfying in every respect. Yet he couldn't help but notice how urgently he needed to get back in the habit of regular exercise, and start to go easy on the constant trips to the pantry and wine cellar.

This was something that became clear especially when he said goodbye to Cathy: she was already inside her car, and he was leaning over to give her one last kiss. As she kissed him, she teasingly grabbed him by a certain belly roll, a bit of fatty tissue that until then Laurent had considered small and even cute. She didn't have to say anything. That gesture was enough. Then she smiled, gave him a wink and started up her car to go back to Paris, leaving Laurent in the church plaza, anxiously rubbing his abdomen.

Sometimes it's necessary, even for men, to make decisions. He went straight to his room and put on his athletic wear as best he could: its tight fit confirmed the accuracy of Cathy's volumetric analysis. He didn't want to think about it any longer. He put on his trainers and left with no fixed destination in mind. His idea was to run until he collapsed and not think about the trip back. That way he'd be forced to go back the way he'd come.

The air in Berry is excessively clean. There's no industry, the traffic is light, the farmers are mostly aware of the respect due to Mother Nature. The pleasantly rolling hills might even be said to facilitate a purifying wind. Laurent hadn't gone half a mile before his lungs started burning and he noticed signs of gastric discomfort; luckily it was autumn, and the falling leaves would come in handy in case of emergency.

He crossed the main road, determined to make it to Sarzay one way or another. His head hurt, but even so after half an hour he could start to make out the towers of the fortress. He'd only been there on one occasion, and he recalled admiring the architecture and its history. According to the brochure he'd read, it was one of the few fortress châteaux still standing in their original state. Recently it had been bought by a sort of Robin Hood who'd taken on the titanic task of doing a faithful reconstruction, and who'd found himself on more than one occasion going head to head with the bureaucrats at the National Heritage Office. They subsisted on a strict diet of regulations that admitted no exceptions.

As he approached, Laurent recalled that there was a tavern not far from the château. He could easily envision himself seated on the terrace with a beer, admiring the rough-hewn contours of the fortress. Unfortunately, that day he was committed to playing the role of serious athlete and promised himself he'd make do with mineral water.

He walked the last quarter mile but felt he still deserved credit for this first day in pursuit of his erstwhile physical shape. When he reached the little meadow that bordered the church of Sarzay, he performed several approximations of stretches and exercises, and then went to the tavern in search of as much water as he could buy.

Half an hour later he was still seated on the terrace admiring the Château de Sarzay, along with several Berry donkeys with white muzzles and intensely black hides that grazed lazily on the surrounding fields.

'Bonjour, Monsieur. You've come from Saint-Chartier, haven't you?'

An elderly, bald gentleman with lively eyes stood observing him at his side.

Laurent, who always showed respect to the elderly, got up from his chair. 'Yes, that's right, but I don't think I've had the pleasure.'

The gentleman gave him his hand. 'You don't know me, of course, but I know you're the grandson of old Hubert, the *sabotier*. My name is Philippe Lancéole. I used to own the château – I'm the former *châtelain* of Saint-Chartier. And I believe you were a friend of poor Monsieur Shennan.'

What a marvellous coincidence, thought Laurent, *running into the former owner of the château*. He immediately offered a seat to Monsieur Lancéole, who, at Laurent's kind invitation, didn't hesitate to order a beer with Angostura bitters.

They studied each other openly, and finally Monsieur Lancéole lifted his glass.

'To your grandfather, and to Monsieur Shennan. But my

288

God, man, what are you drinking? Water? It's almost the hour of the Angelus! Your grandfather would be ashamed.'

And turning around, he knocked on the establishment's window with his cane, which immediately summoned the waitress.

'Chantal, bring this young man the same thing I'm having.'

'Of course, Monsieur Lancéole. Anything else?' she asked politely.

Ever since he was a child, Laurent had been quite inept at the deployment and use of the word 'no', and that's why a few minutes later he was raising a glass with the old *châtelain*. A short while later they were raising a second glass.

'How do you like Saint-Chartier?' the *châtelain* wanted to know. 'Are you happy there, do they treat you well?'

'I have nothing but kind words to say about anyone,' Laurent said, nose covered in beer foam.

'And what do you think of the château? Quite impressive from the plaza, isn't it? I miss it dearly, but I had no choice but to sell it. I had operations on both knees, and I could no longer go up and down those damned endless spiral staircases. Besides, Shennan struck me as the only person really capable of restoring it, and I wasn't mistaken.'

'How did you know it was me?' enquired Laurent.

Monsieur Lancéole, who was giving orders to Chantal to refill their glasses, answered distractedly. 'Someone pointed you out to me at Shennan's party. As you can imagine, I'd been invited as well. I was there chatting with some old childhood friends, and Tonton Boussard told me who you were.'

Laurent squinted. He'd run eight kilometres on no breakfast, and now had put back three pints of Pelforth with bitters into his sweaty body, so he thought maybe he'd misheard him. 'I'm sorry, Monsieur. You know Tonton?'

'Of course. Saint-Chartier is a small town. Everyone knows everyone, and unlike in cities, there are no social differences, and age doesn't matter much, so we all used to play together. Besides, Tonton was in my gang. We both liked hunting, so we were in the same club. As children we'd always steal pastries and cookies from the château kitchen, and then go and eat them in the basement or the secret passage.'

Laurent gave a start. 'The secret passage? But the builder said it was walled off when Shennan bought the château.'

'Yes, it's true, we walled it off because we used to get horrible draughts, and when we lived there we didn't have the heating system that Shennan installed. But I'm surprised by what you say, because I told him about them myself when I showed him the château, and he seemed excited.' As he said this, he looked at his watch and slapped his thigh. 'It's almost one o'clock! My wife is going to kill me. I promised I'd pick her up from the hairdresser's in La Châtre. It's been a pleasure, and I hope to see you again soon.'

He made a gesture to ask for the bill, but Laurent stopped him.

'This one's on me, Monsieur. I insist. I'll remind you next time I see you.'

And a broad smile spread across the gentleman's face as they shook hands.

'Thank you. Hopefully next time will be in La Cocadrille, and Le Juanch will serve us something hearty that sticks to your ribs. My wife serves me nothing but vegetables and steamed fish. I can't stand it.'

Laurent sat back down, and as he stretched to loosen up his muscles, he thought for a long time about Tonton's feigned surprise at the existence of the passage, a secret he knew all too well. He recalled perfectly how the man had told him he thought they were a legend, and that a previous owner, Monsieur Lancéole's ancestor, had sealed them all off. Tonton had told him a bald-faced lie. And he was the second one to do so, after the abominable, preposterous Monattis. How many more lies had he been told? What did the two suspects he had yet to visit have in store for him? He shuddered to think about meeting Yael again.

On the other hand, why would Shennan feign surprise at the discovery of the passage, as though he didn't know about it himself? Perhaps he'd planned to put it to some other use, and that's why he'd kept it a secret, something he could no longer do once Rataille discovered it during construction.

Chantal arrived with a new pint of beer and, seeing Laurent's surprise, explained, 'I saw you raise your arm, but if you'd like I can take it back.'

Laurent stopped her. 'No, no, let's not be hasty. Leave it here, it'd be a pity to let it go to waste.'

It was the end of autumn, but the sun still shone over the round, pointed rooftops of the proud towers of Sarzay. Laurent could make out the owner in a window, operating an electric pulley to raise a wooden beam.

He left the money on the table and got up, perhaps a bit too fast, because he felt a slight wooziness. He knew then that the return trip would be an inferno comparable only to Napoleon's retreat from Moscow.

PIA DE LA TRESSONDIÈRE

Laurent couldn't have imagined Pia de La Tressondière living anywhere else. The architect's Parisian apartment was one of those elegant eighteenth-century buildings that had survived Haussmann's zealous reforms, and it must have been an expensive one, too, because it was one of the few that still had a doorman. The very entryway was a profusion of construction details, with a coffered oak ceiling and a hardwood floor inlaid with exotic woods. After showing his identification to the doorman, a tall, broad-shouldered Senegalese man apparently dressed by Armani, he stepped into an elevator that seemed modelled after a cabinetry catalogue, and when he reached the fourth floor, he noted that the building had only one apartment per floor, which gave him an idea of its soaring price.

A maid dressed in an old-fashioned uniform opened the door, took his coat, led him to a waiting room and offered him a coffee, which Laurent accepted. Paris at this time of year was usually rather chilly.

The sitting room was the very essence of lavishness: tobacco-coloured walls rose up to impossible white cornices that seemed to pour out over the room from the ceiling, while a plush rug adorned the floor, its elegant designs unobstructed by furniture or decoration. On the northern wall hung a large bronze Tibetan relief that must have cost several years of Laurent's former salary, while on the southern wall, in a stark but singular contrast, hung a painting similar in size to the Tibetan bronze, a mixture of several techniques whose striking use of colours created a hypnotic juxtaposition. The long western wall, by contrast, held a single piece of art: set in a beautifully carved antique ebony frame hung a hyper-realistic painting, not more than sixteen by twelve feet or so, showing the face of a woman shouting for joy.

As he studied it, Pia de La Tressondière walked into the room.

'Do you like the painting? It was done by a Mexican friend of mine, Fernando Motilla. It's titled *The Howl*.'

Laurent studied the work more closely.

'Yes, I like it very much, and now I see that it's you. It's hard to recognise you laughing. Whenever I see you, you have a serious look on your face, and last time, if you don't mind my saying so, you were even rather sad.'

'It's true, I was sad, and also angry. But please, sit down.'

It wasn't hard to choose a seat: the minimal decoration meant there were only two black leather chairs in one corner.

Now settled, Laurent looked around. 'Madame, everything you touch turns into something elegant and unusual. Promise me that the day I have money you'll decorate my humble home.'

Pia put her hands together and looked down, accepting the compliment. 'Please, I'm not so expensive. The results may look that way, but there's really more set design than investment.'

Laurent gave her a sceptical look, but he spoke politely. 'I appreciate your meeting me, and with your permission, I'll explain the reasons for my visit, which I hinted at over the phone.'

With a somewhat indifferent gesture, Pia invited him to continue, and he proceeded to lay out his motives and objectives, omitting what he didn't want to reveal, such as the names of the others on the list.

'Really, Laurent, I'd suggest you find a serious occupation and stop playing Marlowe, because even though you look the part, I don't think you could make a living at it. You're missing that touch of nastiness. You're handsome, strong and quite a drinker, but you don't inspire any fear.'

Laurent nodded, granting the point, but then he took out his most fearsome weapon. 'What did Carlos Shennan inspire? Was he also a good guy, or was he the tough type that you seem to like?' He awaited her reply, trying to make an insolent face.

'Laurent, poor thing, don't tell me my innocent comment's wounded you,' she said sarcastically. But then, taking pity on him, she answered his question with an unusual metaphor. 'Carlos Shennan was a cross between a crocodile, a bird of paradise and a mongoose, all covered in an impenetrable, solid shell.'

'So I take it you're still angry with him. Can you tell me

what he did to you to make you hate him so much even now that he's dead?'

Madame de La Tressondière's eyes were burning. 'Well, if it's really of such interest to you, I'll tell you. Actually it will do me good to vent.' She pressed a hidden buzzer and immediately the maid appeared.

'Brigitte, please bring us the reserve Calvados from my study, along with two glasses.'

'I have to admit, people of your class know how to live well,' remarked Laurent.

'Please don't play the poor man with me. You're living as a rentier.'

'Living off my savings, Madame, just off my savings. I wish I had some rent. But let me tell you what I'm looking for while we wait.'

Pia listened patiently to Laurent's questions about the passageway.

'Yes, that's right, we knew about the secret passage,' she confirmed once he'd finished. 'But we weren't the only ones. One of the organisers of the music festival, Gimbault, also told me about it. Apparently before they held events in the château they'd go with electricians throughout the château, so he was certainly aware of it. I remember he even offered to show me.'

'Gimbault knew about the secret passage too?' Laurent was starting to have a sense of humour about the subject. 'But did no one, not even you, have the decency to tell the police that they knew about the passageway?'

'Listen, Monsieur, I don't know what you're insinuating, but I was never asked about that passageway.

And in any event, you should know that the reason I didn't want to be implicated in the matter was that you weren't the only one who heard me badmouth Carlos at the party.' Pia de La Tressondière had lost part of her armour. 'I was even afraid they'd come across a call I made where I really let him have it. I told him I wished he were dead, but in that way you never expect will come true. That's why I preferred not to get involved.'

'But Pia, you still haven't told me why you hate him so much.'

Madame the architect poured herself a second glass of Calvados, saying she was going to need it. Laurent saw that, when necessary, she could certainly drink.

'At first, the job in Saint-Chartier was a godsend,' she said, starting her story. 'I restore historical buildings, and with the recent government cutbacks my work had dropped off. I needed money because I'm still paying off this apartment. Carlos contacted me because he'd called the National Heritage Office to request résumés of architects who specialise in historic preservation. He chose the top three and interviewed us one by one. There were two women and one man. He dismissed the other woman and asked the other two of us to come to the château for a second interview. My colleague arrived just eleven minutes late, but Carlos told him on the spot he could go home, because he didn't make his customers wait and he wasn't about to tolerate that behaviour from his suppliers or employees. Then he told me that I had the job. He'd reserved a room in the Hôtel de la Vallée Bleue, just outside the town, a very nice mansion that once belonged to Dr Pestel, George

Sand's personal doctor. Within a few days I was crazy for him, something very unusual for me, because I usually have a high degree of self-control. On the third day he came to my hotel and we spent the night together. His family still hadn't arrived, and in any case I honestly didn't give a damn. I hadn't had sex like that in years.

'Working with him was a bit irritating. I have to admit, he amazed me with his knowledge about historic buildings, but professionally it was frustrating how he never accepted my ideas the first time around but always fought me on them. He also didn't take advice when selecting suppliers. But to his credit, whenever we did reach an agreement about some aspect of the work, he wouldn't interfere any more and would heap praise on me, as if the idea had been mine. The worst thing was, he often managed to convince me he was right.' Here she paused, and Laurent seized the opportunity.

'What you're telling me doesn't seem reason enough for such anger,' he pointed out.

'That's because the story doesn't end there. I was still smitten with him, and we'd meet whenever his schedule permitted, which wasn't often. So for the first time in my life I began to feel jealous. I concluded he must be seeing other women, and I became so pathetic I even considered hiring a detective to have him followed. But I dismissed the idea because I didn't want to feel even more ridiculous.

'One night, at a dinner he organised in Vallée Bleue, it finally all made sense. There were some fifty of us altogether, and he spent the evening speaking to different women, alone or in groups. I had plenty of opportunity to observe him, and I set to work spying on him to see how he behaved with the others. That was when the scales fell from my eyes: he treated them exactly the same as me, listening with interest, giving compliments when appropriate, making a gallant gesture or naughty joke at just the right time . . . At a certain point he always forced some physical contact, mostly taking them by the arm, as if to prevent them from stumbling. So I concluded that if I, who was sleeping with him, hadn't been treated the slightest bit differently from any of those other women, the most likely explanation was that he was rolling in the hay with a few more of them. I grabbed my handbag and left.

'The next day, during the work meeting, Carlos spoke to me as if nothing had happened. Clearly, he hadn't noticed that one of the sheep from his flock had gone missing. I asked him if I mattered to him, and his look said it all: it was as though he were thinking to himself, *Oh God, another foolish girl in love!* I couldn't control myself; the tears flowed and dripped onto the blueprints. Shennan offered me a handkerchief and said, "I thought you were an adult and understood from the start that we were just having fun." His lack of empathy was the best thing that could have happened to me, because my infatuation vanished all at once, as if it had been exorcised. "Don't worry, Carlos," I answered. "I'm sorry for making a scene, and I won't cross the line again in what should be a purely professional relationship." He was unfazed. "Wonderful, Pia, now hand me the blueprints for the cellar, I want to see if we can make it bigger." And that's how our short fling ended, neither happily nor ever after.'

Laurent didn't know what to say. 'I'm truly sorry, Pia. That must have been a hard blow. And yet, even so, on the day of the party the way you spoke made it seem you'd also had some sort of professional row with Carlos.'

'Yes, now I remember. The day of the party, he repeatedly congratulated me on my work. He was radiant, receiving praise from everyone, and perhaps because of the euphoria, he seemed to suffer from emotional amnesia – he got a bit handsy, you understand. Yet even though he'd spoken to me on several occasions about having me do his summer home in Corsica, that very day I learnt he'd hired a very cute but very inexperienced architect for the job. And that's when I finally told him to go to hell.'

'That must have happened before the two of us spoke in the park, right?' Laurent interrupted her. 'I assume you didn't see him again, because you told me you were going to work on another project somewhere else.'

Pia gave him a piercing stare. 'Given that you're looking for a culprit for Carlos's death, it's not very smart of me to tell you what I'm about to tell you. But I don't care: as I was heading to the exit, I saw Shennan from afar, as he was saying goodbye to some guests. I felt awful, I had an unpleasant sour feeling in my gut, and I couldn't help myself. I walked over to him. I was wearing a very pretty gold watch with emeralds that Carlos had given me – perhaps you noticed when we spoke. In any case, I walked up to Shennan, and when I saw him greet me with that look of amiable indifference, I said nothing: I just took off the watch, dropped it into his cocktail and left.'

The end of the story was met with applause by Laurent. The architect smiled as she raised the back of her hand to dry a little tear struggling to well up.

'The truth is, you were right, Laurent. It feels good to vent. Do you need anything else? I'm meeting my mother to go shopping, and . . .'

Laurent took hold of the armrest to hoist himself out of the chair. In designer furniture like that, aesthetics always took priority over comfort.

'Don't worry, I appreciate your time. If you're interested, I'll keep you posted on what I find out. And buck up, a woman like you can't let a man get her down.'

'Thank you, Laurent. If you come through Paris again, don't hesitate to call, I'd be delighted to see you.' When she said goodbye at the door, she gave him a kiss on each cheek. As Laurent descended the marble staircase, he thought to himself that he'd just met someone quite different from what he'd imagined – and not for the first time in these last few days.

Pia came across as a tiger, but was a wounded gazelle; Solange seemed like a little white hare, when in truth she was a hawk; Cathy pretended to be a praying mantis, when in fact she was just a purring cat. And Madame Mayumi . . . she remained unclassifiable.

YAEL GOLANI

Laurent planned to interview Yael the next morning, so he decided to spend the night in Paris, an occasion he always took to stay in a cheap Ibis hotel on the boulevard near the Druot Auction House, which he always visited when he found himself in the city. He never intended to buy anything, and all he knew about antiques was that he liked them, but he made up for his ignorance with enthusiasm for attending the heated bidding sessions.

But on that occasion, the hotel's location was doubly convenient, since from there the walk to the Marais, where he had news that Yael now worked, made for an interesting route, both architecturally and for the shops he could find on his way.

He sat in on a new bidding session, dined reasonably well and slept in the hotel, and the next day, straight after breakfast, he decided not to postpone the encounter any longer and headed straight for the Judaica shop where, from what he'd heard, the woman he'd once thought he was in love with might be working. He couldn't help wondering why Yael was taking refuge or hiding in that neighbourhood. The woman he'd met months ago in Saint-Chartier didn't go on about her ethnic heritage, much less display any remotely religious beliefs.

As he approached the Marais, Laurent saw more kosher restaurants and more kippahs on men's heads. All of a sudden he felt transported to a nineteenth-century ghetto in Galicia or Chełm. Laurent saw men in shtreimels with long earlocks waving in the wind, with baggy trousers, white or black socks and kaftans tied with a sash. The most outwardly pious wore their phylacteries tied to their forearms, while many women carried enormous handbags and wore crude wigs or headscarves with designs from the Caucasus. Buildings showed their mezuzahs at the entrance, and although the Hebrew script mostly alternated with French, some posters also advertised events or theatre performances in Yiddish.

Laurent was so absorbed observing the people filling the streets that when he reached Yael's shop he realised he'd arrived too early. Luckily, across the street was a cafe for devotees of the Singing Rabbi, Shlomo Carlebach. There were few customers inside, so he managed to get a table with a view of Yael's shop.

An ageing blonde waitress with a friendly demeanour and an American accent asked him in Hebrew what he wanted, and Laurent replied in English, ordering a strong coffee and a sesame pretzel.

The pretzel came fresh from the oven and would have

earned the blessing of the Grand Rabbi of Krakow. He dipped it in the coffee and took a bite as he looked out of the window and tried to see into the storefront across the way. This was no easy task, as the shop window was crammed with objects: seven- and nine-candle menorahs for the Sabbath, bookstands for the reading of holy scripture in Yeshivas, silver placeholders for books, amulets with the Star of David, framed photos of men with mane-like beards and round glasses, along with anything else one might find in a Judaica shop. It was a world not wholly unknown to him, since Chile has a large Jewish community, and one of his great loves had been Judith, a beauty with devilish green eyes who was flexible and liberal in her everyday life but had surprising fits of religious observance. Sometimes, after a session of lovemaking, she'd tell him about the significance of the festival of Purim or Rosh Hashanah, and Laurent would listen rapt as he stroked her breasts; at other times, however, she turned away from his attention and caresses, complaining that Laurent wouldn't get circumcised as proof of his love.

As his mind wandered back to those memories, Laurent almost failed to notice the shop door open as an old bearded man with the air and manner of a rabbi made his way outside. The woman holding the door open was Yael.

Laurent couldn't believe his eyes. There she was, in a long dress, a blouse like those worn by the devout, and her hair hidden under a headscarf. The man stood in the street saying something, and she leant against the door, arms crossed over her chest and looking down at the ground, nodding at what the old man said.

Laurent knew that her modest attire covered a sculpted body with cinnamon skin, that her headscarf concealed a cascade of jet-black curls, and that he – he himself – had made love to her. That's why he couldn't get over the shock of seeing her now as some kind of religious prude, nor could he make sense of her transformation. He simply couldn't fathom what could have caused such a drastic change.

The last time he'd seen her, she had just slapped Shennan and was heading for the château gate. She was sensually dressed in a long gown with cut-outs on the front that revealed her legs, and from behind showed off the rhythmic swaying of her taut buttocks. But now he had trouble gathering the strength to go into the shop and walk up casually to her, even though that was the purpose of his visit: he was afraid of how Yael might react, since she was so unpredictable. And he was afraid of how he might react too.

Fortunately, he'd let his beard grow, and thinking ahead, he'd put on a black beret and sunglasses. He had a studious air he hoped would let him escape notice in the apparently large shop, where he intended to slink about and spy on her. Suddenly it occurred to him that if there was no one else in the shop, the employees might pounce on him and try to sell him on an edition of the Mishnah, so he decided to wait until he saw someone else go in.

He was in luck: ten minutes later a group of Talmudic students led by their teacher entered the shop, and he took the opportunity to leave the cafe, march across the street and follow them in.

* * *

The shop turned out to be enormous, and his impression from outside was mistaken: it was full of people, many more than he expected. They weren't easy customers, he noticed: they studied each object as if their lives depended on it, completely focused, even checking to see whether the branches of a menorah were aligned, or whether the leather in the phylacteries was of good quality. Laurent stopped in front of a display case and pretended to be interested in a tallit. From there he spotted Yael, speaking to a hunched old woman. Her unflattering clothes were unable to conceal her beauty, and Laurent couldn't help grimacing as he saw her struggling with an unruly curl and forcing it back into its confinement.

Behind her was a bookshelf, and he slowly moved toward it, trying not to be seen. He placed himself practically beside Yael's back and stood there, looking over the books as he listened to her speak to the woman in Hebrew.

Who was that woman, really? In Saint-Chartier she'd lived as a modern, liberated artist, and in the Marais she was a prim standard bearer of the Lion of Judah. He studied her out of the corner of his eye and saw her lift her head and wrinkle her nose, as though sniffing the air, and then look around, disconcerted. Finally she seemed to dismiss a thought and turn her attention back to the old woman, who was taking her hand tenderly.

Laurent knew Yael thought she'd recognised his scent, since the cologne he put on after showering was by a little-known brand with a very particular fragrance. Then he heard her call over another shop assistant, who she asked to help her find something he didn't understand.

He couldn't delay any longer. He turned to Yael and in a polite voice asked, 'Could you help me find a book on spirituality? Specifically I'm looking for something about helping women repent after they've strayed from the true faith and rolled around in the mud of carnal sin with men like me.'

Yael gave a start but instantly recovered her composure. Her face did not betray the slightest excitement or joy at seeing him.

'I wasn't mistaken. That was your scent. What are you doing here? I hope you have a very good reason for coming to disturb me at work. Besides, you're a goy, you can't touch these objects, you have no right.'

At this point Laurent was in no mood to take lessons from anyone, least of all Mademoiselle Yael Golani.

'I'm moved by your warm welcome.' He stepped dangerously close to her. 'I'm here because I want to talk to you, and don't you tell me what I can or can't touch, after you jerked me around with your lectures, stories and lies.'

She gave him an icy look. 'If you don't leave, I'll have them call the police.'

Laurent raised his eyebrows sarcastically. He had just about closed the door on his former passion for Yael, but this stupid reaction of hers was the perfect way to bolt the lock.

'Ha. If you don't calm down this instant and ask for a break, saying I'm your cousin and we're going to get coffee across the way, I'll start yelling that you're the whore of Babylon. And believe me, I know enough about Judaism to come up with such a story that afterward you won't even find work as a cleaning lady at a bris.'

She studied him, and for the first time since he'd met her he could see she was hesitating.

'And if I do go with you, what do you want to talk to me about?'

Laurent's bluff had worked, and he could tell that Yael had lost the match, but he still wanted to make sure. 'We'll talk about whatever I want to talk about, because I deserve it. And I want to explain some things and hear your opinion about them. If I don't get the answers I expect, I'll come back here and go through with my initial plan. Café. Now.'

The American from the cafe met him with a smile.

'I knew you'd like our place. What can I get you?' She looked at Yael, and added, 'You look like you're a Yemenite. So is our cook, and he makes some very good Yemeni pastries. Why don't I bring you some, along with some anise and cardamom tea?'

Laurent had to admire the server's business acumen. If Le Juanch had a waitress like that he'd be rich.

'Sounds perfect,' he said. 'The same for you, Yael?' She gave a nod, and Laurent held up two fingers.

After a short silence, he decided to begin.

'Look, Yael, I don't know what sort of mystical sect you're mixed up in, and I don't give a damn. I don't think I treated you so badly to deserve such a shitty, threatening welcome, nor to have you suddenly vanish from Saint-Chartier. Besides, maybe you're unaware, but after Shennan's death I was the only idiot hauled in for interrogation, while you, my one-time neighbour and lover, didn't have the decency to speak up on my behalf. Imagine how grateful I am. How does it look to you? But what a silly question! As if I didn't know you'd gone there with a plan, and that I was nothing more than an extra in your show.'

Yael seemed to be slowly regaining her calm. 'Finished with your tantrum? Ask me whatever you want. The sooner I get out of here, the better.'

But Laurent was in no mood to let her off easily, and he decided to make his second bluff. 'No, my dear, I haven't even started. Don't think you're so pretty or untouchable, because guess what: I was nice enough not to mention the story of how you yelled at Shennan and slapped him in the face just before he died. But as I suppose you know, the case has been reopened, and since I don't want to go through that inferno again, I won't hesitate to spill everything. Maybe that way you can experience what I did. You're a smart girl; you'll have guessed I'm not joking. I'm sick of being the "collateral damage", as you once called me.'

Yael seemed to evaluate the situation. 'Fine, you're right. I didn't treat you well. I'll tell you whatever I can, and I'm sorry for what you went through. You may not believe me, but I swear I left town right after Shennan died, and since I wasn't in contact with anyone, I had no idea you were a suspect.'

'No one ever knew that I was the scapegoat, it seems! Let me rephrase the question. If you had known, would that have even slightly altered your plans? Have the decency not to lie to me.' Laurent stared her straight in the face.

She closed her eyes, then lowered them. 'No, I don't think that would have changed my plans.'

308

'Such a shame, Yael.' He looked ruefully out onto the street. 'I was genuinely in love with you, and there's nothing I wouldn't have done for you. But silly me, I'm just a goy. In short: throwaway material.'

This confession did seem to reach her sensitive fibres.

'Don't say that,' said Yael, placing her hand beside his. 'And I do feel sorry, as much as I'm able to.'

Laurent withdrew his hand. He wasn't about to lose his dignity for such an insignificant gesture of affection that for all he knew might have been feigned.

'You're as sensitive as a fossilised amoeba, Yael. It doesn't matter; let's get down to business. Have your pastries and listen.' Laurent once again explained what he'd told everyone else on the list. To his surprise, she found the whole thing extremely interesting.

'So the Monattis also saw me slap him? Strange that they didn't tell the police, but then of course they weren't interrogated, and they risked having their theft discovered. From what you've said, it sounds like no one was involved in Shennan's death, so maybe the police theory is right. And I don't understand how I can help, since you told me yourself you saw me leave before anything happened to Shennan.'

'Look,' said Laurent, licking his fingers after devouring the last pastry. 'What I want is for you to tell me the truth about your story, in this order: what were you doing in Saint-Chartier? Why did you have sex with me? Why were you so furious at Shennan? And finally – and I admit, this is what really gets me – what on earth are you doing dressed like that?'

Yael looked out toward the shop. 'It's a very long story and I have to work. Can we meet later?'

'We've got all morning, and I doubt you're so indispensable in that orthodox emporium. You'll come up with an excuse. The sooner you tell me everything the sooner you can go, and hopefully we'll never see each other again.'

A sarcastic smile blossomed on Yael's lips. 'You know, when you play the bad guy, you're much more attractive than as the clean-cut ski instructor. You should work on that; you'd be irresistible.' Then she studied him again, and again smiled. 'Now I see. You've found someone else.'

'My love life isn't on the agenda today. Just answer the questions. Women only pay attention to men who ignore them.'

She thought about this. 'Not always, but that's pretty close to the truth. Listen, I'll tell you everything, and hopefully this will stay between us. Do you mind if I order a raki?'

'Order two and get to the point.'

Yael seemed to sink into a trance. She closed her eyes, put her hands together and murmured something that had the cadence of a prayer.

'Before I moved to Saint-Chartier, I'd worked in this shop for two years. Before that I wasn't religious, or rather I was in the way non-practising Israeli Jews are: we carry on traditions because that's what's allowed us to survive for centuries. Yemenites like me are seen as the gypsies of Judaism, partly because many of us make music and art. I myself studied voice and worked as a model in the School of Fine Arts to earn some cash. Had my parents known, they would have stoned me. Still, perhaps because of our common past with the Arabs, we hold the family in very high regard and are very close.

'In my case, I was very close to my sister Myriam until she went abroad to study. I did my military service in the Nahal Brigade, where I met a lieutenant in the special forces, in a Palsar unit, a Sephardic Jew who I eventually married. I was madly in love with him, and I desperately wanted to have his child. But Eliah was very reluctant, and spent a lot of time in the north, crossing into Lebanon to fight against Hezbollah – you're familiar with the situation. Three years ago he disappeared in combat, and shortly thereafter I was notified they'd recovered his body, with clear signs of torture. He'd been emasculated, something they often do to their prisoners, even dead soldiers.

'I felt very alone, and one day I ran into a friend from university who'd married a Lubavitcher. Little by little, they brought me into their way of living Judaism, and it was a great consolation. You may think I'm lying, but I don't miss my past life.'

Laurent raised his hand to interrupt her. 'All right, I understand what you're doing in that shop, and believe me when I say I'm sorry about your husband. But now the rest makes even less sense: why did you come to Saint-Chartier? Were you taking a sabbatical from your orthodox life?'

'That's because of my sister Myriam. As I said, she'd gone abroad for school, to Buenos Aires, which has a huge Jewish population . . .'

'Ah, Buenos Aires . . . so I suppose this is where Carlos Shennan makes his entrance.'

'Exactly. No doubt you also know that Shennan was a very successful arms trafficker, specifically in chemical weapons, and he didn't turn up his nose at any clients. On one occasion Myriam was invited to a big party in honour of a Jewish Argentine painter, and there she met Shennan, who turned out to be the host. I don't think I need to explain the effect he has on women when he deploys all his tactics of seduction. My sister Myriam is stunningly beautiful but, unlike me, she's quite innocent and tends to believe what she's told.

'A few months later, she wrote and told me all about it: she said Shennan was the love of her life, and she didn't care if he was married, they were going to go travelling together . . . Through my late husband, I had my contacts in the army, and didn't have trouble getting my hands on Shennan's notorious file. As you can imagine, the first thing I did was act like a big sister. I called Myriam to alert her and suggested she get away from him as soon as possible, but it was already too late: she was pregnant with his child and sounded deliriously happy. I begged her to leave him and come back, but she told me I was just jealous because I hadn't been able to have a child with Eliah. I hung up on her and didn't hear from her again until much later.

'Predictably, Shennan wasn't thrilled about the pregnancy and began to distance himself from Myriam with various excuses: his business, his family, his endless trips . . . all the while, the pregnancy progressed, and Myriam felt increasingly abandoned. She decided to visit

Shennan at his office with her already very noticeable belly. When they met, he took on the cold, emotionless manner he was famous for in these situations: he said their relationship was no longer the same and even cynically told her she'd changed. He advised her to abort. He opened his desk drawer and handed her twenty thousand dollars. Myriam spat at him, threw the dollars in his face and marched out.

'Her pregnancy was difficult and she didn't have a penny. Out of pride, she didn't let me know and wound up living in destitution, but determined to carry the child to term. Her health deteriorated until in the seventh month of her pregnancy she was rushed to the emergency room.

'To make a long story short, the girl (because it was a girl) was stillborn, and my sister, as a result of a poor diet, a lack of adequate medicine and the sorrow of knowing her daughter had died, fell into a state of depression and had to be hospitalised. She'd given my name when she registered at border control, so the Israeli embassy tracked me down, and when I learnt of her situation, I left to find her right away. When I saw her I understood that she'd never again be the same: my sister was lifeless, deathly pale, with glassy eyes and trembling hands. As soon as she recognised me she told me she wanted to call her daughter Yael, and I broke down and cried, holding her until nightfall. With our community, we managed to get her admitted to a house run by the Lubavitchers, and I hope to bring her here as soon as possible. Now do you understand why I went to Saint-Chartier? I went to find Shennan.'

'To kill him?' asked Laurent, struck by the story. 'Tell me the truth. If it was you, I won't say a word, because I'd understand, even though I don't approve.'

Yael shook her head.

'No, I really don't know what for. I had several plans. On the one hand, I did want to kill him, or at least make him suffer, to find some legal or fiscal irregularity to bring him down – anything to hurt him. I spied on him, I tailed him and I witnessed many of his infidelities and strange meetings. At night at home I gathered all the information I could on him. I even sent letters to those leeches the Monattis. I used a false name and said I was an employee of his, tormented by the secrets of his chemical weapons companies, and I slung as much mud as I could. The Israeli intelligence services found out I'd requested his file, and they contacted me, ordering me to keep an eye on him as best I could. So every two weeks I had to submit a report in Blois, Bourges or Tours. Meanwhile, I'd even thought of punishing Shennan through his family, but when I saw his daughters and wife I knew I just couldn't.

'Shortly before the party, I'd decided I should return to Israel. I couldn't go on with this foolishness. My plans went against everything I'd been taught in synagogue. I decided I'd simply tell him he was a selfish bastard, and that one day soon, when he was a decrepit old man, he'd be alone with nothing but the memory of the women he'd used to make himself feel more like a man. But in the end, when I finally had him in front of me, I lost my cool. I shouted Myriam's story to his face, and slapped him, trying to convey through my eyes the hatred I felt.'

Laurent stroked his chin. 'I apologise for being so brusque earlier in the shop. I never imagined any of what you've just told me; I'm truly very sorry for Myriam, though perhaps you could have told me earlier. Two questions. When you left for long stretches at a time, was that because you were coming back here to work in the shop? I'd been imagining ghastly things involving the Israeli Secret Service.'

'Yes, I'd come back here, explaining my absences by saying my sister was ill, which was partly true,' admitted Yael. 'And the other question? I suppose you want to know why you, right?' Before he could respond, she launched into another explanation. 'I hadn't been with a man since Eliah died. I'm a woman and a Yemenite, we're a sensual people, and before my husband my life was somewhat dissolute in that regard. The day we met at Caroline's – remember? – I found you attractive, and I liked that you knew a thing or two about us. I often saw you walk past my door, and I won't deny I even fantasised about the future. But – don't get angry – you're not Jewish, and for me that carries a lot of weight at the moment. Years ago it wouldn't have mattered, but right now I need my faith. That may not always be the case, but for the time being it is.

'The day I slept over at your place, I meant it as a farewell. I liked you quite a bit, I felt a real affection. You'd been really good to me, and I thought you deserved that night of love. And I can't lie, I wanted to treat myself, too, not just out of physical attraction, but also as a sort of last hurrah. My rabbi has decided I have to marry, and I need to follow his recommendations on my future spouse. But I've had a glimpse, and I know it will be hard, very hard. That's why I want to say again that it was all my fault, Laurent. You're a wonderful man, and I'll never deserve you. Forgive me.'

Laurent was a magnanimous, generous sort. 'I accept your apology, and I appreciate your finally opening up to me, though I still think you were wrong not to do so earlier. Probably everything would have been easier that way. As for my not being Jewish, isn't that what the mikveh are for?' he joked. 'But seriously, I'm sure you're right when you say that what can't be can't be, and that there's no one wiser than providence in bringing people together or pulling them apart. Don't worry, Yael, I won't bother you again, and I'll cross you off the list. The bad thing is, I don't have any suspects left.'

Yael smiled mischievously. 'I'm sorry to disagree, but from everything you've just told me, I've come up with a sketch of the culprit. But it wouldn't be right for me to tell you their name. It's just a hunch with no evidence to back it up, and besides, I can't help sympathising with their actions.'

'How can you say that? Please, give me a clue, even a small one,' Laurent begged her.

'No, really, I can't. Don't insist. Maybe one day, but not now. I should go, Laurent. It saddens me we won't see each other again, though who knows . . . Let me give you a hug.'

And as she did she showed a feeling she'd never shown before.

For the first time since he'd met her, Laurent felt Yael's warmth. Meanwhile, the waitress looked on, entertained and oblivious to their sad story.

REVIEWING SUSPECTS IN
LA COCADRILLE

A week had gone by since his short trip to Paris, and Laurent hadn't found time to go over his notes, so his investigation had reached a standstill. He went down to the living room to get to work, but he realised with a shiver that an unpleasant cold had settled into the house. It was December, and he'd forgotten to order fuel for the boiler.

Annoyed, he phoned the fuel suppliers in La Châtre. They were conscientious, obliging people, but they said they were overwhelmed with orders, since no one wanted to be without heat over the approaching holidays. They couldn't tell him with any certainty until the following day when the tanker truck would arrive.

Laurent wasn't the sort to be daunted by such a trifle, and decided that La Cocadrille could become his temporary study. He'd talk to Le Juanch about using the little spot in the back of the tavern, a pleasant corner consisting of a room that had been extended with a glass wall and a large stone hearth on the inner wall that they kept permanently lit. Of course, he'd have lunch, tea and dinner right there.

On the way to the tavern he passed by the city hall. The mayor was trying to post some pages on the outside bulletin board. Laurent stopped for one of those brief, inconsequential conversations that are the soul of small towns.

'Morning, Monsieur de Rodergues,' said the mayor. 'Looks like you're heading to Le Juanch's. How I envy you . . . My wife's worried about my cholesterol, and has forbidden me to set foot inside if she's not with me.'

'Good morning, Monsieur Jancelle. Don't tell me you're announcing some new tax, or worse, some new septic tank regulations. I'll have you know I've had it up to here with that issue.'

'I assure you, I don't know anyone, myself included, who isn't sick of it,' laughed the mayor in reply. 'But no, what I'm posting are the results of the latest land auction. Lands that were seized by the bank or belonged to farmers who died without a will or next of kin. I expect Tonton Boussard will be especially happy when he sees them.'

'Why's that?' asked Laurent, intrigued.

'He successfully bid on the Chanceau farm, with 126 hectares, and in my opinion, he got it for a song.'

'What does he want it for? He already has more land than he needs, and he lives alone. He's going to work himself to death.'

'Farmers are like that, Monsieur de Rodergues. They complain all day, but they're always buying up land. As I understand it, Tonton's had his eye on the plot for years, but he thought he might not get it, because Monsieur Shennan also wanted to bid. Apparently his lawyer, Jablard, on the express orders of Madame Shennan, stopped bidding, against the instructions he gave before he died. That's understandable, though. Madame's in charge now.'

Laurent hesitated a few seconds before asking his question. 'Do you know what Shennan planned to do with that land, Monsieur Jancelle?'

'No, I can only guess that perhaps he wanted it to grow barley and other grains for the beer he was making with Le Juanch. Or maybe he just wanted them to annoy Tonton. The truth is, I have no idea, but as you know he was constantly dreaming up projects.' He turned to leave. 'Well, I've got work to do, I'm going back inside. Take care, Monsieur.'

La Cocadrille was half full that morning. The cold made people not want to go outside, and it still wasn't lunchtime. Laurent explained his problem to Le Juanch, who, with his usual good humour, led him to the back room. But first he gave him some advice: 'Don't order beer this morning, Laurent. Have a light wine instead, a Chablis, for example. Today's menu will be heavy, for men with hair on their chest. And on no account should you miss it.'

From his table Laurent smiled, and once he was alone, he began to spread out his papers. He reread everything twice, jotting down notes that he immediately crossed out. Frustrated, he put his head in his hands to see if it helped him concentrate, but he still couldn't come to any conclusions.

He decided to write the list out again, adding details and questions he hadn't foreseen the first time, which he gleaned from the information he'd gathered. Next he'd examine each suspect and cross them out if he couldn't find any possible sign of guilt in them. But first he needed to order a very strong coffee, so that he wouldn't fall into a coma after the gargantuan feast he knew Le Juanch was preparing for lunch.

After a long while working intensely, adding his latest conjectures and inferences, Laurent arrived at the following conclusions about his suspects.

Jean-Pierre Gimbault: he'd strike him off the list. Not only had he come across as convincing during their meeting, Laurent also couldn't see what he had to gain from Shennan's death. On the contrary, Gimbault would be adversely affected, since he'd indicated that they'd discussed potential future plans.

True, Gimbault had, on the other hand, known about the secret passage, as he'd been organising the festival since he was a young man. That position had given him access to the château from top to bottom on several occasions, not to mention the old floor plans of the premises provided by the Historical Archives of Châteauroux, which clearly indicated the passageway.

Silently Le Juanch slipped in and left some warm punch and cheese petits fours on the table. Laurent, absorbed in his work, didn't noticed his fleeting presence, but when he saw the cup, he raised it an imaginary toast and sipped the punch, which, like everything that came out of that kitchen, was of the highest quality. He couldn't help eating all the flaky pastries one after another. And with his strength restored, he set about tackling the next suspects on his list, the outlandish instrument-maker couple.

Jeannette and Claude Monatti: Laurent couldn't deny he couldn't stand them and would have happily saddled them with any crime at all. They were a despicable pair of petty con artists who pretended to be artisans, but in fact brazenly lived off slander, defamation and a motley assortment of scams and swindles. Still, they weren't guilty of anything more than that.

He crossed them off the list too. They were vultures, but they didn't have the instinct or the guts to commit a crime like Shennan's murder. The murder – because even though Laurent still lacked any conclusive evidence, he was ever more convinced the death was premeditated and malicious – bore the traces of genius, whereas the Monattis were rank amateurs.

Thierry Chanteau: Laurent closed his eyes in thought after reading his name. In the forester's case too, he lacked any evidence against him, though he did have two possible motives for committing the murder: first, his brother's suicide, which Thierry didn't blame Shennan for, but which Shennan had been involved in as one of Thierry's sister-in-law's lovers. Second, the question of Shennan's advances on Solange Vartel, Thierry's current girlfriend. The *arboriste-grimpeur* had admitted to feeling irritated and jealous, and while Solange had defended his innocence, during his meeting with her, Laurent had caught her in a statement that he found unbelievable: she'd claimed that Thierry had never set foot in the château. But that seemed impossible, especially since during the restoration the area was in chaos, with people coming and going unmonitored.

Last, there was one more detail to take into account: Thierry had a way with children, and Shennan's daughters were crazy for him, because he was constantly performing tricks and stunts. Whenever he showed up, the three girls stuck to him like glue and laughed at his jokes, since his circus experience and innate affability made him a natural with them. Laurent knew them well, and he'd bet that the little girls, to win him over, had told him about the passageway. This was just conjecture, and he had no evidence to back it up, but it meant that not only did Thierry have one of the strongest reasons to hate Shennan, he was also the one most capable of killing him. And even though his looks and his limpid eyes made him look like an angel, Laurent, who hadn't had occasion to see him angry, could easily imagine him turning as diabolical as Lucifer himself.

Suddenly another detail against Thierry occurred to Laurent as he remembered he was involved with the circus: 'Of course,' he whispered aloud, 'his profession, and his work at the Cirque Bidon, require a high degree of dexterity, and no doubt he knows his way around a tightrope, and wouldn't have had any trouble climbing up somewhere to get into the château when no one was looking.' Then he threw his pencil down on the table in frustration. 'No, that's impossible. The garden was packed, the security team were roving the grounds and Thierry was probably with people the whole time. It couldn't have been him. His motives weren't serious enough to murder Shennan, and even Solange herself admitted that Shennan had long ago given up on her.'

In the end he struck his name from the list, and turned his eyes back to the page where he'd written 'Final Suspects'. Below this heading he had written nothing. He got up to go to the bathroom and chat for a bit in the kitchen. He liked to watch Le Juanch and his two assistants cook and maybe nab a bite to eat while he was at it. A quarter of an hour later, after a successful kitchen raid, he returned to his work station.

The next name was Solange Vartel, who'd turned out to be the most enigmatic and underrated suspect on his list. Months back Laurent would have sworn to anyone that Mademoiselle Vartel was the quintessence of virtue, a little songbird covered in onyx and ruby feathers who only opened her golden beak to make a beautiful trill. But no: once again outward appearances, what we think we see in others, had turned out to be so many layers of an enormous onion.

Laurent knew that Solange had nothing to do with Shennan's death. She was amused by his doting, and no doubt he was a romantic trophy on her list, but nothing more. She'd noted that outside a brief period of embarrassing pushiness, when he sought to reprise that single night of love or sex, Shennan had left her in peace. Laurent therefore guessed that what she'd interpreted as an infatuation on his part was simply the flattering reading that some women make of men's attention. From what he knew of Shennan, he felt certain he hadn't been at all obsessed with her. What had bothered the man was simply that his lover's tricks hadn't turned the landscape architect into another admirer. As for Solange, she'd never know this 'romantic obsession' was nothing more than a game for him, a simple pastime. Laurent laughed as he imagined his neighbour trying to think up a ploy to win over Solange. And because Shennan was a man of tangible, immediate things, he would have given up, slightly annoyed that he couldn't achieve his objective.

As for the outright lie that Solange had told him about Thierry, that was excusable and could be called love, or simple friendship, because ultimately lying for a loved one is not a sin or misdeed, especially when the person who prompted the lie is innocent, as Thierry was.

He crossed her off his list, thinking that no doubt Cathy would say he was a pushover who'd fallen under the spell of Solange's apparent fragility. Maybe so, but even though he lacked poetic gifts, Laurent was no novice in love and could have spoken at length about melancholy and the moods of the heart.

The next candidate on his list was the wildcard in that deck, his friend Tonton Boussard, with his menagerie of do-it-yourself taxidermy. Looking back on their meeting, Laurent decided he must not look very intelligent, because people kept trying to feed him falsehoods left and right. Even that boorish farmer with his coypu hides had had the nerve to lie to him about the passageway.

On the other hand, aside from his primitive way of looking at life and his phobias about everything, on the list of suspects he was really the only one who had something to gain from the man's death: once Shennan was out of the auction, Tonton had acquired an enormous estate at a ridiculous price. Still, Laurent had trouble believing that Boussard could attain the degree of criminal sophistication that a death like Shennan's entailed. Tonton Boussard was also set free.

Yves Rataille: he was without a doubt the only one who shouldn't be on the list in the first place. He'd added and interviewed him just to get to Ahmed El-Kubri. Besides, not only had the businessman not benefitted from Shennan's death, he was actually worse off, because Shennan had promised new projects that now would never take shape. Add to that the fact that he'd acquired several important projects in the area through his work on the château and Shennan's contacts, and the only conclusion was that Yves Rataille, far from harbouring murderous hatred, could have only felt gratitude toward the man. Therefore there was no point in wasting another second wondering about him.

Ahmed El-Kubri: unfortunately, thought Laurent, the individual most likely to be the murderer was the hardest to incriminate. El-Kubri had turned out to be a diehard Salafist who hated anything that didn't fit in his world. Not only was he the one who'd torn down the false wall that led to the passageway, but he'd been publicly slapped by Shennan, who, to add insult to injury, had used the language of the Prophet to threaten his family.

But as Yves Rataille had told him and Cathy had confirmed, he was the subject of an active search by Interpol and the CIA, so he couldn't have made it through the château gate on the day of the party – he'd have set off alarms from miles away.

Pia de La Tressondière: she was perhaps the only one on

his list who had truly been straight with him. She was also one of the few who'd earned his respect.

While Pia had plenty of reason to despise Shennan, she was too smart to let herself be carried away by spite. Cold and calculating, with the intellectual faculties needed to devise such an exquisitely planned death, she was also, as Laurent could see, a woman of great sensitivity and passion, emotions she hid under her mask of sneering Paris snobbery.

The image of Hercule Poirot came to mind, sententiously repeating the line *'Cherchez la femme!'* Yes, perhaps the instigation had come from a woman, but the execution seemed to require a man, and none of the women involved in the case had much physical strength to speak of.

He drew a thick red line through the architect's name. Only one name remained, that of a woman who had meant a great deal to Laurent, a woman he had come to despise as fiercely as he once thought he loved her.

Yael Golani: after the Mauritanian, she was the one with the most motives to hate Shennan. Because of him, her little sister had been institutionalised, and her niece had been stillborn largely as a result of his indifference. That's what had led her to spend all those months observing him from the house she'd rented across from the château, and ultimately to confront him and hit him the night of the party. Also worth noting was that, like every non-Orthodox Israeli citizen, Yael had military experience. Not only had she been stationed on the northern border, which implied she had abundant experience under fire – she herself had said as much – but her late husband had been in the Israeli special forces. What's more, Yael had the intelligence, the motives, the mettle, the physical training and a flair for the convoluted that would have allowed her to plot the crime. If that weren't enough, she'd been the Shennans' neighbour for long enough to pick up any other necessary information.

Still, she wasn't the culprit. Laurent felt certain she was innocent, and not just because she'd assured him she was, but above all because the security team had seen her leave before the crime was committed, as Cathy had confirmed.

Once again he took his red marker and drew several lines through her name until it was no longer legible. Then he tore out the page, crumpled it up into a ball and threw it into a distant rubbish bin, not making a basket. He felt discouraged. There were no more suspects left standing. He had no one, and still Laurent believed, despite what everyone else said, that his friend Carlos had been murdered.

From the other room he heard Le Juanch calling out to him to clear away his things because the food was on the way.

Laurent did as he was told, and as Le Juanch set the dishes on the table, he asked with his usual chattiness, 'How's the investigation coming along? Figured out who did it yet?'

'How do you know what I'm doing?' asked Laurent with a start. 'Who told you?'

'Who do you think? Tartarin. He told us all about it after your visit to the station. He came for the Town Preservation and Promotion Society meeting, and after a few beers he blabbed so much he had to sleep on a cot I keep upstairs for emergencies.'

'But . . . that's unacceptable!' Laurent was beside himself with indignation. 'I told him it was a private matter that called for the utmost discretion! What else did that knuckle-dragger say, and how many people heard him?'

'I don't know . . .' Le Juanch stroked his chin thoughtfully. 'Honestly, the place was packed. As for what he said, there wasn't too much.'

But seeing the look of rage on Laurent's face, he began to twist his kitchen rag awkwardly, realising he'd stuck his foot firmly in his mouth and might not be able to take it back out.

'Look, don't get angry, we're like a great big family here, and nothing will leave this restaurant, but the truth is, he told us everything. He even told us about your list. In fact, along with Sandrine Jamet's tavern in Saint-Août, we've set up a pool betting on who your culprit will be. Tartarin's bet a double round of Carterius Magnum for all the regulars that his theory, that it was all an accident, is going to win out. Even Thierry and Tonton are betting, and they're implicated.'

Laurent was mute with rage, but finally he spoke. 'This is beyond the pale. No respect for privacy and discretion! This is humiliating – I must be a laughing stock.'

'Not at all, Laurent.' Le Juanch put his arm around his shoulder. 'You can't imagine how much fun we've had thanks to you. It's like we're all playing Monopoly! Madame Triflerre's embroidery group has also joined in, with different variations, and every Thursday we get together to see how the ranking is going. At the moment your friend, Mademoiselle Yael, is winning. Honestly, we thought you knew, because even your new girlfriend has money in the pool.'

This news was too much for Laurent. 'Which girlfriend would that be? Because I don't recall having one.'

'Don't be like that, Laurent. You can't lie to me, not to your Le Juanch. I mean the curly blonde beauty, with that killer body and those huge green eyes. By the way, you should know we all think she's great for you. Hopefully she won't brush you off like Mademoiselle Yael. The morning she left your place she stopped here for a coffee – she said the one you made wasn't strong enough. She saw us drawing up the pool and asked about it, so we told her. She laughed and bet ten euros on Mademoiselle Yael, five on Mademoiselle Solange and two on the architect in Paris. Personally I'm leaning toward the worker from Mauritania, Thierry's betting on Tonton, and Tonton says it was the skinny Chinese secretary.'

The fact that Cathy was having a ball taking part in the pool, that even Thierry and Tonton had placed bets . . . Anyway, the damage was done, and he might was well draw his conclusions as soon as possible and find a stable, paid occupation.

'It's fine, it's nothing. Don't worry about it, just let me have lunch in silence. Lord knows I need it,' Laurent pleaded, crestfallen and feeling thoroughly ridiculous.

'I'm sorry, I didn't realise you'd get so upset,' said Le Juanch contritely, though he quickly seemed to perk up. 'And while we're at it, since you're going over your files, couldn't you give me a clue for Thursday?'

The look Laurent gave Le Juanch could have wiped out all

the legions of Scipio Africanus at a single blow. The barkeep, tail between his legs, scurried off to tend to his stovetop.

Laurent, with all that food before him, let himself be intoxicated by its aroma, which is always soothing. As much as he hated to admit it, ultimately he'd have to agree that Tartarin was right.

THIRD CHORD

A LETTER

Not four months after the dark day of his disappointment in La Cocadrille, Laurent received a certified letter signed by Xiao Li: Madame Shennan and her daughters would be visiting the château and asked him to call on them to discuss his acceptance of the inheritance.

Laurent hadn't expected to hear from Madame Mayumi and had completely forgotten about the gift from Carlos Shennan's estate. He reread the letter several times. The prospect of seeing the victim's wife was daunting, even if he had to admit that she was the only one, aside from Cathy, who'd spoken up for him. He also knew it would be sad seeing the girls, who were now fatherless. No doubt they'd have grown quite a bit over the last year, he thought with a rueful smile.

Ever since he'd reviewed his list of suspects for the last time, just before finding out the entire town had been following his investigation, Laurent had tried to put the whole thing out of his mind by intensely occupying his time. He was again exercising, taking brisk hour-long walks every day and going to La Berthenoux to ride three days a week. For practical reasons, as well as out of financial necessity, he decided to open up the building behind the vicarage that housed his grandfather's workshop, with all its tools still meticulously in order. From the mayor he heard about some courses in traditional crafts and grants offered by the prefecture that led to his professional reinvention as a *sabotier*, or clog maker, a job that left him a lot of free time, since despite showing himself to be a remarkable craftsman, his product did not yet have mass appeal.

His love life followed a meandering course to which Laurent was not averse: Cathy stepped in to fill many of the roles usually reserved for a girlfriend but wisely did so with a light touch. She never imposed her presence, and cleverly punctuated it with absences largely made necessary by her work. Laurent thus had to put up with long periods of abstinence, sprinkled with calls or surprises that she ably rationed to whet his appetite. Cathy was often on the road, and many of their encounters took place in other cities, like Orléans, Paris or Moulins. Then he'd return to the vicarage and eagerly await the amusing postcards she sent from abroad, which he'd grown quite fond of. His love life was peaceful, and from Olympus a buxom Aphrodite looked on in satisfaction as a devoted Cupid massaged her bunions.

Although he hadn't managed to finish his memoir, or even write a single line, he'd at least come to the conclusion that he wanted to stay in Saint-Chartier. He publicly admitted defeat at the hands of Tartarin, and even raised a glass to his health on each of the two rounds that Tartarin had promised to pay if his theory on Shennan's death won out. That night, once he'd admitted that Carlos's death couldn't have been anything but an unfortunate accident, he put on a good face and accepted the ribbing from the regulars. They even begged him to come up with another, equally entertaining idea as soon as possible.

In short, he'd led a peaceful life until Madame Shennan's letter arrived asking him to meet with her three days later. Laurent was shaken again. He sighed: he clearly couldn't turn down the inheritance, and he realised he had to start thinking about where to store it and how to make the most of it.

Suddenly he recalled that Madame Mayumi knew nothing about his investigation, and it occurred to him that she might be interested in hearing about it. Laurent thought for a long while, weighing this possibility, and in the end he decided to go to La Châtre: he wanted to buy some presents for Shennan's daughters, as well as order a bouquet of flowers for Madame Mayumi.

IN THE MUSIC ROOM

The day of the meeting arrived, and Laurent endeavoured to dress nicely so he'd be as presentable as possible to Madame Mayumi. He hoped she and her daughters liked the gifts he'd made: he'd worked hard creating a pair of clogs for each of the girls and another for their mother. He was proud of his work, and even though he could only eye the measurements, he could at least take comfort in the thought that wooden clogs always had to be worn a bit loose. Each pair was painted a different colour and had one of girls' names carved in the side. For Madame's, he decided to look up her family crest in Japan, which turned out to be easier than he expected: to his surprise, the history of her family's heroic deeds and its role in the country's military past took up several pages. Apparently, her ancestors had been quite remorseless.

When he arrived at the château he was met by Yammei, the Chinese cook, who could now get by in French, though with a heavy Chinese accent.

'Bonjour, Monsieur Laurent,' she said. 'Madame is awaiting you in the music room. Follow me, please.'

Laurent often ran into her in town, so he felt emboldened to tell her she looked sad, and that made her burst into tears. After she managed to calm down a bit, she choked out a reply.

'I'll never see Tum or the girls again, I just know it! I'm filled with sadness, and Khun Suan is, too,' she sobbed, opening the door to the music room. Laurent wanted to ask what she meant by that, but before he could, she had already closed the door, and a familiar voice called out to him from a corner of the chamber.

'Monsieur de Rodergues, so nice to see you again. Please, come and sit down. What can I get you?'

The voice belonged to none other than Monsieur Jablard, who had already taken over the bar cart, as Laurent saw from the glass of whiskey in his hand. It struck him as a rather generous pour for that hour of the morning.

'No, thanks, it's a bit early for me, Monsieur Jablard,' answered Laurent. He wasn't at all thrilled to see the lawyer.

'You're quite right, it's still early, but it's hard to find whiskey like this in France. Carlos had it brought over from his ancestors' village, in north-western Ireland, and believe me, it's worth a morning tipple. Madame Shennan, who knows my weaknesses, told me to help myself before running off to attend to a small domestic matter. She'll be right here, and asked me to tell you to make yourself at home.'

'I suppose if Madame asked you to come, it's to discuss the inheritance? If she wants to retract the offer

I'd understand, and wouldn't feel offended in the least,' Laurent took the opportunity to say.

'Your attitude does you honour, Monsieur, but that's not what it's about. I think Madame has found a solution for you that you'll find very appealing. Before she gets here, let me sit down and get you caught up. Now, what I'm about to tell you,' he said, taking a seat in the chair across from Laurent, 'is confidential, and I'm only explaining this because you're an interested party, and because you'd find out in a moment anyway from Monsieur Shennan's widow, who was never in favour of this medieval caprice of her husband's, as you well know. And now, as you can imagine, it's not just a place she dislikes, it's the place where her husband died under such peculiar circumstances. So you won't be surprised to learn that she feels positively repulsed by it.'

Laurent didn't much like the direction the conversation was taking, but he couldn't deny he wanted to know where it would lead.

'I'm sorry she's not comfortable in Saint-Chartier, but I understand perfectly,' he said. 'What does Madame Shennan plan to do, if I may ask?'

The lawyer had the irritating habit of playing with his glass, which he had now placed on his belly.

'Soon it will no longer be a secret,' he said. 'Madame wanted to sell it right away just to get rid of it. But two things have conspired against her: in the first place, the extent of her late husband's investment in the château makes it very difficult to sell at market prices; and second, her husband, who was sly as a fox, had foreseen this situation. He arranged his will so that, with the exception of a few minor items and a sum intended for distant relatives, his faithful secretary and various charitable organisations he was a member of, his wife would get most of his property – almost all, in fact. But the château, and when I say the château I mean the estate and everything in it, along with the lands and other houses and farms he owned in the area, was to be inherited in equal shares by his three daughters.

'Madame Shennan has usufructuary rights to the château, and as the girls' guardian, she's responsible for maintaining it with the rents from the inheritance she receives in their name. Their daughters, in turn, can't sell the château until the youngest of the three comes of age, and even then only if they all agree. Should any of them wish to hold onto the property, they have the right to buy out the other shares – but only at the price their father has indicated in a sealed envelope kept by the town notary, whatever that may be, which can't be modified. As you can see, Shennan knew human nature quite well, and was furthermore possessed of a peculiar sense of humour. I bet you're curious about that price in that envelope, as am I, but I can guarantee that none of the daughters will ever dare open it. If Shennan wanted to ensure the château remained in his family line, he's succeeded, at least for a generation.'

Laurent looked at the bar cart. 'It's early, but hearing all this I feel like Carlos Shennan is practically here with us, smoking a cigar and laughing at his own will. I'm going to get myself a drink like yours.' And, pouring the amber nectar into his glass, he asked, 'And until the girls come of age, what does Madame intend to do with the château, if she has no interest in living here?'

'Madame Mayumi is a woman of rare resources and intelligence,' replied Jablard, 'and I think that, when it comes down to it, she can be much more ruthless than her husband. With all due respect to Monsieur Shennan, since she won't waste all the time and money her husband devoted to pursuing the fairer sex, I daresay she'll be much more efficient. I don't know how she did it, but within a week the estate will become a high-end Château Relais establishment run by a hotel chain belonging to one of those exasperating recent multimillionaires from Russia. The château has been rented out with all its decorations and fittings – even the sheets and towels will stay where they are. After all, it meets the highest standards of hotel quality, and everything is already embroidered or engraved with the emblem of the château, so for the Russians the deal couldn't be easier.

'Madame has persuaded them that the location is ideal, and in addition to obtaining a very lucrative annual rent, she's managed to have them undertake the maintenance, with a comprehensive insurance policy covering everything, down to the tiniest salt cellar. With her perseverance, and with Xiao Li's help, she's inventoried and photographed each object. The icing on the cake is that the rent is guaranteed for twenty years, with draconian penalties should the Russians withdraw before the end of the contract. I can tell you, Monsieur, I wouldn't want to have to negotiate my fees with her. Luckily Shennan thought well of me and Madame seems willing to continue with my services. And part of that whole caboodle is your inheritance, which is what Madame wants to speak to you about.'

Just then, as though she'd been listening in on them and knew the moment to make her star entrance had arrived, she walked into the room with her ineffable elegance. Laurent found her somewhat thinner, with more wrinkles around the eyes, no doubt because combing through the tangle of Shennan's businesses was like untying a titanium Gordian knot.

Madame Mayumi offered him her hand, and Laurent took it and raised it to his lips, which brought a smile to her face.

'I'd almost forgotten your gallantry, Monsieur de Rodergues. In the world I move about in now, if someone brought my hand to their lips I'd fear they were trying to rob me of a ring, or bite me. You'd be a smash in my country.' With a good-natured smile she turned toward Jablard.

'And you would too, my dear, if you were a few years younger and had a better haircut. Please, sit down, both of you.' She looked at them for a moment, and when she realised they were drinking, said, 'Remind me later, before you go, to have all the Irish whiskey left in the house sent to you two. As I imagine you're aware, Monsieur Laurent, we're soon going to rent out this château to some Russians who will turn it into a hotel, but in the inventory we've provided them we only counted the wine, not the spirits. If I'm not mistaken, we still have four cases of that whiskey, and I hope you'll do me the honour of accepting two cases each, on the condition that you raise a glass to Carlos once in a while. I'm sure he would have liked that.'

'From the bottom of my heart, I thank you for this undeserved gift,' said the lawyer, overjoyed by this unexpected present. 'And believe me, Madame, if this whiskey belonged to me and I were up in heaven, I'd like nothing more than to look down and see it being enjoyed by people who can appreciate it.'

'Carlos, in heaven?' The widow gave a laugh. 'You must be joking, Jablard. That's the last place I'd look for him. But it's very kind of you to say, I appreciate that. Now, on to the matter at hand: the collection of equestrian gear for Monsieur de Rodergues, who I assume is aware of what will become of the château.' When the lawyer nodded, Madame Mayumi turned to Laurent. 'Monsieur Jablard told me you were reluctant to accept what Carlos left you, so I've found a possible solution that requires only that you accept it.'

'Madame, I am honoured by the gift,' said Laurent with humility, 'but I'm familiar with Carlos's collection, which is enormous, and as you know, the vicarage where I live isn't large enough to store hardly any of it. If you don't mind, I'd prefer to choose a few saddles and tack. With that I'd be quite satisfied.'

Madame Mayumi shook her head. 'Under no circumstances. I realise you're unable to store it all in your home, but it's a marvellous collection, and it wouldn't be right to break it up, so I took the liberty of telling the tenants you'd be willing to lease it to them for five thousand euros a year, plus the right to use the saddles, stirrups and whatever else you need, whenever you like. They readily agreed, and I think it's a good solution. The collection is together, you're still the owner, and owning it will provide you money to cover your taxes, fuel and then some. What's more, you'll be able to use any pieces you wish, and there's no better place to display them than where Carlos put them. No matter how you look at it, Laurent, you can't deny it's a good deal.'

He put his hands up and accepted defeat. 'I surrender. You're right, and the solution you've found would make Salomon look like an apprentice by comparison. Now I understand why Monsieur Jablard says he's afraid to negotiate with you.'

'Is that what he says? Well, Monsieur Jablard, don't give me any ideas. So, as you can see, Monsieur de Rodergues has agreed to my proposal, so please make it official in the documents you're drawing up. And don't worry, I won't forget my promise about the whiskey.' The lawyer came over to kiss her hand, copying Laurent's gesture, and as Laurent had gotten up to say goodbye, shook his hand as well.

As Jablard headed to the door, Madame Mayumi pressed a button, and a few seconds later Tum appeared, every bit as pretty as Laurent remembered, but a bit glum, perhaps for the same reasons Yammei had mentioned.

'Tum, see Monsieur Jablard out, and tell Yammei to bring me a hibiscus tea. Monsieur de Rodergues, I don't suppose you want another, do you?'

Tum turned to Laurent. 'Good morning, Monsieur de Rodergues. The girls would very much like to see you. Madame, they asked permission to take him to their game room.'

'Yes, of course, but don't keep Monsieur Jablard waiting. Go on, off with you,' said Madame.

Once Tum had left, Laurent turned to Madame Mayumi.

'I've always been intrigued by that girl's story. She's exceptionally pretty, but every time I see her she gives the impression her soul is pierced by sorrow, despite the fact that you treat her practically like a daughter.'

That remark caught Madame off guard. It was the first time since he'd known her that she was slow to react.

'What can I say, Laurent? I love her and I've cared for her like a daughter. She came to me, or I to her, when she was only thirteen. Her story is very sad, but if sadness were a plant, for some decades now it would be the most widely grown plant in Burma.'

Just then Yammei arrived, serving the tea in a delicate tea set of Chinese porcelain, white on the inside and flamboyantly red on the outside, with a golden dragon at the bottom of the cup that went remarkably well with the reddish hue of the tea. Madame noticed Laurent looking at the set.

'Westerners never seem to understand that tea isn't just for drinking. It's a way of reflection that should inspire and feed all the senses,' she remarked. Then she began to tell him the story of Tum. 'As I suppose you know, my husband's business involved constant dealings with military regimes in many countries about which he didn't speak and I didn't ask. Before we had the girls, sometimes I'd go with him on his trips to Burma, because I'd heard stories about the country from my grandfather, who served there in the war, and it had always intrigued me. On one of those trips, while Carlos was working, his clients arranged for me to have a tour of the country, with a translator and an escort. They took me to several places – Mandalay, Bagan and other names I'd now have to make an effort to recall.

'Burma is a beautiful country with wonderful handicrafts. I was interested in antiques, especially household shrines and chests, but more than anything I wanted to get an antique court dress, because their embroidered fabrics have a richness and exuberance that's hard to describe. One of the driver's contacts gave us an address north of Mandalay, and we went there in spite of the danger – because, as you know, alongside the ruling military junta, and the disorder everywhere, Burma is full of different ethnicities, and at least five of them are at war with the central government, which also has to fight against various drug-running clans, typically led by Chinese descendants of the Kuomintang.

'When we reached the village, we came upon a group of people arguing. One of them was a Spanish or Italian nun shouting at the top of her lungs at a tiny but dangerous-looking man who was holding a girl by the wrist. The girl couldn't stop crying. I was upset by the scene, and I asked the translator to explain what was going on. It turned out that the nun came from a congregation that ran a dress-making workshop in the town, open to people of any ethnicity or religion, that sought to give girls and women a trade, so they wouldn't fall into the sex trafficking networks that ran the area. Sex is a business: everyone's involved, with the blessing of the junta or its local representatives, who profit from it monetarily or otherwise. The girl was an orphan, and the man was a cousin of hers who lived off whoring her out to the nearby rubber plantations. The nun was doing all she could to prevent that monster from taking her away to sell her in the next town.

'I looked at the girl, and she looked at me, and I knew right then that I wouldn't let him take her. Maybe it was a way to atone for some of the suffering my grandfather no doubt inflicted on the area years ago, I don't know. But I did know I wasn't about to let that girl be sold by a "cousin" who treated her worse than a dog. I ordered the translator to tell him my husband was a partner of the junta, and that I wanted to take the girl. I ordered the escort to take out his pistol, and we let that piece of filth know that he had two choices: he could either take one hundred dollars for the girl and disappear, or I'd shoot him in the face. And believe me, I've never been so willing to do so.

'There was no more discussion. Vultures like that know when to beat a retreat. Once he'd left, I spoke to the nun, and she herself urged me to take the girl, because if she'd stayed behind, her cousin would have come back for her. My husband had no trouble getting her an appropriate passport, and we took her with us . . . and she's been with us ever since. Otherwise Tum would have wound up in a network of paedophilia and prostitution, abused, drugged out of her mind, and then, when she was no longer useful, probably sold off for a snuff film.' She said this without betraying any of the feelings that did her honour.

'Now I see why she's so devoted to you, and why she loves the girls so much,' said Laurent quietly. 'You saved her, and you've given her a life she could never have dreamt of. She must feel an absolute loyalty to you. You can tell.'

Madame Mayumi remained silent for a moment. 'Yes, I know she'd give her life for my daughters. And as for her loyalty . . . well, it's the least one would expect, but she's only twenty-three, and at that age, my dear Laurent, one can't expect anything of anyone.' She sipped her tea slowly, then sat for a long time staring into her cup. Laurent imagined the dragon moving about in spirals.

At last she broke her silence, changing topics dramatically.

'From what I hear, you've taken up sleuthing since we left. Is it true, the rumour that you were looking for my husband's potential murderer?'

Laurent turned beet-red all the way up to his hairline. 'You heard about that, too? Really, it was just a way to pass the time. And now that you've brought it up, I'd like to express my thanks for the testimony you gave on my behalf. I don't know how I would have made it through that whole mess had you not stood up for me.'

'Laurent, all I did was tell the truth. Given everything you did for me in the hunt for my husband, there was no way you could have been guilty. Sometimes the police can be so simpleminded . . . but let's not waste any more time – tell me what you uncovered.'

Briefly and succinctly, avoiding embellishments and skipping over the less heroic aspects of his investigation, Laurent summarised his process, going through each of the suspects and explaining how he'd gradually ruled them out, until he'd finally accepted Tartarin's theory.

'Bravo, Laurent,' said Madame Mayumi when he

finished. 'I congratulate you on an impressive job. I also think Lafonnier was correct, though you certainly had every right to investigate on your own. I imagine such excellent mental exercise must have helped you get to know yourself better, and also to make decisions about your own future. From what Yammei has told me, it's also been beneficial for your love life. I'm happy for you. You're a good man, and you deserve to be loved.

'And now you must excuse me; I still have some work to do with Xiao Li so that we can leave everything in order for when we hand the place over to the tenants. I'll have the girls come and get you.'

'Don't bother, Madame. I know the château well, and you have a small staff. I'll find my way up to where the girls are.' He got up and gave a nod to the widow. 'It was a pleasure seeing you again, and I hope I'll get a chance to say goodbye before you leave.'

On his way to the study, which was on the third floor, he ran into Xiao Li, Shennan's secretary, carrying a stack of files, round glasses bouncing on the end of her nose. She stopped.

'Good morning, Xiao Li. I'm going up to see the girls.'

'You're not angry with me, Monsieur de Rodergues?' she enquired.

'No, why should I be?'

'When you discovered the body of Monsieur Shennan, I reacted very badly, and my statement may have led the police to cause trouble for you.'

'Don't worry,' he reassured her. 'Your reaction was perfectly normal, especially given your special relationship to your boss. Don't give it another thought. Madame Mayumi told me you've got a lot to do preparing lists and other things, so you can't worry about that now.'

Xiao Li grabbed him by the jacket sleeve to stop him before he could continue on his way. 'I'm sorry for everything that happened, I truly am. I know you didn't do it.'

Laurent felt a stab of anxiety. 'What do you mean by that, Xiao Li? Is there someone you suspect?'

The secretary shook her head. 'My father was a party cadre during the Cultural Revolution, and if anyone knows the meaning of "hear no evil, see no evil, speak no evil", it's those of us who lived through that period. Best not to go back over those things, Monsieur.' Suddenly her mobile rang, and she answered it. 'Yes, Madame, I'm on my way.' She switched off her phone and looked at Laurent again. 'Excuse me, Monsieur, but I have to go. Take my advice and don't waste your time thinking about that tragedy.'

IN THE WORKSHOP
OF THE *SABOTIER*

Two days after his visit, as he busied himself in his workshop with a new set of clogs, Laurent fondly recalled his wonderful time with the girls. They'd looked genuinely happy to see him, and their shouts of delight when they opened their gifts had been gratifying, despite the inevitable fights when each one said her pair of clogs was the prettiest or that they weren't painted her favourite colour.

Tum also seemed delighted by her gift, a key ring he'd carved that showed the outline of a *chedi* of a temple from her country with her name engraved in Burmese script. Afterward, she and the girls had gone with him to see his workshop, poking into everything and making him promise he'd carve some little horses and send them by post. Then he invited them to his home, where they ate bread with butter and honey from the Green Goddesses. The girls had a lovely time, and he had to admit he did, too.

That morning he was finishing a pair of clogs he wanted to put on display at the tourism office in La Châtre, which showcased pieces by local artisans to promote their work, and he had to be sure it was perfect, because the person who ran the office was exacting in her selection. He stood up to get a thicker gouge, and as he hunted through his grandfather's tools he heard a car pull up outside the shop, followed by a tapping on the window. It was the three girls, all dolled up and wrapped in warm layers.

Laurent went to open the door, and they came in crying.

'What's the matter? What are three pretty little girls like you doing crying? Come now, such beautiful young ladies should always be happy.'

A visibly upset Xiao Li came in after them.

'Mum says that now that we're finished it's best for us to leave now, but she said we could stay longer. She promised!' wailed the oldest of the three.

The middle one grabbed Laurent's leather apron and hugged him, crying, 'We don't want to leave! Let us stay with you! We'll work here!'

'Please!' begged the littlest, who was especially bright. 'We'll be like Santa's little elves.'

'Madame and I have completed the inventory and left everything ready for the handover,' explained Xiao Li. 'It's true we initially planned to stay longer, but Madame is of the opinion, as am I, that if everything is ready and there's nothing more to do, then it's best we leave. Besides, late yesterday evening the Burmese embassy called asking for Miss Tum – something to do with her family. Understandably she became quite upset. Her parents died long ago, but two of her brothers are with the Karen Liberation Army. Madame gave her permission to go, and she herself drove her this morning to catch the first train to Paris. I'll be taking the girls to Tokyo myself, as Madame still has some legal matters to sort out with Monsieur Jablard in Paris.'

'I'm very sorry you're leaving,' Laurent confessed, saddened.

'The girls love you, and though you may not believe me, I'm fond of you too. Now I just hope they behave: it's a very long trip, and I'm not used to dealing with children.' She was clearly terrified at the prospect of the flight.

The three sisters, meanwhile, had let go of Laurent and were looking about the workshop, playing around with everything they found.

'Girls, you heard Miss Li: you have to be on your best behaviour,' said Laurent. 'And you have to promise to write to me, because I promise I'll write back. But above all, I want your word of honour that whenever you can you'll come back to Saint-Chartier. Now, give me one more hug.'

The girls leapt on him and covered him in kisses, and Laurent walked them to the car. At the last moment, he even gave Xiao Li a hug, who first went rigid but then smiled and said, 'You know? That's the first time in my life I've ever been hugged, and I think I like it. Thank you.' She didn't wait for Laurent to respond and got into the passenger seat, cheeks flushed. She seemed like an entirely different woman than the dour secretary he'd first met.

Laurent stood in the street waving goodbye to the girls, who from the back seat blew him kisses. When the car turned the corner, he couldn't help shedding a few heartfelt tears.

CLOGS FOR MADAME MAYUMI

It was dinner time, and Laurent decided he had worked enough for the day. The longer he practised his new trade, the more he liked it, but he was worried that people only bought clogs as a souvenir or a decoration for a country house, so he spent time thinking up new designs and ideas. In fact, he'd started making carved wooden stirrups, in the Chilean style, specifically the kind they call *rugendas*, and he hoped to find someone who could make the piece of steel with silver filigree that could hold the strap. France had a remarkable equestrian culture, and it followed very strict rules, so perhaps riding tack and gear were commercial terrain he could explore. As he walked into the vicarage, he went to hang up his coat.

That's when he noticed a paper bag at the foot of the coat rack that was partly covered by the hem of his raincoat.

Laurent clicked his tongue in annoyance, realising he'd forgotten to give Madame Mayumi her gift. He decided

353

he'd better take it to her as soon as possible, in case she left earlier than planned.

He put his coat back on, grabbed the package and left for the château. As usual, the large gate was shut but not locked, and from far away he saw the Thai gardener in the greenhouse. He reckoned the most sensible thing to do was to enter through the main gate, which led to the terrace. He climbed the steps but found the door locked. Accustomed as he was to always being met there, he didn't notice until now that there was no doorbell.

He walked back down the stone steps and turned right toward the stairs that led to the park, but he also found the door there locked. He was about to give up, assuming that Madame Shennan had gone out to see to some business, when he remembered, as he headed toward the street gate, that behind a large cluster of boxwood trees was the service door in the south tower, the same door the Monattis had snuck in through.

The door was unlocked and he decided to go inside. He liked to believe he enjoyed the Shennans' trust. He reached the hunting room, where a desk lamp cast a soft light over some magazines and papers in Japanese. He didn't dare call out, because he recalled that Madame Mayumi was bothered by voices and sounds. Instead, he called her name quietly but got no response.

He went from one room to the next, until he reached the second floor, where he heard a metallic sound from the guest room. As he got closer he could make out some droning music. He rapped on the door with his knuckles and, getting no response, he turned the handle and entered. Inside the room where they'd found Shennan's body was Madame Mayumi, in front of the passageway, which stood open. The panel had been taken off and set against the wall. A speaker emitted the droning sound he'd heard, which immediately made him think of something religious. But what really surprised him was Madame Mayumi's posture.

She was kneeling on the floor with her back to him, with a container of fresh cement and several bricks next to her. Trowel in hand, she was applying plaster to a wall that she was building to seal the entrance to the passageway. Laurent cleared his throat to get her attention, but she went on intoning a sort of mantra, so he decided to touch her gently on the shoulder, which made her turn and leap up in a defensive pose.

Laurent raised his hands in a sign of peace.

'I'm sorry, I didn't mean to startle you. I tried calling your name, but you were engrossed in the music. I just wanted to drop off a present I forgot the last time I stopped by. I was afraid you'd leave again before I had the chance to give it to you.' Laurent held out the bag to her to illustrate his words.

Flustered, at first Madame Mayumi said nothing. Then after a few seconds she finally reacted, giving him her best smile.

'No, I'm sorry. Forgive me, I was distracted reciting Shinto prayers, and in the constant repetition and the sound of the cymbals I think I fell into a sort of trance.' She pointed to the wall with her trowel. 'As you can see, I'm sealing the entrance to the passageway. I don't want anyone else to have an accident. I'll feel more at ease knowing it's been closed.'

Laurent looked at her work with curiosity. 'I have to say, you've done a very nice job, Madame, but if you need help all you have to do is ask.'

She laughed politely. 'The post-war period in Japan lasted longer than Westerners realise, and there was a lack of strong men, and in every family and neighbourhood people had to help each other out. I was a girl, but I liked to help out my cousins and uncles, and that's how I learnt how to do this, along with many other jobs. But let me see your gift, please. I'm sure if it's from you I'll love it.' She opened the bag and took out the clogs, evaluating them admiringly. 'This is beautiful workmanship! I love them. It was so nice of you to go to the trouble of finding the family crest. Let me try them on.' She took off her shoes, and Laurent could see that she was wearing incandescently white *tabi* socks. The clogs fit perfectly. 'I'm deeply grateful for everything you've done for us, and how warmly you've always treated us. You'll be hard to forget. The girls have already called to tell me they've arrived safely in Japan, and they told me they promised you they'd come back here. The château is theirs; who knows what they'll do with it, but if they ever do decide to return I hope they can count on you.'

'I hope so too. As you know I'll be here to help them. I'm not sure why, but I think that as adults they'll be terrifying.'

'They certainly will,' laughed Madame. 'Now I apologise, but I must say goodbye because I have to finish packing. Later Khun Suan will drive me to the Châteauroux airport. Take care, Laurent. We'll write.' She gave him her hand,

and as he took it, she added, with a laugh, 'And do let me know how things go with your secret agent.'

Laurent pretended to frown. 'The gossip really travels, doesn't it?'

'Listen to me, Laurent. You're like my late husband in many ways, and that's why I think that, just like him, you need a woman who understands you, but who's headstrong and can put her foot down when she needs to.'

Laurent found the remark funny, especially coming from a woman whose husband had been constantly running around behind her back, but then he remembered that, whatever he did, Shennan had never seemed to undermine the dignity of his wife. No one was ever allowed to make a joke about her, and the very mention of Mayumi was always met by everyone with respect and admiration.

'I'll try to take your advice,' Laurent promised, 'but not everyone is as lucky as your husband and can find a woman as exceptional as you.'

'Thank you, it's very kind of you to say so.' Madame Mayumi put her hands together. 'Life with Carlos wasn't always easy. At home he was attentive, fun, affectionate with everyone, and an endless source of humour and generosity, but I never forgot his Janus-like nature, or his Dr Jekyll side, if you will. In Japan we learn from a young age to put up with anything, especially for the good of the family. I loved my husband very much, but I love my daughters more, and I'd never, ever allow anyone or anything to jeopardise their innocence, their future, or their well-being. That was and is my greatest duty. All I've done is try to fulfil my responsibilities.' She remained silent, a silence Laurent had learnt he should respect. 'I'm sorry, I don't know why I launched into that speech. You're very patient with the ravings of an old woman.'

'Please don't say "old",' he protested loudly. 'Not only are you younger than I am, you're a woman whose beauty I shall never forget.'

'That's enough mutual flattery for now. Take care, and please, think fondly of us.'

Saying this, she knelt down to finish her task. Laurent turned to leave, but he suddenly remembered something.

'Have you heard anything from Tum?' he asked. 'Xiao Li said she'd got a call from Burma, something to do with her family.'

'I'm sorry? Tum?' Laurent's question had caught her off guard, as though she didn't know who he was talking about.

'Yes, I think you were kind enough to take her to the train station.'

She raised her finger to her forehead. 'Where is my head today? Yes, poor thing, she received a call about her brother. Yesterday she phoned me from Paris. There's going to be an amnesty in her country, and apparently her relatives got word that one of her brothers is in one of those horrifying Burmese prisons. You can imagine what the people in the military junta are like. Tum left today to see what she could do for him. I'm afraid only money will help, but she's got a lot of savings, and I'll help her out if necessary. It was a miracle that they managed to find her. I'm not sure how they reached us. Maybe the nun I mentioned . . . But don't worry, she's fine, and I'll give her your regards. Have a good evening, Laurent.'

As he tried to find his way out, he stopped to admire the furniture and objects decorating the château. It would have been a shame to take it all down, and Shennan would have approved of the solution with the Russians, he was sure of it.

A KEY RING AND AN
INSURANCE AGENT

Spring had finally sprung, the time of year when Saint-Chartier is arrayed with unrivalled beauty and colour. Ever since the château park had been redesigned, several neighbours, and even the city government itself, impressed by Solange's project, had started to take a more active role in caring for the local vegetation. They'd gone so far as to make the floral decorations of the streets and houses a community activity, and the town was earning a reputation for its greenery. Partly that was the initiative of Miss Heather, a retired British teacher and amateur ornithologist who had seen to it that every resident was assigned a public tree they had to take care of. Partly it was due to the placement and maintenance of a bird feeder in the town, which attracted several birds of several species, whose singing and flitting about notably animated the little plazas and the old public wash house.

Laurent's garden, too, had taken on a more promising aspect, and a relative order had at last taken root among his hens, giving him eggs on a stable, regular basis. What's more, the days were growing brighter, which made it possible to eat outdoors on the patio of the vicarage. All he needed now was for Cathy to come over more often. He'd by now accepted her for what she'd become: indispensable and inescapable. Barring some unforeseen incident, she'd arrive that very night from Clermont-Ferrand, and Laurent hadn't forgotten that she'd been blunt in expressing an acute craving for empanadas, a delicacy that Le Juanch had been inspired to start making. His were a peculiar reinterpretation of the Argentine variety, since they had the chimichurri in the filling.

Laurent headed to the tavern to order them, fearful that if he didn't have them that night, Cathy would deny him the bedroom attentions he so ardently desired. Along the way, he passed by the château and ran into Yammei, who was trying to open the gate while laden with several bags. Chivalrous as always, he stopped to help and offered to hold her things while she looked for her keys. When she found them and took them out of her handbag, Laurent was taken aback: her key ring was almost identical to the one he'd carved for Tum.

'Yammei, could I take a look at your key ring?' She gave me a surprised look but still handed it to him, allowing him to closely inspect it. There was no doubt: it was Tum's, but the upper part of the *chedi* had been broken off.

'I'm sorry, but where did you get that key ring?'

'I found it inside the château, under a sofa. Why? Is it yours?'

'No, but I made it for Miss Tum, it was gift for her.

361

Too bad she lost it; I got the impression she liked it.'

Yammei understood Laurent's disappointment. 'Don't take it so hard, Monsieur. The last few days we were all running around like mad, and Madame was giving orders right and left. You know how Tum always tries to follow orders and satisfy Madame's wishes. Probably she dropped it while running errands. If you like, I can return it to her.'

'No, keep it,' said Laurent. 'But tell me, have you heard from her? Was she able to find her brother?'

'Madame said Tum has to stay in Burma, since the business with her brother is more complicated than she thought. She's very sad, because Tum is such a wonderful girl. She's having trouble finding a replacement who's even half as good. Of course, when she returns, she'll always have a place in the Shennans' house.'

'I'm not surprised. She's an excellent person, and I hope she can get all her family troubles sorted out as quickly as possible. Say hello from me if you're ever in contact with her,' said Laurent with sincerity.

'Of course, Monsieur Laurent. So long.'

Laurent continued on his way to La Cocadrille, and when he arrived he was surprised by the large number of people inside. More surprising still was the smell of Argentine empanadas wafting pleasantly through the air. Squeezing in at the bar, he accidentally pushed someone.

'Laurent! Fancy meeting you here!' It was Blareau, his insurance agent, a friendly chatterbox with an office in La Châtre. Before he could react, Blareau was already hugging him, and his breath testified to a substantial number of libations. 'Everyone keeps telling me about this place, so I decided to come and try it out for myself. What can I get you?'

'A beer, please, but just a glass. How's the insurance business? Hope you're not going to try to get me to sign up for another policy.'

'Pfff, not so great. Everyone thinks they're already covered for everything, and it's getting harder and harder to convince them they need more, or to upgrade the plans they already have. It's crap. Believe me, I actually envy you, making your little wooden shoes here in peace. Which reminds me' – Blareau poked his finger into his chest – 'since you know Monsieur Shennan's widow and the new people leasing the château, couldn't you recommend my services? I think the Shennans owe me one.'

'I know Madame Shennan well enough that I wouldn't dare give her any recommendations. She knows perfectly well what she wants. As for the new tenants, all I know is that they're Russian and coming from there. When I meet them, if it comes up, I'll put in a good word for you.'

'Thanks, you're a good chap. Here's to you.'

Blareau ordered two more beers, and Laurent didn't know how to say no. The clinked their glasses and, after taking a sip, Laurent asked him, 'Why did you say the Shennans owe you one?'

The insurance agent was rather intoxicated and slurred his speech. 'They don't really owe me anything, but I gave the late Monsieur some good advice, especially in view of his subsequent misfortune.'

'Come on, Blareau, don't be so mysterious, it doesn't suit you. You're dying to tell me everything. Would you like another Carterius?' offered Laurent, feeling a bit wretched for using alcohol to refresh his companion's memory.

'I've got no secrets from you, Laurent.' He was totally sloshed, so Laurent assumed nothing he said would be entirely true. 'Two months before he died, Monsieur Shennan stopped by my office and told me a very strange story, then announced he wanted to take out a special life insurance policy on account of the fact he was always travelling to high-risk countries. The premium he wanted to get was very high, and of course I'd never offered policies like that. Besides, there was the question of his age: he was past fifty, and you know what the requirements are like in those cases. I told him for a policy with such a high premium, I'd have to send it to the central office for approval, but if he wanted to save time, he could get a complete medical check-up to attach to the report. He didn't much like the idea of seeing a doctor, or of waiting, so he left. But much to my surprise, a few minutes later he came right back, saying it was lunchtime and he didn't like eating alone, so he invited me to join him.

'We went to L'Escargot, and over good food and better wine, we told each other our life stories. The guy may have been rich, but he treated me like an equal. And I felt bad we'd made it so difficult for him to get his policy. With everything he was doing for the town, and with such small daughters . . .' Laurent could easily imagine a crafty Shennan deploying all his seductive arts on poor Blareau, who was easy prey. Probably before they'd finished the aperitif, he'd had him wrapped around his finger. 'Anyhow, I gave him some advice on how to get a medical certificate right away and talk to an American insurance company that could offer policies with the kind of premium he wanted. He was very grateful, and a week later he sent over a case of wine with a card. What a gentleman, Laurent. They don't make them like that any more.'

The news that Shennan had been looking for better life insurance shortly before his death, and indeed had been so desperate to get one that he'd even had lunch with this bore Blareau, came as a surprise to Laurent. It reminded him of what Father Gérard had said about a supposed illness. He said goodbye to his companion, urging him not to try to drive home, then went to the kitchen to pick up the empanadas he'd ordered by phone. With the precious cargo in his possession, he returned to the vicarage to prepare for Cathy's arrival. He was burning with desire to see her, and to tell her what he'd just discovered about Tum's key ring and Shennan's insurance policy. He decided to ask her to help him track down some information.

As he set the dining room table it occurred to him he should downplay how excited he was to see her. He decided to unset the table and pretend he'd forgotten about dinner, and ask her to help him throw something together. He put away the plates and cutlery, acknowledging, to his credit, that his behaviour would provide plenty of material for any psychoanalyst.

A CONVERSATION
OVER EMPANADAS

Cathy arrived a bit later than planned, and Laurent decided to feign surprise upon seeing her: she found him in his favourite armchair smoking a cigar, cradling a glass of cognac and reading a magazine, as though he hadn't remembered their date. But if he was expecting a scene, he was utterly mistaken: instead of getting angry, Cathy laughed.

'You're a disaster, Laurent! How could you forget I was coming over? But I'm glad, because on my way over I was thinking you were too perfect, too much of a gentleman. I like seeing your boorish side. Come on, let's make dinner. I could eat a literal horse.' No sooner said than done: she threw off her slim gabardine coat and grabbed one of the aprons hanging behind the door. 'I suppose you didn't remember to get the empanadas . . .'

With an impish grin, Laurent showed her the package from Le Juanch's. She smiled, seeing it had all been a joke, and hugged him with joy, as Laurent chided her.

'Woman of little faith! Come on, let's eat. I want to bring you up to speed on my discoveries about Carlos's death.' Laurent felt her shoulders stiffen as she pulled back in his arms.

'Don't tell me you're still obsessing over that. I thought you'd finally forgotten about it. I don't like you going back over it.'

Her reaction caught him off guard. Until that very moment he could have sworn she took an interest in the investigation too, but he realised that Cathy considered the case closed and was irritated he'd gone and dug it up again.

'Don't say that, I never said I'd finished, I just let it go because I saw I couldn't find a way forward. But what I learnt today changes everything. Come on, sit down next to me and I'll tell you all about it.'

She turned toward him in resignation and sat on one of the chairs. 'Fine, I'll hear you out, but this had better be interesting, because I'm really sick of this topic.'

Once they'd sat down at the table, Laurent poured two glasses of chilled Sancerre and told her what had happened just a few hours previously, both about Tum's key ring and the inebriated revelations of Blareau.

Cathy listened to him attentively, without interrupting, and when Laurent was done, she asked, 'All right. What conclusions do you draw from these two pieces of information? Because frankly, to me, they don't prove a thing. As the Chinese cook said, the key ring could easily have gotten lost in the shuffle with the inventory. As for the insurance policy, I don't have a fortune, and I'm younger and less of a globetrotter than Shennan, with no children or husband to worry about, but I always make sure to keep my life insurance policy up to date, not only because my job is more dangerous, but also because I want to make sure my mother will get something if anything happens to me. So it makes plenty of sense that a rich man of a certain age with a fast-paced lifestyle would do the same. And if he then went on to die, and his widow wound up with a fat bit of treasure . . . Well, that's a coincidence, but his foresight is no doubt a comfort to his family.'

Laurent couldn't believe his ears. 'How can someone of your experience not think what I just said is significant? Fine, I see you're not interested. Don't worry, I won't go on about my nonsense any more. Let's finish setting the table and eat dinner.'

'Wow, what a grown-up reaction! The gentleman's gone and got his knickers in a bunch!' said Cathy. 'You're like a child; you're lucky I put up with you. Come here, sit down and tell me your theory.'

'No. I'll pursue my obsessions on my own time. I wouldn't want to bore the lady.'

'Please, Laurent. There's no need to fight.' Cathy was getting impatient. 'Tell me what you're thinking. We'll analyse it and see if there's anything I can do to help. But please, let's do that while we eat.'

'All right,' said Laurent. The smell of the empanadas was making him hungry. 'We'll eat and talk.'

Music soothes savage beasts, and the beef empanadas with chimichurri seemed to have a similar sedative effect. Laurent once again became his usual pleasant self, always happy to spend a nice evening with Cathy.

Once they'd sat down, she said, 'Now you can expound your theory. I promise I'll listen.'

Laurent again summarised what they both knew, this time adding to the details of the policy and the key ring his encounter with Madame Mayumi in the château before he left, and how strange her attitude struck him, not only because she wanted to seal off the entrance to the passageway herself, but also because she looked so surprised when he asked about Tum.

'What are you trying to say? That his wife killed him off for the life insurance policy, and that's why you found her praying in front of the spot where he died? I don't think so. From what you've told me, she's now taken Shennan's place overseeing his business, and it seems to still be going well. Besides, you've told me on several occasions that despite his somewhat loose morals, his wife seemed to be in love with him.'

'Yes, that's true,' Laurent had to admit, 'but put it all together: business wasn't going as well as it once had; the château was a money pit, according to his wife; he was in precarious health, as Gérard told me and Blareau confirmed . . . and add to all that what Madame Mayumi said, about how she'd do anything so as not to jeopardise her daughters' future . . .'

'The only way I can think of to help you is to contact the security team working the night of the party. I could have us all get together again, explain your theory and see what they remember. We could also review everything the cameras and mics recorded, both the ones we installed with the owners' knowledge and the ones we put in without their consent.

Yes, I think that's best – I'll work on my co-workers. We'll spend a few hours reviewing what we have, and if there's anything suspicious I'll call you right away, I promise. Now let's finish this delicious meal and head upstairs.'

Two hours later Laurent decided that stuffing oneself with Argentine empanadas doused in chimichurri wasn't a good idea just before embarking on amorous exploits.

THE PRYING EYE AND OTHER
TECHNOLOGICAL WIZARDRY

Laurent sat in his workshop, happily working on a pair of clogs. Sunlight streamed through the large windows, and the sky above was a deep blue. Chimay dozed at his side, and the aroma of wood permeated the air.

He was sanding a sole when his mobile rang. It was Cathy, and he picked up right away. She didn't give him time to say so much as hello.

'Laurent, where are you?'

'Hi, Cathy, I'm at the workshop. What's the matter? You sound upset.'

'Get home as fast as you can and turn on the computer. I'm sending you something you have to see right away. Trust me. I wanted to surprise you and bring it to you in person, but my car's in the shop and there's a train strike.'

Laurent got up and hurried back to his house without even taking off his apron. His computer was on his kitchen table, and he'd left it on. He checked his email and saw he had two messages from Cathy, one of which was quite large. He opened it, and the message was intriguing, to say the least:

> *I hope you're sitting down while you watch what I'm sending you. Call me.*

He was burning with curiosity.

Unfortunately, the internet at the vicarage wasn't very good, and the connection dropped three times before he could download the file. When he'd finally got it, Laurent called Cathy.

'Hi, I'm about to open the file you sent. Is it really such a big deal?'

'You know I don't like to waste time, honey, so I managed to get everyone together who was working the night Shennan died. I told them about your project and your theories, and suddenly Slawomir, who was team leader that night, remembered something. Apparently the nanny caught his eye – he thought she was hot, and he might have been watching her more closely than necessary. He even said he was tempted to call her later on, but of course, given everything that happened, he figured it wouldn't be wise. And after going over those videos again, I think he was right.'

'Hold on, I've finally got the file open, I'm watching.' Laurent frowned impatiently as the recording started to play. It had been taken in the hallway to the sitting room, where he'd met with Madame Mayumi and Xiao Li before setting out to search for Shennan.

'Watch the video and tell me where you are, and I'll put

it at the same speed on my screen so we can discuss it. Pause yours so they're synchronised.'

'All right,' he said. 'I'm seeing a shot of the hallway, a hallway with a huge tapestry on the wall with mythical creatures. Got it?'

'Yes, one second. OK, on the count of three we'll press play. One, two, three. Here we go, now pay attention to everything.'

The quality of the film impressed Laurent. The image, though in black and white, was crisp and distinct. Suddenly he saw a woman walking from the other end of the hall. It was Tum.

'I can see Tum. It's odd, because from what I see in the time signature, I had just seen her a few minutes before this with the girls and Thierry. What's she doing there?'

'Shut up and keep watching,' said Cathy.

Tum turned quickly, as though checking to make sure there was no one behind her, and then crossed the sitting room and ducked behind one of the enormous curtains that covered the windows. She waited there, and a few seconds later Shennan appeared. Then she came out of her hiding spot, and the two met in a long embrace that gave way to an extended and seemingly passionate kiss. The sound quality in the recording wasn't quite as good as the film, so it was hard to make out more than moans, but there was no need to anyway, because the content left no room for doubt. In the video, Shennan unbuttoned Tum's shirt and kissed her delicate, small breasts as she breathed more and more heavily. Suddenly they stopped. Shennan took his telephone out from the breast pocket of his blazer, gave Tum a kiss on the forehead and hurried out of the room. She stayed behind and started to button up her shirt, then walked to one of the large Venetian mirrors, stood before it and fixed her hair, smiling to herself. The image in the mirror was unmistakable: it was the face of a woman in love.

'Sweet mother of God!' exclaimed Laurent. 'I never would have imagined this.'

'Now calm down and watch the second segment. It's taken from another camera and occurs just seconds after Shennan left the nanny. Watch his face.'

Laurent obeyed, and they followed the same procedure to watch the video simultaneously. This footage, shot from a corner, showed Shennan walking up with his hands in his pockets. Suddenly he looked up, and his face could be seen in perfect clarity: it was the face of a man afflicted with the same ailment as Tum. His enraptured expression was almost ridiculous.

'Cathy, this is pathetic. It's like something out of a Victorian novel where the lord of the manor runs off with the governess. The worst part is, Carlos looks like he's died and gone to heaven. Now this whole thing really makes no sense.'

'Yeah, well, wait until you see the next video. Look for where it says "Recording no. 4" and stay tuned.'

The video showed the same room where Tum and Shennan had given themselves over to passion; according to the time signature it took place barely a minute after the nanny had left.

'Look at the right side of the screen, at the door. Watch very, very closely.'

374

A few yards away from where Shennan and Tum had stood was a door. It opened and Madame Mayumi stepped out. She too walked toward the Venetian mirror, looked at herself and brought her hands up to her eyes. She seemed to be crying. If earlier the mirror showed a girl in love, now it showed a grown woman totally distraught. Madame Mayumi lowered her head, hands still covering her eyes, and a few seconds later she brought them down and raised her head. The change was astonishing. She looked utterly transformed: once again she was the familiar elegant woman. Her eyes were still gleaming, not with tears but with resolve. She raised her finger to wipe her right eye, then walked out of the room.

'Well, Laurent? What do you think now?'

There was a pause as he decided how to respond. 'You want to know the truth? I think it's really sad. I congratulate you on a job well done, but this all leaves a horrible taste in my mouth. In the first place seeing Carlos, who I was fond of and had a degree of friendship with, looking like a schoolboy head over heels for a girl who could be his daughter, and who takes care of his daughters to boot, is awful. Totally inappropriate. But it's even more grotesque to see Tum, who I've always felt affection for – especially now that I know her horrifying story – charmed by that sexual piranha Shennan. And finally, the image of Madame Mayumi betrayed by her husband in their home, on the day that they inaugurated it, and furthermore with someone she had complete trust in . . . know what I think? That it's a such a noxious brew of crime, adultery, humiliation and betrayal that I don't understand how she could feign the stoicism and self-control she showed later.'

'Wake up, Laurent! There's something more important I don't think you realise.'

'What do you mean?' He paused for a moment in thought, then gave a gasp. 'No! Are you suggesting it was Madame Mayumi who killed Shennan? I refuse to believe it.' Laurent was beside himself. He'd found the scene with Shennan's wife looking at herself in the mirror unbearable.

'Calm down and think about it: she always put up with all Shennan's infidelities, but she told you there were things she'd never tolerate, and both you and I know that her honour and dignity were of vital importance to her. You saw her just like I did: that was the face of a woman scorned, yearning for vengeance. In fact, I'm starting to think you may be right about Tum's disappearance.'

'We don't even know if she did anything to her husband, and you're already blaming her for what happened to Tum – and we still don't know if anything bad has even happened to her!'

'You're pathetic. Clearly you're still gaga over the widow and can't stand me questioning her. But I think she did it,' Cathy fired back. 'Look, call me when you've figured it out and decided what to do.' And without waiting for a reply, she hung up the phone.

Laurent sat in front of his computer, silent and upset. He went through the videos over and over, until he had an idea and called Cathy back.

'Don't get mad, although it's very comforting to see you jealous.'

'What do you want now?' Her tone didn't invite joking.

'I was thinking that if you have so much footage, maybe there's a bit somewhere that shows Carlos going into the passageway, or even shows the killer.'

'We've already looked at all of it, and sadly there's nothing,' replied Cathy coldly. 'In any case we only put cameras in the rooms on the first two floors, not in the bedrooms or in the upstairs bathrooms out of privacy concerns. Nor in the guest room with the secret passage.'

'But you did have some in the entryway and by the service door, and that's where you caught the Monattis, right? My question is: couldn't there be footage that shows Shennan's wife inside the château before what the coroner determined was the time of her husband's death?'

Laurent noticed that Cathy found it hard to reply.

Finally she spoke. 'No, there's nothing. But as I said, we only put cameras and mics on the first two floors and the service entrance in the south tower. We didn't put surveillance in the guest room or the second tower.'

'Which tower do you mean?'

'The one that goes from the first to the second floor. There's a small entryway there that goes to a service staircase. There's even a dumbwaiter in the wall for taking breakfast to the third floor. Anyway, our second mistake was not putting any cameras in that entryway.'

Laurent tried to visualise the floor plan Cathy was describing. 'All right, I understand. But you say that's your second mistake, which means there was a first one.'

'I shouldn't do this. What I'm about to tell you, you have to swear to keep to yourself.'

Laurent understood she was risking her job for him. 'Of course, Cathy. I really appreciate for what you're doing for me, and sorry if I was a bit rude earlier.'

'A bit?' she teased, but Laurent relaxed because he noticed in her tone of voice that she was softening up. 'All right, here goes: no one knew about the cameras and mics, and just in case, one of our agents took them all down before the police arrived. Anyway, we placed a small camera in the entryway where we thought we'd see anyone who came in. The problem was that it's a room with an uneven ceiling, and we had to make do with a single camera, so we didn't have a complete view of the entire space, which was rectangular and contained several visual obstacles, like those two large figureheads from ship's prows that were hanging on the walls. In other words, we could see everyone who came into the entry hall and everyone who went up to the second floor, but not anyone who went up through the second tower, since we didn't have any cameras left.'

'That doesn't seem like a big deal. At least you recorded everyone who went into the entry hall.'

'That footage is worthless. The entry hall opens up to the terrace, which was full of guests. That door was open because that's how you got to the guest bathrooms, and on the other side, to the dining room, where they brought out the drinks and food. If anyone wanted to get to the upper floors without being seen, they would have had to go through the second tower, which isn't something that the guests, or anyone other than the hosts, would have known.'

For a moment neither of them spoke. Then Cathy broke the silence. 'What are you going to do now?'

'I don't know, I'm going to watch the videos a few more times. Maybe there's something we're missing,' said Laurent. 'I really appreciate your letting me see these, but really, the only thing they show is that Shennan was even more promiscuous than we thought, that the faithful Tum let her lust get the better of her, and that Madame Mayumi knew everything.'

'So what does that mean?' Cathy insisted.

'Just what I said. I want to watch the videos a few more times, take notes and compare a few things to confirm a hunch I have about something you said earlier. I promise I'll call you later.'

Cathy could tell that something was percolating in his mind.

'Please don't do anything stupid, Laurent. If you have one of your brilliant ideas, call me first, and if necessary I'll go wherever you tell me.'

'I promise, anything you say.' He hung up.

THE COUP DE GRÂCE

Laurent sat at his kitchen table reviewing the footage over and over, but he couldn't find anything new. The fact was, the files Cathy had sent him were a bombshell, and if he forwarded them to the police, he was almost certain they'd reopen the case. Yet he didn't plan to do so. He couldn't put Madame Mayumi in jeopardy: she was his friend's widow, not to mention his own friend and the mother of three adorable girls. Besides, he couldn't be certain she had murdered her husband, even though Shennan had committed more than enough crimes to warrant a shove down the stairs from his wife, especially after what had happened with Tum.

He set aside his computer, took out his notebook from his back pocket and placed it on the table. If the hunch he'd told Cathy about was right, the whole case would fall over the edge of the volcano and be spat out again as magma and rocky debris, and the town of Saint-Chartier itself would suffer the consequences. Nothing would ever be the same for many of those involved. Unfortunately, Laurent believed the truth was at least worth knowing. He opened the notebook.

Laurent was orderly in many things, but not in his papers or his writings. His notebook was mishmash of scribbled thoughts, crossed-out words and ripped-out pages. He looked through the notebook three times before finding the page he needed.

'Here it is,' he said aloud to himself. 'Now let's find information on the train schedule that day, because I just remembered something I didn't pay attention to at the time.' He went to the French railway website and spent a long while looking for the date he'd underlined in his planner. A few minutes later, he gave a roar of satisfaction. Beaming with pride, he picked up his phone to call Cathy.

'Hello, I imagine you're still in front of the computer. Look at what I'm sending you.'

A few minutes later Cathy called back.

'According to this, train service on 18th March was suspended for a partial strike, and the line wasn't up and running again until the next day. I don't understand. All this shows is that there were no trains that day. What's so important about that?' asked Cathy.

'What do you mean? That's why I had a funny feeling. I knew something you told me struck me as odd, but with the videos I forgot about it. Just like I told you, even though it was only a hunch, it turns out I was right. Now you've got to admit my suspicions were correct, because, listen up, the day the girls came to say goodbye, when Shennan's secretary told me how Tum had suddenly left and Madame

Mayumi herself drove her to the station in Châteauroux to get the first train to the Burmese embassy in Paris – that was the day of the strike.'

'And . . . ?'

'You just read it yourself! That day there was no train service, so Tum couldn't have gone to Paris – probably not even to the station. Add to that the fact that I found her broken key ring under a sofa, and you've got to admit there's something strange going on here,' cried Laurent, upset.

Cathy suddenly reacted. '*Merde*! It's true, I hadn't thought of that. But then where's the nanny? You're not suggesting . . . ?'

'Yes, I'm suggesting that Tum may have been killed, and by the same person who killed Shennan.'

'Laurent, you have to go straight to the police and report it.'

'No, first I'll think it all over again, and when I figure out what I should do I'll talk to Madame Mayumi before I take the next step.'

'Laurent, you're insane. What are you going to say to her? "Madame Mayumi, you're simply astonishing. Please tell me how you knocked off your husband and made your nanny disappear, and while you're at it, give me some lessons in Japanese heraldry." Don't be an idiot. I'm going to call Lafonnier myself.'

'Not on your life. This is my case and I'll decide how it's handled. Trust me, please. Imagine the mess I'll be in if I'm wrong.'

Cathy knew that it would be a waste of time to try to persuade him.

'Do whatever you want. Call me later,' she said, and hung up the phone.

Laurent realised he hadn't been very nice to Cathy, but now was not the time to apologise. Night had fallen, and what he needed was to sit on a bench in the church plaza looking up at the stars and smoking a cigar as he meditated on the case.

UNDER THE SHADOW OF ORION

At nightfall, the amber street lamps of Saint-Chartier switch on, and from the plaza, a set of spotlights illuminates the château walls. That night the sacristan had left the church light on, and the stained glass on the façade shone brightly with the four evangelists and Jesus.

Laurent struck a match, lit his cigar, idly played with the band and inhaled deeply, expelling the smoke toward the sky. He tried to blow rings that encircled stars, without much luck. He thought he had the keys to the case, and while on the one hand the possible solution saddened him, on the other he couldn't help congratulating himself, hoping his theory was right.

Sitting on a bench in the plaza, head tilted back, he smoked and silently conversed with a heavenly vault that patiently listened to his disquisitions and theories on the death of Carlos Shennan.

The victim: his first conclusion was that, *contra* the police report, his friend and neighbour had not died in an accident but was the victim of an exceptionally well-camouflaged murder.

Suspects, witnesses and screens: his second conclusion was that the murderer had very cleverly used Shennan's personality and lifestyle to leave an array of possible suspects in the event that the police weren't convinced his death had been a mere accident. These suspects would allow the murderer to get a head start if the plan ran into any hitches. Laurent couldn't even discern to what extent he himself had been manipulated.

The date: the day chosen to carry out the homicide was excessively bold, with the château full of guests and the premises under surveillance by a well-trained security team, but the fact that there were so many people present offered a large number of alibis and at the same time made the police work more difficult.

The location: the passageway was a daring choice because of the difficulties posed by its narrowness and low ceiling, but as only very few people knew about it, it delayed the discovery of the body – indeed, had it not been Laurent searching the house, Shennan's body might have gone undiscovered for much longer.

The motives: on this point Shennan himself had dropped many rosary beads on the trail, and the murderer had cleverly strung those beads together, revealing countless motives among a host of people: clients or suppliers upset with him for one reason or another; women scorned; family members of people he'd hurt, like Thierry and Yael; a radical Islamist slapped in public; farmers who stood to gain with him out of the picture; and even a spurned, humiliated wife.

* * *

Laurent carefully analysed all these points, but in the end, no matter how he looked at them, all the clues led to the same person: Madame Mayumi. He decided to put himself in her place and try to understand her.

Shennan's wife had abundant motives for killing her husband: she herself had said on several occasions that she'd do anything to secure her daughters' future. And as Laurent had heard from Carlos himself, the business had taken a downturn, and the château was a giant leech draining his funds very quickly.

If that weren't enough, Shennan's behaviour had on numerous occasions overstepped the bounds of his wife's patience. His increasingly scandalous entanglements gave the locals plenty to gossip about: an insatiable hunter, he was always ready for flesh, fish or fowl; he'd been fooling around with the architect, and he'd shared a bed with the landscape designer. His notorious affairs had culminated in a liaison with his daughters' nanny, a girl his wife adored. This dalliance hadn't escaped her notice, and she'd become an unwilling witness to a double betrayal that practically had a whiff of incest, given Tum's status as a semi-adopted daughter.

And if Madame Mayumi had still had any doubts about her husband's untamed sexual appetite, the slap that Yael delivered provided further evidence against him. Laurent had spotted her watching the scene from the window, just as in the video he'd seen her go from despair to the most ruthless spite.

With all this, it seemed clear that Madame Mayumi had been the author of her own widowhood. *But how?* he asked. He began to retrace all the details to try to find a clue.

Even when he'd first met her, during the incident with the dogs, she'd let fly a few barbs at her husband.

Then she'd showed him the threats and insults against them, which was a way of revealing to him that her husband had enemies.

Shennan's business certainly hadn't seemed to be going well, but in fact Laurent had no proof save the statements of Shennan himself or his wife. In any event, the fact was that his business, even the most complex deals, now fell to Madame Mayumi, who apparently had taken the reins firmly in hand with a remarkable degree of success. Ever since she'd assumed control, the fear of bankruptcy and the threat to her family's well-being had vanished.

Another detail was Madame Mayumi's open loathing of the château. Now she'd leased it out, generating a modest profit for her family and even for Laurent, turning a former problem into a source of income.

Finally came the issue of Carlos Shennan's possible illness, of which only Father Gérard and Blareau were aware. To be sure, Laurent still had no idea what kind of illness this was, though he did know he'd taken out a hefty insurance policy, an added benefit for Madame Mayumi, who would be the beneficiary and manager of the generous pay-out.

Laurent got up and began pacing from one end of the plaza to the other. Everything he had deduced was tremendously convoluted, not to mention unconvincing, without irrefutable proof, which he lacked.

He decided to ponder it further.

No doubt Madame Mayumi had every motive to murder

her husband, as well as the intelligence and inventiveness to carry it out. He suddenly recalled her vigorously shaking his hand: her elegant, feminine forearm possessed a remarkable strength, and he wondered whether she was strong enough to finish off her husband.

The footage Cathy had provided showed that the day of Shennan's death, Madame Mayumi had witnessed his furtive embraces with the nanny from the next room. After reviewing all the videos, Laurent determined that she wasn't seen entering from any of them, so he could easily conclude she'd come up to the second floor from the staircase in the second tower, which had no cameras, and reached the room from the service hall.

As Sergeant Lafonnier had pointed out, Shennan's body indicated that he'd died while descending the narrow staircase in the secret passage, but as the sergeant also noted, it didn't make sense for him to be going down to the guest room with the three little gifts for his daughters if his original plan was to place them in their room. Laurent concluded he wouldn't find an answer to that mystery, but inspired by the night-time calm and the starry light, he deduced that perhaps Madame Shennan had suggested he go up to the girls' room through the secret passageway to leave them their gifts as if by magic, since after all they thought their passageway was a well-kept secret. Perhaps Shennan had gone up there with his wife, and she'd craftily claimed she'd forgotten something. When he'd turned back to look, she could have given him a hard shove, causing him to hit his head on the rock that jutted out, where the investigative team found remains of Shennan's blood and scalp.

After her husband fell, she just had to break his neck with her hands, arrange his splayed body, then leave again through the guest room and replace the wooden panel, leaving the three leather pouches with the golden bracelets inside her husband's jacket pocket as a way to make his presence in the passageway plausible, given his playful, mischievous streak. Then, retracing her steps, Madame Mayumi would have returned to her guests, chatting with them animatedly until, at the appropriate time, she would have called Xiao Li to express her alarm at her husband's absence.

All that would explain why, in her impromptu meeting in the library with him and the security agents, she'd showed a nerve and sangfroid that had impressed even Cathy's seasoned colleagues. That attitude could be explained only if she already knew what they would discover moments later. Laurent then remembered the call to Madame's mobile and the curt response she gave in Japanese, and it occurred to him that it might not be a bad idea to ask Cathy if they had a microphone planted in the library, and if so, whether they could translate what she'd said. He called her right away, but since she didn't pick up, he left his request on her voicemail. Then he remembered how, in the moments that followed the discovery of her husband's body, Madame Mayumi had the strength of mind to console Xiao Li. Laurent hated to admit it, but the fact was she hadn't acted like an especially distraught wife. She hadn't even seemed surprised or shaken by her encounter with death. Later on she'd cooperated with unflagging energy and never failed in her duties as a mother. What's more, with her noblesse oblige, she'd stood up for Laurent, speaking out on his behalf and ardently defending his innocence.

At that moment, a macabre memory came to mind: how neat Shennan's clothes were even in death. Despite the blood and his awkward position, he looked surprisingly tidy, and now he could imagine Mayumi, with her obsession with order and aesthetics, grooming her dead husband because she couldn't bear to have him look like a slob in front of the coroner.

If she was responsible for her husband's death, Laurent couldn't help admitting he admired how she'd carried it off. Yet his sincere, spontaneous admiration withered all at once when he remembered Tum and her disappearance. She didn't deserve what had happened to her: she was a good girl and Shennan's victim. Clearly Shennan was the only guilty party, since his age, status and charisma had entranced the naive girl and let him take advantage of her. He felt the sour taste of scorn in his mouth as he imagined Carlos seducing Tum.

Laurent kept pondering. Tum had vanished, and her key ring had been found under a sofa in the guest room. Xiao Li's explanation for her departure seemed convincing, as did Madame Mayumi's words, though he hadn't failed to notice her remark about Tum's dubious loyalty: 'at that age, you can't expect anything from anyone,' she had said.

On the other hand, he found it strange that she'd left Tum alone in Paris; even Yammei had expressed surprise at not hearing from her. What's more, she'd lied about putting her on a train, since that day there was a strike.

Several images crowded Laurent's mind: Madame

Mayumi's expression in the mirror after learning about Tum's affair with her husband; her surprise when he'd come upon her efficiently sealing off the entrance to the passageway in the guest room, the same place where the key ring he'd made for Tum had been found; her flustered response when, on his last visit, he'd asked her if she'd heard from Tum.

Where was Tum? Laurent's alarms were all bright red. If the girl really was in Burma, it would be almost impossible to verify.

On the other hand, if Madame Mayumi said she'd put her on a train that never came, that might mean Tum had never left the area, and maybe never even got in the car – which, as Xiao Li had pointed out, had occurred very early in the morning, when everyone was still asleep. A very convenient hour to not be seen.

Laurent again remembered Shennan's widow kneeling before the entrance to the secret passageway, and just then his mobile rang, startling him. He picked up and heard Cathy's voice, full of excitement.

'You're not going to believe this, but we found footage from when we all met in the library. We've managed to translate part of the conversation, the part where Madame Mayumi was speaking. Of course, we couldn't clearly hear the person speaking to her. Even though he was yelling, we can't be totally sure about what we understood.'

'Get to the point, Cathy. What did they say?'

'You have no idea how many drinks and favours you're going to owe my colleagues after all your requests. Now don't get me all in a rush, I've got it all written down here, just a moment . . . Let's see, first there's a male voice speaking in Japanese to Madame Mayumi, but instead of calling her by her name he uses some form of family address. Right away Madame Shennan snaps back, saying something like, "I told you to stay put and not call me for any reason. I'm with people, I can't talk. Stay hidden." Then there's a sort of grunt, like an annoyed response, and the other person tries to talk again, but she cuts off the call. By the way, the call came from inside the house, or from somewhere very close by, and was made with a prepaid French mobile – our tech guy is positive. What do you make of all that, Laurent?'

'What do I make of it? She had an accomplice inside the house. My theory is, they broke Shennan's neck to finish him off after he was knocked out, and while that's not hard if the victim is unconscious, it does require a significant degree of strength. I'd thought she'd done it herself, but it seems possible she had an accomplice. Odd that the police found no trace of that person. Could you find out whether the lists the police made at the exit included anyone Japanese or Asian?'

'I already have. I've checked and there were no Asians. We'd have to watch the footage from the entryway.'

'Who knows if there's some other secret passage, or another hiding place elsewhere in the château. The building is colossal, and it would be easy for something like that to escape notice. See what you can find and we'll talk later. By the way, Cathy, thanks. I can't tell you how much I'm looking forward to seeing you.'

Alone again, Laurent continued thinking. The presence of a mysterious Japanese man, along with Madame Mayumi's orders to remain hidden, showed that something mysterious and secret had been underway almost parallel to Shennan's death.

A shudder went down his spine, and he again recalled Madame Mayumi sealing off the passageway, and a horrifying image came to his mind of Tum trapped alive inside. Only that would explain Madame Mayumi's ceremonious concentration while working, and even the Buddhist music with Shinto mantras seemed to make more sense. No doubt, it would be an appropriately medieval punishment in that château for a disloyal woman who'd taken part in her lord's adultery. But that was impossible, Laurent thought. Madame Mayumi loved Tum. She'd saved her from child prostitution and given her a new life of luxury and affection.

Then he realised, therein lay the answer: all Mayumi's generosity had been repaid with the basest betrayal of her employer, her saviour . . .

Laurent threw his cigar stub on the ground and stamped it furiously out. He'd just decided he wanted to contact Madame Mayumi: he'd lay out all these ideas and see her reaction. It was all too monstrous for him not to give her the chance to explain herself. He went home, intending to call Xiao Li, who still worked for her as a secretary.

POINT BLANK

Laurent called Xiao Li and, without explaining his true motives, told her he needed to meet with her boss to ask a personal favour, something regarding the people leasing the château. The secretary agreed to call him the next day.

As luck would have it, Madame Mayumi had a meeting in Paris coming up, and she graciously agreed to meet Laurent in the bar of the Le Bristol hotel, on the Rue du Faubourg Saint-Honoré.

The time that Laurent had to wait became a veritable torture. As the days went by, new questions and doubts arose, often contradicting one another, and as for the mysterious Japanese man, Cathy's team hadn't found any additional evidence. On the police's list there were no Asians aside from the château service staff, which didn't surprise Laurent: everything seemed to have been planned with such Machiavellian precision, and executed so meticulously, that it was absurd to think that whoever thought up the crime hadn't also figured out how to covertly move an accomplice in and out of the château.

On the other hand, it wasn't at all hard to spirit someone away in that building: all of Shennan's cars were large all-terrain vehicles with tinted windows, and all the gates were automatic, allowing direct access to the garage under the terrace. Besides, the hallway from the garage split in two: one part led to the kitchen, and the other led to the second entrance tower, the same one that had no cameras during the party.

Laurent hoped he was wrong, and that Madame Mayumi had convincing answers to all his questions. In any case, he didn't have a clear idea of what he should do if his theories turned out to be right. If she confessed to her husband's murder, he'd have to report her to the police, a thoroughly unappealing option, because Shennan had gone to great lengths to earn his wife's thirst for revenge, and because he couldn't deprive those three girls of their only living parent. Laurent's doubts only grew when he thought of Tum: if she was dead and he'd helped cover it up, he'd feel to a certain extent like an accomplice, though he still couldn't prove a crime had been committed.

On the day they'd arranged to meet, he arrived earlier than planned and spent a few minutes pacing back and forth in front of the hotel. The moment he feared was approaching, but he had no choice. He went inside.

Madame Mayumi sat waiting for him in the bar. It was completely empty, but she had chosen a table in the back, as if she'd guessed the course the conversation would take. When she saw him she held out her hand, and although Laurent promised himself he wouldn't kiss it, he brought it up to his lips. As always, her skin had an intoxicating scent.

She studied him.

'Laurent, I know you better than you imagine, and I'm sure what you want to talk to me about has nothing to do with the Russians leasing the château. Am I wrong?' She smiled, seeing Laurent blush. 'It's one of the things I like about you. Unlike my late husband, you're transparent and predictable. Have no fear, and tell me the real reason we're here.'

Laurent had to make a great effort not to lie to her about why he'd wanted to meet with her. There, sitting across from her, he felt ridiculous. All his theories seemed like children's games, and he didn't want to offend her by expounding them.

That's when he understood that Madame Mayumi shared her late husband's astonishing talent for seduction, though in a more sophisticated, less obvious way. When he realised this, he composed himself, ordered a vermouth, and began to speak.

'As you no doubt recall, Madame, I told you a while back I felt intrigued by your husband's untimely death, and in spite of my limitations and total lack of experience, I set about investigating the circumstances of the tragedy.'

'Of course I remember, and you shouldn't be modest; you did an impressive job,' she said encouragingly. 'Unless I'm mistaken, you told me you ultimately concluded that the police version was right, and even publicly admitted defeat by raising a glass to Sergeant Lafonnier.'

'Well, the fact is that I continued to investigate, and a stroke of luck led me to discover a series of facts that have forced me to reconsider the case. Therefore, and out of the respect I have for you, I wanted to lay them out to you.'

Madame Mayumi did not look the slightest bit surprised. 'I appreciate that very much, but you don't have to do me such courtesies. If you think you have something that might concern the police, don't hesitate to go to them. I more than anyone have an interest in clearing up my husband's death.'

'Thank you, Madame, but since we're here, if you don't mind I'd rather present it all to you, with your permission. I've taken the liberty of bringing my computer so I can play some video footage and audio recordings for you.'

Laurent opened up his laptop, and turned it on. Then he recounted in detail everything he had uncovered since the last time they'd met. Shennan's widow listened without interruption, only moving a hand once in a while to sip tea or read one of the messages that silently appeared on her mobile. Only when Laurent showed her the footage of her husband passionately kissing Tum did she show any signs of discomfort, though not as much as might be expected.

Laurent continued presenting his case, played back the call from the Japanese man, and finally asked her about Tum's whereabouts, though he didn't go so far as to suggest he feared she was no longer alive.

Then Madame Mayumi gave him an impressed look, and with a slight smile, began to speak.

'Laurent, you've done a magnificent job, and I'm deeply grateful that you're willing to keep all this information secret to protect me and my daughters, but that won't be necessary. I think I owe it to you to tell you a different story. It might be a good idea for you to order another vermouth.'

MADAME'S STORY

Laurent was dumbfounded by Madame Mayumi's self-control. Not only had she not moved a muscle when presented with the mountain of evidence that to a greater or lesser extent incriminated her in her husband's death, but she'd even suggested he order a drink before hearing a story that could apparently refute his theory.

He hadn't expected this reaction, and he didn't know how to respond. He'd imagined inconsolable tears and an out-and-out confession, a speech he'd receive with gentlemanly magnanimity, so that they could find a decorous solution together – as long as Tum was still alive. But no, here sat this ethereal woman delicately sipping a cup of white tea. Her carefully drawn eyebrows wouldn't budge a centimetre even if she came upon a triceratops with fuchsia lipstick. In any case, he decided her suggestion about the vermouth was wise, so with masculine self-assurance he called the waiter over and, once he'd been served, raised his glass to her.

'Madame, I don't know if you'll be able to convince me, but I raise my glass to you, your sangfroid, your courage, and –' he looked her clothes up and down – 'and your *couturier*, who never fails to surprise me.'

'Thank you, Laurent, and now I'm going to ask you to please listen to me, even though you'll no doubt find what I'm going to tell you hard to believe, just as any jury would find the story you told me hard to believe.

'As I suppose you realise, the only thing that could . . . not incriminate me, but certainly surprise anyone, is the fact that after witnessing that scene I didn't kill my husband right then and there. You'll admit, though, that no matter how intelligent or crafty you think I am, the time between Carlos and Tum's encounter and the subsequent accident is so short that I would have had a hard time hatching a plan as diabolically perfect as the one you've described. You'd make a great novelist, Laurent, and in fact this could perhaps be the plot for that book you've never gotten around to writing.

'So I'm going to reveal something that you may or may not believe, but which is no less possible than your version. In the first place, nearly everything you've said about my lack of enthusiasm or interest in the château is entirely correct. So is your observation that it was hard not to be exasperated by my husband's often childish whims, since his compulsion to rub up like a dog in heat against the leg of any woman who crossed his path was not only disgraceful but also an affront to my good taste. But even so, those weaknesses were mere trifles compared to how he progressively lost interest in his business, until he eventually let it go adrift. Fortunately, Xiao Li kept me informed about everything she heard, and she followed my instructions, tempering or averting Carlos's foolish decisions. The château totally absorbed him, and seemed to monopolise his attention to such an extent that he thought of nothing else but its renovation.

'To top it off, the sedate character of the locals had such an effect on him that he forgot that the deals he made required quick decisions and the reflexes and reactions of a tiger. But in the arms of the French countryside, Carlos let himself go, and our financial world began to collapse. As you can understand, I was not happy; I told him as much on several occasions, but he preferred to devote himself to hitting on women and making banal, trivial conversation with the locals.

'Sadly, he learnt he was ill and his days were numbered. That brought him back to reality. I lashed out at him, and didn't pull any punches. I told him his death would only bring us misery, and when he realised this, he was distraught. I once told you that hiding under a layer of narcissistic, childish egotism was a good person. He was ashamed and he asked for my help to save us from being ruined. That's when he once again became the Carlos Shennan I fell in love with, a man who took bold decisions and could find the most convoluted solutions to any problem – a man who didn't fear anything and whose willingness to put family above all else made him capable of the greatest sacrifices and the most audacious actions. Am I boring you with this show of conjugal admiration?'

Laurent was absorbed. 'No, go on, please.'

'Carlos found a way to take out a comprehensive insurance policy with a scandalously high premium. Of course, he was sick, and it must not have been easy, but medicine is a profession that has lost the heroic glamour it once had, and many doctors have buried their Hippocratic oath in the dung-heap of youthful ideals.

'Carlos was going to die, that much was certain. And he had no illusions: the policy he took out was so generous and so recent that there was no way the insurance company wouldn't send their experts to review the case in depth. He couldn't take that risk. That's when he came up with his plan and decided to share it with me when he realised he needed more than one accomplice and various scenarios to create a maze of heavy veils that would confuse anyone who dared enter.

'My husband adored the château and knew its most secret corners, so for his plan he had one condition: if he had to die, he'd die inside. In his half-madness he also thought the château would help him in his plan: he said it was only fair, since without his restoration the building wouldn't have survived. So he began to discreetly seek advice to get everything ready, and as he was an intelligent man, he soon understood the path he had to take.

'He prepared everything to carry out his plan on the day of the celebration, and when he hired the security agency he knew all too well, since he'd always worked in the field of defence, that the agency would place cameras and microphones inside.

'That's why he decided we needed to act out a series of scenes specially intended to be filmed by those cameras, which would corroborate our plan if anyone ever methodically watched them all in search of a culprit. If you look closely at the footage, Laurent, you'll see that at some points we walk through one location, then later through another, then back to the first, and so on, always trying not to look at the cameras. All that was to pretend we didn't know they existed, and to confuse any spectators with our movements inside and outside the château.

'With the same care, Carlos also planned to have a line-up of people who could become hypothetical suspects. Some of these he sought out intentionally, but others were brought by chance, and my husband was a virtuoso at the art of using them. That's why, for example, he made a point of hiring Thierry, because he knew perfectly well he was the brother of the baker who killed himself in Lignières. He found a way to make the landscape designer believe she'd seduced my husband, not realising she was just a pawn in his game. The business with Pia was a pity, but he had no choice but to attract her, use her and dispose of her to give her grounds for spite. As for the Muslim construction worker, he was an unexpected windfall, and it was too bad he later disappeared. The Monattis were guided without realising it: they don't remember that someone in a bar in Montgivray planted in their minds the idea of robbing an instrument, and they'll never know that that someone was sent by my husband. The same goes for many others: that dreadful farmer filing his complaints, the festival organiser . . . they all played their part as planned. Except for one person: your Israeli neighbour,

403

who we didn't at all expect. In the end that theatrical slap in the face that you and the Monattis witnessed became another ace in our hand.

'The only really horrible part of the plan was that he had to die without raising any medical suspicions – that is, he had to be killed. After considering all the possibilities, he concluded that the stone jutting out in the passageway was the most believable option: the darkness, the narrow space with irregular steps . . . it was an ideal setting. Carlos was brave, and he was willing to throw his own head against the stone, but I couldn't ask him to do something so horrible, so I persuaded him to at least use a local anaesthetic, the kind that disappears from the blood immediately. He wanted me to push him, but I didn't have the nerves, and neither Xiao Li nor Tum would ever have agreed to play an active role, even if they did help out with the rest of the preparations.

'That's where the Japanese man on the recording comes in: that was my younger brother, who came expressly for this purpose. It was hard to get him to help, but my husband managed to convince him. My brother is a sensei, a teacher at a Shorinji Kempo school in Nagoya. Carlos appealed to the chivalrous spirit of our ancestors, explaining he was soon going to die and that by helping him he'd be safeguarding the future of his sister and nieces. With such an argument, he couldn't refuse. He arrived two days before the party and stayed hidden in an extra room in the attic, which is why no one saw him. When the time came, he crept down to our daughters' room to wait for Carlos, and when my husband arrived as planned, coming up through the secret passage, he thanked him, embraced him, and then turned to go back down the way he came. My brother is very quick and inordinately strong, so he waited until Carlos was off balance with one foot in the air and gave him a single shove. He fell to his death. My brother thinks he died from the impact, but since he didn't want to leave anything to chance he broke his neck cleanly and laid out the body in case I had to see him.

'As for the rest . . . you know the story. Everyone was partly right, in fact: in a way it really was an accident, as Lafonnier said, but it was also a murder, as you now insist. Though in truth all it did was move up Carlos's imminent death. It may comfort you to know that those last few weeks he had a tremendous time organising his death, and he loved combining it with the preparations for the party, which as you saw was spectacular.'

Laurent had tremendous difficulty finding words. 'Madame, this is incredible. I don't know what to say. It's madness, but extremely methodical madness. I'm very sorry I doubted your good name. I hope you can forgive me.'

Madame Mayumi waved away his apologies. 'Monsieur Laurent, I'm not proud of what I did, but I am proud of the love my husband showed us. I'm also not happy about the harm we caused innocent people, like the architect – or like you yourself, who were even considered a suspect.

'Xiao Li, Tum and I were upset, and that's why I went to the police to testify for you. And believe me when I say that, had things gotten any worse, I was prepared to confess everything.' She paused. 'Laurent, I free you from your promise. You have my permission to tell all this to the police. I don't care if they lock me up, because my daughters' inheritance is safe. I ask only that you not implicate anyone but me. Xiao Li acted against her will, and only because Carlos begged her. As for Tum, she was distraught. And my brother I should say is now in Japan. They're guilty of nothing. Only I am.'

'You have my word of honour that I'll take this to my grave, Madame,' Laurent reassured her. 'There's just one thing I don't get; it has to do with Tum. Her performance as Carlos's lover was so masterful that I have a hard time believing it was faked. But aside from that, what worries me now is that she's apparently disappeared: her key ring turned up broken in the guest room where you were walling off the entrance to the passageway. And then . . .' Laurent hesitated. 'Then there's the fact that you said you drove her to the station, when in fact that day she couldn't have left, because there was a train strike.'

'Laurent, think back. Did I at any point tell you I dropped her off at the station in Châteauroux?'

He tried to recall and had to admit he hadn't heard that from Madame Mayumi's lips.

'No, Xiao Li told me. But then I mentioned it to you and you didn't deny it.'

'You see? Xiao Li thought that's what happened because that was the original plan, but when we got there and found out there was a strike I drove her to Paris myself. I think I could even find expressway receipts from that date, if that's of interest to you. When you mentioned it to me I didn't think it important enough to waste time contradicting you, since you wanted to find out about Tum, whom you think I killed and walled up in the passageway. Isn't that right? Well, I'm sorry to disappoint you, Laurent, but she's alive and well in Burma. I'll try to have her contact you. That way, with proof of her existence, you can exonerate me.'

Laurent tried to reply as best he could. 'To be frank, I really would like to know that she's safe in her country and has been able to locate her brother.'

Mayumi smiled at his failed attempt at chivalry. 'Monsieur Laurent, you're quite a case, but that's part of your charm. Say no more – she'll call you, you have my word.'

With that she seemed to signal that the conversation was over, but suddenly she remembered to add something. 'You remarked on how well Tum and Carlos did the kissing scene . . . I was surprised myself, actually, by their feigned ardour. Not on his account, since he had the appetite of a satyr, but on hers. I even wondered if she wasn't secretly in love with my husband, which would have been in terribly, unpardonably bad taste, don't you think? And now, if you have no more questions . . .'

'No, Madame, you've been very kind, both with your time and your honesty. You have my word that the police will never hear a word of this.'

Laurent accepted everything Madame Mayumi had told him. Not only did it make sense, it truly seemed like a ploy contrived up by Carlos's convoluted mind. Besides, his self-esteem as a detective was at its peak, because he'd finally been right: Shennan's death was the result of a crime, an extraordinarily complex crime that he would forever keep silent. He motioned the waiter to ask for the bill, but Madame Mayumi stopped him.

'Not at all,' she said. 'The drinks are on me. After all, I'm the one staying in the hotel. Go and enjoy your life in

Saint-Chartier. I'm sure we'll cross paths again soon.' She again gave him her hand and got up to leave, but before she did, she asked, 'You came by train, I suppose? Are you going back to Berry today, or will you be staying a few days here with Mademoiselle Cathy?'

Laurent smiled.

'No, she's not in Paris today, and as for me, I'll fly back this afternoon. I found a very cheap flight to Châteauroux leaving at five-twenty. Farewell, Madame.'

AND CATHY

He'd never been in the Châteauroux airport before, and he didn't plan on going back: with all the hurry-up-and-wait, it took almost as long as by train or by car. Once he landed and got off the plane, he took the first free taxi and headed to Saint-Chartier.

When he opened the door to the vicarage, he was surprised to find three enormous suitcases sitting neatly in the entryway, next to a large duffel bag. Then he heard Cathy singing softly to herself in the living room and called her name. She rushed down, threw herself into his arms and began trying to remove his shirt.

Laurent dodged politely and pointed to the suitcases. 'What's all this doing here?'

She looked him in the eyes mischievously and said, 'Isn't it obvious? I've decided to move in with you. I know you've been longing for this day, but you've got some sort psychological issue or trauma from childhood that keeps you from telling women that you care. You can help me unpack and put everything away later.'

Not much would have shocked him at that point, but this invasion of his space came as a surprise. On the other hand, he didn't exactly think it was a bad idea. He decided to let her undress him. In fact, he had always wanted to do it on the stairs.

A few hours later, lying comfortably on the queen bed in his room, Laurent thought to turn on his mobile, which he had switched off on the plane. Cathy lay with her eyes closed and her head on the large bolster pillow and asked him how the meeting in Paris had gone.

He gave a detailed account of his conversation with Madame Mayumi and the information she'd given him. Then he gave a little shout.

'Look, what a coincidence. I've got a missed call with a voicemail from a foreign number. Let me listen. I'll turn up the volume.'

First there was a sound like an engine or gears, and then came the clear voice of Tum.

'Monsieur Laurent, it's Tum, calling from Burma. Madame Mayumi asked me to call you to let you know I'm all right. Thanks for your concern. My brother is also all right, so I'm very happy. This phone belongs to a neighbour who doesn't speak English. Tomorrow we're going to our village. Take care. Goodbye.'

Laurent shut off the mobile and looked at Cathy.

'See? In the end everything has a reasonable explanation, and Tum is fine. I'm glad, but I feel like a bit of an arse for all the trouble I've caused.'

Cathy sat up on the mattress.

'Right. Shennan's widow gave you her version, and of course you, as always, swallowed it without a second thought.'

'What do you mean? I know you hate her, but as far as I can see, everything's been cleared up. I just want to forget about the whole mess and burn my notes in the barbecue.'

'Yes, sure, that's all well and good, but first I'd like to give you my theory. You'll love it, you'll see.' Laurent looked at the ceiling as though praying for forbearance as she began. 'Everything Mayumi told you is very logical, but I suppose you realise she's the only one who can back up her story.'

Laurent sat up against the headboard. 'What are you insinuating, Cathy?'

'Nothing, just that what she told you is a perfect explanation for everything that was bothering you. There are no loose ends. Too bad you can't prove any of it: you have no idea where her brother is, nor whether he was even in the château beyond that call we listened to.

'As for Shennan's supposed illness, you heard about that from the priest, and he could have heard about it from Shennan directly or even from his wife, because, if you recall, he stressed that he learnt about it outside confession. But what's even stranger is that all your suspects have turned out to be her puppets, including your Israeli girlfriend – to say nothing of the perfect timing of the fatal blow. And finally, it turns out Tum and Shennan's passion was merely a performance for our benefit. I'm sorry, but those kisses were real, on both sides.

'And one more thing: it's curious how Mayumi gave you such a warm goodbye and enquired how you'd get home – a smart question she asked after she promised she'd have Tum call. Sure enough, predictable as always, you go and tell her what time your flight is. And what do you know? Tum just happens to call while you're in the air, leaving you an uncompromising voice message. Not only that . . . hold on.' She typed something into her mobile, looking for information. 'You received her supposed call at six in the evening. Unless I'm mistaken, that was one in the morning in Burma, and Tum doesn't strike me as the kind of girl who'd be awake so late. In those countries people usually go to bed at ten.'

'I don't see where you're going with this, Cathy.' Laurent seemed confused.

'You're the one who likes to dream up intrigues and conspiracies. Here's one: everything she told you is a lie. Shennan wasn't ill, and she was the one who spread that story. Nor was there any Japanese brother – she could have had anyone call her, or she could have ordered Tum to call her using a recording in Japanese. You heard it, it was practically inaudible. And last, maybe Tum really is dead, and the master strategist Mayumi, predicting you'd be uneasy, convinced her to record something neutral enough not to arouse suspicions if she had to use it. That's why she so cleverly got you to tell her your flight time, so you couldn't return her call – a call where, even more damningly, she says you can't contact her in the future.

'As for Tum's trip, the business about her getting a call from the Burmese embassy could also be a set-up, a lie to dupe Tum herself. The only thing we know for certain is that the girl really was in love with Shennan and may indeed be walled up in the château. What do you think of my conclusions? I defy you to refute them,' she said, sitting up on her knees on the bed in front of him.

Laurent snorted and then reduced her theory to a single sentence. 'So you *are* jealous of Carlos's wife. Come here, I'll give you something to be jealous of,' he joked, grabbing her by the waist and drawing her toward him.

She closed her eyes with her arms around him. She couldn't wait until they had more interesting topics of conversation than Shennan's death. She regretted saying what she'd said, and prayed Laurent wouldn't put too much stock in her version of events.

Laurent pulled away from her and held her by the arms, staring at her intensely.

'Cathy, there's something very important I want to ask you.'

Heart aflutter, she thought she saw a great passion in his eyes, and she hugged him again even more tightly than before.

'Of course, my love, whatever you want.'

He gently pushed her back again and took her by the hands. 'Do you think your friends can locate Tum in Burma?'

AFTERWORD

This novel is set in and around the Château de Saint-Chartier, a medieval fortress located in the historic Berry region of France (Department of Indre), in a town of just over six hundred inhabitants named after the castle or château whose walls protect it. A bit weathered now, those walls still retain an elegant, austere majesty, having borne witness, over their long history, to innumerable events both inside and out.

While the characters are all fictional, they are inspired by actual people. The geography is entirely real, as are some of the establishments and shops that appear in the story. Others, such as the tavern La Cocadrille, are not – though we have it on good authority that a handful of them will soon acquire a physical and fiscal existence.

This book's sole aspiration is to generate a bit of income and kind words, not to mention – since there's no harm in asking – to help revive this lovely French town, for we would be remiss if we failed to note that it is a constant source of comfort and joy for the troubled spirit.

Spanish businessman and historian, IVO FORNESA is known for his work as a consultant in China, as well as for his many collaborations with newspapers and publications. His fascinating life has seen him volunteer in the Spanish Foreign Legion; train as a parachutist; live as a Catholic friar in the Holy Land; restore traditional houses in South America, Morocco, China, Thailand and Burma. Fornesa now lives in France, in a chateau in Saint-Chartier.